The Spectacle and Passion of the Epic Battle for a New World

ANA The Spanish conquerors destroyed her world, but never her pride. To the end, she was her people's beautiful queen.

TAHÍACA Cherished princess, despoiled by slavery in faraway Spain, she'd return to her home with a Spaniard who loved her.

DANIEL Separated from his betrothed by religious persecution, he joined Columbus in the quest for adventure and riches.

RACHEL Her heart went with Daniel across the seas, where their love would reunite them in the settlement of a new land.

SAMUEL Son of Daniel and Rachel, he was father to a son whose blood mixed the heritage and destiny of two worlds.

Crying in the Wilderness

THE CARIBBEAN CHRONICLES

Floydene Partain

AVON
PUBLISHERS OF BARD, CAMELOT, DISCUS AND FLARE BOOKS

CRYING IN THE WILDERNESS: The Caribbean Chronicles is an original publication of Avon Books. This work has never before appeared in book form.

AVON BOOKS
A division of
The Hearst Corporation
959 Eighth Avenue
New York, New York 10019

Copyright © 1983 by Floydene Partain
Published by arrangement with the author
Library of Congress Catalog Card Number: 82-90546
ISBN: 0-380-82271-7

First Avon Printing, March, 1983

AVON TRADEMARK REG. U. S. PAT. OFF. AND IN OTHER COUNTRIES, MARCA REGISTRADA, HECHO EN U. S. A.

Printed in the U. S. A.

WFH 10 9 8 7 6 5 4 3 2 1

*Dedicated to
my daughter Martha,
who prodded me to write.*

The voice of one crying in the wilderness,
Prepare ye the way of the Lord,
make his paths straight.

Luke 3:4

ACKNOWLEDGMENTS

To all the librarians and keepers of archives who preserve the rich treasury of history;

To Cecil Beach and the Broward County Libraries for assisting me in obtaining valuable and sometimes rare research materials;

To the Spanish Government for permission to research their archives;

To the Archivo General de Indias, Sevilla, Spain, for making available certain old and precious documents;

To the Biblioteca Nacional, Madrid, Spain, for making available certain old and precious documents;

To Benjamin Keen and the Rutgers University Press for permission to use quotations from Professor Keen's translation of *The Life of Admiral Christopher Columbus, by his son Fernando Colón*;

To the United States Commission on the De Soto Expedition for their fine map;

To all these, my sincere gratitude and heartfelt thanks.

F.P.

TO ENCOURAGE readers to see well-known history with different eyes, I have used old Spanish spellings for names and places. Thus Christopher Columbus is Cristóbal Colón, and De Soto becomes Soto. Place names change as the novel progresses. Both historical and fictional characters appear in the novel, each playing a part in keeping with the times.

FLOYDENE PARTAIN

BOOK I

An Affectionate and Generous People

They are such an affectionate and generous people, and so tractable that I assure Your Highnesses there are no better people or land in all the world. They love their neighbors as themselves, and their speech is the sweetest and gentlest in the world, and they always speak with a smile.

ADMIRAL DON CRISTÓBAL
COLÓN,
La Española, 1493; from
*The Life of Admiral Christopher
Columbus, by his son Fernando
Colón,*
translated by Benjamin Keen

CHAPTER 1

Cuba, 1479

LATER, AFTER Anacaona became a legend and spread herself upon the winds of Huracán's wings, people began to speak of her as if she were a goddess; but in the beginning, before the Spaniards came, she was just one of Caonabó's wives—the favorite one. Ana might have ruled the Taino village in Cuba after her uncle the Cacique had his awful vision and ordered his own execution, but that very night, as Ana sang her uncle's funeral areíto, Caonabó attacked the village, captured her, and took her back to Haiti.

Caonabó had traveled far to find Ana—all the way from the gold-bearing mountains of Cibao, across the sea of the Caribs to Cuba in a long canoe with twenty oarsmen and fifty fierce Carib warriors, each wearing a buzzard's white tuft attached to his forelock. Caribs believed the first warrior had been born of the union of a woman and a giant buzzard. To prove himself, a Carib warrior had to snatch his tuft from a live buzzard.

Cacique Caonabó, whose father's tribe had been man-eaters, ruled many villages in the gold mountains, but not in all his villages did he have a singer like Ana.

Everywhere the long canoes traveled, even as far away as the mainland, the tobacco traders talked about Ana— the sweet singer, the graceful dancer, the composer of the song-poems called areítos which told the history of her people, the Tainos.

Soon the Caribs would conquer all the islands in the sea, just as the Tainos had conquered the Ciboneys, who were now their servants, and as the Ciboneys had once conquered the Guanajatabeyes, who lived now only in the dim memory of the oldest singers of areítos. No one knew anything about how the Guanajatabeyes had lived, for no one had composed great areítos honoring them. Caonabó wanted Ana to be his wife, to bear him strong children, and to compose such fine areítos about his deeds that people would still be singing them long after the Caribs were only memories.

On the morning of the day Caonabó attacked the Taino village in Cuba, Ana's uncle went to commune with his cemís—those manifestations of life's mysteries which call forth awe and worship from trembling, insecure humans. Everyone had cemís, although every cemí assumed a different form in accordance with the needs of the worshipper. Some people kept cemís in their homes, such as the carefully cleaned bones of ancestors stored in covered baskets, or the lucky stones the buhuitihu took from the body when they healed the sick or delivered a baby.

Some cemís lived in trees, especially in giant ceibas. People built their villages around gnarled, fluted trunks of old Mother Ceibas, playing ball and dancing areítos in the batey clearing under Her spreading branches while the spirits of the ancestors whispered among Her leaves. Mother Ceiba is a cemí more powerful than the god Huracán, for the ceiba is the only tree in the forest never struck by lightning, never uprooted by storms.

The old Cacique left the village shortly after dawn, walked slowly up the mountain, stopping often to catch his breath and to lean on the fire-hardened stick he had used to cultivate his fields. Finally he reached the cave of the cemís, stooped, and entered, hitting his head on a boulder. Bats squeaked, and he slipped on accumulated guano as he made his way through the darkness—reentering the womb of Mother Earth from which mankind had escaped on that long-ago day when Marocael, son of Yocahu, had left the door ajar.

Shortly after the Ciboneys had been subjugated, the Cacique's people had found this cave filled with Ciboney cemís. In his youth, the Cacique had seldom come here, but in his old age he came to seek whatever wisdom lay under the droppings. He did not disturb the cemís of forgotten people. Instead, he sought out his own cemí—beloved and familiar to him after a lifetime spent creating it.

"Well, old cemí," said the Cacique, running his hands affectionately over the familiar shape, "you are not what I started out to make, and I am not what I started out to make, but now that we are nearing the end of things, let us share one last cahoba dream."

The Cacique had discovered his cemí many years ago when the cemí had spoken to him from a fallen mahogany tree, telling him to come back at night to clear away the vines and begin carving the hard wood to release the cemí. The Cacique had worked the rest of his life shaping his cemí, carving it patiently, little by little, until his old fingers could no longer hold the obsidian knife.

Now the Cacique knelt before his cemí to make his last cahoba—the ceremony of communion, called by the same name as the forked instrument used to inhale the sacred powders. From a little sack around his neck he poured a few grains of tobacco dust mixed with certain hallucinogenic herbs. He leaned over and trickled the dust into a small mound in the saucerlike depression atop his cemí. Then he placed the hollow, forked bone to his nostrils and sniffed. He sneezed, his eyes watered, he coughed. Then he sniffed again, this time without sneezing. Finally, he settled back against the cave and began chanting, waiting for the cohaba to work.

Light began to fill the cave, multicolored light, and he could hear the finches singing inside his head. His spirit lifted, joining his cemí and moving outside and up...up...up...until the mountains seemed flat and the clouds floated lazily below him. Then he saw Huracán, the mighty one-eyed storm god, swirling nearer and nearer.

Never had there been such a storm. Huracán's clouds writhed with masses of people so ashamed of their bodies they were fully clothed. Lightning was the flash of their weapons, and thunder the noise of their destruction. Even during the calm of the eye before the worst winds struck, the Cacique could hear the moans of the people. The Cacique knew he was being given a great vision. Many such storms would sweep his island, devouring the land and destroying the people, barely leaving time to begin again before the next storm.

The Cacique knew his people would need strong leaders if they were to weather such storms, so he made the only decision a great cacique could make. He bade an affectionate good-bye to his cemí and left the cave.

The first stars were coming out in the velvet tropical sky when the Cacique entered the batey under the ceiba and began to sing. First he sang and danced his vision—the warning to his people about the clothed men with beards who worshipped strange cemís; then, strong and clear, sweet and sad, he sang his own death song. Afterward, he ordered his son Hatuey and his nephew Behechio to carry out the deed. The saucer moon was high in the sky when the executioners returned with his body and hung it to dry above a fire under Mother Ceiba. The body had a mystic quality now, twisting and bobbing in the wisps of smoke.

All the villagers gathered around Ana as she brushed her sadness into the corner of her heart and began to sing. Tears trickled down her cheeks, for she had loved her uncle as a woman always loves the man who awakens her to the joys of her own body. The people danced slowly as Ana danced, sang as she sang.

Then the dreaded Carib war cry shattered the areíto, terrifying the dancing mourners as Caonabó and his warriors, brandishing their shark-tooth spears, ran into the batey. Few people stopped to defend themselves; peaceful Tainos were no match for Caribs.

Ana ran swiftly through the darkness, underbrush snatching at her, tearing her, whipping her. She could hear someone behind her, and she tried to run faster. A stitch came into her side, and she knew he was gaining. She looked back fearfully, tripped over a fallen log, sprawled into a bed of leaves at the base of a tree. She tried to scramble up, but Caonabó was standing over her.

Like the Tainos, the Caribs wore few clothes—although Caonabó seemed to be clothed. His lean, muscular body was tattooed and scarified on every available space. Even his face bore a blue iguana with red eyes, clawing its way up his cheek and curling its tail around his determined mouth. A gold pendant swung under his nose. He reached for Ana, and she bit her lip to keep from crying out. She believed she had come face to face with the opia—the dreaded spirits of the dead who walk about at night taking whatever shape they please.

Instinctively Ana drew herself into a ball, her legs held together tightly. Although he was not much more than five feet tall, he seemed to tower over her. She scuttled away crablike until her back scraped against the tree trunk. Her heart pounded in a throat so dry only an animal whimper escaped her lips. Caonabó's tattooed skin seemed alive as he reached for her. Ana knew she was trapped.

Caonabó did not grab her and drag her away as she had expected. Nor did he vanish into the air as opia sometimes do after frightening their victims. Instead he held out his hand and stood waiting.

"Give Caonabó your hand," he said.

Ana drew back, putting her hand behind her to feel the reassuring roughness of the tree trunk.

"Caonabó will not harm you," he promised.

Almost as if it had a life of its own, Ana's hand came out from behind her and reached for Caonabó.

All that night and the next day and into the next night Caonabó marched them rapidly through the forest. Ana's whole body ached before he called a halt, and

7

she was asleep before her hammock stopped swinging. Caonabó lay down beside her hammock on a mat.

Toward morning the opia visited Caonabó. Her face was Ana's face, her body Ana's body, her appetites those of a bitch in heat. The moment he tried to embrace her, she vanished, leaving only the throbbing ache of his erection. He was ashamed of himself for not recognizing the opia, who roam the forests at night seeking the pleasures of the living. Caonabó knew he should have felt for her navel, for the motherless opia have no navels. He watched Ana still sleeping, curled in the hammock with her shapely hips toward him and the nipple of one breast sticking invitingly through the mesh. He masturbated to keep from taking her in her sleep. He wanted her to come to him as willingly and as passionately as the opia of his dream.

When she awoke, he was squatting on the ground talking trade with her brother Behechio and her cousin Hatuey. She had never seen so many golden crowns and masks and ornaments as Caonabó was offering Behechio.

"A bride price for Ana," said Caonabó.

"Why buy her?" Behechio asked. "We are your prisoners. Take Ana whenever you wish."

"Caonabó wants a wife, not a concubine," he said. "If Ana is happy, she will compose areítos for Caonabó. Life in Cibao is good for Caonabó's wives. Caonabó also has a sister. You shall have Caonabó's sister, and Caonabó shall have Ana. We will be brothers. Caonabó will make you ruler of many villages in the province of Xaragua. Caonabó is the greatest cacique in all the Sea of the Caribs."

Behechio looked at all the gold and thought about what Caonabó had said about ruling all the villages in the province of Xaragua.

"Done," Behechio said. "I will give you my sister Ana."

Ana was furious. How dare he trade her for a few gold trinkets! Would her beloved uncle the Cacique have made such a bargain? Yes, Ana knew he would. Men commanded. Women obeyed. Ana made her face as still

8

as one of the golden masks lying on the grass, her body as cold as a cemí. Caonabó, sensing her hostility, made a bold decision.

"Would Ana like to return to her village?" he asked.

Ana looked up at him, bewildered. Would he let her go? Caribs ate people. If she went with him, would he fatten her children for the cooking pots?

"Caonabó gives Ana a choice," he said, and his eyes beside the iguana were honest eyes. "She may return to her village, or she may come to Cibao and be Caonabó's wife."

"Has Caonabó many wives?" Ana asked, slipping into his way of speaking of himself in the exalted third person.

"As many as the greatest cacique," he answered.

"Ana shall not be subject to Caonabó's wives," she announced.

"Caonabó's wives are subject only to Caonabó."

"And Ana?" she asked. "Will Ana be subject to Caonabó?"

"Ana will be subject only to the song in her heart."

"Ana will come to Haiti and be the wife of Caonabó," she said, reaching out to touch the iguana on his cheek.

Caonabó turned and swung off down the trail.

Late that afternoon they reached the mangrove-lined bay where Caonabó's canoes were hidden. After they had eaten and swum in the surf, the men began pairing off with the women from Ana's village. Soon Ana and Caonabó were alone, trying to bridge the awesome gap into intimacy, talking about impersonal things like the coming sea journey. Uneasy silences lay between them. All the miles Caonabó had traveled to find her seemed short compared to the distance now between them. Finally, Caonabó unrolled his hammock, looking around for two likely saplings, but the mangroves were too thick. He began tearing at the underbrush. Ana arose and unrolled his mat on the soft sand.

"Why does Caonabó need a hammock?" she asked. "This mat is big enough for both of us."

He turned, smiling, the iguana flicking its tail around

his mouth. He strode over, knelt beside her and cupped her bare breast in his palm. She twisted and moaned, and he fell on her hungrily. He was all she had ever heard about the carnivorous Caribs, the child-man feeding at her breasts, the hungry lover devouring his love.

Ana writhed in ecstasy as his lips found her secret place. She had never known such pleasure. Her coupling had been stolen in the brush with young men still exploring the woman bodyscape. Even her beloved uncle had never taken her to such heights. Caonabó gifted her with the accumulated wisdom of five wives and numerous concubines. Playing with her, teasing her, caressing her, provoking her, teaching her, rousing her higher as she fondled him, stroked him, devoured him. Time and time again he carried her to worlds she had not dreamed existed. Each time he was there before her, waiting for her.

Yet something was lacking. Her pleasure was incomplete, unsatisfying. Her womb, aching for his children, was one vast emptiness only he could fill. The one-eyed moon mocked her. Wind and water, sand and sea swam around her as she floated in her ecstasies, but still Caonabó held back. She traced the lambent patterns on his scarified body, the circles around the tiny nipples on his chest, the fluted ridges outlining the ribs, down the spiral carved on his stomach and into the navel where he had been separated from his mother to become a man.

Man! Yes, man. Not opia, man! Wondrous, joyous, miraculous man!

Ana moaned an animal moan as she opened her legs and clasped her lover to her, willing him to come into her, to become part of her Oneness—the Oneness that was before time began. Caonabó still held back, smiling. He, too, must feel his way from breast to navel, must be sure she was not the opia that can come between two lovers more swiftly than a cloud blots out the moon. So, just before Caonabó made Ana his wife, he traced that beloved symbol of her beginning.

Woman! Yes, Ana was woman!

Ana fitted easily into the sisterhood of Caonabó's wives and concubines. Wondrous womanly things were always happening in Caonabó's bahío—the long palm-thatched house where they all lived. Someone was always becoming pregnant, giving birth, nursing a child. Caonabó dutifully attended to each wife's needs, sometimes inviting traders to share his hospitality, sometimes giving one of his concubines to a youth who needed to lose his virginity. When Caonabó was making love with Ana, he liked to think of all the other wives and of all the other men who had made love with his wives. It stimulated him. The night was always peopled with erotic murmurings—and whimpering children. When morning came and the children awoke, the women always shooed the men away so they could get on with their living.

It seemed only yesterday Ana had come to live in Caonabó's bahío, and now she had three children. Tahíaca had seen six seasons when the people looked anxiously at the clouds and danced areítos so Huracán would not visit the island. Higueymato was a season younger than her sister, and only a few months ago Ana had taken Mayabaño to the river for his first ceremonial bath, then fastened his head securely into the headboards that would shape his skull high and his forehead wide like his father's.

Caonabó's wives and concubines divided up the work. One grandmothered all the children, another decorated the bahío with wood carvings and bronze masks and wicker cemí baskets. One tended the cooking, another the weaving, the pottery-making, the wood-carving. One wife supervised the servants as they dug holes to plant yams, peppers, peanuts, potatoes, corn, beans, yucca, and manioc. Another made sure the children on the scarecrow platforms urinated in the right spots to fertilize the crops planted among fallen trees in the forest clearing.

Jealousies were few, confidences many; they loved each other and thought of themselves collectively as Caonabó's family. They had known no other way of living and sought none. Caonabó might rule the villages of Cibao, but the wives ruled Caonabó's home.

They left the spiritual training of the children to Ana. The children on the platforms in the fields, assigned to scare away the parrots, were always happy to see Ana walking among them, singing her areítos, teaching the myths and legends, dancing the Huracán dance until the platform shook as if it would fall.

Men had little part in those first yeasty years, but little by little the boys would sense their isolation from the womanly things and slip away to sit with the elders at eventide under the ceiba, listening to the exaggerations. One by one the men would snatch the boys away to teach them to draw a bow or make a sword edged with shark's teeth. Before a young man reentered the world of women via the sanctuary of a concubine's arms, he would have caught half the fish in the rivers, paddled halfway to the mainland, turned half green trying to smoke long black cigars. No matter how far he wandered, he would always come back—tied irrevocably by life's umbilical cord to Woman.

When the whimpering of fretful children became too much, or the women's companionable laughter became too isolating, the men would go hunting for gold in the rivers—first carefully observing the fasting and celibacy taboos. No one from Caonabó's villages questioned the full moon of celibacy required before hunting for gold, nor the fasting during the rituals in the caves of the cemís. If a man could rise above sex, why not above food? If above both, will he not have conquered life itself? Will he ever need women again?

In the night, a baby began to cry. Caonabó buried his head against Ana's soft breasts, trying to shut out the commotion in the crowded bahío as all the other children joined the chorus and all the wives tried to hush them. Caonabó had built such a large bahío it should have held many wives and their children comfortably—a strong house with mahogany posts set deep into the ground, with smooth pine floors, and roof and sides thatched with palm fronds to keep out wind and rain. Now the bahío was not even big enough for one crying baby.

Ana stirred, knowing it was Mayabaño who cried. A few days before, a butterfly had lighted on Mayabaño's forehead just above his nose. That evening all the wives had chattered about his good fortune. Mayabaño would live many lives, see great changes, and have his greatest glory in his final days. Such an auspicious prophecy must be dutifully recorded; so, with a fishbone knife, Caonabó had scarified a butterfly on Mayabaño's forehead. The baby had screamed when Caonabó poured in the acidic dyes; but no matter how much Ana protested, Caonabó had not stopped. Now Mayabaño fretted and cried almost every night.

"Ana's baby is crying again," said First Wife peevishly. "Let Ana see to her butterfly boy."

Caonabó reluctantly released Ana, and she hurried through the dark bahío to Mayabaño's hammock.

"Hush, my butterfly boy," she crooned, kissing his tear-stained face, giving him her breast, and holding his little hand to keep him from pushing at his headboards. Ana wished children did not have to wear these headboards. They always cried, but the boards made their heads long and aristocratic. No mother wanted her child to look like the round-headed Ciboney servants.

Ana kissed the angry tattoo on Mayabaño's forehead, rocking him back and forth until at last he slept. Ana held him close for a long time, listening to him snub back his sorrows, even in his sleep. Gradually the bahío became still. The night crawlers came out from among the fronds, and Ana heard one of the concubines slip quietly into Caonabó's hammock. Next day, Caonabó and the men began their fast before hunting for gold.

After many days of fasting, the men went to commune with the cemís in the sacred caves from which mankind had first emerged. After appropriate orations, Caonabó placed the cahoba to his nostrils, sniffed the hallucinogenic dust, then passed the instrument on to the next man while he began singing Mother Earth's areíto. No man knew who had first sung this areíto, just as no one knew who had made the first cemí.

In the darkness of his Mother's womb, Caonabó lost track of time. Her heart pulsed. She shivered. A few ancient rocks, Caonabó's brothers, rolled down the mountain outside. A fine sulfurous dust sifted down on their heads, confirming Caonabó's faith. His Mother lived! Mother Earth was alive. Her molten heart still beat. Her fury spews up through anger holes. Her breathing makes whole continents disappear. Legend says these islands were once mountains down the spine of a vast land that disappeared one day beneath the waves.

Caonabó wanted a piece of his Mother's golden heart, a drop of the gold in her veins running through the rocks. Caonabó revered his Mother, and She rewarded her son. Other men might not find gold, but Caonabó never left the mountains without it. Other men might not value gold, tossing it aside as unfit to make anything useful, but Caonabó loved the soft metal.

Caonabó's painted, scarified body glowed. The cave echoed with his prayers. Men and cemís moved freely through time and matter as Mother Earth embraced them all. Caonabó concentrated to keep from being swallowed up by his mother.

Caonabó danced out into the sunshine. He squinted as First Man must have squinted when he escaped the darkness into painful light. A double rainbow arched over the waterfall newly created by the quake. Caonabó came to himself later, lying with one foot in the new stream bed. He knew the gold would not be far away, but he was in no hurry to find it.

Caonabó slept.

The first few days the men were away, the women enjoyed themselves, letting their work go, watching the children's undisciplined play, chattering among themselves with no thought of what the men might think. They retold the old legend of the island where women lived by themselves, allowing men to visit only once a year. They giggled at the thought of having a man after a year of abstinence. They wondered whether they might have to find themselves woodpeckers to create men, as legend said the men had used woodpeckers to create women.

Then the nights began to be lonely and the days empty. With no one to please, why plait flowers in your long, black hair, why search out the most fragrant leaves to anoint your body after a bath? Soon they grew snappish with each other, like a woman whose husband has brought home a new bride and forgotten he has wives with previous claims.

Word must have spread throughout Haiti that Caonabó was hunting for gold, for the traders from other provinces began to gather under the ceiba, spreading their wares and watching the women work. Flowers appeared again, and women wore their prettiest skirts. Only Ana was allowed to wear a long skirt. Most of the women wore only the briefest covering, but it covered enough to intrigue, bringing smiles and knowing looks to the traders' faces.

The women began preparing for the areíto to celebrate Caonabó's success, for they knew he would be successful. The men began to choose which wife they would accept as Caonabó's hospitality gift for the night of the festivities.

Ciboney servants grated manioc root and hung the flour to drip in long stockinglike sieves. Other women kneaded the flour into bread and baked it on hot, flat rocks. Wives wove wooden withes into grills called boucans, and soon Muscovy ducks and succulent jutía sputtered over the coals. Pieces of cazabe bread were dipped into pots to see if the stew was tasty; fat iguanas simmered in sweet manioc sauce. Ciboney servants scurried about carrying trays of papayas, bananas, avocados.

Before Caonabó returned, canoes lined the river banks. Visitors milled about laughing, talking, feigning fights, sharing family news. Babies slept in string hammocks under Mother Ceiba. Visiting caciques sat on intricately carved stools, cheering rival teams playing stickball. Traders regaled children with tall tales ....*Did you know there is a magic spring on the*

island of Bimini? Drink from that spring and live for-
ever.

Areítos began forming themselves in Ana's mind,
and she sent Tahíaca to find her father and bring him
back to the feast. Tahíaca flipped her fat little rump as
she walked too close to the traders, who nudged each
other and laughed. She could feel the pull of their male-
ness and wanted to finger her cemí—that tiny bit of
flesh she worshipped because it felt so good when she
touched it. Tahíaca often lay awake at night fingering
herself and listening to Caonabó pleasuring his wives.
She was a precocious, provocative six-year-old who could
not wait to grow up.

Ana's daughter was at home in all worlds—playmate to the children, respectful helper to the wives,
budding child-woman to disturb all the men. Tahíaca's
mouth smiled even when she was serious.

Caonabó was kneeling beside the river when Tahíaca
found him, working quickly and surely, washing away
silt, throwing away pebbles until two gold nuggets lay
in his cupped palm. One was the size of a grain of corn,
the other the size of a duck's egg.

The iguana lashed into a smile as Caonabó tossed
the smaller nugget back. He fondled the larger nugget
as a man fondles a woman's breast. He was about to
lie back and begin masturbating when he heard a noise
behind him.

Tahíaca! Tahíaca never stayed where she belonged,
or rather Tahíaca never believed she did not belong
wherever she wanted to go.

Caonabó looked up and frowned, but when he saw
the baked yam she held out to him, he realized how
hungry he was. In three strides he was back into the
world of women. He picked Tahíaca up and set her on
his shoulder. All the way down the mountain, Tahíaca
warmed his heart chattering about the coming areíto.
When they came into sight of the village, Caonabó set
Tahíaca on the ground and showed her the nugget.

"For me?" she asked, dancing around and squealing
with delight.

"No. For your mother Ana. Go find her and tell her Caonabó waits."

Later, Caonabó came down the mountain hand in hand with a radiant Ana. Tahíaca and Higueymato ran quickly to get his carved wooden throne and place it among the caciques under the ceiba. His wives brought his tall golden crown—an intricately designed crown three feet tall, with scrolls and swirls hiding mythical animals and great staring eyes. Caonabó signaled the areíto to begin.

Softly Ana began to sing. The crowd quieted and only the rustling leaves of the ceiba accompanied Ana's dancing feet as she performed the areíto of Cacique Caonabó, mighty Carib warrior, father of many children, wise ruler of Cibao. The last rays of the sun gilded Ana's lovely body. At the end of her song, she knelt before Caonabó, looking up expectantly as he surveyed the waiting wives and the lusty traders.

"May the wives and concubines of Caonabó make him many happy children tonight," he said, waving his hands in benediction.

Joyous lovers vanished into the twilight, leaving only Caonabó and Ana under the ceiba. Ana took away his heavy crown while he slowly traced her navel.

CHAPTER 2

Córdoba, Spain, 1491

"RAV JOSEPH will never do it" said his wife with a worried look on her usually serene face. "Never. You know him. He is your brother."

"You can persuade him, Sefira. He will listen to you," urged Rafella. "You have to make him understand how easy it is. All he has to do is say a few words and let the friar baptize him. It will take only a few minutes. Then you go to confession once in a while, attend Mass sometimes, and give a little money to the special projects. It's easy. Aram did it, and so did I. Nothing's changed. We're still Jews, and we keep the Law, the fasts, and feasts. Of course, we have to be very careful who knows, and we can't teach Daniel until he is old enough not to betray us. You can become Christians and still be Jews in your hearts."

"He won't. I know he won't." Sefira's voice showed the strain. "To become a Christian just to stay in Andalucía would violate his conscience. He will never do it. Never."

"I know," sighed Rafella. "My brother is a stubborn man. Even when we were children studying Hebrew together, Joseph was the devout one. Even then he knew he wanted to become a rabbi. Rabbis know too much for their own good. It is not good to take even the Law too seriously."

The two women sat on the little balcony looking down into Rafella's flower-filled patio where their husbands sat talking. It seemed to Rafella that women were always sitting on balconies isolated from the men who made all the decisions. Even in the little synagogue a few doors away, the women sat on the balcony while the men prayed.

Siesta was almost over now, and afternoon shadows cooled the patio. Soon she would have to wake her son Daniel and send him down to keep the bodega. People would begin coming in to buy wines, or medicinal herbs, or amulets to cure their sicknesses and ward off evil spirits. Some would come hoping to fetch her husband, Aram Torres, one of the most respected doctors in Córdoba. Daniel would tell them his father was not at home; and, of course, no one could expect a seven-year-old boy to know the prices. So, by sending Daniel to tend the bodega, the New Christian Torres family could keep the Sabbath and still seem to be working.

Jews who converted had to learn to live a double life. On the Sabbath, Rafella always sat with her spindle in her lap so she could begin spinning if strangers came into the patio. To be found not working on the Sabbath was to be accused of judaizing. People were burned at the stake on such evidence of heresy.

Of course, the Church washed its hands of all blame for the death of heretics. All the Church did was establish the Holy Office of the Inquisition to identify the judaizers, to torture confessions out of them and, if they refused to recant, to "relax" them to the civil authorities, who were expected to burn them. *Relax!* A strange word to use to cover up such horrible deeds! And they called the whole ceremony an "act-of-faith"!

"Aram was always different, wasn't he?" asked Sefira. "Aram had eyes only for you. Aram always does what he thinks will make you happy."

"Aram is a good husband," Rafella agreed. "So is Joseph, Sefira. He loves you. I am sure he does."

"Perhaps, but he loves God more. Even at midnight on Sabbath eve, when love between a man and his wife is supposed to reunite God and His Shekhina, Joseph seems to be thinking more about that mystery than he is about me." Sefira blushed to be speaking so intimately, even with her good friend and sister-in-law Rafella.

"Isn't every Hebrew supposed to love God above everything else? Isn't that why they find ten men to make up a minyan and recite the Shema morning, noon, and night? Isn't that why the Shema is the most sacred of Hebrew prayers?"

"Yes, but some men only say the Shema with their lips. 'Hear, O Israel, the Lord our God, the Lord is One...' Rav Joseph has the words engraved on his heart. He truly loves God with all his heart, with all his soul, and with all his might." Sefira sighed. "He will never become a Christian, even outwardly. Never."

"Then you may have to leave Andalucía if the Cardinal persuades Queen Isabela to sign the expulsion order," said Rafella.

"How can I?" cried Sefira. "Can an olive tree live if it be uprooted? My family came to this land when the Roman Emperor Titus destroyed the Second Temple in Jerusalem, fourteen hundred years ago. Fourteen hundred years! How can I leave? I know nothing of Jerusalem except the stories Joseph reads from the Torah in the synagogue. I know only my home warmed by the Andalucían sun shining down on our olive groves. How can they expect us all to leave? How dare they force us to give up our faith? What shall we believe? Where shall we go?"

"Calm yourself, Sefira. Aram says there may be a way out. Luis de Santángel is coming here today to meet the mapmaker Cristóbal Colón, who thinks he can sail west to find Cathay. Marco Polo said there were Jews in Cathay. If the Queen approves his voyage, and if Colón finds Cathay, perhaps you can live there."

"I don't want to live in Cathay. I don't want to live anywhere but Andalucía. I am not a child of the Exile to go wandering around the world thinking that even if I die, my bones will be gathered up in the resurrection and taken back to Jerusalem. Córdoba is my home, not Jerusalem. If I have to leave my home, I shall surely die." Sefira was almost in tears.

"It is time to wake the children," said Rafella, to get her friend's mind off her troubles. "If we don't open the bodega soon, someone will be sure to tell the Inquisitor we are keeping the Sabbath."

Rafella woke Daniel and his five-year-old cousin Rachel, then settled down to cheer Sefira with family talk. The family, always the family. Marrying and begetting, carrying on the traditions.

Great-grandfather Efram ben Torres ibn Chincillo had been baptized Santángel during Fray Vincente de Ferrar's great crusade after the 1391 pogrom, when so many Jews had been massacred. Luis de Santángel, who was coming today, was a distant cousin. Another cousin by the same name had assassinated the Inquisitor Pedro de Arbués while he prayed in the Cathedral, so all the Santángels were still under suspicion, even Luis, the financial secretary to King Fernando.

The Abravanels, Rav Joseph's family on his mother's side, were financial wizards and "tax farmers"—as tax collectors were called—who had helped raise money for the Moorish wars. Gabriel Sánchez, the Queen's Treasurer, was a distant cousin. Another cousin named Sánchez had also been involved in the assassination plot. The illustrious history of the Sánchez family went back even farther. Some of their relatives had been martyred at Massada.

Few people of influence in all the Iberian peninsula were without Jewish blood. Even King Fernando was part Jewish, as had been the Grand Inquisitor himself, Torquemada. But not all the Torres and Sánchez family were as illustrious. Not all were court advisors. They were also physicians, carpenters, shoemakers, and weavers. They had fought in Christian armies against the Moors, and they had risen to high positions in the Church. Why then would not the Church be satisfied to let some of them, men like Rav Joseph, keep their ancient faith?

Whenever Rafella and Sefira talked, they came back to the same question: Why were the Jews always persecuted?

To get away from such dismal talk they began to gossip about Cristóbal Cólon, who spent a great deal of time at the bodega drinking wine with Aram and the Harana brothers and talking about his dream to sail across the Western Ocean to Cathay.

"Is Cristóbal going to marry his mistress, Doña Beatriz de Harana, now that his wife is dead?" asked Sefira.

"I don't think he will ever marry again," answered Rafella. "Cristóbal is married to his dream, and when such a Lilith possesses a man, he can have no other wife."

"What of her son Fernando? Isn't Cristóbal going to legitimize the boy? How old is he now?"

"Oh, six or seven. About Daniel's age, I suppose. Cristóbal takes care of Doña Beatriz and the boy, though he leaves his older son, Diego, with the friars at La Rabida when he goes off on a voyage."

"Doña Beatriz is better off not married to a man who wants to sail over the edge of the world. Rav Joseph may be stubborn, always studying the Torah, but at least he stays at home." Sefira comforted herself by comparing her husband with men of less admirable character. Certainly Cristóbal Cólon was a fool, if not a madman.

Don Luis de Santángel always traveled with a retinue of caballeros, for not only was he a favorite of both King and Queen, he was also very rich. He had once courted Isabela, but had stepped aside gallantly for handsome young King Fernando of Aragon. Both King and Queen had been very poor at the time of their wedding, and Santángel had brought the necklace Fernando gave Isabela upon their betrothal. So Santángel was a very powerful man.

Santángel stopped his retinue at the dusty little plaza outside the old Roman walls, the place where they burned the heretics. People were already calling it the

23

Field of the Martyrs. Santángel shuddered as though someone had walked over his grave.

"Take the horses to the stables at the Alcázar," he ordered. "We shall stop there for the night and get an early start tomorrow for Santa Fé. I have business now in La Mezquita."

Santángel dared not disclose his true mission, but his attendant, dressed almost as richly as he in velvet bloomers and brocade doublet, did not question the King's secretary. Both King and Queen often sent him on secret missions. So Sántangel disappeared around the corner and started up the cobblestone incline past the barnlike building with the mudejar gates—La Mezquita. Three Mohammedan rulers had been two centuries building this mosque, enlarging it to accommodate all the faithful who had gathered on Friday nights to say the special prayer for the khalif. The marble pillars and building stones had been taken from demolished Christian churches in conquered cities. Built by Christian slaves, it had been conceived to remind mankind forever of the greatness of God.

Surely La Mezquita had been built on holy ground, for once a pagan temple had stood here, then a Gothic church, then La Mezquita, and now somewhere in the bowels of La Mezquita a Catholic cathedral was rising to glorify the Crucified One. La Mezquita covered thirty-three thousand one hundred and fifty square cubits—a third again larger than St. John's apocalyptic New Jerusalem. The largest library in the medieval world had been assembled in Córdoba, and the greatest professors in the world had been attached to La Mezquita, sitting up against the marble columns to teach science, literature, mathematics, astrology, medicine, and religion.

Santángel always stopped in La Mezquita to say a prayer, to walk through the forest of marble pillars with their red-and-white-striped arches intertwining with each other into the dim recesses of the building, and to imagine the people in jeweled turbans and flowing white robes listening to the long-dead Imam read from the Khalif's copy of the Koran—the one he always carried into battle to remind the faithful that their names would be instantly inscribed in the Book of Life if they died fighting for Allah. Santángel could almost hear them chanting: "God is great. There is no god but God."

But today, Santángel hurried on, feeling the pull of the judería. In such twisted streets with iron-grated balconies and hanging gardens, Santángel had been born. The lives of all the Jews of Spain were hidden behind such gates, securely locked in at night. All were forced to convert or wear the red badge of shame. No matter how high they rose in the service of the King, they would all joke with each other about the indelible stamp of the judería.

His ties to the judería, rather than the Queen's secret commission, had brought Santángel to Córdoba this Sabbath day. For Santángel had seen Talavera's draft of the order expelling the Jews from the land they had called home for so long. Their Catholic Highnesses had not yet signed the order, but it was only a matter of time until their confessors persuaded them to do so. It was imperative that this Genoese mapmaker, Cristóbal Colón, be right. The Jews would have to find a new Jerusalem.

Little Rachel Sánchez saw Santángel first, and she ran to tug at Daniel's shirttail as he stood just inside the bodega door listening to his elders on the patio. It was nearly sunset now, and the patio was completely shaded. Honeysuckle filled the air with its cloyingly sweet perfume.

"Daniel, come quickly." Rachel tugged again.

"Hush! Leave me alone. I want to hear what they are saying."

"They are only gossipping about the family. Telling stories you have heard a hundred times."

"But I want to hear. How else am I going to have anything to talk about when I become a man and sit in patios? Now go on. Don't bother me."

"But he's here!"

"Who's here?"

"Don Luis de Santángel. He's outside in the street looking for the right gate."

"Why didn't you tell me? Get out of my way. I have

25

to be sure it is Don Luis de Santángel before I let him in on the Sabbath."

Santángel came into the patio and embraced Aram and Rav Joseph like a man who has not seen a good friend for a long, long time. They exchanged blessings, pleasantries about weather and traveling in Andalucía, and bits of family gossip, while Rafella served wine and little fish cakes. Then a silence developed. After a bit Santángel broke it by asking:

"Where is Colón? Is he coming?"

"Oh, yes, he will be here. You can be sure of that," Aram said. "He has been here every day this week to see if you had arrived. Doña Beatriz will see that he doesn't forget. For the chance to have such a friend at court as Don Luis de Santángel, who would not come— even on the Sabbath?"

They passed the time with family talk, and they could not avoid talk of family members who had already been victimized by the Inquisition—like the Santángel cousin and the Sánchez cousin, both drawn and quartered, with their arms and legs tied to four horses pulling in different directions. Two questions demanded answers: Why do the Christians hate us so? Will the Exile that started so long ago when our fathers were carried away into Babylon begin all over again? Santángel was close to the throne. Perhaps he would know.

"Cousin Luis," asked Aram. "When Granada falls, what will happen to the Jews?"

"Who knows?" shrugged Santángel, not wanting to raise their fears by talking about Talavera's order. Powerful Jews like Abravanel were trying to raise money enough to bribe the King not to sign.

"If I knew, would I be asking?" Aram said. "Tell us the truth, Cousin Luis."

"You think the Rum bastards will be satisfied with the fall of Granada?" Santángel sounded bitter. No one used the old Arab slur word "Rum" to talk about the Christians unless he despised them; for "Rum" meant Roman in Arabic, and the Arabs had good reason to despise the Romans.

"Why do the Rum hate us so?" asked Aram.

"For seven hundred years," said Santángel wearily, as though he were instructing a retarded child, "every time a new Sultan came to power, he had to prove himself by laying waste Rum cities, burning Rum crops, making slaves of Rum captives—castrating some to make harem eunuchs—and blinding the musicians so they could play for the sultan's wives in their baths. Why do you think victorious Christians hung those slave chains on the walls of the Cathedral in Toledo? To remind themselves that their rage had stopped the Moors at the Pyrenees. Rum revenge spawned the Crusades. Rum determination has built the city of Santa Fé in only three months so Queen Isabela and her ladies can be near the siege of Granada to pray for the Christian victory. What do you think will happen when Granada falls?"

"We have sinned," said Rav Joseph. "We have gone a-whoring after false Gods. We convert because we fear for our lives, or because we don't want to leave our comfortable homes. We say we can be Christians and still keep the Covenant, but we deceive ourselves. Be not deceived. The Most Holy One, blessed be He, will not be mocked. Israel will suffer for our transgressions even unto the third and fourth generations."

"With all due respect, Rav Joseph," said Santángel, "conversion is the only way. Isabela is a pious woman. She will not tolerate a people who are not Christians living in a united Spain."

"Why?" asked Aram. "Why can't we live in peace together?"

"They blame us for the seven hundred years of Moslem rule. They say Jews conspired to invite the Berbers to cross the Strait of Gibraltar. Perhaps it is true. The Sultans always left Jews in charge of conquered cities. We were court advisors and tax farmers. They say we built palaces like the Alhambra with money wrung from the Christians, and we did!"

"We are not all tax farmers," cried Aram. "We were court advisors to *Christian* kings too. Why, Santángel? Why?"

"We are their scapegoats," said Santángel in a soft voice. "We have always been the scapegoats. When a

27

people need to send their sins into the wilderness and cleanse themselves of their own failures, they look for scapegoats. Afterward, for a little while, they feel righteous. That is why we are God's Chosen People. To be scapegoats for everyone else!"

"You border on blasphemy," said Rav Joseph.

"You have to believe in God to blaspheme," said Santángel. "We have only one world. We are born, we live, we die. That is all! If there is a God somewhere, he is a monster who sets us against each other, then laughs to see us destroy ourselves."

"Blasphemy! You are one of the Averroists!" shouted Rav Joseph. "Why are you so interested in this mapmaker's project if you do not believe in God?"

"Because we are the only Messiah we will ever have. Because I am a Hebrew from my mother's breast. Because I cannot live with myself if I do not do whatever I can to keep my people from perishing. But don't talk to me about God. I spit on God!"

"Blasphemy! Blasphemy!" shouted Rav Joseph.

"I spit on a God who killed Egyptian babies so Pharaoh would let our people go! I spit on a God who destroyed women and children in Jericho and became peeved when a poor Israelite took a few trinkets and hid them in his tent! How can we be proud of such a vicious God? No wonder Israel suffers. If you kabbalists are right and souls are sent back to earth time and time again to atone for sins, the cycle will never end. We have so many sins to atone for. Will we ever stop killing each other in the name of God?"

"Blasphemer! Blasphemer!" cried Rav Joseph, jumping up and running around the patio with his hands over his ears. "Woe to the Community of Israel, for the Most Holy One has departed from us. We are nothing but a nation of tax collectors and whoremongers and winebibbers. Judgment is come upon us. How shall we escape from the wrath to come?"

Sefira rushed down the stairs into the patio to cradle Rav Joseph in her arms. Rachel heard her father shouting, ran out of the bodega, stumbled, and fell. Daniel picked her up and stood with his arms around her, holding her back while Sefira led Joseph away. Then Daniel led Rachel back into the bodega and gave her a licorice root to suck to stop her crying. A red-haired man with a bundle of sheepskins under his arm was standing in the doorway. Two boys peered out from behind his simple country shirt.

"Señor Colón!" said Daniel.

"The same," Colón answered. "How are you, Daniel? Ready to sail to Cathay with me?"

"Oh, yes," said Daniel, his eyes shining with the wanderlust he had caught from Colón, a disease he would never outgrow.

"Did Don Luis de Santángel come today?" asked Colón.

"Yes, Señor. They are waiting for you in the patio. Please do me the favor of coming with me."

"You boys stay here," said Colón. "Mind your manners, now. Behave like gentlemen as the friars taught you."

"Yes, Papa," said Diego, nudging his little half-brother.

"Yes, Papa," echoed Fernando.

"Lead the way, Daniel," said Colón.

Daniel had never felt more important. He tried to walk as he had seen caballeros walk, with an insolent swagger. When his father introduced Señor Colón to cousin Luis, Daniel stood close by proudly, hoping they would let him stay to hear.

"That will be all, thank you, Daniel," said his father.

Daniel turned reluctantly and went back into the bodega.

"Let's play Christians and Moors," said Fernando when Daniel returned. "Rachel can be the beautiful Christian girl, and I will be the mean Moorish sultan. Daniel, you and Diego can be caballeros trying to rescue Rachel."

"I don't want to be the beautiful Christian girl," said Rachel. "I want to have another licorice root to suck."

"Be quiet, Rachel," said Daniel. "I want to hear what they are saying on the patio."

"Why can't I have another licorice root?" Rachel asked.

"Why can't we play Moors and Christians?" asked Fernando.

"I don't want to play Moors and Christians," said Rachel, crossing her arms over her chest and puffing out her cheeks. "I want another licorice root. If I can't have another licorice root, Daniel Torres, I won't marry you when I grow up."

"Here, take your licorice root," said Daniel, reaching for the jar on the shelf beside the Lilith amulets. "Suck it and be quiet. Papa says this conference with Don Luis is very important. We must not disturb them."

"Oh, thank you, Daniel," said Rachel, throwing her arms around Daniel and kissing him.

"Don't kiss me, Rachel," he ordered, as his face turned scarlet. "How many times have I told you not to kiss me! Especially in front of people."

"It is all right if I kiss you," said Rachel. "We are betrothed. Papa says so. I am going to marry you someday."

"No, you are not. I am not going to marry anyone. I am going around the world with Señor Colón."

"You are going to make a fine Hebrew husband."

"No, I am not. I am a convert. I was baptized in La Mezquita when I was a baby. I haven't even been circumcised!"

"Your mama washed the chrism off the minute she got you home. I know. You're a Hebrew, all right. If you're not circumcised, then show me you're not."

"Girls!" scoffed Daniel.

Girls were always talking about getting married and other boring things. He liked his cousin Rachel, and one day he had bloodied a Christian boy's nose for making fun of her, but he wished she were a boy so they could talk about going to sea together. They did everything else together.

Like sneaking into La Mezquita and munching on the stolen wafers of the Host, then running through all those marble pillars with young Fray Dominic chasing them. They had escaped into the Patio of Oranges and scooted out the back gate into the judería, then hidden in the ladies' gallery of the synagogue while the friar went running up and down all the narrow streets crying blasphemy. He hadn't really gotten a good look at their faces, because Fray Dominic could not see very well. They had gotten away with it, but both would have been disciplined severely for such dangerous behavior if their parents had known.

Daniel had been afraid Rachel might tell, but she never did. Even if she was a girl, she could be trusted. One day he probably would marry her. They had been betrothed when they were babies; but in the meantime, he wished Rachel had been a boy. Even if boys could never be as pretty as Rachel.

"Girls!" Daniel muttered again, then walked to the door of the bodega to listen to more important things.

The mapmaker's red hair was already graying, and his ruddy face was lined from squinting at the sea. He wasted no time after being introduced to Santángel, but spread his maps and began to talk, catching them all up in his vision. He was like a mystic who, having seen God, no longer doubts Him. He knew he could find Cathay by sailing west. Fabulous treasures awaited only the building of a few ships.

"How did the Queen react to your proposal?" asked Santángel, although he already knew she had referred it to a commission of churchmen. "Does Her Catholic Highness share your strange dream?"

"I remember the first day I saw her," Colón began. "It was the first of May, right here in Córdoba in the garden of the Alcázar. Such a pious woman, Her Highness. So beautiful. So gracious. So dignified."

"Enough! Enough!" said Santángel. "Every Andalucían reveres the Queen. Are not our highways now safe? Has she not melded warring fiefdoms into one mighty kingdom? Now, what did she say?"

"Her Highness was interested," said Colón, but the joy had gone out of his voice. "She has many pressing problems...the Moorish wars...the Inqui—"

Colón let the sentence trail off, embarrassed that he

had almost mentioned the Inquisition, which must cause pain to the Torres and Sánchez families, to say nothing of Santángel.

"She put me on the payroll," Colón continued, a trace of bitterness in his voice. "A modest salary...my wife died recently...Doña Beatriz and my sons...you know how it is. A man cannot sacrifice everything for his dream."

"What if the commission reports unfavorably?" asked Santángel, although he knew they already had. He wanted to know what Colón's plans were. The Queen had been very specific about that. She might not want to approve the venture herself, and she certainly lacked the funds to back it, but she did not want any other Christian prince taking up the project.

"It is a crazy scheme," said Aram. "They say no one can live in the tropics. As a physician, I believe them. The human body can stand only so much."

"The Portuguese have proved the tropics of Africa are inhabited," said Colón, enthusiasm coming back into his voice. "Everyone knows the world is a sphere. Pliny...Ptolemy...Have you read Marco Polo's book about the riches of Cathay? Or Pierre d'Ailly's *Imago Mundo*? In the name of the Blessed Virgin, I know I can find Cathay."

Daniel had been edging closer to Colón. He was ready to follow the explorer anywhere.

"Who will man such ships?" asked Aram.

"I will, Papa," said Daniel.

"Ah, Blessed Virgin María," said Colón, ruffling Daniel's hair. "To have the faith of a little child."

"Truly, God's Shekhina is guiding you," said Rav Joseph, who had come back into the patio when Colón arrived. "You may find the ten lost tribes. Didn't Marco Polo find Jews worshipping in Cathay?"

"Don't launch into a sermon, Rav Joseph," said Santángel. "Sephardic Jewry is reeling before the Inquisition, and what do you rabbis do? Put on your phylacteries and your prayer shawls. Sit meditating on the Tree of Life. Bah! I spit on you."

Colón started to roll his maps.

"Perhaps I should be on my way. I have taken too much of your time, Don Luis. My brother Bartolomé is in London, and I may go to see the King of France."

"Don't be in such a hurry," said Santángel. "Perhaps I can persuade the Queen. I do still have a certain influence with her. But you will need money to outfit your ships, and the Queen has spent all she has raised in the siege of Granada. Gabriel Sánchez, her treasurer, is privately wealthy. He is interested, and so is Abravanel. Perhaps he can raise the rest."

"We will raise the money," promised Aram. "You persuade the Queen."

Colón's face brightened as he clutched his maps. His eyes had a faraway look, as though he saw farther than any other man would ever see.

"And you, Cristóbal," said Santángel. "What do you want from all this, besides the pleasure of being right?"

"To be Admiral of the Ocean Sea and Viceroy of all the domains I acquire for Castilla. To govern those domains and pass the reigns of power on to my heirs." Colón had become another man now. Not the mystic, but a man with an old score to settle. "To receive ten percent of all the revenues from the lands for myself and my heirs forever and ever..."

"Impossible!" Aram warned.

"And," said Colón, with his head held high and a determined look on his face. "And...to entitle myself Don Cristóbal Colón."

"The Queen will never agree," said Aram. "Your blood is not pure enough to be called Don."

"Leave the Queen to me," said Santángel, smiling slyly.

"Don Cristóbal," said Daniel, looking up at him with adoring eyes. "Take me with you."

"Perhaps on the next voyage, Daniel," Colón said. "You can be my cabin boy. We will visit the Great Khan together, and you can pick up gold and emeralds from the seashore."

Daniel turned away to hide his disappointment. He saw Rachel standing in the doorway of the bodega, holding a licorice root and sticking out her tongue.

CHAPTER 3

Granada, 1492

A FEW months later, on January 2, 1492, Granada was finally starved into submission. People who studied the stars said 1492 was a tiny crack that would split the world in two; nothing would ever be the same again. Spain was Catholic. The silent mosques became cathedrals. After eight hundred years of Moslem rule, Spain was finally united under one flag and one faith. No, not completely united—there was still the question of the Jews.

The breeze off the snow-capped Sierra Nevada stirred the flag of Their Catholic Highnesses King Fernando of Aragon and Queen Isabela of Castilla. Cristóbal Colón had been summoned to court, and marched proudly in the triumphal parade through the crooked, narrow streets of Granada to the walls of the palace crowning the crescent city. The cross gleamed atop the Alhambra. *Alhambra...Alhambra...to whisper "Alhambra" calls up exotic visions....Alhambra...*

Isabela's heart overflowed with gratitude, and she spent a great deal of her time on her knees praying.

"Holy Mary, Mother of God, pray for us sinners now and at the hour of our death..."

Sometimes Isabela could not believe God had chosen her to work such miracles, to drive the Islamic infidels from the land, to unite the peninsula under one rule and one faith...well, almost one faith. Her confessor kept reminding her she must be humble in the face of such an outpouring of God's blessings. How could she, an obscure princess with little chance of inheriting the throne, have accomplished so much except with the help of God? She was troubled in her dreams about the series of poisonings that cleared her way to the throne, but she had nothing to do with them, and had not been able to find anyone who did. She comforted herself in the still of the night by the thought that it was God's will she was on the throne of Castilla and had kept it firmly in her grasp even when married to Fernando of Aragon. Women need not always be subject to their husbands, at least not if they are queens.

God had a wondrous work for them to do, and neither she nor Fernando could have done it alone. Isabela knew this, and she was grateful to God. She spent so much time on her knees to fight the sin of pride. It would be easy to become proud.

"Holy Mary, Mother of God, pray for us sinners..."

It was Maundy Thursday, March 29, 1492. Isabela had been walking in the gardens of the sultan's summer palace atop the mountain behind the Alhambra, silent and empty now except for the birds, the butterflies, and the ever-gurgling water running through the underground channels to the numerous fountains of the Alhambra.

Isabela was troubled. She walked down the gallery of the Patio de la Acequía and climbed to the guard tower. Below her was Granada; above her, the cross gleamed beside the fluttering colors of Castilla and Aragon. She could not see the cross on the roof of the tower, so she turned and walked past the pool and the spraying fountains before looking back. Then she made her way down the mountain under the covered oleander walkways. She stopped to pick a rose in the garden, then passed through the silent harem into the Alhambra itself.

All about her she saw disturbing evidence of Moorish decadence...subterranean baths where blinded musicians had played while sultans and their ladies walked through steam baths on floors so hot they had to use wooden shoes...airy towers and marble fountains in the middle of chambers whose crowning beauty was their lacy ceilings carved in a matrix of lime mixed with marble and alabaster. Niches in the walls still smelled of heady perfumes. Everywhere carpets, cushions, and draperies whisper of ravished maidens—ravished Christian maidens taken captive in the wars, released now into the custody of the caballeros who besieged Granada.

Isabela paused to pray in the sultan's mosque, now being converted into a chapel. "Holy Mary, Mother of God, pray for us..."

Isabela left the chapel, still fingering her rosary, still praying for guidance as she walked toward the Court of Lions. Sunlight blazed down into the courtyard, gilding the lions, gilding the mudejar lacework, gilding the fountain. Gilding everything except the twelve poor Dominican friars who stood awkwardly around the fountain waiting for their Queen to fulfill an ancient custom first performed by our Blessed Savior. A hint of Arabian perfume lingered in the air.

The Queen took a basin, filled it with water spurting from the mouth of one of the lions, girded herself with a towel, knelt, and washed the feet of each of the twelve. The last man, a nearsighted young friar named Dominic, drew back as if to say, with the disciples, "Not me, Lord." Isabela grasped his foot gently but firmly and put it into the water.

Then, having proved even a queen is humble before God, she walked to the shaded portico at the end of the courtyard and knelt before her confessor, Cardinal Talavera. Her rosary beads felt like great drops of blood. Was this her Gethsemane? Was Torquemada right about the thirty thousand ducats the Jews were offering Fernando not to sign the expulsion order? Are we betraying our Lord as Judas Iscariot betrayed Him? She murmured her confession and began the prayers of her penance.

"Holy Mary, Mother of God, pray for..."

The Queen did not sleep well that night, and when she awoke on Good Friday, her heart still ached remembering Christ's Passion. Oh, Merciful Savior! What gift can compare with your gift? What tribute can be laid before so Compassionate a Lord?

After morning prayers, the Queen spent her day in matters of state—organizing the subjugation of a conquered people. Toward evening she made her way again to the sultan's private mosque. She knelt at the balcony rail and looked down where Friday night prayers used to be said in the sultan's honor—infidel prayers.

Cardinal Talavera was saying Mass. How marvelous it was that the power of the worshippers of Allah had been broken, that the scimitar no longer cut across Spain! As the Host was uplifted, Isabela felt a surge of gratitude.

It was nearly sundown. No meuzzin would call the faithful to prayers in mosques that Friday night, but the Jews would still be lighting their Sabbath lamps all over Andalucía. Isabela felt a surge of shame. Andalucía? If every knee bowed, and every tongue confessed...

Isabela fingered her beads as she prayed, "Holy Mary, Mother of God, pray..."

Holy Saturday dawned bright and clear. Isabela no longer felt a burden on her heart, for she had selected her Easter gift to the Crucified Christ. After Mass, Cardinal Talavera solemnly handed her the parchment, and she affixed her signature: *I, the Queen.*

It was finished. The Royal Cédula became the law of the land. The sons and daughters of Abraham, of Solomon's traders who came to Spain when it was called Tarshish, would now become Christians or find another home. Isabela picked up her rosary, looked up at the cross, and began to pray.

"Holy Mary, Mother of God..."

Easter was a triumphant Sunday in 1492.

Two weeks later, on April 14, Luis de Santángel persuaded Queen Isabela to authorize Cristóbal Colón's expedition. Gabriel Sánchez, the converted Jew who was the Queen's Treasurer, told her the kingdom's coffers had been emptied by the Moorish wars. The expedition must be financed privately. The Queen offered her jewels as collateral, but Sánchez told her they would not be needed. He guaranteed private financing for Colón's venture, assuming the Queen knew it would be Jewish financing. The Queen did not ask whose money Sánchez would add to his own. Perhaps it would be some of the money raised to offer a bribe to Their Catholic Highnesses not to sign the expulsion order. If it was, the Queen did not want to know.

CHAPTER 4

Córdoba, 1492

"HEAR, O Israel, the Lord our God, the Lord is One. And thou shalt love the Lord thy God with all thy heart, with all thy soul, and with all thy might..."

Sefira could hear Rav Joseph praying, all muffled up in his prayer shawl and bound up in leather straps. A stab of jealousy pierced her heart. Immediately she was ashamed of herself. She had known when she stood under the wedding canopy with Joseph that she would always occupy second place, and she had told herself then that it didn't matter. Can the moon refuse to shine because she occupies second place to the sun? Sefira did not know what was wrong with her.

True, they had had only four months to leave Andalucía. Only four months! By July 31, 1492, Jews must convert or leave Spain forever. There had been no doubt in Sefira's mind that Rav Joseph would leave rather than convert. Why, then, was she so upset?

Sometimes she felt as if it were winter and she had been out in the cold so long she had turned to stone, as Lot's wife had turned to salt. Sometimes she felt as if she were burning up, as if the fires of Hell were inside her. Sometimes she would move about the house like a shadow, not speaking for days. Sometimes she would lash out at Rachel until the poor child cowered like a wounded animal.

Rav Joseph would come then and try to make peace between his normally patient wife and his bewildered daughter. Sometimes Sefira would be so worked up she would lash out at Joseph as if she hated him. Then she would be so ashamed. She would cradle Rachel in her arms and apologize to Joseph.

Sefira didn't hate Joseph, she loved him. Sefira hated God, but she would not allow herself to even think such a thought. No, she loved God. "Hear, O Israel, the Lord our God, the Lord is One. And thou shalt love the Lord thy God..."

Half of the four months allotted to the Jews had passed, and Sefira could not even help Joseph with the packing. Sometimes she would just sit in the patio, moving only as the sun moved, trying to keep in the shade, for it was summer now in Córdoba.

Sephardic theologians had a tradition for what was wrong with Sefira. One of the great thirteenth-century kabbalists had described her condition perfectly: As a soul descends from the curtain of souls around the Throne of Glory to inhabit a body, it must acquire a shield. That shield, called a *zelum,* is made up of the deeds of one's life. When the zelum ceases to protect the body from its immortal soul, the body is consumed in its fiery brilliance. Sefira's zelum was becoming frayed.

Rav Joseph and his family lived in the ruins of the Medinatu-az-Zahra, an Arab palace her family had bought and given her as both a dowry and a wedding present—for even in ruins, the Medinatu-az-Zahra had great value. Sefira was in the patio, taking cuttings from various plants, when Aram arrived for one last talk with Rav Joseph. Aram stood under the grape arbor over the gateway watching the little family in the false security of their walled garden, trying to think of something to say to change Joseph's mind. Jews had lived in such gardens for centuries, making their homes the center of their lives, safe from the prying eyes of gentiles, but now the walls were crumbling.

Rav Joseph was packing books in panniers, some to be carried by mules; the most precious, except for the Torah, to be carried on Rav Joseph's back. From time to time the rabbi's wife stopped to wipe away unbidden tears, streaking her face with the yellow ochre of the Spanish soil. Knowing she would soon have to live without servants, she took a perverse satisfaction in doing such work herself.

Rachel flitted back and forth between her parents, excited about the journey. She had never been farther from home than the city of Córdoba five miles away. Now they were going all the way to Lisbon, Portugal. Rachel could not understand why her mother was so upset.

"Joseph," Sefira called, "what do we do if we run out of saffron?"

"Did not God provide manna in the wilderness?" Rav Joseph asked, trying to be patient. "Must you complain even before we start on our journey? What is a pinch of saffron or two?"

"Don't you like your Sabbath dishes flavored with saffron?" she asked.

"Have you not said enough, woman?" Rav Joseph clapped his hands, looking sternly at his wife lest he break under his love for her and go running off to La Mezquita to be baptized. "Enough, I say! Enough!"

Sefira took her basket of clippings and went into Az-Zahra. Rachel looked up questioningly at her father.

"Don't they have saffron in Portugal, Papa?" she asked, skipping along beside her father as he went for another armload of books.

"Who knows what they eat in Portugal?" said Rav Joseph. "Is this Egypt? Can we not trust Him who brought the plagues on Pharaoh and delivered His children out of bondage? Now go into the house and see if you can help your mother."

Rachel skipped across the wine-red marble flagstones into the old palace. Sefira was standing beside one of the pillars, her face leaning against the cool marble, running her hands up and down the delicate tracery of the Arabic carvings.

How she loved Az-Zahra, even in ruins! Az-Zahra was a woman's palace, built and named for the mistress of a sultan, begun with money willed by a rich concubine to redeem Moslem captives. Miraculously, not one Moslem captive had been found in all the Christian countries, so Medinatu-az-Zahra had been built on the south slope of the mountain called the Bride of Córdoba. Sefira had wanted to live there ever since she discovered an old Arabian manuscript and painstakingly translated the wondrous tale.

Ten thousand workmen had labored to complete Az-Zahra, and it had cost a third of the sultan's annual revenues—half the money being raised with a per-capita tax on Christians and Jews living in Moslem domains. Marble for the four thousand pillars had come from Rome, France, Constantinople, Carthage, Tunis, Africa—and of course, Andalucía, where marble was plentiful. Its fifteen thousand doors had been plated with iron and brass. The fish in the ponds of the gardens of Az-Zahra had consumed twelve thousand loaves of bread daily.

Most splendid of all the rooms had been the Hall of the Khalifs, where they entertained frightened Christian ambassadors with displays of lightning from the quicksilver lamp in the middle of the room. The roof of this splendid room had been tiled with gold and silver, reflecting the sunlight so brilliantly it was said observers had to shield their eyes to keep from being blinded. The sultans had justified such splendor by saying that their subjects, seeing their rulers dwelling in such quarters, might get some idea of the delights of the celestial paradise reserved for true believers.

Once an entire city of such palaces had lined the River Guadalquivir, in the valley of Córdoba, forming a strip six miles wide and twenty-six miles long. That was before civil war destroyed them all.

Now nothing remained of Az-Zahra except the Hall of the Khalifs, minus its magic lamp and its gold-and-silver dome. Sefira had been just a young schoolgirl when she first read about Az-Zahra, but she had made up her mind to live there. Somehow her father, a rich tax farmer, had bribed the authorities to let his daughter and her husband live outside the walled judería in Az-Zahra—his wedding present to her. It was as close to paradise as Sefira ever expected to come, for she could not believe in that mythical resurrection when the Jews of all ages would be gathered back to Jerusalem, no matter what the kabbalists like her husband taught. Ezekiel's dry bones had no magic meaning for Sefira, and the farewell, "Next year in Jerusalem," never comforted her. Sefira believed only in Joseph and Rachel, and in the life they had built together at Az-Zahra.

Aram Torres had braved the Inquisition to come here. If they suspected he was a judaizer.... Yet, even before leaving Córdoba, Aram had had little faith in his mission. He knew Rav Joseph would never convert.

Rav Joseph had let Aram talk, uttering not a word in reply, walking back and forth packing... always packing. The Talmud...the Mishna...Maimonides' *Guide to the Perplexed*...the *Zohar: Book of Splendor*...all the rabbinical writings used to adjust daily life to that most sacred book of all: the Torah.

Of course, Rav Joseph did not pack the Torah he had taken from the little synagogue in Córdoba when they closed the doors. When the community of Israel left Córdoba, the Ark containing the Torah would travel in a cart in their midst. The Shekhina would go with them on their journey, just as She had accompanied all the Children of Israel in the Exile of all the ages. Rav Joseph's face was resolutely set.

"Will you listen to me, Joseph?" said Aram. "The community of Israel is not dead in Andalucía. We still keep the Covenant in secret."

"You have gone a-whoring after other gods," said Joseph, looking like one of the prophets.

"Even David ate the showbread in the Temple to keep from starving," Aram rationalized lamely. "Will God judge His Sephardic children so harshly for trying to stay alive?"

"Can you serve two masters?" Rav Joseph put his arm around Aram's shoulders and looked into his eyes. "No, Aram, my brother, you must choose. Do you know what they call you? Marranos! Can it find favor in His sight to be called swine?"

"Converts, Joseph. We are converts." Aram's voice was filled with despair. "Outwardly we have converted, but inwardly we keep the Faith. We worship in secret."

"Hear, O Israel, the Lord our God, the Lord is One," said Rav Joseph. "The arm of the Inquisition is long. Their judgment is swift. Their punishment is death. How shall you escape?"

Aram had been talking for hours, trying to persuade his brother-in-law; but instead he had half convinced himself Rav Joseph was right. How staunchly Joseph defended his principles! Aram was ashamed.

Aram wished he could be as strong as the rabbi, but he had his wife Rafella and his son Daniel to consider. In Córdoba he could provide them with a good life. He hated the sham and the hypocrisy. He had become secretive and withdrawn, and had fallen into the habit of answering a question with a question, never daring to speak straight lest his words betray him.

Even with Daniel, Aram had become close-mouthed, for the Inquisitors often tricked children into betraying their parents, but one day...one day, Aram promised himself...when Daniel was old enough, Rafella would light the Sabbath candles. They would eat the Sabbath meal, say the prayers...then Aram would take Daniel into the secret room he was building and open the Bible. His house would become Daniel's yeshiva, and the Shekhina would hover over them as he taught his son Daniel to be a Hebrew. Without the covenant of Abraham, of course. To circumcise the boy would be to sign his death warrant. The first thing the Inquisitors did was strip a man.

Aram hung his head, ashamed of himself, wishing he never had to make the sign of the cross again, never had to confess when his only sin was the confessional itself. He wanted to wave his circumcision under Cardinal Talavera's nose, perhaps piss on the cross as Jews

46

were always accused of doing when Christians wanted to start a pogrom.

Trumpets interrupted Aram's fantasy. Up the hill over the ruins of Az-Zahra rode a detachment of the Holy Brotherhood, led by Don Miguel Sandoval, Conde de Córdoba, dressed in the silks and satins of the Order of Santiago, riding a prancing black Arabian stallion. Although they did not wear the hooded masks they wore when they went after heretics, Aram knew instinctively they were the Holy Brotherhood. Their Catholic Highnesses had created the Brotherhood to restore order to the countryside left lawless in the wake of the Moorish wars, but their authority had quickly been expanded to the prosecution of heresy. They rode, as they had ridden on the scorched earth at Granada, with the arrogance of conquerors who despise the conquered.

Yet Don Miguel's small stature seemed to need armoring. His high forehead, bulging eyes, hooked nose, and mean mouth marked him as a man born to make war. Without a battle to ennoble him, he would always go looking for enemies and creating pitched battles. He had gained knighthood for his services at Málaga, and been granted the Order of Santiago for his services at Granada. At Málaga he had directed the ditch diggers for the blockade that starved the city into submission. At Granada he had been chief arsonist for the destruction of forests, towns, and villages on the broad plains at the foot of the mountain—and the crops on which Granada depended for food.

Famine, not the sword, had won the Moorish wars. The Knights of Santiago had fought only a few mock battles with the forces of the sultan—tournamentlike battles. Granada had been betrayed by its own sultan and his scheming mother, who sold out the city for their own advantage.

Rav Joseph stepped outside the arbor-shaded gate to meet Don Miguel and the Holy Brotherhood as they came riding full-tilt up the hill, pulling up short, brocaded caparisons fluttering in the breeze as their horses snorted, pawing the air. Rav Joseph cleared his throat and spat. Aram stood just out of sight behind the gate.

"So, Rabbi, you stand your ground," Don Miguel snarled.

"The Most Holy One, blessed be He..." Joseph began.

"Silence!" Don Miguel ordered. "If you must blaspheme, speak not at all."

Don Miguel always traveled with a large retinue of lesser knights, all ready to back him up. One of them rode forward and prodded Joseph with the point of his lance. Another dismounted and routed Aram out of the gate with his sword.

"So, another Jew cowering like a dog," Don Miguel said, backing Aram down the hillside in front of his horse.

"A Christian, Don Miguel," Aram said, making the sign of the cross. "A convert, I swear it. Ask Fray Dominic at La Mezquita. He baptized me and my wife and son."

"Marrano!" Don Miguel spat, then motioned to one of his aides. "A bit of pork for the Jew convert!"

Aram looked at the proffered slab of slimy meat, but he could not bring himself to reach for it.

"So, you are not a true Christian, you convert?" Don Miguel sneered. "Perhaps you are not hungry enough to eat pork."

Aram knew he had to take the meat, had to eat it to keep Don Miguel from arresting him as a judaizer, but he saw white maggots wiggling, and the stench was overpowering.

"Eat it, Jew!" Don Miguel ordered. "If you are a Christian, you will find it delicious. If you are a Christian..."

"He is a Christian," Rav Joseph said. "He came here to try to get me to convert."

"And will you?"

"And lose all hope of salvation?" Rav Joseph cried. "Never! My people know how to go into Exile; we do not know how to be defeated!"

"You have not much time left to leave the country, Rabbi. Will you be gone in time?"

"We must settle our affairs, make provision for our

48

journey. It is not easy to find a buyer for a property like Az-Zahra."

"I have come to buy Az-Zahra," said Don Miguel, tossing a small bag of coins into the dust.

Rav Joseph bent down to pick up the bag, knowing it was only a pittance and knowing he had no choice but to accept. Just then Sefira ran out of the house and fell on her knees before Joseph.

"Don't take it, Joseph," she pleaded. "Don't sell Az-Zahra. I shall die if I have to leave here, Joseph. Oh, Joseph, please! What does it matter which God we worship? Oh, Joseph, can't you see what you are doing to me? You are killing me."

Joseph reached down and tenderly pulled Sefira to her feet. He put his arms around her and hid her face in his beard. She leaned against him like a half-filled sack of grain. He murmured a few words to her; and she turned and stumbled back into the patio. Joseph fingered the bag of coins, knowing he would get no better offer. A little money was better than no money at all.

"Don't take it, Joseph," Aram broke in. "I will give you much more. Rafella has always wanted a home in the country."

"You haven't tasted your meat yet, Marrano," said Don Miguel.

Aram closed his eyes and stopped breathing while he bit off a small piece of the rancid meat, trying to keep from gagging. He almost choked, then he chewed slowly as the gall rose in his throat. His eyes watered, and he was sure he could not swallow, but Don Miguel's lip was curled sarcastically. Somehow he managed to swallow the lump, but he had to swallow again and again to keep it down.

"Give the rabbi the deed papers," Don Miguel ordered, as he turned his attention back to Joseph. "Sign it, Rabbi."

Rav Joseph affixed his signature, in Hebrew.

"Be careful of the company you keep, Dr. Torres," Don Miguel said, using Aram's name for the first time. Then he turned and spurred his stallion down the hill, followed by the Holy Brotherhood, their silks fluttering around their horses' flanks.

"My wife is not well," said Rav Joseph, to break the awkward silence.

"May I send you some herbs, or perhaps a little Lilith amulet to drive away her demons? My servant can bring them after dark."

"Send them, for all the good they will do," Rav Joseph said. "Sefira's roots grow too deeply in Andalucían soil. See that they do not dig up her bones for an act-of-faith."

Aram nodded. Nothing was left except to say good-bye. He could not safely visit Az-Zahra again. If the Holy Brotherhood caught him here, he would be brought before the Inquisition for judaizing. Aram and Joseph embraced each other, holding close for a long time. Then Aram walked away. Rav Joseph followed him a little way down the hill.

"Next year in Jerusalem!" Joseph called as Aram rode away.

Aram did not look back, but he found little comfort in the old Hebrew good-bye. Jerusalem seemed a long way off. At the bottom of the hill, he stopped his horse and vomited.

CHAPTER 5

River Guadalquivir, 1492

RAV JOSEPH led his little Córdoban community into Exile down the winding valley of the Guadalquivir past the towering castle of Almodóvar, keeping close to the river, stumbling along among the briars and up and down the yellow-clay gullies. The cart carrying the Ark joggled down rutted roads; any time it swayed, a dozen hands were there to keep it from falling. Even so, the new Hebrew Exile trickled down the roads toward the safety of the borders.

Past marble quarries, along roads lined with yellow-blooming Spanish broom, over endless hills covered with cork-oak forests, past olive and almond groves, skirting vineyards and wheat fields, through patches of melons and leeks and garlic. Around jutting castle-crowned mountains with villages huddled against their walls, past anxious towers—round for Moors, square for Christians. For centuries people had peered anxiously through those narrow slits and across those serrated battlements, watching suspiciously from behind iron bars and casement windows, looking at the patchwork of their land. So the Andalucíans had developed their souls—closed to strangers, to the outsiders who are different. They closed themselves into their patios, into the walled gardens of their hearts—in with the flowers, the singing and dancing, the poetry and drama. Woe to outsiders when the iron gates clanged shut!

Prodding donkeys, carrying bundles on their backs, herding sheep and cattle and little children, supporting the elderly, the Sephardic Jews walked in the sun, slept in the rain, and died quietly, to be buried in hastily marked graves.

Rav Joseph, a physician-rabbi like the great Maimonides, was needed everywhere. Someone had festered feet. Someone's old mother could not get up this morning. Someone had seen his father slip and roll down a steep incline. Rav Joseph bound their wounds, soothed their sorrows, and reminded them who they were.

"Hear, O Israel, the Lord our God, the Lord is one..."

Rav Joseph ministered faithfully to his people, but he failed to notice his wife's naked soul shining out of her eyes. Once Sefira had locked the door of Az-Zahra, she never once looked back. She could not bear to look back, for she knew she would have been blinded by the sun glinting off the gold-and-silver dome of the Hall of the Khalifs.

Sefira had changed. While other people stumbled, Sefira skipped along as lighthearted as Rachel—rummaging in the byways and coming back with armsful of wildflowers: blue gentians, yellow daisies, white baby's-breath, tall bluebells. Never a strong woman, she now spilled her energy recklessly. She became the clown, the trickster, the pixie spirit that had gotten the morose Hebrews through all their Exiles by forcing them to laugh at themselves. Even to laugh at the Most Holy One, blessed be His Name, and to gently chide Him for playing such tricks on them.

Sefira gave things away. First the flowers, then her jewels—which Rav Joseph recovered—then the useless little mementos of a lifetime that she had packed so carefully before leaving Córdoba. She was even generous with her saffron, using it lavishly, flavoring everything with saffron until the food was as golden as Spanish sunshine. When her supply began to run low, she began hoarding it, so even her Sabbath bread was pale and tasteless. When Joseph complained, she flew into her first and only rage.

"Saffron! You want saffron in your bread...and saffron...and saffron in your stew. Do you see a crocus blooming so I can pick the stamen? Have the oak leaves fallen yet? What...where will we be...when the cold winds...blow...blow out of the Pyrenees? Andalucía is my home! My home! Not Jerusalem. I spit on Jerusalem. I don't want some Promised Land I have never seen. I want Andalucía, do you hear me, Andalucía!"

She was shouting, red-faced and dry-eyed. Joseph tried to put his arms around her to comfort her, but she pushed him away. People were beginning to gather around them, shaking their heads and clacking their tongues. Rachel was frightened.

"Papa," the child wailed, "I want to go home. My feet hurt. I want to go home to Córdoba and play with Daniel. I want a licorice root. Daniel always gives me a licorice root. Why can't we go home to Córdoba, Papa?"

Rav Joseph straightened himself and did what had to be done.

"Enough, both of you!" he ordered, clapping his hands. "Are we in the Sinai that you should complain about a little saffron? The river is full of fish, and Sevilla is only a few days' walk away. We will take a boat to Cádiz, and we will be in Lisbon before you know it."

Rachel hid her face against her mother's skirt, but Sefira stood there unmoving, deep hatred simmering behind her eyes. She seemed oblivious of everything around her. Rav Joseph turned to the curious crowd.

"Come, all of you, recite with me: 'The Lord is my shepherd; I shall not want....'"

The people looked at him curiously, but a few of the old ones joined in the psalm: "He maketh me to lie down in green pastures: he leadeth me beside the still waters..."

53

Rachel joined the recital, but Sefira just stared at the deep cleft the river had made in the land.

Sevilla was jammed with fleeing Hebrews, and Rav Joseph could find no boats for his little congregation. Time was running out. Between Sevilla and Cádiz lay the treacherous marshes; between here and Portugal rose the formidable mountains of Extremadura. Rav Joseph decided to lead his people through the rolling foothills down to the Río Tinto at Palos de la Frontera, where Cristóbal Colón was outfitting three caravels for his first voyage across the Western Ocean. Rav Joseph had contributed to help finance Colón's dream. Perhaps now the explorer could help them find a little boat to take them to Lisbon. Time was growing short, and the money was running low.

Two days out of Sevilla, Rachel's mother made a blessing of the saffron to a woman who had just joined the company—sharing the last of it because the blessing of sharing was too deeply ingrained in her soul to refuse. The travelers survived on this blessing. If someone caught a fish, they shared fish stew. If someone traded an heirloom for a late spring lamb, they waited until the eve of the Sabbath, then the whole company feasted on roast lamb—dancing and singing as if khalifs still ruled Andalucía. As if the hummingbird's nest was not empty. Always someone had a little something sweet, baked with honey, to share with the rest. Life somewhere would be sweeter.

One evening, after Rav Joseph had washed his hands and pronounced the benediction, someone began strumming on a mandolin while the women cleared away. Soon the people were clapping and singing the old romantic ballads. Sefira came out with her tambourine, and Joseph lifted his hands over his head as they danced the old folk dances. Soon the valley echoed with Andalucían love songs, as the valley had echoed that night long ago when Joseph had first seen Sefira dance. He had known that night he was going to marry her.

They danced until after midnight. Sefira's eyes shone brightly as they lay down together beside the sleeping Rachel. Things might have been different if Joseph had made love with his wife, but he was tired, and it was not the Sabbath.

Before dawn Rav Joseph wrapped himself in his prayer shawl and walked up through the olive grove to join the minyan for early morning prayer. The sun woke Rachel, and she sat up—frightened. The tent was so quiet. Mama was still in bed, curled up facing the tent wall.

"Mama?" Rachel whispered.

Her mother did not stir.

"Mama?" A little louder. "Mama, wake up."

Rachel tried to shake her mother, but the body was stiff and cold.

"Mama? Oh, Mama!" she begged. "Wake up, Mama."

Rachel crawled around her mother's body to see on her face the startled eyes and astonished "Oh!" of the recognition of Death. As long as she lived, Rachel would never forget the feel of her mother's cold cheek. When Rav Joseph returned from his prayers, Rachel was sitting beside her mother's body, rocking back and forth.

Joseph knelt, took his wife's cold hands in his, and choked on his thoughts. Always before he had been able to focus his attention on God, while his wife quietly did all the trivial things necessary to make his life run smoothly. Now Lucifer, Archangel of Darkness, lowered a veil over him. Joseph was cut off from God, drowning in his own despair. Unclean! Grief possessed him, hiding him from the face of God.

The women of the burial society came, pouring out the water, washing the body, sewing up the shroud. Women are exempt from the laws of uncleanness, for women have work to do. Women closed her eyes, laid silver coins on her lids, placed the gold coin on her tongue to pay her passage, before tying a napkin around her chin.

The Shekhina spread Her comforting wings around Her son Joseph. The sun hung low in the west when the men shouldered his wife's hastily built coffin and walked up the hill toward her grave where the people of the Exile had met to join hands and dance and sing, to shield Rachel from whatever demon-children Joseph had fathered in the embrace of Lilith the night demon. Joseph was also drawn into the protective circle around his wife's grave.

The men had searched for another rabbi to say a few words of comfort, but had not found one. So Joseph himself spoke of Moses forbidden to enter the Promised Land, and of the coming resurrection in Jerusalem. Rachel stood a few feet away, bewildered, as Rav Joseph picked up a dry clod of yellow clay and crumbled it into the grave. Then he lifted his little daughter up on his shoulders, up above the crowd where the setting sun glowed ruddy on her face.

"Next year in Jerusalem," he shouted, in a voice carrying over the hills.

"Next year in Jerusalem..." A wave of voices took up the cry. "Jerusalem...Jerusalem...Jerusalem-salem-lem-lem." The gray-green olive groves echoed with the voices of Jews who had stopped to perform the blessing of comforting the sorrowing. As Rav Joseph carried Rachel on his broad, strong shoulders toward the feast tables, a multitude of hands reached out to touch them.

When Rachel saw her father sitting shivah on the flat rock at the door of their tent, his clothes torn and ashes on his head in the old manner, she slipped easily into her mother's housewifely ways. The child Rachel had been left behind somewhere among the wildflowers beside the Guadalquivir. The woman Rachel walked too sedately as she built fires and carried savory dishes to her father. Women patted Rachel's head and called her La Matronit.

Matronit—dearly beloved mother of the family, companion, helper, a woman of wisdom and years who takes charge. Rachel was all these.

On the next Sabbath, Rachel put her mother's lace mantilla over her head and lighted the candles. When Rav Joseph had said the prayers and was breaking the bread, tears filled his eyes. How could there be a Sabbath without his dear Sefira? When midnight came and all the other couples were performing the blessing of reuniting God with His Shekhina, who would comfort

Joseph? Rachel seemed to sense his need, and when the meal was finished, she crawled up into his lap.

"When are we going back to Córdoba, Papa?" she asked. "I am lonely for Daniel."

"We can't go back to Córdoba, Rachel."

"Not ever?"

"Not ever."

"Why not?"

"Because we are Jews."

"Aren't Uncle Aram and Cousin Daniel Jews?"

"They have converted...become Christians."

"What is a Christian, Papa?"

Rav Joseph did not know how to answer that question.

The footsore Córdoban community arrived at Palos de la Frontera only a few days before the deadline. Exiles swarmed over the little village at the top of the hill, clogging the narrow streets, pitching their tents on every available space on the hillside—all the way down to the edge of the river. All the seaports in Andalucía were now crowded with such families. There were few ships. Food was scarce and cost dearly. If Rav Joseph's little community were to get out of Spain in time, it would take a miracle.

However, most of the fishermen of Palos were busy ferrying Jews around the Rock of Gibraltar and up the coast to Lisbon—a lucrative if brief business. The July sun had baked the tidelands clay a hard, dull gray.

Three caravels—the *Niña,* the *Pinta,* and the *Santa María*—lay at anchor below the friary where Cristóbal Colón always left his sons when he made a voyage. As they came around the hillside on their way down to the river, Rachel saw their high decks and fat round hulls. Rachel went everywhere with her father, clinging tightly to his hand, frightened amid the mass of jostling strangers.

"Halt!" ordered a burly man with arms stained the color of oaks—a tanner. Also a Jew who wore the red badge of shame. "Where do you think you are going?"

Joseph halted. Rachel peeked out from behind her father's long black robes.

"Let us pass," Rav Joseph said. "We must see a friend in yonder caravel. We must find a vessel to take us to Lisbon."

"A vessel, is it?" the tanner laughed. "The rabbi wants a vessel. Do you hear him? One of the Queen's ships, perhaps? Their Highnesses are even pardoning criminals who will agree to sail with this madman who now calls himself *Don* Cristóbal Colón. You will have to convert if you sail with him. Become a Marrano. And you will never come back. Never!"

"We can never come back, anyway, my son," said Rav Joseph. "Do not question the ways of God. Turn your face toward the West. Who knows what lies beyond the Ocean Sea? Trust in the Most High, blessed be His Holy Name."

"A thousand pardons, Rabbi," said the tanner. "See what they do to us? Set us at each other's throats. Are there many in your community, Rabbi?"

"Not as many as there are here," Rav Joseph replied, waving his hand at the sea of people all waiting for miracles.

"Have you a vessel?"

"Would I be looking for one if I did?"

"Do not be so testy, Rabbi. Don't you recognize a friend when you meet a friend?"

Joseph looked at the tanner skeptically. He had met many such friends on the road from Córdoba, and most of them had lightened his purse considerably. Sefira's jewels were almost gone. Two things are unclean, say the sages: a thief and a tax collector. There were sure to be tax collectors in Palos, too.

"We will need a good-sized fishing vessel," said Rav Joseph.

"Can you pay?"

"Doesn't a Jew always have to pay?"

"I know a man named Sandoval," confided the tanner. "Rodrigo Sandoval, son of the Conde de Córdoba. Perhaps you know the Conde?"

Rav Joseph spat on the ground. Yes, he knew the

count of Córdoba. He thought of Sefira on her knees begging him not to sell her ruined palace to the Conde de Córdoba.

"Rodrigo Sandoval got into a little trouble a few months ago, but the Conde was able to secure his release, provided he sail with Colón," the tanner continued. "While he is waiting for the caravels to be outfitted, he has bought up most of the fishing boats in Palos. If you want to get to Lisbon, you will have to deal with Rodrigo Sandoval."

"Through you, I presume," said Rav Joseph.

"A man has to look after his own interests, Rabbi."

Joseph started to turn away. He felt unclean, and he knew he would not be clean again until they were out of this country. The whole nation was unclean, and he shuddered to think what judgment God might bring upon their heads. Yet, what choice had he except to deal with the tanner?

"Can you get us passage before the deadline?" he asked.

"Who knows?" said the tanner. "A man can only try."

"How much?"

"Who knows?" the tanner waved his hand toward the milling crowds. "I shall let you know."

Joseph agreed, then started to walk away.

"Rabbi," said the tanner, tugging at his sleeve.

Joseph turned. What did the filthy tanner want now?

"Are you a scribe, Rabbi? Can you mend scrolls, write a mezuzah?"

Rav Joseph nodded, wondering what this infidel wanted with a mezuzah.

"I shall find you when I need you," said the tanner, smiling and winking his eye before he disappeared into the crowd.

Rav Joseph cleared his throat and spat. During the next few days he earned a little money as a scribe, money he needed badly. He did not see the tanner again until the day he was contacted about the boat, but he felt sure the tanner collected a fee for referring people who needed a scribe.

* * *

Using the same methods used by the great Saint Vincente de Ferrar, whose evangelistic crusade a century ago had been so successful, the Holy Brotherhood and the friars at La Rabida offered one last hope of salvation to the stubborn Jews. Fray Dominic, who had ridden horseback all the way from Córdoba to assist in the work, ranged the hillsides around the river looking for unattended children, baptizing them and farming them out to knights like Don Miguel Sandoval to be raised as Christians.

Fray Dominic hoped by doing this great work he might have a mystical experience, perhaps be visited by the Holy Virgin Herself. To catch one glimpse of the Eternal with his myopic eyes, only one glimpse, would be enough. Fray Dominic had dedicated his life to the Church in hopes of that one moment of glory.

He had been born near Triana, the fortress home of the Inquisitor of Sevilla, and named Abdu-l-Rahman by his mother—a descendant of the Omayyads who had ruled Andalucía for centuries. If his ancestors had not fallen to quarreling among themselves, Abdu-l-Rahman might have been sultan of some Andalucían city, hearing special Friday-night prayers said for him in the mosques.

Instead, by the time Abdu-l-Rahman was born, his mother was a street woman. Who his father was Allah only knows.

Soon his mother had grown too old for street competition, although she was still a young woman and very pretty. So she had attached herself to the court of the Inquisitor, doing whatever dirty work needed doing: laundering holy vestments, scrubbing the spiral ramp up the inside of Giralda Tower in Sevilla's cathedral, serving young friars who had not yet become corrupt enough to keep mistresses openly. She and Abdu-l-Rahman lived in a hole-in-the-wall up against Triana Fortress.

When Abdu-l-Rahman was five years old, he saw his first act-of-faith. He was awed by the pomp and pageantry and fascinated by the flames. A few days later plague swept Sevilla, and young Abdu-l-Rahman was orphaned. The Dominicans took in the boy, baptizing him Dominic after their patron.

The Dominicans, of course, blamed the Jews for the plague; and young Dominic imagined he saw visions as he laid the wood for the fires of their acts-of-faith. Some of the Dominicans began to call him a mystic.

Torquemada himself noticed the boy, and Dominic served the Grand Inquisitor until his death in 1489, always seeing that the unicorn horn was on his table to protect him from poisoning and dutifully eating the first bites from Torquemada's plate. As a reward for his service to her former confessor, Queen Isabela had brought him to Santa Fé to pray for the fall of Granada.

The myopic young Dominican felt his cup running over with joy when he was summoned to the Court of Lions in the Alhambra for the Maundy Thursday royal foot-washing. He had thought he would be asked to wash the feet of the Queen; so when the Queen knelt before him, he had withdrawn his foot, feeling unworthy before such a saint. Now he was at La Rabida preaching the gospel in the streets of Palos, baptizing as many Jews as he could, unable to understand their refusal to accept the Blessed Lord as their Messiah.

The late July heat and the smell of unwashed bodies almost stifled Rachel as she clung to her father's hand while he made his way through the crowds trying to find the tanner. When Rav Joseph heard the crowd haggling with the captain of a fishing boat, he let go Rachel's hand to get closer. Rachel looked up into the vacuous rabid eyes of Fray Dominic, who grabbed her hand and started dragging her away.

"Papa! Papa!" Rachel cried, but her voice was drowned out by the crowd.

"We will find your Father," Fray Dominic assured her. "Our Lord has said, 'No one comes to the Father, but by me.'"

Rachel kicked at his shins and clawed at his arm with her free hand, but Fray Dominic had a good grip. He strode up the hill, elbowing the crowd aside. Rachel dug in her heels, but the friar was too strong for her.

She could see the whitewashed walls and red-tiled roofs of La Rabida at the top of the hill. Ahead, on the road winding up to La Rabida, Rachel saw two men staring at them curiously.

Rachel recognized one of the men. He was Diego de Harana, the brother of Colón's mistress, Doña Beatriz. Rachel had seen him several times in the Torres bodega in Córdoba.

"Señor Harana," she cried. "Help me. Please help me!"

"Say, isn't that Rachel, Rav Joseph's daughter?" asked the other man, Luis de Torres, who was going with Colón's expedition as an interpreter. He was just coming from being baptized at La Rabida, a condition of his employment on the expedition.

"Yes, that's Rachel," said Harana, "but where is her father?"

"She will never see him again once the Holy Brotherhood gets their hands on her," said Torres.

"We can't let that happen," said Harana.

"What can we do?"

"Watch me! I'll bump into the friar. You rescue the child. I'll meet you back at the dock after I find her father. Ready?"

"Ready!"

Rav Joseph had been frantic when he realized Rachel was gone. He went through the mob shouting her name, stopping everyone he knew to ask if they had seen her. He was tearing his beard when he bumped into Diego de Harana.

"Rachel?" he cried. "Have you seen Rachel? I barely let go of her hand, and she has disappeared."

"She is all right, Rav Joseph," said Harana. "Come with me."

"Are you sure?" asked Rav Joseph, disbelieving as one disbelieves when calamity piles on calamity.

"The Most Holy One, blessed be He, has preserved her," Harana said, forgetting he was a Christian and shouldn't use such language.

Rachel was standing at the side of the tall, red-haired

Colón when Rav Joseph saw her. He rushed forward and swept her up into his arms. She flung her arms around his neck as if she would never let go again.

"How can I ever thank you?" he asked the three men who had returned Rachel to him.

"Pray for the success of our mission," said Colón. "Pray we find a land where everyone can live together in peace—where little children will not be snatched from their parents, and men will not have to hide to say their prayers."

Rav Joseph cleared his throat and spat, then added, "Amen."

Luis de Torres and Diego de Harana spat, too, to clean their mouths before joining him in the Amen.

The Jews paid a handsome sum to the authorities to secure a two-day extension of their deadline so they could observe the Ninth of Av, their bleakest festival, commemorating the destruction of the Two Houses. First King Nebuchadnezzar of Babylon had destroyed Solomon's Temple and carried the Jews into captivity; then Titus, the Roman Emperor, had destroyed Jerusalem and the Second Temple, scattering the Jews. Now, at the anniversary of these two disasters, the Sephardic Jews felt keenly the meaning of the Ninth of Av. Not until the second of August did they board their little boats and sail out of the mouth of the Río Tinto.

Rav Joseph looked up as they passed near the *Santa María* and saw Don Cristóbal Colón and Luis de Torres leaning on the quarterdeck rail. Rav Joseph helped Rachel wave at the explorers. When she was an old, old woman, Rachel would remember only three things about their Exile: the feel of her mother's cold cheek, the rabid look in Fray Dominic's eyes, and the friendly wave of the tall red-haired man at the rail of the *Santa María*.

"God go with you," Rav Joseph shouted.

"Go with God," Colón shouted back, waving his stocking cap.

On August 3, 1492, the *Niña,* the *Pinta,* and the *Santa María* sailed. In his log entry for the day before, Colón had written about seeing the little boats of the Jews.

CHAPTER 6

Haiti, 1492

TO REASSURE herself when the trader told the amazing story of invaders in winged canoes, Ana looked around for her children. How they had grown these past years! Mayabaño, her butterfly boy, was a sturdy six seasons old now, just learning to build fish weirs. Higueymato—ten seasons, plus one—sat quietly among the wives, her hands folded in her lap. Higueymato was shy, apt to disappear if one of the village boys approached her, but Tahíaca was never shy. Oh, no, Tahíaca was never shy. Her inborn smile and way of walking always made men squat down and turn away to hide their desires.

Caonabó understood Tahíaca better than anyone else. He knew her being was so filled with love she could not have behaved otherwise. She was only twelve seasons, but already she seemed as wise as a woman. Yet she had chosen no one man because no man had yet measured up to her love. She used them up quickly and spent a great deal of her time daydreaming about the right man. Caonabó often confided to Ana that he feared what might happen when Tahíaca met that man.

"Ana," Caonabó spoke, interrupting her walk into her children's future by his own need to have Ana's opinion of the trader's strange news.

"Yes, my husband Caonabó." Ana reluctantly pulled herself back.

"What does Ana think about the winged canoes?"

More and more lately, Caonabó relied on Ana for advice. People expected him to know everything, and when he was younger, he had thought he did. People expected him not to be afraid, and when he was younger, he had not known how many things there are to fear. He told himself he was not afraid now, but he did not like surprises unless they were of his making. How could canoes grow wings? Caonabó could not afford to show doubts or fear, so he turned to Ana. Ana understood him. With Ana, it was not necessary always to be the fierce Carib cacique. Ana loved him.

"What does Ana think?"

"Ana thinks the trader's story will make a good areíto," she said, "but Caonabó is neglecting his hospitality."

"Caonabó smoked the cigar of friendship with his guest," he said defensively.

"But Caonabó has not offered his guest food or drink. Let Tahíaca brew cocoa. Perhaps drinking it will clear the trader's head of visions."

Caonabó motioned to Tahíaca to brew cocoa, and as Tahíaca worked, she looked boldly at the trader. He in turn watched her lovely budding breasts rising and falling as she ground the beans, mixed them with just enough hot water to make a thick brew, then poured it back and forth until it was frothy just the way Caonabó liked it. Tahíaca smiled as she served the brew in small, ceremonial wooden cups. She saw the trader squirm to hide his erection, and she decided to sleep with him that night to see if he was the man she was looking for.

"What does Ana think?" Caonabó asked again when they had finished the cocoa ceremony.

"Ana finds the trader's talk hard to believe," she

said, "but perhaps the cemís have granted him a great vision."

"Not a vision," insisted the trader. "The Guanahaní man and I do not lie."

"Tell the tale again," Ana requested. "Whether or not it is true, such a wondrous tale is worthy of becoming an areíto."

"The Guanahaní man rowed across from his island to our island after the hairy-faced men came," the trader began.

"Enough!" Caonabó held up his hand, stopping the trader's story as if to prove to himself he was still in control, even if only of how and when the story would be told. "Caonabó has heard enough for now. Caonabó will decide later whether or not the story is going to be true. Then Caonabó will decide whether the story is important enough to become an areíto."

Caonabó rose majestically from his carved stool, strode slowly to his bahío with Ana following him solicitously. The trader squatted on his hammock-wrapped trading pack, watching the sun probe the shadows of the valley. Caonabó and his people were not yet prisoners of time, so there was no hurry to solve this riddle. With such an important tale to tell, the trader could wait.

The Admiral Don Cristóbal Colón's three ships—the *Niña*, the *Pinta*, and the flagship *Santa María*—had come to the Caribbean over two months ago, landing on the island the natives called Guanahaní. Some of the gentle Tainos received the strange men with courtesy, others fled into the forest. None attacked the strangers. By the time Admiral Colón left Guanahaní, a man was paddling for the nearest island to warn his neighbors. The Spaniards had captured some of the people of Guanahaní and carried them away in their canoes. The families of the captives, left with a few hawk's bells and some rosaries, never expected to see their loved ones again.

Ana knew how to soothe her troubled husband. To all the rest of the world he was Caonabó, the great Carib cacique who had conquered Cibao with a small band of

67

warriors when he was just a young man. To Ana he was a lover whose marvelous body never failed to awaken her desires and whose wisdom and understanding never failed to move her to awe and devotion.

On that long-ago night when they had first come together, it had not seemed they would ever be able to improve on their loving, but they always seemed to be finding new ways to please each other. Whatever pleased one, the other found great joy in doing. It seemed as if they created love anew each time they came together. Their love was an aura surrounding and protecting them. When they exhausted their bodies, their hearts would begin to sing. They would lie in each other's arms in the everlasting prayer only love can voice.

They would arise from their loving strong and wise, able to meet whatever came because they had each other. Whenever they came back from the outside world into that world they created together, they would find their ardor miraculously increased by the absence. Their love for each other never diminished, even when they were apart, even when Caonabó serviced his other wives or Ana extended his hospitality to a guest. Their love only grew stronger and more satisfying—as uncontrollable as Huracán sometimes, but also as compelling.

Ana and Caonabó stayed in their bahío most of the day, drawing strength from their love. Toward evening, Ana went out again to talk with the trader.

"Show Ana the talking bells," she said, falling easily into the royal third person. "Tell Ana about the winged canoes again, and leave nothing out."

"Yes, Cacica," the trader said. People had learned that Ana often spoke for her husband, and they worked as well with her as with Caonabó. The trader opened his pack and held up a little ring of bells used for falconry in Andalucía. He jangled the bells and said, "Chuque! Chuque!"

The crowd drew nearer, murmuring to each other about this marvel. The trader glowed in their attention as he rang the bells for them again and again. Ana tied a string of bells to her ankle and danced a few steps of the new areíto she was composing about the arrival of the winged canoes. The villagers nodded their approval. Then the trader held up a rosary with a dangling iron cross.

"Cemí," he explained, then showed how the strangers knelt, fingering these beads and muttering strange prayers.

"Cemí?" Ana held the rosary up to the sun.

The beads glistened like great drops of blood. The trader held up several other rosaries exactly like the first. Cemís, all of them, strange and unimaginative cemís exactly alike. Yet their cemís must be very powerful if they had marvelous things like canoes with wings. Ana hung the rosary around her neck. The iron cross felt cold to her skin as the little iron man nestled between her breasts. She danced the new areíto of winged canoes and strange clothed men with hair on their faces, officially entering the story into village history.

"Do they commune with their cemís?" asked Ana. "Or smoke cigars in friendship?"

"No, tobacco is new to them," replied the trader.

"How can they go on long sea journeys without tobacco to stave off hunger and relieve loneliness?" the people wanted to know.

"Have they a friendship ritual?" Ana asked.

The trader made the sign of the cross, and mumbled a few words. Ana made the sign and added it to her areíto. With a *Chuque! Chuque!* and a *Hail Mary Patre et fille,* Christianity came to the Caribbean. Ana danced away the fears none of them wanted to recognize. So they also laughed and danced, making the sign of the cross and pretending their world had not changed, as if the strangers in winged canoes were spirit dreams to be blown away on Huracán's wings. Then a runner came into the batey demanding to see Caonabó. Caonabó stepped out of his bahío.

"They are here!" the runner gasped.

"Who?"

"The hairy-faced ones from the winged canoes!"

"Where? When?"

"In the mountains north of here only a day's journey,

perhaps two. They are coming to Cibao. Someone has told them there is much gold to be found here."

"Caonabó will go to meet the hairy-faced ones when the sun begins his journey tomorrow," Caonabó announced, then retired again to his bahío.

Ana and Caonabó tried to soothe away their anxieties, but neither of them slept much that night. By daybreak Ana had roused the wives and concubines and set them to work painting Caonabó's body for the reception. Men wore paint according to rank—some a streak or two down cheek or arm, some an eye patch or, if old and venerable, perhaps the entire face. Only provincial rulers like Caonabó painted their whole bodies.

The wives' busy fingers worked to create Caonabó's image of himself—an image that until now he had found good. Caonabó kept finding fault with the painting, making the concubines wash it off and the wives do it over again until the floor of the bahío was streaked with paint and the wives were shouting at each other to keep from shouting at him. Ana sent them all away.

"Caonabó is afraid," she said boldly. "Why is Caonabó afraid?"

Caonabó glared at her, and she felt such an outrushing of love she could hardly keep her head. She forced herself to be stern.

"Why should Caonabó be afraid? He has only to speak and the invaders will be killed. Some people are saying they are opia, or even cemís, but Caonabó knows they are only men."

Still Caonabó said nothing, but his gaze softened. How wise she was! Caonabó himself had a powerful talking cemí all the people feared—but it was only a hollow image with a speaking tube through which he had taught Hatuey to talk. Caciques had to deceive people sometimes to maintain control, and people seemed to like being deceived.

"What does Ana think?" he asked again.

"Ana thinks Caonabó is very wise. Perhaps he will kill all the invaders, or perhaps he will decide to let them live until they can teach him to make wings for his canoes."

"Perhaps," said Caonabó.

Ana painted his body herself this time, massaging out his tensions as she worked. She knew why he was troubled, and he knew she knew. Not only did he not have winged canoes, but he had never in his wildest cemí visions seen such a thing. A man cannot make something he has not envisioned. The coming of the invaders had made Caonabó seem less than he had always been—the greatest cacique in the Sea of the Caribs. Yet in one thing, he thought, he was still superior. No one had a wife like Ana. *Ana-caona.*

Yes, he would give her a new name. Ana-caona— the woman of Caonabó, who rules beside him. She who, when Caonabó shall go to the valley of the everlasting areítos...Caonabó did not finish the thought, lest the prospect of his own mortality become so attractive he order his own execution while he still had his power. Caciques always knew when the time had come for dying, and Caonabó had decided he would call upon his cemís when the time came. To die must be a glorious occasion.

Ana finished the painting, then knelt before Caonabó looking up at him with all the adoration and love stored in her heart. No areíto she could ever compose in his honor would convey what she felt for this man.

"Ana loves Caonabó," she said simply.

"I love you, Ana-caona," he said.

"Ana-caona?" She was startled and pleased by the new name.

"Yes, Anacaona. Woman who is part of Caonabó. Cacica who will rule after Caonabó..." He did not finish his thought. "Come, Anacaona, we must tell the people your new name. Then we will go to see the hairy ones."

Tahíaca walked along beside her mother's litter bearers wondering about the young men strutting through the forest. Is he the one? She knew—as all girls did—her destiny was tied to some man who would make her as supremely happy as Anacaona and Cao-

71

nabó or as miserable as the syphilitic women who lived in lonely bahíos far away from the villages. Who will he be? What will he be like? Will he love me? Will he be wise? Gentle? Cruel? Indifferent? Every time a new man came to the village, all the girls playfully asked themselves that important question. Is he the one?

Young males like Rodrigo Sandoval played no such games, forgetting until it was too late how important pleasure is to love and love to life. True sons of the Church, they would spend their lives pursuing glory and honor, only to find they have missed the most important thing of all—happiness. Rodrigo had never in his life asked himself: Is she the one? When he had amassed enough riches, he would marry the daughter of another Christian knight, as his children would be expected to do—knighthood and the Church being the only alternatives to such arrangements.

So it was that Tahíaca and Rodrigo Sandoval met at the bend of the river below the fluted bluff against which Caonabó held court. Tahíaca saw the handsome young Spaniard and knew he was the one. Her heart spoke to her in that mysterious language only the heart understands. Rodrigo was the one.

Rodrigo stumbled into an Arabian fantasy as he rounded the bend to become the first Christian to see the splendors of Cibao. He blinked his eyes, but when he opened them the court was still there. Caonabó's gold crown stood three feet high, scrolled and decorated with birds and mythical creatures with oversized eyes. Anacaona wore a similar crown, not quite as tall. All the village caciques subject to Caonabó also wore golden crowns. Long, thin, blue-gold banners fluttered in the winds, crackling like flashes of lightning from the gathering storm in back of the bluff.

"Jesucristo!" murmured Rodrigo, crossing himself. "Look at all that gold. For me! For me!"

Rodrigo Sandoval was the second son—the second legitimate son—of Don Miguel Iago Carlos Rolando Sandoval, Conde de Córdoba. He pledged a pilgrimage to Santiago de Compostela in thanks for his good fortune. Never had Rodrigo expected to see so much gold.

Tahíaca, standing near her father's litter-throne holding a golden banner, looked at Rodrigo. Yes, he was the one. Never had she seen anyone so splendid. Never seen a great moustache and carefully trimmed pointed beard, never seen silks and satins and velvet clothing, never seen a gilded engraved sword such as hung at his side.

Dazzled by so much gold, Rodrigo had failed to notice they wore not a stitch of clothing. Now he saw Tahíaca, wearing only the nugget necklace Caonabó had once given her mother. For me, Rodrigo promised himself. The men with him were also looking at the Taino girls and having similar thoughts.

Have they no shame? Bare breasts for all the world to see. Enticing a man with those eyes. No Christian modesty! That girl with the tantalizing smile. See how she sways her hips as she shifts that banner. Mother of God! So young! Perhaps still a virgin. Rodrigo thought it fortunate he had spent some of his Jew profits buying indulgences at La Rabida.

"Caonabó welcomes you to Cibao," said the Cacique, and the Spaniards understood the tone if not the words. "What is ours is yours. Caonabó has spoken."

Tahíaca had watched as long as her nature would allow. Ready for love, eager to be loved, she gathered unto herself all the men's thoughts as she walked across to Rodrigo Sandoval and touched him.

"Santa María!" he breathed, crossing himself again.

Tahíaca had bridged the gap, and now the Tainos crowded around the Christians—touching them, chattering like parrots, keeping the interpreter busy.

What do the strangers call this? A sword. Careful, it cuts at the touch!

What is this? A lace point.

And that and that? Hawk bells...brass bracelets called wives...rosary beads...

The Tainos rolled these strange sounds around in their mouths, laughing and nudging each other, making fun of the strangers' speech. They made the sign of the cross as the trader had taught them to make it, but they laughed as they did.

73

They felt the Christians to see if flesh lay under their clothing. Grasped arms, slapped shoulders, nudged thighs. Tahíaca tried to lift the hem of Rodrigo's shirt to see if he had a navel. Hands reached out for groins. Why would they cover themselves if they had all their parts? Were they really men?

Young sailors from Palos and young rancheros from Extremadura backed away giggling like a covey of nuns, embarrassed to admit they gloried in the touching. Too long at sea. Too many hoarse-breathed masturbations. Too sharp the division between virgin and whore.

How well the Church does its work! How well chivalry protects ladies! But these girls? Naked as God placed Eve in Eden! Fair game.

The storm rumbled closer now, and the trading became lively as Tainos uncorked even their nose pendants to trade. How simple these Indians are! How easily taken in! What do they need with points of lace when they have no clothes to sew them on?

This nugget as big as my thumb for your lace point, another for your spirit bells. A bracelet of gold for your rosary beads. Such fools these strangers are! Never has Cibao heard the cemís talk more clearly than in these bells. Soon we shall also have wings on our canoes.

The Castilians would not trade their swords, nor the Tainos their crowns. More and more Tainos came out of the forest bringing gifts of fruits and vegetables, of brightly colored bolts of cotton cloth, of wicker cages filled with rare colored birds. Even when the strangers had nothing left to trade, the Tainos plied them with gifts. Who can say what value to put on telling the grandchildren you once touched the men from the winged canoes?

Only Caonabó and Anacaona stood apart, watching, skeptical. Caonabó watched the faces of the invaders. How their eyes glittered! Like the eyes of Caribs when a baby was roasting on a spit. Caonabó had left his island and come to Haiti to get away from the glitter in such eyes, for Caonabó's people had been man-eaters who captured women, bred them, and cooked their children. Caonabó had never regretted changing his way

74

of life, and he knew no good could come of this visit of the strange men with the hungry eyes.

"Tahíaca, come here," Anacaona called.

She, too, had seen the hungry eyes—a different kind of hunger. These men were not accustomed to Taino ways. They would not know how to respect Caonabó's wives and daughters, how to wait for his hospitality before availing themselves of his women. Tahíaca seemed not to hear her mother. She was chattering away with Rodrigo Sandoval—neither understanding the words of the other, yet both understanding perfectly.

"Tahíaca!" Caonabó ordered.

Tahíaca reluctantly detached herself from Rodrigo, walking toward her mother and father as if part of her had already become part of the young Castilian. She looked back over her shoulder at Rodrigo, promising with her smile. Rodrigo understood. The first patter of rain from the gathering storm fell on the glade, and a breathless messenger ran up to Caonabó.

"More winged canoes," the messenger reported. "Three or four days away."

"How many?" Caonabó asked.

"Two."

"Caonabó will go there as soon as the storm flies over," he said as his people began scattering for cover.

Eyeing the storm to see whether it was the kind that uprooted trees, flattened houses, and killed whole sections of the forest with its blue spirit-light, Caonabó urged his bearers to the safety of a cave. Only when they sat huddled around a fire discussing the invaders did they miss Tahíaca. In the confusion she had slipped away. Tahíaca was always slipping away.

Captain Pinzón ordered his men back to the *Pinta*. They needed to secure their gold before they faced Admiral Colón, who was entitled to share in their prize. Each man makes the same mistake about gold. Each thinks gold is his to keep. Mine...mine...mine...

Huracán knows. Gold belongs to Mother Earth, and to Her bosom it will return. For a while She lets a man keep this small part of Herself, even lets him dream he owns part of Her heart. Then She watches how he tries to protect it and keep it. Mine...mine...mine...

The men from the *Pinta* argued about the gold, spied on each other, squirreled it away to keep from sharing it. Not one speck for that Genoese, Colombo, who now calls himself Don Cristóbal Colón. Who does he think he is? He's not even Spanish! Could he have gotten here without us? What gives him the right to ten percent of my gold? How much do you suppose Their Catholic Highnesses will take?

The Jews are gone now, so there will be no tax collectors. Nonsense! There are always tax collectors. And the Church? The bishops will demand the tithe—ten percent to the Church, ten percent to Colón, a fifth to the King and Queen! How much does that leave for me? I'll bury it where no one can find it.

Huracán rumbles closer. Mother Earth is patient. She has plenty of time to gather all things back unto Herself. Mine...mine...mine...

Tahíaca caught up with Rodrigo after the storm. The Spaniards were drying their clothes on the bushes, cavorting among themselves in the nude like little children just beginning to discover their bodies. Tahíaca watched for a while. One of the Spaniards had caught a young Taino girl, and Tahíaca saw them taking turns with her. Just before it was Rodrigo's turn, Tahíaca ran into the glade and presented herself to him.

CHAPTER 7

Cibao, 1492

PERHAPS TAHÍACA loved him because he came from a different world, a world she had not yet visited—exciting and mysterious. Perhaps because his eyes were blue and his skin white, while hers were brown and her skin bronze. Perhaps because the language he spoke sounded like soft music to her heart. But love needs no explanations and no excuses.

His companions backed away when Tahíaca came up to Rodrigo, and the Taino girl lying on the ground smiled up at them. Another man quickly took Rodrigo's place with the other girl, as he devoted himself to Tahíaca. She wanted him to take her immediately, for she was already excited from watching. He reached out and plucked the flower from behind her ear, held it in his teeth, and did a little dance to show her he could wait—to make her want him more.

She reached for him and he backed away, then ran around the glade like a shy girl, with Tahíaca chasing after him while his companions clapped their hands, cheering the game. Tahíaca had never played so exciting a game. She chased after him as he ran into the woods laughing. He hid behind a tree, waiting for her, and as she darted past, he stepped out and caught her in his arms. She leaned against him, feeling the urgency of his desire throbbing between them. He kissed her hard, cupping her marvelous little budding breast in his hand.

"Beloved," he murmured.

"Beloved?" She imitated him, looking up quizzically, wanting to learn his words so she could tell him how much she loved him.

Tahíaca could not wait. She had to have him. She pulled him down upon the grass. She ached with her longing for him. She believed that in all her life only one man would ever be able to still that longing, and Rodrigo was that man. He had never bedded such a woman, although he had left two women pregnant in Spain: One was the daughter of a Marqués, whose chaperone he had bribed, and the other was the daughter of an innkeeper. One entered a convent, the other did not. Of course, Rodrigo could not consider marrying either of them. He and his family respected the Sacrament of Marriage, and he had pledged himself to marry only a virgin. It did not take him long to decide Tahíaca was not a virgin—even before he took her.

"My little whore," he said, amazed at her passion. "So young, and already a whore. Por Dios, this is a heathen world in need of Christianizing!"

"Little whore," she repeated, smiling and nodding, thinking it another endearment, wanting to please him but, of course, not understanding what he said. She only heard his heart talking through the gentle insult.

Rodrigo enjoyed his little whore again and again, and when he was finished, he wanted to share her with his friends. She considered it a compliment that her man wanted to show off her talents, so she did her best to please. She enjoyed the others more, knowing he was watching.

At last they all slept, Tahíaca and Rodrigo in each other's arms. She had fallen asleep before he did, and he felt her soft breath against his chest. He looked down into her childish face. How innocent she looked in sleep, like the dark Virgin of Guadalupe. He felt a rush of emotion he did not even want to identify. Women were so deceptive—especially whores, who could almost make a man feel loved even when he had just witnessed her take on all of his companions. Mother of God! Was there no virtue in this strange new world?

When morning came, of course, he saw not a virgin but a whore. He and his companions woke first, dressed themselves quickly, hiding behind bushes, embarrassed and not looking at each other. The birds were barely awake when they gathered up their gold and slipped away, leaving the two Taino girls still asleep. They marched swiftly back toward the *Pinta,* talking little. Later they would brag, but not to each other. To other men.

Anacaona tried not to worry about her eldest daughter. Tahíaca was always slipping away. Women were free to come and go as they pleased in Cibao. The stony mountains offered few dangers once a girl had learned to climb safely. Haiti had no predatory animals. No poisonous reptiles. Just easy-to-catch birds like the biaya and the Muscovy duck. Just rodents like the hutía that scurried around the bahíos making their homes in thatched walls, waiting to be killed and eaten. Just blinking iguanas and squawking parrots and singing yellow finches. Everything in this paradise seemed made for the comfort of the Tainos. Life was easy and no one had to work hard. So women were free to come and go as they pleased. Women, too, needed time to commune with their cemís. Tahíaca would find her way back.

When the storm passed and Tahíaca had not returned, Caonabó sent scouts to look for her. When the scouts returned without her, Caonabó angrily sent them out again, telling them if they returned without her they would be executed. Anacaona's heart welled up in the separation song. Not the birth song, which is a joyous separation, but the going-away-into-adulthood areíto—the tearing of the fabric a mother's heart wraps around her child. Why had it come so soon? A suckling babe once toddled at her feet, and now a woman ran toward her man through the forest. Anacaona had seen the way Tahíaca looked at Rodrigo.

"Tahíaca, my firstborn, a woman? No. Oh, no! Not yet!"

Anacaona tied the spirit bells around her ankle and danced the child-grown-into-a-woman. Come back, my baby. Stay a little longer. Let me tell you how much I love you. Did I ever tell you I love you? Do you know you must grate the manioc to drain away the poison before you make the bread? If you let all the poison drain away, it makes a fine bread that lasts a long time without spoiling. Shall I sing of the poison in the bread, or of all the other poisons? Who will teach my daughter about all the other poisons?

Anacaona's sad wailing, her death-of-childhood areíto, struck Caonabó's heart a blow a Carib cacique could not afford to show. The fierce iguana pawed his wrinkled brow, and when he felt his grief waters threatening to overflow, he waved away his bearers and started walking down the broad valley toward Marien—the province where the hairy-faced men had come in the two winged canoes. Behechio and Hatuey walked with him, with Mayabaño trotting behind to keep up with their quick strides. The cornfields and potato patches in the valley were crowded with Tainos hurrying to see the strangers.

By the time Caonabó reached Marien, Colón's flagship, the *Santa María,* had gone aground, and the people were unloading the doomed caravel. Caonabó pushed his way through the crowd on the beach. Tainos crowded around the strangers, calling "Chuque! Chuque!" and offering to trade gold family heirlooms. The price of a single hawk's bell had risen to four gold nuggets.

Caonabó stood looking at the funny-shaped canoes with leafless trees growing out of them, at the cross-branches wrapped in cloth, at the hammocklike webbing fastened up the sides on which men climbed up to stand in a wicker basket and look out to sea. Caonabó tried to imagine how you could build such a canoe. He thought this must be a cahoba vision. His world was changing too fast.

"Where are their women?" Behechio asked.

Caonabó shrugged.

Hatuey shook his head. Were they the legendary men whose women permitted them on their island only once a year? The ones who one rainy day had set woodpeckers hammering out substitutes?

Where was Tahíaca?

Caonabó forced himself to think about Cacique Guacanagarí, that strutting peacock in whose province the ship had been wrecked. Guacanagarí had always been a fool. Now Guacanagarí walked about as if the strangers had crossed the sea just to do him honor! Huracán had tossed Guacanagarí a bone, and he was carving himself a cemí.

Admiral Don Cristóbal Colón had been enjoying a well-deserved sleep that Christmas Eve in 1492 when the flagship *Santa María* drifted onto a reef and tore a hole in her bottom. Now the explorer who called himself Admiral of the Ocean Armada had only one available ship—the little *Niña*. The *Pinta* had disobeyed his orders and gone off looking for the mythical island of Babeque. So Colón, who knew he had not yet found Marco Polo's Cathay, but thought Cuba was Japan, had become Adelantado of the territories he had discovered.

"Adelantado" was a very old Moorish title, meaning one who anticipates the future, who accelerates everything, a man of progress who enters and leaves always running. Certainly Colón fitted this description; but the Adelantado must also be governor of territories, chief justice of a frontier province, captain-general in time of war. Colón was the explorer who looked beyond the next star and saw what no one else could see, but he was not qualified to be an Adelantado. Power—there was too much power in the word "Adelantado," and the red-haired Genoese mapmaker Colón was not a man who valued power, or who knew how to use it.

Cacique Guacanagarí called the Admiral "Adelantado," not knowing the meaning of the word, but Caonabó did not. Caonabó had himself been an adelantado without ever having heard the word. He knew about caciques like Colón who established villages in new territories. Once Caonabó had landed on Haiti's coast in long canoes, and now he ruled the gold-bearing mountains. Guacanagarí was a fool!

Admiral Colón built his fort and called it Navidad. Guacanagarí's people had not stolen so much as a lace point from the salvaged cargo stored in bahíos. Colón wrote his sovereigns that there were no better people in the world, being truly lovers of their neighbors. Only a little Christian instruction would be needed to turn these people into hard-working servants of Their Catholic Highnesses.

Colón divided up his crews, leaving behind thirty-nine men, including the troublesome Basques, under the command of his mistress's brother, Diego de Harana. He gave Cacique Guacanagarí a red velvet robe, some gloves, and bright-red Córdoban leather buskins. Guacanagarí promised to give the Admiral a cemí of pure gold as large as a man. Just before the Admiral sailed away in the little *Niña,* he gave a demonstration of power. He brought the lombard ashore, along with a supply of marble balls used for ammunition.

Caonabó drew near, pushing through the crowd, fascinated and awed by the hollow tree-trunk made of iron bars held together with rings and bolts. The whole thing was attached to a carriage. Until then, the Tainos had never seen a wheel. The marble balls weighed so much two men were needed to pick them up. They pointed the lombard toward the *Santa María* and lit the fuse.

The thing roared and belched smoke. There was a whistling and a boom, and the *Santa María* began to sink, a gaping hole in her side. The Tainos began to run, or fell to the ground in fright. Caonabó hid behind a tree until he was sure the Adelantado was not going to point the thing at him.

Caonabó told Guacanagarí he was a fool to let them build the walled village and to let them bring such a weapon ashore. How could the caciques defend themselves against it? They should kill all the invaders now. Haiti would soon be swarming with them. Did Guacanagarí really believe the Admiral when he said this weapon would be used to protect the Tainos from their enemies, the man-eating Caribs?

Caonabó knew. He had tasted flesh. Give men such weapons, and one among them will turn the weapon to his own use. Caonabó did not wait to see the canoe take wings. He returned to Cibao to set guards on the passes and to begin making more fishbone spears. Caonabó knew he did not have much to fight with, but no one would be able to say Caonabó was afraid to fight.

Where was Tahíaca?

When Tahíaca awoke and reached for her lover to find him gone, she felt as if a piece of her had been torn away, leaving her as empty as the opia who must wander the forest forever in search of love. Having found him, how could she ever be complete again if she lost him? She could do nothing except go in search of him, for without him she was nothing.

She stumbled up the valley with her heart aching and tears blinding her eyes. Women stopped working in the fields to wave at her, but she did not see them. Flocks of golden finches darted in singing clouds around her, but she did not hear them. She followed Rodrigo for three days, stopping only when too exhausted to move, sleeping restlessly only as long as her body demanded, then waking up ashamed of having slept and afraid she would have lost him forever because she had not had the strength to go on.

By the time she caught up with him, Rodrigo Sandoval had begun to miss her. He had never known a girl like her, such a combination of innocence and ardor. With such a girl he might easily forget all the preachments of the Church and stay in this paradise forever.

They were getting into the longboat ready to shove off for the *Pinta* when Tahíaca found them. Captain Pinzón was eager to rendezvous with Admiral Colón and make peace with him for having left the fleet and gone exploring for the mythical golden island of Babeque the Indians kept talking about. They had not found the island, but the gold they had gotten from

Caonabó's people might placate Colón. Pinzón was hiding half of it and sharing the rest with his commander.

Tahíaca cried out to Rodrigo as she ran onto the river bank. She flung herself into his arms, clinging to him like a little child, babbling in that strange tongue of hers, but he understood she loved him. The intensity of her need frightened him, and when he looked up to see his companions smirking, he pushed her away. She looked at him as if he had wounded her. She felt as if she were bleeding inside from a wound that would never heal.

Caonabó's scouts had been following closely behind Tahíaca, and before the longboat could push off, they attacked with a rain of bone-tipped arrows. The Spaniards fought back, killing two of the Tainos and capturing five others, including the girl who had been with the Spaniards in the glade. When the rest of the Tainos ran away, Rodrigo turned to Captain Pinzón.

"What shall we do with these?" he asked.

"Bring them along," Pinzón ordered. "Admiral Colón is not the only man who will return to Spain with tattooed natives. The girls will help relieve the lonely hours on the homeward passage."

Pinzón ordered the captives confined below decks and placed Rodrigo in charge of scheduling the girls for recreation duty. The men were too busy with sailing to require their services for the first few days, but by the time they had sighted the *Niña,* the men had begun to make demands of Rodrigo. He scheduled the other girl, but he found excuses not to schedule Tahíaca. His Spanish soul had asserted itself, and he could not bear to think of her in someone else's arms. Neither could he approach Tahíaca himself. He had not yet sorted out his feelings.

No female had ever moved Rodrigo as deeply as this simple savage girl. He began to dream of jumping ship and going back to live with the men at Navidad. If they worked it right, they could be in control of the entire island before Colón returned on his next voyage. Rodrigo could have both Tahíaca and all Caonabó's gold— including the crowns.

Tahíaca could not know Rodrigo was thinking about her. When the caravel sailed, she had been desperately frightened. She never expected to see Haiti again, and she was homesick. She cried frequently now, for she had not seen Rodrigo since she came aboard. She could not understand what had happened to her romantic dream. During her growing up, she had listened to her mother sing and dance the areíto of how Caonabó had invaded Cuba to capture his favorite wife. Rodrigo had captured her the same way, but now he acted as if he had never given himself to her in the glade. How could a man give away part of himself and feel nothing?

Rodrigo's chance to jump ship came when Admiral Colón ordered the Pinzón captives put ashore. Colón wanted to be the only one returning to Andalucía with natives to show off. Pinzón put Rodrigo in charge of the longboat to take them ashore. Tahíaca sat huddled forlornly in the bow of the boat. Rodrigo longed to put his arms around her and comfort her, but he did not dare, lest he tip his hand.

They landed on a cape Admiral Colón would name the Cape of the Lovers. Scarcely had the boat touched shore when Rodrigo jumped out, grabbed Tahíaca's hand, and ran for the forest. When they stopped running, Tahíaca looked up at him with shining eyes. Her heart was singing its own areíto.

Next morning Rodrigo left for Navidad, and Tahíaca awoke again to find her lover gone. This time the pain was not as sharp. It was just a dull ache sapping away her will to live. Tahíaca came home in the dark of the moon, slipping from rock to rock, from tree to tree, so not even Caonabó's guards saw her. She huddled around the remains of the fire under a boucan waiting for morning, hugging her knees. There was a tree in the Haitian forest called the manzanillo, whose shadow was believed to be so poisonous that anyone who slept under the tree would awaken in the beautiful valley of everlasting areítos. Tahíaca imagined herself asleep under that tree.

"Rodrigo...Rodrigo..." she whispered, hugging herself and trying to forget his touch. "Rodrigo...Oh, Rod-rigo!"

When Anacaona saw the woman huddled beside the cold boucan, she knew her Tahíaca—the Tahíaca they had all watched flirting on the edge of tomorrow, her Tahíaca—would never return. She never asked her daughter where she had been.

CHAPTER 8

Navidad, 1493

Huracán...first winds...

Christ has come to the Sea of the Caribbee. Saints and sinners have come. Santa María—*the flagship...San Salvador—the landing place once called by the heathen Guanahaní...the Sea of Saint Thomas, discovered on Saint Thomas's Day. Crack the whips, ring the bells, wear grotesque masks to frighten away the demons...Fernandino, Isabela, La Española...These lands, bearing new names, have been claimed in the name of the Father, the Son, and Their Catholic Highnesses of Aragon and Castilla. Advent has come and gone, leaving thirty-nine men on a lonely shore amid a million Indians.*

But Haiti still belongs to the caciques. Caonabó begins fashioning fishbone spears to battle lombard, harquebus, crossbow, and sword. Anacaona composes a new areíto.

Huracán! Moaning of lost souls...flickering of strange blue lights...shaking of the powers of Heaven...

The men of Navidad were mostly farm boys who had left the lonely mountains of Extremadura and the rolling cultivated plains watered by the Guadalquivir to seek their fortune. Juan, the tailor...Vizcaino, the cooper ..."Chachu," the Basque boatswain and his bunch of highwaymen...young, illiterate, lustful. Driven to prove manhood in all the ways young men have always tried to prove manhood—drinking, swearing, fighting, fornicating. Young, very young, all of them. Even Torres, the interpreter, and Gutiérrez, who had been the King's butler, were young.

Not one of them could admit fear. Not one of them could accept Diego de Harana as commander of Navidad. By Santiago, could a man command just because his cousin had opened her thighs for the Admiral? If she were such a saint, why hadn't Colón married her and made his son Fernando legitimate? By the Virgin, a man did not marry a whore—and a man did not obey the son of a whore.

Diego de Harana was not the son of a whore, but the cousin.

Not important! A whore is a whore, and a lady is a lady!

Not one of them could admit he had ever been a farmer or a woodcutter. Now they were all gentlemen, every one of them. They held ceremonies knighting each other into the Order of Santiago. The blessed Saint James had been the first to bring Christianity to Europe, and his image had lain buried in the ground for the seven hundred years of Moorish rule, only to be found by a simple farmer. Spaniards had built a shrine on the site, and the rallying cry for driving out the worshippers of Allah had been "Santiago!" Now all the Christians of Europe made pilgrimages to the Cathedral of Santiago de Compostela, and every patriotic Spanish lad dreamed of joining the Knights of Santiago and fighting for the glory of Spain. Surely the men of Navidad deserved this honor for having braved the dangers of the Green Seas beyond the Pillars of Hercules.

For claiming all these islands for Their Catholic Highnesses. All these islands... all these God-forsaken, mosquito-ridden, hot, stinking islands. Oh, Andalucía! Oh, beautiful mountains! Oh, fertile vegas of Castile! Oh, blue skies above Sevilla! The men were so homesick they wanted to die. Give the islands back to the Indians, by God!

"Give me a drink of your wine," a sailor from Huelva demanded of Chachu the Basque.

"Drink cazabe beer. There's not much wine left. If you can find wine, you can get it for yourself."

"Gentlemen don't fetch wine. Knights of Santiago don't dirty their hands with work. Who do you think you are talking to? I am an hidalgo! Jesucristo! Where is that Indian woman?"

They were called Indians now.

"What is the matter with you, hidalgo?" Chachu asked. "I thought we were friends, but you yell at me like you yell at your Indian whore."

"Five women that old Cacique Guacanagarí gave me, and I can't find one when I want some wine to cool my throat."

"Are you sick, too?" Chachu asked, backing away from the sailor, who was lying in a hammock the Indians had given him.

"Yes, my throat's sore. I ache all over."

"How about your penis? Got an ulcer on your penis?" Chachu asked.

"How did you know? But it's getting better. Now my bones ache. Who hasn't got an ulcer on his penis? Nothing like this ever happened back home. Half the men in Navidad can't piss, their pecker's so sore. Wish we had a doctor to tell us what it is. Some plague of these stinking God-forsaken islands. Wish we had a priest. Maybe confession and the Host..."

"Didn't you buy your indulgences before we left?"

"Yes, at La Rabida, but now I have this rash. My mouth is full of sores. I ache and I can hardly swallow. I'd feel better if I could talk to a priest."

"Don't worry, man. Indulgences cover anything. What do we need with a priest? You know half the priests need indulgences themselves. You should have seen the ones flocking to Compostela. Always slipping women up to their rooms."

"Still, when a man comes to die, and there's no priest to hear his confession... Why didn't the Admiral bring a priest? Who will pray for my soul when it is in purgatory?"

"Who says you are going to die?" Chachu asked. "You are going to get up out of that bed and go with us to find Cibao. The gold, man! Gold! Think about gold! Think of what you can buy with all that gold. All the women in the world. All the doctors you need. All the forgiveness for all the sins you will ever commit. Why, man, you can buy the Pope himself with enough gold. The Pope can pray anyone out of purgatory. Here, drink the rest of my wine."

Rodrigo had left Tahíaca at the mouth of the river Colón had named the River of Gold—the river draining the mountains of Cibao. He had walked up the vega through the farming villages to Navidad. By the time he arrived, most of the men at Navidad were sick. Short-tempered quarrels broke out over the slightest thing: women, wine, the last of the moldy biscuits. Diego de Harana had almost given up trying to keep discipline. Yesterday, Escobeda the King's Secretary and Gutiérrez the Royal Butler had killed the sailor Jacome before they left the fort to look for more women and gold.

By the Virgin Santa María, you might not find much gold, but the island was swarming with naked women. Why depend on old Guacanagarí to send more? If you tired of what you had, find new ones. Why should a man limit himself, among so many women? A man had to make up for all that time at sea.

Guacanagarí had sworn friendship with the Admiral and protection for the men of Navidad. So when the men demanded women, Guacanagarí had supplied the women—women from the ragged, round, thatched cañayos tucked away in the forest. Women without men of their own. Women banished from Guacanagarí's village. Women the traders could visit without anyone's permission. Syphilitic women!

Although no one at Navidad knew what the disease was, never having come across it in Europe, half the men in the garrison were suffering from syphilis. Half the men in the two little caravels returning to Andalucía were carrying syphilis germs back to their wives and sweethearts.

Huracán...first winds...

CHAPTER 9

Cibao, 1493

CAONABÓ CONTROLLED his emotions as carefully as he controlled the fire at the base of the tree. Too much fire and the whole tree would burn; too little and it could not be felled. He sat on his haunches watching the coals eat away the base of the royal palm. He tried to forget why he was felling these trees, or why he had gathered the vines to tie them together, or why he had piled palm fronds at a certain place outside his village.

Building a cañayo for Anacaona's eldest daughter should have been a happy time. Cañayos were round, thatched dwelling places used by the Ciboneys as homes, but by the Taino and Caribs as temporary ceremonial shelters until the rectangular bahíos could be built. Not for a long time had Caonabó built a cañayo—not since he built the traditional wedding cañayo for his first wife. Now he was building a cañayo for Tahíaca, but not for her wedding.

Oh, Tahíaca, my joy, my life. Where are you, Tahíaca? A man should not allow himself to become so attached to the daughter of one of his wives. Caonabó's wives had many children, but none of them had ever gripped his heart as Tahíaca had. Now Tahíaca was gone.

Someone resembling Tahíaca wandered around the village, but the enchanting girl he had loved was gone. Caonabó had heard her sobs in the night. He had heard the name she murmured over and over again.

"Rodrigo!" Caonabó muttered between clenched teeth, the iguana pulsing.

At first Caonabó had been suspicious of the invaders in the winged canoes. Now he hated them. How dare they come here with their spirit bells and their lace points, saying some far-away cacique ruled these islands! How dare they raise their crossed cemí on Haitian soil and say they came from Heaven! Had the stars fallen? Had the sun left off chasing after the moon?

"Tahíaca!" he moaned, knowing no one could hear him.

Caonabó gritted his teeth and stood up. A Carib cacique does not allow himself to cry over a lost child. Tahíaca had made her choice. Now that her man had sent her away, she must go to live in the forest like the other women without husbands. She should have been left to build her own cañayo, but Caonabó was building it for her.

His heart ached because he would never be able to sit down with the strong nephew of some worthy cacique and discuss the man's fitness to be Tahíaca's husband. A man's sister's son was always in line to inherit the caciquedom from his uncle, for only then could anyone be sure of the blood lines. Caonabó would want to know more than blood lines. Could a man build a fish weir? Did he know how to use the remora fish to catch larger fish? Could he snare an iguana? Catch a parrot? Did he know how to build a bahío to withstand Huracán? Did he have a cemí who could tell him where to find gold? Could he row a canoe across long stretches of water with nothing to sustain him except tobacco? Could he make fishbone spears? Could he protect his village from invaders?

"Stop this!" Caonabó told himself sternly. Such a conversation would never take place.

The Tahíaca he had known would never return. Soon traders would begin visiting her cañayo. Perhaps one of them would take her away, but now he would not have to ask Caonabó's permission. Hopefully, while she was still young and pretty, one of them would make her his concubine. If not, soon the sickness would come upon her. One day she would wander away into the mountains, muttering to the opia, and then... and then...

Caonabó bent his back to the tree, exerting all his strength to topple it. The fire had not quite done its work, but he gloried in the strain as his face turned a deep red. Finally the tree began to sway, and his muscles bulged with the last hard push. He felt the tree slip away from him, toppling of its own weight. He stood back to watch it fall.

So it had been with Tahíaca. She had slipped away from him, and now he could only watch. That was what happened when people came who did not know the customs. Even if Caonabó killed them all, Tahíaca would never come back to his bahío, never be his little girl again. What kind of men were these who had no respect for a man's family?

The last night before she left Caonabó's bahío, Tahíaca lay in the darkness listening to Caonabó with one of his wives, to the sounds that had pleasured her all the nights of her growing up. Some of the other wives were already snoring softly, and some were pleasuring themselves to the rhythm of Caonabó's lovemaking, trying to disguise their pleasures by breathing in spasmodic harmony. Tahíaca's body ached with remembrance of Rodrigo. She ground her fist into her mouth to keep from shouting his name.

For so it is with women. A man enlarges, acts, is satisfied. A woman grows moist, receives, is never satisfied. When she is gone, he still has his fullness. When he is gone, she has only emptiness. So she will sell her soul to fill her emptiness.

Anacaona had tried to make the building of Tahíaca's cañayo a joyous occasion, a family affair. Mayabaño, who did not understand why Tahíaca was moving away, tied fronds on the roof. Anacaona gave her daughter clay jars of cazabe flour, a pair of Muscovy ducks, a family of hutía, baskets of fruit, and a fine carved mask cemí for her wall. Higueymato helped string the hammock, and they swept the dirt floor until Anacaona was satisfied. When no footprints except her own marred the surface, Tahíaca looked across the lonely cañayo at her mother, wanting to go back and knowing she could not.

Anacaona had no song in her heart, only the malicious whispers of the wives and concubines as they grated cazabe roots. Anacaona wanted to ask them what Tahíaca had done to deserve their contempt. Had none of them been strangers to Caonabó when he captured their hearts? Was it so bad Tahíaca had chosen one of the strangers? No! But what mattered was that Tahíaca had been sent away by her man. Now the women must shun her lest whatever opía had driven him away affect them, too. Who could live without the protection of a man? Nothing Anacaona could say or do would change anything, so she crossed the vines over Tahíaca's door and went away leaving her alone.

Mayabaño hung around the cañayo hoping Tahíaca would come out and play. Higueymato walked by a hundred times a day. But on Anacaona's orders, no one disturbed her. No one was allowed to build a fire or to cook for her. No one was allowed to uncross the vines and talk with her. Mayabaño wanted to keep watch at night, but Caonabó would not allow it. A few days later, Anacaona began to worry because no one had seen her daughter. She approached the door with the vines crossed over it, standing a respectful distance away.

"Tahíaca," she called, then a little louder: "Tahíaca, come out."

No sounds except the scurrying of a hutía in the dry thatch. A chameleon on the doorpost flashed his red blanket, raised up on his forefeet defiantly, then scuttled out of sight and stood rigid, trying to look like a twig.

"Tahíaca, are you here?"

Still no sound, except the sighing of the fronds. Only

in emergencies did any Taino violate the crossed vines over a door. A family could go away for many moons and come back to find everything in place. Anacaona decided this was an emergency.

She uncrossed one of the vines, feeling ashamed of herself for invading her daughter's privacy. She peered into the darkness in the little round, thatched cañayo. It was empty. Even Tahíaca's hammock was missing, but not one footprint marred the smooth surface of the sandy floor. As Anacaona had always taught her to do, Tahíaca had left the new home neat and clean, carefully sweeping away every trace of her passage. Anacaona carefully recrossed the vines before going to find Caonabó.

He was supervising the men making shark-tooth spears, and when he saw Anacaona's face, he knew what she had to say. He, too, had been watching those crossed vines.

"Tahíaca is gone," she said, watching his face for a reaction, but the iguana was strangely still.

"Did you hear me, Caonabó, my husband? Tahíaca is gone."

"Caonabó has ears," he snapped.

"What will Caonabó do about his daughter?"

"Caonabó is making spears, Carib spears. Caonabó will go to Navidad and kill all the invaders."

A sad song formed itself in Anacaona's heart.

Rodrigo and Chachu the Basque were sitting beside the river waiting for the Indian to carry the rest of the Basques across the stream on his back. Neither of them had yet put back on his clothing. The cool air felt good to their skins. More and more the hidalgos were leaving off pieces of the heavy, ornate Spanish garb. Yet they were very careful with their clothes, for where could they get new ones in this wilderness? So they always forced Indians to carry their clothes across on their backs, then swim back and carry the hidalgos across on their backs. Few of the Spaniards could swim.

"What is so special about this Indian girl?" asked Chachu. "What did you call her?"

"Tahíaca," answered Rodrigo, making it sound like a musical phrase. "Tahíaca is like Eve must have been in the Garden of Eden."

"And you, Don Rodrigo, carry a wicked serpent between your legs, eh?" laughed Chachu, and the strange hungry look came over his face—the look he always had when he thought about another man with a woman, a frightening look.

"Don't get any ideas, Chachu!" Rodrigo warned. "I am serious. Eden must have been like this. Have you watched these simple people? Do you ever see them working? The land feeds them. Plant a few beans, and tomorrow you have beans for the pot. Three times a day they stop everything and go for a swim. Have you seen any of them unhappy? No! Where are the priests to remind them they should be unhappy? No, my friend, you will find no hair shirts here. No one has ever told them what sin is!"

"You are talking sacrilege, Rodrigo," Chachu chided. "Be careful. Even on the road to Compostela, a man could not talk like that about the Church without answering to Chachu!"

"But Chachu could lift the purse of every pilgrim he found on the way to Compostela," Rodrigo charged.

"A man must live," said Chachu, "but someday a man must also die. It is the dying that keeps the priests in business."

They became silent, neither of them wanting to talk about dying. They lay back and looked up at the cocoa tree with its dark green leaves and its masses of fragrant pink blossoms. Towering forty feet into the air, sheltered by a bluff, this cocoa tree had defied Huracán for more than a hundred years. Women came twice a year to gather and sweeten the cocoa beans, piling them under green plantain leaves. The women of Haiti knew how to sweeten many things—cazabe, cocoa beans, men. After the bitterness had drained away, the women would sort the beans into little pouches their husbands carried to even out their trades. Without knowing it, Rodrigo and Chachu lay under a money tree!

Rodrigo was not thinking about money. He was

thinking about Tahíaca, the way she moaned just before that final ecstasy, the way her eyes teased for more. Rodrigo turned over to hide his sudden need.

He would marry Tahíaca, he told himself. Marry her and never go back to petty Castilian wars. Marry her as soon as priests came to La Española. Surely Colón would bring priests next time. Yes, Tahíaca would be baptized, receive instruction, learn to clothe herself modestly, and behave like a Christian. They would kneel for the Holy Sacrament of Matrimony, then Tahíaca and all of Caonabó's gold would belong to Rodrigo Sandoval.

He would build himself a Moorish castle on one of these mountain peaks, teach Cacique Caonabó how to really defend Cibao, then live like a sultan with Tahíaca as his First Wife. Rodrigo never entertained the thought that Caonabó might not welcome a Knight of the Order of Santiago as his daughter's husband. He would be doing the Indians a favor to marry her. With such daydreams, Rodrigo drifted off into a contented sleep....

Slivers of moonlight probed the valleys, changing the face of the mountains, awakening the opia. Tahíaca could see them, hear them, almost feel them. Those tree roots? Were they writhing? Should she stop and speak to the cemí of the tree, ask what it wanted of her? Promise to come back with a stone ax and free it, to set it up in the caves of the ancestors?

Cibao nights held many terrors for the young Taino girl who had never been away from Caonabó's bahío at night until she ran away with her handsome...her handsome...what had he called himself? Cabal... caballero...yes, that was it. Caballero! Caballeros rode horses, he had told her, then tried to describe a horse.

Tahíaca could not imagine such a wondrous creature as a horse. They had all sorts of strange animals in that place called Andalucía. Horses, cows, pigs. Perhaps they were all opia who had crossed the water and taken strange shapes. Opia had that power—unlike cemí they were not prisoners of their shapes. Cemís had to wait for someone to recognize them, to carve and shape them, to set them up and worship them. The opia had wills of their own—mischievous wills.

Suddenly a boulder loomed against the night sky, seemed to grow larger, to breathe. Perhaps it was a dragon. Rodrigo had said caballeros fought dragons and rescued ladies. Tahíaca backed away, but the stone dragon leered at her, panting as the clouds passed over the moon.

Oh, how she wished she could go home. Go sleep again among the sounds of Caonabó making love with his wives.

Tahíaca looked for a way to escape the dragon and saw a giant, waving fan-shaped hands—hundreds of them. Trying to catch her. She turned and ran from the monsters she had created, and she saw Rodrigo on the ridge riding his horse toward her in the moonlight.

"Rodrigo," she called, beginning to run. "Rodrigo, you have come back to me. I knew you would."

She scrambled up the slope toward her lover. Her feet slipped on gravel, but she got up again—tears of joy blinding her to everything except that Rodrigo had come back. Through her sobs she heard him call to her, and she opened her arms to embrace him.

"Rodrigo, beloved!" she moaned, relief flooding her heart.

Her face scraped pocked granite thrown up during some long forgotten volcanic eruption. She looked up at a stunted pine whose limbs had been twisted by Huracán. The opia! Dead spirits luring her, trying to find love in the arms of the living. Tahíaca ran back down the slope, trying to outrun them. She stumbled, rolled in a small avalanche to the foot of a spiked-leaf pandanus. The roots of the pandanus, because of their strange way of growing down from the limbs, had always been used as love charms. Tahíaca cried herself to sleep nestled against the roots of the pandanus.

When morning came and the sun probed the valleys looking for the last vestiges of the moon, Tahíaca felt better. She had started out to find Rodrigo, and she knew in her heart she would soon see him. First she must make her morning prayers to the spirits of the water. She tossed her skirt over the pandanus and ran across the glade to a pool at the base of a waterfall. It was in the glade of the ancestors, and behind her were the two caves where people had first come out into the sunlight. The chiseled face smiling out of the boulder did not frighten her now. It was no dragon, it was Marocael—who had been turned into stone for neglecting to keep people penned up in darkness.

Bathing three times a day was a religious ritual for Tainos. As they washed sweat and dirt from their bodies, the water soothed their souls. Who could have an evil thought while floating in a pool watching a flock of golden finches circling an old ceiba? Tahíaca splashed about, reviving her spirit with memories of her mother's areítos, the comforting old myths of creation—like how the seas were made...how a man and his son quarreled, and the father killed the son and hid his body in a calabash hung from the ridgepole of his bahío...how from the son's bones sprang all the fish of the seas, and how three brothers, all born after their mother had died—delivered by the buhuituhu's knife—had stolen the calabash, dropped it, and been swept away when all the waters of the seas came rushing out.

Tahíaca swam lazily to the edge of the pool, then climbed to the top of the cliff to dive off the waterfall. Rodrigo saw her rising like Venus from the waves. Quickly he stripped off his clothing and ran toward her. He had never seen anything more beautiful than Tahíaca gilded by the sun.

"Tahíaca, wait for me," he called.

Tahíaca looked up, startled. Was it the opia again? Everyone said the opia roamed only at night. Here was Rodrigo standing nude in the sun on the bank of the pool below her.

"One moment, amigo," called Chachu in an ominous voice, from the opposite bank of the river, where he had also been watching Tahíaca. He had a strange, mad look in his eyes, a look Rodrigo had seen once before on the road to Compostela. "Chachu saw her first. She is Chachu's woman now. Chachu knows what to do with such women."

"No, Chachu! No! Not this woman!" Rodrigo shouted, wishing he had his sword. He knew Chachu.

Chachu had once been an altar boy, dedicated to the Church by his mother, who had been barren and prayed many years for a son. She had kept him so pure he would be fit to serve God; as Chachu grew up, he was afraid to tell his mother about his impure thoughts. One day he told his confessor he could not keep his thoughts pure when little girls made their first communion. The kindly old friar assigned Chachu a penance he thought would rid him of his sins. Chachu was to go to his mother's patio and flagellate himself until he drove such thoughts out of his head.

When his mother learned why he was beating himself, she pushed away the contrite little boy with the thick black curls and the sad Moorish eyes, telling him she wanted nothing to do with such an evil child. After that, Chachu began having visions, sinful visions. Sometimes he was the angel who had impregnated the sainted Virgin María! Often when he was alone in the chapel, the Virgin baring her breast to the Christ child would seem to be offering herself to him. Every Holy Day, Chachu saw men throw kisses at paraded Virgins. He stopped serving as altar boy and took to the streets, but every time he saw a girl behind barred windows or patio grilles, she looked like Santa María—smiling seductively.

Once he went with a whore and saw the Blessed Lord on the Cross hanging above her bed. Before he knew it, he was beating the poor woman. He was afraid she would set the Holy Brotherhood on him, so he killed her. Then he went to his mother's patio and flagellated his back raw.

Next morning a friar found Chachu lying in front of the altar. The Inquisitors questioned him, but could find no traces of heresy. So Chachu joined the regimented life of the friary—praying, fasting, chanting.

Gradually, his torment returned. Plaster Virgins uncovered their breasts and opened their thighs. Chachu spent feverish hours on cold floors trying to purge the evil from his soul. One night a kindly friar lifted Chachu up, led him into a dark confessional, and knelt before him. When Chachu realized what the friar was doing, he gave an agonized groan, but he was powerless to stop the ecstasy.

Brothers, they were brothers in Christ, the friar told him, sharing everything, sustaining each other, answering each other's needs. When the friar finally left, the languid Chachu had his final vision of the Virgin. She appeared to him sorrowfully, crying crystal tears. Never again, she told him, would she appear to him, and never again would he taste the joys of a woman.

Chachu had broken all the plaster saints in the chapel, stolen the gold plate, then taken himself to the mountains around Roncesvalles where, like some apocalyptic evangelist, he preached the corruptions of the Church. No one listened. Some threw stones. Others threatened him with the Inquisition. Chachu the altar boy became Chachu the highwayman—terrorizing pilgrims as he courted Death and Final Judgment.

Chachu became known as the celibate bandit. Never taking a man, never keeping a woman. When his passion became too great, Chachu would capture a young girl and give her to his band, watching through slitted eyes while they raped her, but never touching her himself until he carried out the judgment he had pronounced on her. He would flog her until he found his release. Few girls survived Chachu's sins.

"Come, my friend," said Chachu the bandit, standing on the river bank looking longingly at Tahíaca. "We can share this girl. Did we not share a young virgin once on the road to Compostela?"

Even Sandoval blood did not run so darkly in the veins. Once Rodrigo had participated in one of Chachu's rites, and when he saw what Chachu did to the girl, he had been sick. He had vowed to kill Chachu rather than see him do it again. The Holy Brotherhood had arrested them both soon afterward. Now Chachu wanted Tahíaca.

"Chachu is waiting!" He laughed the chilling laugh without mirth Rodrigo had heard many times in the mountain passes near Roncesvalles. Rodrigo looked toward the bank. Did he have a chance of reaching his sword? Chachu laughed again, stepping out from behind a palmetto holding a drawn Turkish bow. Chachu was very good with that bow!

"No, Chachu, not this girl. You can't—"

Evil recognizes danger to itself far more quickly than does good. Rodrigo started toward the sword on the river bank, and Chachu let go his bowstring.

Twang!

Twang! Thud! Thud!

Tahíaca heard the hiss of the two arrows thudding into Rodrigo's heart. Water splashed up red as his body fell and rolled into the pool.

"Rodrigo!" she screamed, diving into the water already stained with his blood.

Chachu felt the old familiar excitement in his loins.

CHAPTER 10

Cibao, 1492

TAHÍACA WAS unconscious when Mayabaño found her in the caves of the ancestors, where she had crawled after Chachu had left her for dead. Mayabaño drove away the finger-long roaches that had gathered to feast on her lacerated body. He tried to move her, but he was still too young to carry such a burden. He covered her with fresh palm fronds, then started back toward the village to get help.

Anacaona was digging cazabe roots, jabbing the digging stick into the earth's bosom as if it were an enemy. Scraping away dirt...pulling up roots...filling her basket to fill her mind and keep out the thoughts crowding themselves into her unsung areíto. The cyanide poison in the cazabe roots was only a breath away. Anacaona took them back to the village, grated them savagely, filled the stocking sieve and hung it to drip. Sad notes pushed themselves into her mind. Sad notes of a poison not draining away...lost souls moaning on Huracán's winds.

Anacaona could no longer keep her song inside. She donned her dancing feathers and tied the spirit bells around her ankles. Then, singing her sad song, she danced out of the village and up the road toward the caves of the ancestors.

The wives looked at each other, puzzled. Had the opia possessed Anacaona? They had heard no one coming who merited a dancing welcome. Whoever was coming must be bringing bad news. Anacaona had never sung such a mournful song, but Anacaona was always hearing things they did not hear, and knowing things they did not know.

So Anacaona danced to meet Mayabaño, singing the areíto of Tahíaca, her lost child...a song to echo down the centuries...the dance of the doomed Tainos her uncle the old cacique had danced so long ago.

Bats had begun their nightly exit from the caves when Caonabó and Anacaona reached their daughter. Caonabó knelt beside her, saw her bruised and torn body caked with blood.

"Tahíaca!" Caonabó's agonized voice rolled out over the mountains like the deep-voiced instrument they used to call the men to make cahobas. "Tahíaca! Tahíaca!"

He gathered her into his arms, tears spilling out of his eyes as he rocked her back and forth, muttering her name. The men who had done this thing did not know it yet, but they were already dead. Caonabó had killed them.

They laid her tenderly in a hammock and carried her gently down the mountains to the village. They sent Hatuey into the forest to find the buhuitihu, hoping against hope he would be able to bring her back from the brink of death.

"Buhuitihu!" Hatuey called, standing before the lonely cañayo of the healer. "Buhuitihu! Come and bring your healing bag. Caonabó commands it!"

No one answered, but a green parrot flew out of the buhuitihu's dilapidated cañayo and perched on the vines crossed over the door.

"Buhuitihu! Buhuitihu!" mocked the parrot.

So the buhuitihu was at home. Everyone knew the parrot went wherever the buhuitihu went.

"Buhuitihu," Hatuey called again, annoyed at the old man's silence. "You must come at once."

"Go away," said a cracked old voice.

The parrot flew back into the hut, muttering, "Go away, go away, go away. Buhuitihu, buhuitihu, buhuitihu. Go away, go away."

"Why should the buhuitihu take such a chance?" the old man asked. "The buhuitihu has not yet recovered from the beating given him by the family of the last patient who died."

"Caonabó has spoken," Hatuey urged, reaching toward the crossed vines, then stepping back. Even on such an urgent mission, he must respect the buhuitihu's privacy.

"Would Caonabó take my other eye and smash my other testicle?"

"Only if his wife's daughter dies," Hatuey said, "and only if her voice accuses you after death. Only then can a family have their day of revenge. You know the laws of healing."

"And if I do not choose to treat Anacaona's daughter?"

Hatuey was startled. How had he known it was Anacaona's daughter who was in need of a healer?

"Caonabó will surely kill you if you do not come," said Hatuey.

Silence. The only sound was the twittering of finches in the jacaranda shading the old man's cañayo.

"Buhuitihu! Buhuitihu!" the parrots muttering interrupted the silence. "Kill the poor buhuitihu!"

Hatuey knew the buhuitihu would come. What choice had he? Hatuey had little faith in these healers, but he felt sorry for the buhuitihu. Relatives of patients who died were allowed one special day to beat the buhuitihu for causing the death—to break his arms and his legs, to tear out his eyes, to smash his testicles trying to kill him. Hearing the old man stirring around in his cañayo, Hatuey cleared his throat to remind him he was still here.

"Very well, the buhuitihu will come," the old man said. "Tell Caonabó to send a litter."

"Only caciques and their favorite wives are entitled to be carried on litters," Hatuey reminded the old man.

"The buhuitihu must assume the sickness of the patient in order to heal," the old man scolded, as if speaking to a retarded child. "Tahíaca was carried home in a litter, so the buhuitihu must go to her carried in a litter."

Again Hatuey was astonished that the old man knew it was Tahíaca who was ill. Hatuey had not mentioned her name, nor that she had been carried home on a hammock. No one could have gotten here quicker than he had, except perhaps the parrot. Every time Hatuey resolved to pay no attention to superstition, something incredible happened. Perhaps the parrot. Yes, it must be that the old man sent the parrot out to spy for him.

"Buhuitihu! Buhuitihu! Call the buhuitihu!" scolded the parrot.

While Hatuey went for the litter, the buhuitihu limped painfully around the cañayo gathering up his medical supplies. Why had he ever wanted to become a healer? He had studied with the best buhuitihus in the islands before he blackened his face and took his first case. He knew all the healing herbs, where they grew, when to gather them, how to prepare them.

Most of his patients recovered, and he had outlived buhuitihus much younger than he. But when someone died, the family sometimes beat him unmercifully. He had had so many beatings now that the healing snakes did not come so quickly, and even another buhuitihu would not tend him after a ritual beating. One of his testicles was permanently swollen now, so he walked spread-gaited; but as long as he still had at least one good testicle, they would not be able to kill him. He dipped his hand into the soot pot and began blackening his one-eyed, bruised face. People expected a buhuitihu to look like a buhuitihu.

Sometimes patients cured themselves. He knew that. He had seen people live who should have died, and he had seen people die who should have lived—living or dying in spite of the buhuitihu. Yet people always sent for him—awed by death, puzzled by life. They seemed soothed by a buhuitihu who looked like a buhuitihu, and they were comforted by the ceremonies. The buhuitihu knew most of what he did was nonsense, but he always behaved as people expected him to behave.

When the buhuitihu finished blackening his face, he took a handful of herbs and chewed them until Huracán began churning at his stomach. He ran outside and vomited, clearing himself of evil. Back inside the cañayo, he selected a stone he had been carving in his spare time, one with the Huracán symbol—a frightful one-eyed face with no body, one hand curved over the head, and one under the chin, with motion featherings and furious arrows. He wrapped the Huracán stone in a bit of meat from the boucan, then in banana leaf. He stuck the wad into his cheek, neither chewing nor swallowing. The lump became just another lump on his battered face.

When Hatuey came back with the litter bearers, the buhuitihu was cutting aloe leaves. He washed his hands in the thick, golden flow from the cut ends of the fat leaves. He lay down on the litter and began imagining he was Tahíaca. Hatuey was impressed by the tortured look on the buhuitihu's face.

Tahíaca lay on the floor of Caonabó's bahío with all her family around her—her mother and father, her father's wives and concubines, her sister and brother, her half-sisters and half-brothers, Behechio and Hatuey. The bahío looked as if they were having an areíto rather than a healing.

"Go away, all of you," ordered the buhuitihu, shouldering his way painfully through the crowd.

Higueymato followed the wives and children outside, where they stood peering back into the bahío, but Mayabaño stayed close to his beloved older sister, a frown on his butterfly face.

"You, too, butterfly boy," the buhuitihu said sternly. "Be gone. Get out of my way. Go and play. Leave sickness and sorrow to others. You will have your turn. Do not run too quickly down the bitter path of the buhui-tihu."

Caonabó refused to leave, and Anacaona stayed with him. They stood back a respectful distance while the buhuitihu began his ritual. First, he took the cahoba and blew a pinch of powdered herbs up Tahíaca's nose. She sneezed and coughed, but did not regain consciousness. As soon as the drug took effect, she ceased moaning and lay deathly still. Then a smile flickered over her face. The buhuitihu quickly mirrored her smile. He put the cahoba to his nostrils and sniffed. To heal her, the buhuitihu must make her journey into the spirit world. He picked up his torch and began chanting, walking round and round Tahíaca.

He walked in the glade and saw the young stranger poised at the waterfall. He took the two arrows in his breast. He fought the rapist—kicking, biting, cringing, crying, clamping his legs together. Only if he took her pain upon himself could he heal her.

He took the aloe leaf, cut it, and anointed her body from head to toe with the sticky sap. He massaged her breasts, caressed her loins, filled his hands with the evil possessing her. Then he ran to the door of the bahío. The onlookers scattered as he threw the evil into the wind, blowing on his hands and shouting:

"Be gone! Let Huracán take you if He will!"

He knelt and sucked the rest of the evil from her body—her neck, her breasts, her stomach. He licked each of her wounds tenderly, then he fastened his mouth on the little cemí at the center of her being. Seeing the buhuitihu do this obscene thing, Caonabó stepped forward to stop him, but Anacaona held him back.

Tahíaca writhed, moaning in pain or ecstasy, they could not tell which. The buhuitihu continued his ministrations as Tahíaca tangled her hands in the old man's long gray hair, clutching him with her thighs. She opened her eyes on some faraway vision. Her breath came in half-sobs, half-gasps as she muttered incoherently. She began to cry out...one name, over and over.

"Rodrigo...Rodrigo...Rodrigo. Ah-h-h, Rodrigo!"

Caonabó could not bear to watch. He clenched his

fists, wanting to strike the old man, pacing up and down the bahío, his head turned away to keep from seeing what was engraved on the back of his eyelids. How many times had that old man treated women in this manner?

Suddenly, Tahíaca gave an ecstatic cry, and the buhuitihu sat back on his heels, triumphantly holding up a mess of meat wrapped in a slippery bit of banana leaf. He stripped away leaf and meat and held up the saliva-wet stone inscribed with the cemí of Huracán raging.

"Here! Behold her cemí—the cause of her trouble," he cackled triumphantly. "Build a shrine to this cemí, feed it, worship it. When Tahíaca conceives a child, rub her breasts with this cemí every day so she will have plenty of milk. When she comes to deliver the child, lay this cemí on her belly to make the delivery easy. This cemí is most sacred, because it has come from within. Such a cemí will always protect Tahíaca."

The buhuitihu turned to Anacaona and began prescribing Tahíaca's diet, a rich diet including stewed iguana, usually reserved for caciques alone. From now on the lecherous old healer would have to follow the same diet as his patient.

Tahíaca lay conscious, but not moving. Caonabó decided to tear out the old man's remaining testicle if Tahíaca did not recover, but before he could voice his vow, Tahíaca opened her eyes.

"Papa?" she whispered.

"Yes, daughter," said Caonabó, kneeling to take her hand.

"Papa," she whimpered, and the pain in her voice smote Caonabó a mighty blow. "Papa, he...he..."

"Papa knows. Papa knows. Do not talk about it."

"He...he killed...he killed my Rodrigo, Papa. Oh! Papa! My Rodrigo is dead."

Caonabó took Rodrigo into his family because Tahíaca had loved him. To avenge the handsome Spaniard became as important as to avenge Tahíaca. To wreak such a vengeance would now require him to wipe Navidad off the island. Caonabó would have his revenge.

"Rest now, my daughter," he said.

CHAPTER 11

Cibao, 1493

"LET MAYABAÑO go with his father to make the war ceremony," asked the boy, who had slipped back into the bahío to be with his beloved sister.

Mayabaño tried hard to look stern. The butterfly wrapped in the cocoon of his bangs had grown part way up into his hair. He was not yet allowed to cut his hair to the tips of his earlobes, but wore it long and tied back like a woman. He wanted to be a brave man like his father, but no one called him anything except the butterfly boy.

"No one can make the war cahoba with Caonabó," his father said, wondering when Mayabaño had grown so tall.

"Hatuey will go with Caonabó. The elders will go. Why not Mayabaño?"

"When it is time for Mayabaño to make a war cahoba, he will not have to ask permission. Hatuey is going because he must call up the opia so they can guide Caonabó to the valley of everlasting areítos. The elders are going to watch over Caonabó's body while he is on his journey."

"You are going to visit the dead?" Mayabaño felt a chill down his back at the thought of the mystical valley of everlasting areítos. "Let Mayabaño go with you. Please, let Mayabaño go with you."

"No man, not even Hatuey, can make this journey with Caonabó. Mayabaño is not yet a man even if he has grown tall while Caonabó was not watching."

"Let Mayabaño sit with the elders and watch over Caonabó's body while he is on his journey."

"My son." Caonabó smoothed back the bangs, coaxing the butterfly out of its cocoon. "Someday you will fight your war. Do not run to meet it."

The look of disappointment on Mayabaño's face touched Caonabó's heart. Why not let him go? The boy had to become a man someday.

So he allowed Mayabaño to go with Hatuey and the elders to the sacred caves to sit in darkness while Caonabó fasted, sniffed the cahoba, and chanted the ancient prayers. After seven days, Hatuey blew on the sonorous instrument called a mayohavau, which could be heard in villages far away. In a loud voice he called for opia to guide Cacique Caonabó into the valley of everlasting areíto on a mythical island not far away. Mayabaño felt chill winds in the windless cave as Caonabó's head dropped between his knees. He slumped over, and they stretched his body face-up on the cave floor.

First, Caonabó saw the Old Cacique from Anacaona's village, still trussed up in his funeral bundle, sitting like a rock in the corner of the cave. Opia began marching across the ceiling of the cave—the opia of all the people Caonabó had killed in battle, the babies his family had bred for the stewpot, the boys they had castrated, all danced around him. The Old Cacique from Anacaona's village slowly unfolded himself and walked across the ceiling, circling three times and peering down at Caonabó. Caonabó could see the old man's bones shining through his green skin, fluorescent like the phosphorus sea.

Caonabó saw this through the transparency of his eyelids; but when he tried to rise, his body did not move. Only his soul rose slowly and stood upon the ceiling looking back down upon himself, and on the solemn little group keeping guard. He suddenly wished he had taken his son Mayabaño with him, but he knew Mayabaño would have his own journey to make—perhaps sometime in the future, perhaps sometime in the past.

"Welcome," said the Old Cacique in a surprisingly young voice. "We have prepared an areíto for your pleasure."

"Caonabó has no time for feasting and dancing," he said. "Caonabó must find out whether he will have victory over his enemies."

"Time does not exist here," said the Old Cacique. "Caonabó may dance areítos forever if he wishes, and still be reborn in time for the next battle. There is always a battle to be fought. Is Caonabó so eager for war?"

"No," said Caonabó truthfully.

Caonabó hated war, for he knew what few warriors know. Men fight wars to conquer death, but Death always wins.

"Who can tell Caonabó whether he will win this battle?" Caonabó asked.

The Old Cacique summoned up the cemí who had led him through this same cahoba many years ago in Cuba—the day Caonabó had captured Ana. He showed Caonabó the coming Huracán, and the clothed invaders who were destroying the people of the Sea of Caribbee. Only yesterday the Old Cacique had seen this same vision, and tomorrow someone else would see it, for it had many verses like a long areíto.

Caonabó saw the bones of the dead making miracles, and he heard the voices of the dead in the winds of Huracán. He saw stones become cemís, and he heard the dead accusing their murderers, raining their ashes on the guilty until the flesh rotted off their bones. He ate the fruit the opia gather during their long night walks in Cuba, and he felt as free as they—free to take any shape he wished, to do anything he desired.

Yesterday and tomorrow were one with today, and the living and the dead danced wondrous areítos. How sweet their music! How vibrant the beat of their timeless hearts! Mountains dissolved into clouds radiant with sunlight, and stars exploded into spirals. Tarry not too long in this valley—this world without dimension, constantly changing, beyond imagination. So thin is the veil, so sharp is the edge of Eternity!

The Old Cacique urged Caonabó to make the same decision he had made. What man can say he has conquered death unless he chooses when death will come to him? Caonabó did not think everlasting areítos would suit him, but the Old Cacique assured him he could leave the valley any time he chose. He himself had done it many times in the past and many times in the future. As he had chosen the hour of his death, so he could choose to dissolve and enter once again into a woman's womb before birth. He could be born again to whomever he pleased, and to whatever winds Huracán was blowing at the time.

Caonabó chose to return to the world where his job was not quite finished. Someday, he told the Old Cacique, he would choose his own death. Caonabó readied himself, for the Old Cacique had told him the way back was blocked by Huracán himself. Wave after wave of the past and the future hit Caonabó as if the eye of the storm had just passed over and he were plunging into the storm again. Wave after wave, people after people whirling by; but in the distance, like a warm fire on shore marking the end of a long sea journey, Caonabó saw Tahíaca standing alone, singing an old Carib lullaby to the child in her arms.

Caonabó gathered up his strength to reenter his body and take up the awful burden of his vision. Mercifully, before he passed back through that breathless curtain, all memory of his journey was blotted from his mind.

While Caonabó was away making his cahoba, Anacaona ruled Cibao. Sitting on the carved stool under the ceiba, she received the complaints of the village caciques. All of them talked of the atrocities committed by the Spaniards. Someone's home had been broken into, the crossed vines torn from the door and the bones of their ancestors spilled from the wicker baskets onto the floor. Did not these people respect the dead? They told Anacaona of children kidnapped, wives ravished, food supplies stolen. What kind of people were these?

By the time Caonabó returned, Anacaona had decided that although she was a Taino, she would claim the right of a Carib woman to fight beside her husband. She knew it would be difficult to win against people with such weapons, so she suggested they ask Manioc to help them.

Manioc had been a fisherman long ago when the great god Yocahu had gone on his journey during which his lazy son Marocael let the people escape. Yocahu had been so angry when he returned and caught some of them outside that he had turned some into plants and animals to feed the rest. Manioc, the fisherman, had been turned into the fleshy-rooted plant with poisonous sap that would stupefy fish, making them easily caught. When Yocahu got over his anger, he taught the women how to separate the poison from the pulp, which made a fine bread. Anacaona suggested they use the manioc sap, a deadly poison if used in concentration, to trap Tahíaca's attacker.

Scouts brought word to Anacaona that the Basques had camped on a river bank not far from the village. Before sunrise next morning, Caonabó positioned his court in all their golden splendor on the other side of the river, and his warriors with spears, poisoned with the sap, behind a cedar brake. Anacaona carried a large covered jar of manioc poison. They waited patiently for Chachu and the Basques to wake up.

"Jesucristo!" Chachu murmured when he awoke to the dazzling sight on the other side of the river.

Chachu had never believed Rodrigo's tale of the gold in Cibao, and now he rubbed his eyes and looked again. It was still there. He put his cockleshell pilgrim's hat over his heart and crossed himself. He had taken that hat from a Dominican friar on the road to Compostela, and its band was adorned with the rosaries taken from his virgins.

"Gold!" he whispered, then began kicking the sleeping Basques awake. "Gold! Wake up, you bastards! Gold! Look at all that gold!"

Chachu and these Basques had almost aborted the Admiral's expedition only a few days short of the discovery. Now they awoke to see the morning sun shining on more gold than they had ever expected to see.

"Mother of God! The gold of Cibao!"

"We're rich," they shouted. "We've found paradise."

"Quick, give me some hawk bells," Chachu ordered. "And the beads. Indians go crazy for beads."

No one seemed to have hawk bells. They had stopped carrying trade goods. Chachu grasped the ornate pectoral cross hanging around his neck and dropped to his knees. The cross had once belonged to a bishop who had the misfortune to meet Chachu while on his pilgrimage to Compostela.

"Salve Regina..." Chachu began, then noticed the men were stripping off their clothes preparing to cross the river.

"Kneel, you bastards," Chachu ordered. "Thank the Virgin for such luck. Show these Indians how to pray. Kneel, damn you."

The Basques reluctantly knelt, crossing themselves and holding their rosaries, every one blessed by Pope Alexander himself before Her Catholic Highness gave them to Colón. Caonabó sat majestically on his carved litter-throne watching the Basques through slitted eyes. The iguana on his cheek pulsed slightly.

"Let us see if their cemís can protect them from Manioc," Caonabó murmured to Anacaona.

Caonabó knew the Spaniards would summon Tainos to ferry them across the river. He was ashamed of his people for still according this hospitality to such men, but most of the people were afraid now. Some were even beginning to say the invaders were cemís and did not die. Today Caonabó would prove they were men and could be killed. Caonabó waited patiently for the Basques to finish their prayers, marveling at Chachu's clothing.

Chachu wore the tattered, elegant finery that had earned him the title of "the handsome highwayman":

a Sicilian nobleman's red-and-white-brocade surcoat, a young crusader's doublet with the Red Cross blessed by Pope Urban himself, a Medici's parti-colored hose, puffed and slashed breeches, and a Córdoban leather belt once belonging to a Jewish financier on his way to confer with the relic sellers whose stalls crowded the courtyard of the Compostela Cathedral. At his belt he wore a silver perfume ball and a small enameled Cairo cosmetic case containing the mummified thumb of a sultan taken in one of the first crusades. Boxes of such relics had been shipped back from Jerusalem to be sold as souvenirs. Chachu needed only one thing to complete his costume—Cacique Caonabó's golden crown.

"Amen." The Basques completed their prayers, crossing themselves.

Chachu held up the Bishop's cross, and Caonabó took Anacaona's nugget necklace and held it out toward Chachu.

"By Santiago," said one man, nudging Chachu. "Each nugget is worth thirty castellanos or the Virgin María is a whore."

"Don't blaspheme the Mother of God." Chachu gave the man a cuff.

Caonabó rattled the necklace, and some of the Basques plunged into the river waist-deep before remembering they could not swim.

"Send over some Indians," Chachu ordered.

Caonabó pretended not to understand.

"Can't swim." Chachu ducked the nearest Basque, held his head under while he thrashed about, then let him go.

"Bastard," the youth sputtered. "Trying to drown me?"

"Come on over, you heathen," Chachu shouted. "Carry us across. We can't swim."

Caonabó nodded his head, and his best swimmers dived into the river. Quickly they swam across and bent their backs to the naked Basques.

"Now we shall see whether they are from Heaven," Caonabó said. "Is Anacaona ready?"

"Forward, horse." Chachu kicked his Indian.

"Forward! Forward!" The other Basques joined the fun, yelling as though riding into battle. They were little more than children, all of them except Chachu. None was yet twenty years old.

As the river deepened sharply, the Tainos dived under—slipping easily out of the clutch of the Basques, swimming underwater, and surfacing safely upstream.

"Help!" gasped the Basques, trying to stay afloat. "Help us! We're drowning, drowning."

Caonabó nodded to Anacaona. She tipped the jar, careful not to inhale the deadly fumes. Soon five unconscious Basques floated to the surface. Caonabó fished them out with long poles and stood waiting for them to regain consciousness. He wanted them to know they were going to die.

"Holy Mary, Mother of God," murmured Chachu as he saw the awful iguana on Caonabó's face.

"Tahíaca-a-a-a!" Caonabó's anguished cry rumbled over the mountains.

Caonabó plunged his poisoned spear into Chachu's belly just below the navel. Chachu convulsed once before his eyes glazed, but he did not feel much pain.

"Now let us see how powerful their cemís are." Caonabó motioned to Hatuey.

Caonabó and Anacaona waited patiently while the giant condors circled the five blue-tinged bodies tied to the crosses, and when after the third day the men had not come to life again, as some of the Tainos had begun to believe they would, Anacaona made a great areíto to celebrate Caonabó's triumph over the men from Heaven.

The legend of Anacaona, the singer of great areítos mirroring the spirit of her people, began to grow after the celebration. In the coming years when her people needed courage, they remembered Anacaona. When they needed inspiration, they evoked her image. When they needed a leader, they turned to her. Even after the Spaniards killed her, she did not die. She lived wherever a spark of freedom lived and wherever mercy cried out against injustice.

She had always enjoyed areítos. Even when she was a little girl, she had sat watching the old singers and dancers while the other children played, absorbing the myths and legends and creating new ones. Her whole life had been an areíto, lived joyously. She felt more deeply than most people. She loved more passionately. A sunset was not just a sunset, and a child was not just a child. Tahíaca, torn from her body, was still part of her, the continuing bridge of generations. Anacaona belonged, not just to herself, but to all people.

Anacaona's victory areíto lasted three weeks. Never had Haiti seen such celebrations, and never would such celebrations be seen again. Dignitaries came from all five provinces. People came from all the villages in Cibao, and even from as far away as Xaragua, Behechio's province.

Women brewed cazabe beer. Men built fish weirs. Smoke rose from a hundred boucans where fat Muscovy ducks sputtered over spits. Sweet potatoes baked in the coals and juicy ears of corn roasted in their shucks. Mayabaño even captured one of the giant sloths called a megaluccus, and he stood proudly and unflinchingly while Caonabó scarified the outline on his chest, then sat proudly with the caciques to eat its meat. Now perhaps people would stop calling him "butterfly boy."

Caonabó's wives rolled giant cigars as long as a man's arm and almost as thick, and Caonabó proudly passed them around among the visiting caciques. Mayabaño accepted the honor of smoking, but had to run away when he got sick.

Anacaona watched the ball tournaments from a place of honor beside her husband under the old ceiba where the spirits of the Tainos whispered. The celebration had a perfection so sharp it almost frightened her. She stroked Caonabó's arm as she often stroked it, loving the feel of his scarified skin.

"Remember the areíto in my village in Cuba, my husband?" she asked.

"When Caonabó came seeking a new wife who could sing areítos?" he asked, smiling at her.

"Yes, that areíto."

"How sweetly Anacaona sang her uncle's funeral areíto," said Caonabó, "but Anacaona will sing even more sweetly today when she sings Caonabó's areíto."

Anacaona looked at her husband, adoring him, wondering how she could have been so fortunate as to have had him choose her for his wife. She wanted to hold this precious moment, yet a feeling of doom gripped her heart. She looked up at the crosses and shuddered. No matter how she tried, she could not hear a happy melody. Sad notes kept coming into her heart, she kept hearing her uncle's death song. She kept hearing the moaning of the lost souls on Huracán's winds. Anguished notes kept crowding themselves into the triumphant melody of the areíto composing itself in her heart—the areíto of Caonabó, great Cacique of Cibao.

"Caonabó," Anacaona said, and he heard a great urgency in her voice. "Caonabó, I must tell you something before it is too late."

"What is it, Anacaona? What is so important?"

"I love you," she said simply.

Caonabó felt a rush of pride, a swelling of love. Never had she said it this way before. No royal third person, just woman to man. Caonabó, who had so much love in his heart he sometimes had to confide his love to his Mother, the Earth, looked at his favorite wife Anacaona. He loved all his wives and all his children, but he had never known what love was until Anacaona came into his heart.

"I love you, Ana," he said.

Dancing the areíto of a village sometimes takes days, for the singers and dancers must not only present the pageant of their present cacique, but also all past caciques so the people will remember their history and know they are proud and worthy of honor and respect. Anacaona waited politely until all the other villages had presented their areítos. Then, just before she danced, Caonabó announced that he would retire for a while to his bahío. Today, for the first time in his life, Caonabó wanted to appear before his people fully clothed—in the cast-off finery of Chachu's victims, the pilgrims to Compostela.

Anacaona ceremonially washed Caonabó and anointed his body with the fragrant cabo leaves before she laid out the clothes on his hammock. Caonabó did not dress at once. He sat holding the brocade surcoat, fingering the textured embroidery and running his palm over the velvet. What kind of people had woven such cloth? Not in all the storehouses in Xaragau, where Behechio's people wove cloth to trade, was there a bolt so intricately designed. A two-headed bird with a man's torso and a beast's hindquarters? Were there such creatures? Strange markings were embroidered around the edges of the crusader's doublet. What did they mean? Caonabó smoothed the pretty design some Catholic mother had woven into the hem, not knowing the Arabic script read: "Only Allah is God, and Mohammed is His prophet."

Caonabó wanted the best, wanted to be the best, but he held in his hands proof he was not the best. The invaders knew things he did not know, had powers he could only imagine. Yet they had not come from Heaven, as they claimed. They died the same way other men died. Caonabó wished they could have been friends, so he could have learned from them. Perhaps if he put on their clothes, some of their power would become his.

Caonabó dressed slowly, awkwardly, with Anacaona's help. They forgot the hose until after the short breeches and had to start over. They put the soiled, once white, lace-trimmed shirt over instead of under the crusader's doublet. They slung the Córdoban leather belt over his left shoulder and wound the heavy bronze chain around his arm so the Bishop's cross dangled from his elbow. He refused to put on the pointed-toed shoes. He hung the perfume ball around his neck and mused at the mummified thumb inside the cosmetic case. Whose cemí was this?

The surcoat Chachu had stolen from the nobleman had been too big for Chachu, and it dragged the ground in front of the stocky, compact Caonabó. When he stood up, he took one step and tripped over the flowing coat, sprawling on his face at Anacaona's feet.

Anacaona laughed. "Does Caonabó need to make a fool of himself? Should Caonabó cover the record of his great deeds with a bundle of cloth?"

Caonabó began stripping off the clothes. With each garment shed, he grew in stature and dignity until he stood before Anacaona in the most magnificent garment she ever hoped to see—his own scarified skin. Pride welled up in her.

"Bring the clothes to the batey under the ceiba," Caonabó said. "Caonabó will make presents of them to his caciques."

Anacaona and Caonabó quarreled about the rest of the men at Navidad. She felt there had been enough killing. Tahíaca had been avenged. They should now try to heal, to make friends and understand the strangers, to learn from them. Caonabó said there was nothing he wanted to know about such people. What was there of honor in such men? They had to be killed, all of them, and if more came, they would have to be killed also—before they conquered the islands and made servants of his people as the Tainos had once made servants of the Ciboneys.

Yet Caonabó was in no hurry to attack Navidad. Tainos and Caribs lived their lives according to planting seasons and Huracán winds. Their moons and suns had not yet been fragmented into hours and minutes and seconds. The time for war on Navidad would announce itself. Later, much later, after news of fresh atrocities came to Caonabó, he summoned Anacaona to apply his war paint—bold-fingered black lines, broad-palmed vermillion planes, yellow splashes, and delicate traceries of stark white.

Mayabaño watched his mother preparing his father for war so that even his appearance would strike fear into the hearts of his enemies and give him an advantage. Mayabaño felt his Carib blood hammering in his heart. Caonabó looked strange, taller and more frightening—exciting beyond any excitement Mayabaño had ever felt. Was this war? This frightful mask transforming his father? No more a father, but a warrior. Unapproachable.

Mayabaño again asked Caonabó's permission to go to war—to paint his face and wear the war mask. Caonabó told his son he was not ready. No one need ask permission to put on war. A man was part of war or he was not. Mayabaño would know his war when it came.

October draped a velvet curtain hiding the sun from his lover the moon. Caonabó, wearing his war mask, squatted in the bushes watching Navidad. His spies had told him only eleven men remained at the fort, most of them delirious with fever and running sores. They drank cazabe beer, played cards, quarreled, and fornicated. No one obeyed the cacique called Harana. Caonabó had decided to attack at night, so Guacanagarí, in whose province the fort lay, would be at home avoiding the opia. Now Caonabó waited, listening to the night sounds, lulled by the waves breaking peacefully on the beach.

Diego de Harana lay in his hammock trying to shut out the noise of the birds. Lately he kept hearing birds when there were no birds, even at night. Cheeping, squawking, warbling, chirping, flapping, everlasting birds! The birds and the loneliness. No one had warned Harana about the loneliness. A million Indians on this stinking island, all the women a man could handle, and not one could carry on a decent conversation in Spanish!

How long had the Admiral been gone now? Seven months? Eight? Harana had lost track of time. To think he had begged, actually begged Colón to give him command of Navidad, promised to collect the gold and hide it in the well if the Indians attacked. By God, no one ever brought any gold back to the fort, so what was there to hide?

Stop those birds!

Can anyone shut up the birds? Don't they ever stop flying, even at night?

Where is everyone? Who is standing guard? Can't

you bastards obey me even long enough to stand guard? What if the Indians attacked, for Christ's sake!

Harana tried to remember how many men were left now. One had died raving mad with this fever. Luis de Torres had taken two with him when he went to Cuba. He wanted to get samples of the tobacco he had found when they stopped there. Torres would soon have all Europe smoking cigars. Let the others dig for their gold, the Jews like Torres would make more money trading. Trading, hell! Who was Torres going to trade with? Colón was never coming back.

There would be no more supplies, no food. Food! Chickens... eggs... Some of the men even dreamed about pigs, but Harana didn't like pork. Some of the men had planted a garden that matured faster than anyone could have believed, but what they needed was meat—good red meat. Harana was tired of duck, and his stomach turned at the thought of eating the squeaking little rodents called hutía that the Indians kept underfoot.

Bread! What he wouldn't give for a crusty loaf of wheat bread warm from Friday's oven. The wheat they had planted sprouted all right, but soon dried up in the heat. Now all they had for bread was that flat, bland cazabe bread—as tasteless as a dirty shirt.

The birds! Get them away from me! There's one now... a big one... no, not a bird... never saw anything like that before... a monster! Straight out of hell... the devil himself...

"Run! Run for your lives! Jesucristo, run!" Harana yelled, lucid now as he stared into Death in Caonabó's war mask.

So swift was Caonabó's attack on Navidad the young Castilians had no time to defend themselves. Harana and two others died in their hammocks. Eight men fled into the sea clad only in nightshirts, fleeing Caonabó's war mask. Caonabó patrolled the shore until the last splash ceased. He fired the fort and sat watching the flames reflected on the waves while Anacaona led the victory areíto.

CHAPTER 12

Another World—1493

Another world is emerging from the winds of eternal change. Huracán broods, and a blue light shines over everything. His Holiness Pope Alexander VI, one of the Borgias, divides up this world never before under the dominion of Christian Princes. The Vicar of Christ, the keeper of the keys, the Spanish Pope, presuming the world is his to divide, gives it to the Catholic sovereigns of Spain and Portugal.

Papal Bull Aeternis Regis, 1481:
...to the faithful Don João of Portugal, sovereignty of the territories beyond the Canaries, also known as the Fortunate Isles, and this side of Guinea...
In the name of the Father...
Wait, Your Holiness, says the Spanish Ambassador, may I respectfully point out that a certain Admiral Cristóbal Colón has discovered certain islands, undiscovered by others...except, of course, by the people previously dwelling there...
Papal Bull Inter caetera, May 3, 1493:
...to Their Catholic Highnesses of Castilla, full sov-

ereign power over certain very distant islands and even mainlands where dwell a people well disposed to embrace the Christian faith ...

In the name of the Father, and the Son ...

Wait, Your Holiness, with all due respect, the definitions are too vague. These and other unknown islands will shortly be subjected to Christ by messengers of Their Catholic Highnesses King Fernando and Queen Isabela. There is a great island inhabited by naked people without any skill of fighting, but some of whom it is said have tails ... In the island are rivers of gold. Surely, Your Holiness ...

Papal Bull Inter caetera II, May 4, 1493:

... to Castilla all lands west of a line drawn from the North to the South pole one hundred leagues west and south of the Azores ...

In the name of the Father, the Son, and the Holy Spirit ...

Wait, Your Holiness, says the Portuguese Ambassador. I must protest. Without our great Prince Henry the Navigator, none of these discoveries would have been made ... truly, I must protest. Oh! How can one do business with a Spanish Pope?

Papal Bull Dudum siquidem, September 26, 1493:

... we amplify and extend our aforesaid gift ...

In the name of the Father, the Son, and the Holy Spirit, Amen!

CHAPTER 13

Haiti, 1493

THE BODIES still lay on the beach at Navidad when Admiral Colón, his red hair now turning gray, returned to the islands. Only a few months had passed since the massacre, and Anacaona knew her beleaguered people had no hope the day the Spanish fleet of seventeen ships returned to the Sea of the Caribbees. Colón, perhaps trying to establish his Christianity in the minds of the pious, went about venenating the islands with new names, christening them *Santa María de la Galante, Santa María de Guadalupe, Santa María de la Antigua.* The Spanish soul had special need of God, the Mother.

Nuestra Señora de los Nieves ... Snow? In the Caribbean? Perhaps the Admiral was homesick for the perpetual snows of the Sierra Nevada above Granada, or perhaps he remembered the legend of the sultan who planted almond groves so the mountains would turn white in the spring to cheer up his homesick Scandinavian concubine.

Santa Cruz ... Is that a proper name for the island where the carabelli are said to live? A new word has come into the language: carabelli, cannibals, derived from the man-eating Caribs who were Caonabó's ancestors. How many

Christian swords were sharpened by legends of cannibals who sickened and died after eating friars. Exter-
mination must somehow be justified.

So the islands receive their names. Some names stick:
Antigua, Guadalupe, Nevis. Some islands remain persis-
tently Indian: *Jamaica, Haiti, Cuba;* and the sea is never
called anything except the *Caribbean.*

When Admiral Colón discovered the ruins of Navidad, he moved his capital up the coast to a place he
called *Isabela* after Her Highness, the Queen of Castilla. Exploration was coming to an end. The Spanish
had come to stay. The conquest had begun; the Indians
must be pacified. In everyone's mind it was Cacique
Caonabó and his Cacica Anacaona who stood between
the Indians and their conquerors. Perhaps they were
right. As long as Caonabó lived, his people resisted; as
long as Anacaona's areítos were heard, the people remained proud. Proud people died hard.

Anacaona knew the legend was growing up around
them, but she was powerless to stop it. People needed to
believe Caonabó was the fierce cacique who could destroy the invading army as he had destroyed the men of
Navidad. People needed to believe Caonabó was invin-
cible. With their world shaking under their feet, there
was so little to believe in. Only Anacaona knew Caonabó
also stood on shaky ground. Anacaona's heart bled for
her husband, who was being torn apart inside, losing
confidence in himself every time he saw something new
the Spanish had—like the horse-man creatures.

Caonabó and Anacaona stood with their people high
atop a bluff watching the millipede Spanish army
marching up the broad valley through pink-blossoming
cocoa orchards. Gentle breezes furled and unfurled colorful banners; sunlight glinted off sword and lance and
wickedly curlicued alabardas. From time to time they
stopped to terrorize villagers with volleys of harquebus
fire.

Captain Alonzo de Ojeda enjoyed terrorizing the Indians. Ojeda commanded the van. He was a cocky little
man who had once pirouetted atop a high beam in Gi-

ralda Cathedral. He considered himself very brave now, too, conducting Colón's March, 1494, campaign of fear: twelve hundred knights in armor against Tainos armed only with digging sticks and fishbone spears. The Tainos did not fight.

Caonabó knelt dangerously close to the edge of the bluff, talking with Hatuey about the creatures that seemed to be men growing out of animal backs. Nothing so frightful had ever appeared in Haiti, where large animals were the slow-moving megaluccus sloth or the scaly iguana. Anacaona stood behind her husband admiring the play of sunlight on his back.

Had anything ever been so beautiful as Caonabó's skin rippling under his scars and tattoos? Anacaona was deeply moved by Caonabó's body, golden, pristine, unashamed. No higher majesty than Caonabó moving with grace and dignity...free...only sunlight clothing his life's work...

"What is Caonabó going to do?" Anacaona asked the question everyone in Haiti was asking.

Caonabó looked up at her, concern showing on her usually smiling face, her full lips now set and grim. How he loved her! How he wanted to go back to the time when there were no winged canoes!

"Horse-men, but no women," said Caonabó. "Very strange."

"They will take our women again," Hatuey warned.

"Let them come," Caonabó said grimly. "Let them touch my Anacaona. Caonabó will drive them all into the sea."

Anacaona heard the hollow fear behind Caonabó's brave words. She knew he was remembering Tahíaca, who still wandered through the forests as if she were looking for Rodrigo. In spite of his reputation, Caonabó was more like the peaceful Tainos than like the Caribs. Sometimes he had to be pushed into action.

"Perhaps Caonabó does not remember Tahíaca," she goaded him.

"Mayabaño remembers," said the boy, standing a few feet away, his face solemn under the blue-black bangs barely concealing his butterfly. He clasped and unclasped his hands, watching his mother and his father.

"A butterfly boy must be silent while Caonabó decides," he chided his son.

"Let the boy speak, Caonabó," Anacaona urged. "When you and I are dancing everlasting areítos, Mayabaño will be dealing with these people. Let him speak."

Caonabó frowned. Anacaona asserted herself too much lately, cutting his manhood from beneath him. Perhaps he had given her too much power. He felt himself buffeted by the remembrance of his cemí vision— more and more invaders coming like Huracán's winds, uprooting and destroying everything. He turned to Hatuey, who coordinated Caonabó's intelligence forces. Nothing happened in the Caribbean without Caonabó's being aware of it.

"Tell Caonabó about this Cacique Ojeda," he ordered.

"Ojeda takes, but does not give," Hatuey said. "He is crafty and treacherous, like the quicksand bogs. When he enters a village, his men rip away crossed vines and take whatever they please—gold, food, women. When our people try to conclude the trade by taking whatever they wish from the Spaniards, Ojeda cuts off their noses."

The people sucked in their breaths, murmuring at this indignity. Did the Spaniards not know how to trade? How could a fair bargain be struck if they did not follow the customs?

"They have banners of woven cloth, not of beaten gold," said Caonabó, clutching at the one thing that made him superior to his enemies.

"Wherever people sing of great caciques, Caonabó's name will always be first," Anacaona reassured him, her heart praying it would be true.

Caonabó frowned. He did not like to have Anacaona reassure him. "Prepare an areíto, Anacaona," he ordered. "Invite all the caciques of the five provinces of Haiti. Together we shall be able to stop these horse-men!"

With a heavy heart Anacaona prepared an areíto, to which only Behechio and Hatuey came. The caciques of the other three provinces, all of whom had attended Mayabaño's naming ceremony here in this very batey, all of them made excuses. Guacanagarí, cacique of Marien, was a friend of the Admiral. Cacique Mayobanex and Cacica Cotibanama of Higuey were too busy watching for Carib raiders. Guarionex, Cacique of Magua, had his hands full with the Spaniards. Already they had built two forts on his land. All the caciques had fought too long among themselves to unite against the common enemy, and of all the caciques in Haiti, Caonabó was the only one who could have led them to victory, but also the one they feared most. No one wanted to subject himself to the Carib cacique who had conquered part of their island.

"It is everyone's war," cried Anacaona. "Can't they see that?"

"Guacanagarí is angry because Caonabó invaded his territory to kill the men at Navidad whom he had sworn to protect, and Guarionex is angry because Caonabó came into his province to watch the invaders build their Fort Santo Tomás," said Hatuey.

"Does Caonabó invade homes, or capture children?" Anacaona asked sharply. "The invaders have taken boys as young as Mayabaño and forced them to take care of the horse animals. My butterfly boy would die of fright."

"Mayabaño is not afraid!" asserted her son.

"Guarionex says it is his fight, not Caonabó's," Hatuey said. "Every man in his province will fight, but not as warriors under Caonabó."

"Guarionex is a fool," Anacaona said. "Only a Carib can lead this fight. This is not a handful of sick men. This is an army with dreadful weapons. Many of our people will die."

"They have other animals besides horses," warned Hatuey. "Animals called dogs, with big jaws full of teeth as sharp as a shark's. They play a game with these animals—a game called *aperrear*."

"Game?" asked Caonabó. "What kind of game?"

He thought if these were people who played games, they might be people who could learn to live with the Tainos and respect them, perhaps participate in their areítos.

"When one of our people has done something to displease them," Hatuey said, "they turn these sharp-toothed animals loose. Then they wager with each other over how long it will take for the dogs to kill and eat the victim. That is the game called aperrear! They keep these animals in special pens and feed them only the flesh of dead Tainos they keep hanging from great hooks. They boast about owning the winning dog. Sometimes they play the game just for sport, choosing one of our people who happens to be walking by."

Caonabó's face clouded over, and he sat for a long time in silence, looking out toward the mountains. He longed for the bosom of his Mother, the Earth. He was not a young man anymore. Defending his territory did not offer the excitement he had felt when he had conquered it.

"Does Caonabó need the other caciques?" Anacaona prodded. "Only a handful of men have been left at Fort Santo Tomás. Let Caonabó plan an attack. We can surround the fort with four groups of warriors commanded by Caonabó, Behechio, Hatuey, and...and..."

She paused to let them think of the fourth commander. Caonabó looked at her, seeing the light of battle in her eyes. No Carib woman could have made him more proud.

"And Anacaona?" he asked.

"And Anacaona," she replied. An areíto began forming itself in her heart.

The Admiral Don Cristóbal Colón paced the foundations of the new government house he was building at Isabela as if he were pacing the poopdeck of his flagship, the *Maríagalante*. He could almost feel the sea swells. His hair had gone gray now, and his arthritic bones complained. It was April Fool's Day, 1494.

He hated the land. He longed for the spray in his face and the pull of a far horizon. He mused to himself as he often did, for no one had ever been able to share his vision. He knew a great continent could not be far away. He felt it as a woman feels a child growing within her. Colón was a man born to the sea, happy only at sea. All he had ever wanted to do was to prove he could find Cathay.

But a man had the right to profit from his discoveries, didn't he? To leave something for his children? Colón had been poor all his life. What did he have to leave his boys except the land he had discovered? Why couldn't these Indians accept that? Be peaceful...learn Christian ways...go to work...wear clothes and be modest, for God's sake! Turn over the King's gold without a fight, and leave the hidalgos to do battle against invading Caribs.

Pacify them, that's what Colón had to do, if he killed every last one of them. Pacify that Carib Cacique Caonabó, and all the rest would be docile like old Guacanagarí. Colón felt a lump in this throat when he thought about the affectionate, generous Gaucanagarí, who had salvaged the *Santa María* without stealing so much as one lace point. By the Blessed Virgin, that Gaucanagarí was a prince!

"Admiral..."

Oh, to be at sea again. Cathay was out there somewhere. The Indians pointed north and west and said that there was a great land mass. If Cuba was Japan, as he was convinced it was, then the continent must be Cathay.

"Admiral, with your permission..."

An explorer was meant to explore, not govern. Why couldn't they understand that? If not now, then later, he knew he would discover something new of great value. Who could be trusted to govern while he explored? No one outside the family, that was certain. Oh, if only his brother Bartolomé were here. Bartolomé was the organizer. Diego was the mystic. Cristóbal was the explorer. Dreamers, all three of them, but Bartolomé was the practical one.

"Admiral, please, listen to me..."

Who could be left in charge of La Española while he put to sea again? Who could make the men work and pacify the Indians? Gorbalán? No, he couldn't get any work out of the hidalgos, who thought they were too good to soil their hands. How they had complained when Colón made them widen the pass in the mountains— the pass he had sarcastically named Pass of the Gentlemen. No, Gorbalán could never make the men build the buildings and plant the crops.

Margarit? No, too vicious. Dr. Chanca? Too busy writing his journal. Fray Buil? Too much of a complainer, schooled by the Inquisitors.

"Admiral, this is important..."

Perhaps Ojeda. No, not Ojeda. Too devious. Too quick to fight.

"Admiral." The messenger tugged at his sleeve. "Admiral, please, listen to me!"

"Speak up, man. Stop mumbling."

"Admiral, the Indians are going to attack Fort Santo Tomás!"

The Admiral stood waiting for the man to cry "April Fool!" Surely he was joking. But the man's face was not the face of a trickster.

"Impossible! Who says so?"

"One of Guacanagarí's agents. He said Cacique Caonabó—"

"Caonabó! That murdering cannibal? The cacique who burned Navidad?"

"The same."

"Find my brother Diego."

"Yes, Admiral."

"And send Ojeda to me—Alonzo de Ojeda."

Ojeda had been itching for just such a command. His orders: Take Caonabó, alive if possible. Treachery might help. Offer the cacique a lace-trimmed shirt. The Indians were easier to hold when they wore clothes. Ojeda left, whistling, and Colón prepared to go exploring.

Anacaona and Caonabó scrapped their plans to attack the fort after Ojeda's army arrived—four hundred of them, one-third cavalry, plus a pack of trained hounds. The systematic pacification of Haiti had begun—merciless slaughter, unspeakable atrocities. Caonabó was not a coward, neither was he a fool. He had never lost a battle in his life, because he had never attacked unless he had the advantage. He carried out sporadic raids, always successful. He did not talk much these days, but at night Anacaona could hear him groaning in his sleep—deep, agonizing groans.

Spring passed, summer ripened the bananas. Yam vines with heart-shaped leaves spread over the fields. Orioles and cardinals flew north. Parrots squawked. Colón returned without finding Cathay. A cacique was arrested for stealing clothes at a river crossing. Fortunately, Guacanagarí was able to secure his release, but not before the Spaniards cut off his ears and slit his nose.

Many Indians wandered in the forest now, homeless refugees whose villages had been burned and whose families had been killed or captured. The Admiral had built huge cages at Isabela in which he kept the captives he was collecting for the slave markets in Sevilla. He wrote the Queen that the trade would be profitable and might help offset the cost of continuing explorations, if she would give her consent. The Indians were, after all, prisoners of war.

Mayabaño spent a lot of time these days with Tahíaca, who still woke up every morning with tears rolling down her face, and who still roamed the island peering down narrow roads as if expecting to see Rodrigo.

Sometimes Mayabaño and Tahíaca would talk; but more often they sat listening to the birds, perhaps eating a piece of fruit. Once in a while they swam in the river and rubbed each other down with cabo leaves. Sometimes they just walked.

One day they came upon a pregnant woman trying to hang herself, a girl not much older than Tahíaca. She told them she had been a young bride nursing her first child when the Christians raided her village. To escape, she had had to run very fast into the dense woods where the horse-men could not follow. When she realized they were gaining on her, she laid her baby on the ground, certain not even the Christians could be so cruel as to harm a baby.

From the safety of the thicket, she had seen her infant son impaled on a lance and held aloft triumphantly. She had run screaming toward the horse-man, who captured her and made her his slave. Now she carried his child. She had managed to escape so she could kill both herself and the hated child.

Tahíaca took the girl into her cañayo and talked with her almost all night. A child was a child and could not help who its father was. She knew other women were also committing suicide rather than bear the invaders' children, but perhaps if the girl raised the child in the mountains away from the Christians, it could not learn their evil ways. She should not blame herself because her first baby had been killed. Now she had been given a second chance. Tahíaca would help her. They would plant a garden, weave another hammock for the girl and a small one for the coming baby.

Finally the girl agreed, and Tahíaca went to sleep feeling good about herself. Mayabaño slept just inside the door. If the Christians came again, he was sure he would be able to protect his womenfolk. He had the young male's absolute certainty of his own untried power.

Next morning Tahíaca awoke without crying, and it was noon before she thought of Rodrigo. Thinking of him now was not a pain, but a bittersweet memory she would visit from time to time.

The girls were happy together waiting for the baby. Mayabaño liked the girl because she did not call him butterfly boy, but treated him as if he were a man. He built a fish weir in the river and kept them well supplied with fish for their boucan. The three of them were happily planting manioc the day Ojeda came. It would be two years before these cuttings matured, but they thought they still had all the time in the world. The baby would need bread to chew on when he began to cut his teeth.

Mayabaño heard the dogs while the girls were still chatting happily. He stood up and cocked his head to listen, then he grabbed their hands and tried to lead the girls to safety. Fear disoriented him, and he led them into a clearing to meet the dogs.

"Aperrear! Aperrear!" shouted Ojeda, loosing his hound and spurring his horse.

"A castellano says my dog strikes first blood," yelled one of his men.

"You're covered," Ojeda cried. "Aperrear! Aperrear!"

CHAPTER 14

Cibao, 1495

THREE YEARS had passed since the winged canoes first sailed into the Caribbean, and Ojeda was systematically rounding up Indians with hounds and driving them into ambush to be slaughtered by the harquebusiers. Caonabó had known the end was near the night the moon disappeared. When the moon turned to blood, the sun would cease to shine. Huracán would send his blue light, and all would be over.

One final flash of blue light! Then nothing! No more sea. No more islands. No more world. All would melt away in Huracán's blue light. Caonabó had seen the blue light once. Not the long flashing tongues of white light, but the eerie glow of a circle of blue fire. Nothing burned, but the next morning all the trees were dead. Now the moon had been eaten by a giant frog, and tomorrow the sun might not rise. Then would come the blue light...nothing but Huracán's blue light...

The sun had risen as usual the morning after the eclipse, but that afternoon Anacaona had brought Caonabó word that Tahíaca and Mayabaño had been captured during a game of aperrear. The pregnant girl with them had been devoured by the dogs, but, having satisfied the hounds and their own need for sport, the hidalgos had taken Tahíaca and Mayabaño back to Isabela to become part of Antonio de Torres's next slave shipment to Sevilla. Not enough gold had yet been found to begin to pay for the expeditions, but every noble family in Andalucía now wanted an Indian slave, and although Queen Isabela had expressly withheld her approval, the trade was already brisk.

Tahíaca was placed in the slave cages with the others. The Spanish had too many women to even bother using her, but one hidalgo took a fancy to Mayabaño and kept him for a body slave. He called the Indian boy Mariposito, which is Spanish for little butterfly. Among his other duties, Mayabaño had to clean the stables and groom the hidalgo's stallion. Mayabaño was deathly afraid of horses, but he did not want anyone to know. One morning before his master awoke, he hobbled down to the corral still in his ankle chains—determined to conquer his fear.

One of the mares had foaled during the night, and Mayabaño watched, enchanted, as the spindly-legged colt struggled to its feet. When the colt zigzagged to the fence as though he wanted to make friends, Mayabaño lost some of his fear. If you could tame a parrot with a wicked beak, why not a horse? Especially such a lovable little horse. Why, someday, he, Mayabaño—son of Cacique Caonabó—might even ride a horse! Mayabaño's mouth felt dry and his palms slippery as he took hold of the fence to climb over.

Suddenly his master's stallion thundered up behind the colt. Mayabaño froze, watching in disbelief as the stallion grabbed the little colt by the neck, holding it in his powerful jaws and shaking it up and down. Only a few shakes were needed to snap the fragile neck, then the stallion dropped the colt and cantered away. Mayabaño stood transfixed, staring at the still form on the ground.

"Get up, little horse," he pleaded. "Please get up. Don't be dead!"

Death had come quickly, and the little horse did not get up.

Mayabaño refused to go near the horses again, even when the hidalgo whipped him. He refused to do anything for the hidalgo. He spent his days sitting on a rock, chin in hand, butterfly brow drawn up in a frown.

When they loaded the slave caravels for Sevilla, they thrust Mayabaño aside. He was too young to survive the trip or to bring a handsome price. Tears trickled down Mayabaño's face as he watched Tahíaca shuffling along in the line of shackled captives. When the caravels had been filled to capacity, hundreds of Indians were left over. The Spaniards did not want to feed them until the caravels returned, so they gave the hidalgos their pick for servants and drove the rest away. No one chose Mayabaño. As he watched the caravel sail away, he vowed someday to kill all the Christians or die fighting.

That night he plucked the hairs from around his butterfly. So they called him Mariposito, did they? Everyone had always called him butterfly boy, and he had hated it and been ashamed. Well, now he did not hate it, and someday he would make the Christians fear Mariposito. Next morning he slipped into the fort to awaken the hidalgo who had captured him.

"Look at Mariposito!" he demanded as the hidalgo rubbed his sleepy eyes.

"Go away, Mariposito," said the hidalgo. "You are a lazy good-for-nothing."

"Look! Mayabaño will make the Spanish fear Mariposito!"

"By Santiago's sword, you are a strange one," mumbled the hidalgo, rolling over to go back to sleep.

Mayabaño slipped out of the fort and went back to Cibao.

Antonio de Torres sailed regularly from the Indies to Spain now, bringing out supplies and new settlers, carrying back Indian cloth, fruits, spices, parrots, tobacco, a little gold, and slaves. Gold was not yet being mined, and the few nuggets found had a way of disappearing into the pockets of the finders, so Colón again petitioned the Queen for permission to sell Indians, assuring her they were prisoners of war, therefore legitimate slaves. The slave trade flourished, even though many of the Tainos sickened and died during the long, cold sea voyage, and few survived their first winter on the peninsula. Next year in February, Torres brought out a few Spanish women.

Meanwhile Caonabó fought running battles, killing isolated bands of marauding Christians, but never attacking Ojeda's main army and never allowing the army to find him. Anacaona fought at her husband's side, learning to throw a spear almost as accurately as he and commanding raiding parties in his absence. Then one day word came that Ojeda wanted a truce. He was coming to Cibao, not with an army, but with an honor escort of only a few men—like an ambassador to the court of the great Cacique Caonabó. Anacaona was deathly afraid.

"Do not believe the little hidalgo," she said.

"Caonabó will wait to hear what he says."

"Lies, all lies," Anacaona warned. "They know not truth, nor would they tell it if they did."

"Caonabó will listen."

"Caonabó grows foolish in his old age. Perhaps Caonabó wishes to become like the hidalgos, having great buildings for his cemís with bells on the top and cemí crosses guarding everything."

Caonabó was tired of fighting his own vision in the war he knew could not be won. If a war was lost, a wise man made the best peace he could. Caonabó had heard about the bronze bell atop the church at Isabela, a great metal voice that could be heard two villages away. Caonabó wanted that bell for the cave of his ancestors. Caonabó also wanted to go see for himself the great rulers across the water, Cacique Fernando and Cacica Isabela. If he could just talk with them as one cacique to another, he was sure he could get them to return Tahíaca safely. Caonabó had not confided this dream to anyone, not even to Anacaona.

Ojeda, the feisty little commander of Fort Santo Tomás, rode into Caonabó's village on the prancing rogue stallion that had killed the little colt. The magnificent animal, caparisoned in green silk and red Córdoban leather, gave little Ojeda much needed stature. Ojeda invited Caonabó to go with him to Fort Isabela to see the Admiral and talk peace, promising him the great bronze church bell.

"Do not listen to his lies," Anacaona warned. "Do not go to Fort Isabela. It is an evil place fit only for the opia. What is a piece of bronze? Even before the invaders came, our traders brought back bronze from the continent. Now our artisans have seen a bell, they will make one for Caonabó. Do not listen to this quacking little duck."

"Enough, Ana!" Caonabó always called her Ana when he wanted to reduce her authority. "Compose a new areíto about Caonabó, the cacique who brings peace to Haiti. Make a big areíto and invite all the other caciques to come ring Caonabó's bell."

Caonabó would not allow Anacaona to accompany him when he left with Ojeda, but he kissed her tenderly and tried to reassure her. After all, Ojeda had but a few men, and Caonabó was to be accompanied by his army. Despite his reassurances, the old feeling of doom settled over Anacaona, and no peace areíto arranged itself in her heart. Two days out of Cibao at a rest stop, Ojeda showed Caonabó the handcuffs.

"Wives," Ojeda said in Spanish. The men with him laughed at the joke. "Wives of the finest Viscayan brass."

"Wives?" Caonabó rolled the strange word over his tongue, and rattled the iron handcuffs Ojeda had called black Viscayan brass. "Wives. Very fine wives. Caonabó likes wives."

"Cacique Fernando of Aragon always wears wives on occasions of great ceremony," Ojeda lied.

Ojeda handed Caonabó the handcuffs—two thick black rings attached to each other by a thick black iron bar. Caonabó turned them over and over in his hands. Obviously they were not head ornaments. They were too thick and heavy for nose pendants. How did Cacique Fernando wear them? What power did they give him?

Whatever the great foreign cacique had, Caonabó wanted. He had always wanted the best. Was not Anacaona the best composer of areítos in all the Sea of Caribbee? Anacaona was the best wife a man ever had. Yet neither his wives, nor all his children, nor all his golden crowns and banners had really comforted Caonabó after the invaders came.

They had taken his Tahíaca, but they had made him want all the things they had—weapons, machines, tools, horses. Caravels flying before the wind, and pieces of paper that talked without making a sound. The big bronze bell to call people to worship their cemí, perhaps the most powerful cemí any cacique had ever had. Caciques always stole each other's cemís. If a cacique had a more powerful cemí, he sometimes buried it to keep it from being stolen. Caonabó had heard that the cemí they called Santiago had once been buried to hide him from the caciques who worshipped another cemí called Allah.

Caonabó wanted the best—the best singer of areítos, the tallest gold crown, that bronze bell, and these black wives. Whatever made Cacique Fernando so powerful, Caonabó wanted.

Ojeda had been studying Caonabó's face. He could tell by the twitching of the iguana that he had the cacique in his power. By trickery, he, Alonzo de Ojeda, had captured the man-eating Carib Caonabó! Ojeda felt the same exhilaration he had felt that day in Giralda high above the cheering crowd. Imagine what they would say when he took the cacique back to Sevilla and all the people turned out to welcome him. "Ojeda! Ojeda! Viva Ojeda!" they would shout. "Ojeda has captured the Navidad murderer." What a story to tell in the bodegas! He might never have to buy himself another bottle of wine.

"Would the great Cacique Caonabó like to see how the cacique of the Christians wears the wives?" Ojeda asked, smiling and bowing obsequiously with the flourish bred into generations of caballeros.

Caonabó nodded, trying to keep his eagerness from showing.

"Come with me," Ojeda said, backing toward the caparisoned stallion, stopping every few steps to bow to Caonabó.

Caonabó hesitated. Ojeda was being too...too ...Caonabó did not trust him. He was like a trader who knows he has the advantage and can afford to be polite. Yet Caonabó's men far outnumbered Ojeda's men. He did not want Ojeda to think he was afraid of the horse, so he strode boldly forward, clenching his teeth as he neared the stallion.

"Don't, Papa!" Mayabaño shouted. "Don't go near that horse. Please, Papa!"

Caonabó ignored his son's warning, and Hatuey put a restraining hand on the boy's shoulder. Mayabaño was so ashamed of his outcry, ashamed of his own fears of the stallion. He clamped his teeth together lest his voice escape again to shame his father.

Ojeda swung into the saddle, and immediately became more commanding. Caonabó tried to calm his racing heart as one of Ojeda's men helped him mount up behind the little caballero. Caonabó thought riding behind someone on the horse was a very strange way for Cacique Fernando to travel on state occasions, but all the Spanish customs seemed strange to Caonabó.

"Now you shall see how the wives serve His Catholic Majesty," said Ojeda, clamping one of the iron rings around Caonabó's wrist.

Caonabó looked at the dangling iron ring. He tried not to shake, but he was filled with fear and foreboding. The same kind of fear he always had of Huracán, a fear he dared not voice. The horse snorted and reared impatiently, and Caonabó clung to Ojeda to keep from falling off. Quickly Ojeda snapped the other handcuff into place and put spurs to the stallion's flanks.

"Forward, by Santiago, forward!" Ojeda yelled as the stallion galloped away.

Ojeda's men dropped to their knees and began firing on Caonabó's army. Without their cacique to lead them, the Tainos fled. Hatuey managed to get Mayabaño to safety, but the Spaniards got away with most of Caonabo's crown gold. Ojeda did not stop riding until he rode triumphantly into Fort Isabela.

After Caonabó's capture, Anacaona fled to Behechio's province of Xaragua, taking all his wives and children with her and establishing her headquarters there. With Behechio and Hatuey, she plotted to attack Fort Isabela and rescue Caonabó; but before her plans were complete, Ojeda marched on Xaragua and captured Behechio. Still Anacaona refused to admit defeat. She issued another call to arms to all the caciques in the provinces of Haiti.

Meanwhile Caonabó, caged at Fort Isabela, drew the attention of all the hidalgos—especially one Fray Ramón. No Indians had yet been baptized, and Fray Ramón wanted to learn why. So day after day Caonabó told Fray Ramón the myths and legends by which his people lived, and night after night he paced his cage praying to Huracán for deliverance.

Huracán was power beyond all power, the creative force of the universe unleashed. Wind...water ...lightning. Battering...uprooting...destroying in order to build up again. Anger to be reverenced. Vengeance to be feared. Awesome presence to be invoked only if one stands ready to become part of Huracán.

Caonabó knew all the old prayers, but he had never known anyone who had dared invoke Huracán. Old Carib wise men who feared Huracán above all else had warned him. Huracán will roar through space and time until nothing remains except Huracán. Nothing! Absolutely nothing. Prepare to become Huracán, or call not on Huracán's name.

Caonabó called Huracán day and night, remembering his vision of destruction and wanting to become part of those waves after waves that had been his own vision. Better to become Huracán than be destroyed by Huracán. Better to bathe in the blue light and become part of Huracán's force. Only Huracán could destroy the Christians.

Caonabó believed in Huracán. Voices spoke out of

Huracán's winds. Caonabó never ceased to call Huracán's name.

Yet the days remained calm and serene in Isabela. Gentle breezes cooled the nights as May passed into June. The Admiral prepared to return to Spain. Fray Buil, the disgruntled complainer, had preceded him and told Their Catholic Highnesses Colón was not fit to rule. He could not even pacify the Indians. Strange word, pacify, thought the Admiral. We say pacify when what we mean is exterminate.

Their Catholic Highnesses wanted action. The Indians must be subdued, Christianized, put to work. Now Colón had something to show the Queen and her confessor. He would parade Cacique Caonabó in all his golden finery through the streets of Sevilla. Caonabó would be baptized in Giralda and swear allegiance to Castilla and Aragon. With Caonabó a Christian, the Indians of La Española would surely also become Christians—docile, hard-working, pious—fit subjects for Christian rulers.

Caonabó continued to pray, but nothing happened.

The day before the scheduled sailing, they chained Caonabó in the hold of the flagship *Maríagalante*. Just before they pegged shut the hatch, Caonabó saw a flock of frigate birds wheel and fly inland. Huracán comes, he thought. The birds know. They feel it in their bones. They screech warnings, but leave their young in the nests. The sky leadens. The sea foams. The air presses down so breathing is difficult. Midafternoon seems like twilight and the crabs venture forth, only to scurry away from the murky water. Mosquitoes find a hiding place. The first gales rattle the palms. Iguanas dig into the lee side of trees.

Caonabó heard the wind moaning. He could not see the trees bend, but he heard the rain battering the deck above. The caravel began lurching uncontrollably, and Caonabó braced himself against a beam. He tried to visualize how Huracán would take him. He prayed it would not be in a wall of water, for life had already overwhelmed him. If the caravel broke up, Caonabó would be crushed. So he prayed Huracán would claim him whole and undamaged, ready to join in the fight against the evil ones.

Caonabó wished he had a cahoba pipe. Perhaps Huracán would grant his wish if he made a cahoba; but they had taken away all his belongings, dressed him, and hung a cross around his neck—which Caonabó had thrown away. Now Caonabó tore off his clothes, ripped them to shreds, and dropped the rags at his feet. He straightened, his sweaty body glistening in the dim light of the hold, the iguana barely moving as he prayed. Huracán tore his prayer from his mouth. The caravel rocked precariously, tore loose from its mooring. Water began filling the hold. The caravel was breaking up.

"Huracán-n-n-n-n!" Caonabó gave one final shout.

Suddenly the back of his neck began tingling, and his hair seemed to stand on end. The glory of the blue light filled the hold. Not jagged fingers of lightning, but a consuming, flickering, blue charge. Caonabó's spirit became one with Huracán, and they vented their wrath on Fort Isabela, leveling the settlement, destroying the fleet, opening the cages and freeing the captives.

After the storm, Anacaona came to Fort Isabela to claim Caonabó's body. But Caonabó was nowhere to be found, for Huracán had taken him.

BOOK II

Act of Faith

If a man abide not in me, he is cast forth as a branch, and is withered; and men gather them, and cast them into a fire, and they are burned.

John 15:6

CHAPTER 1

Córdoba, Spain, 1495

TAHÍACA HAD not expected to live through the cold March passage from La Española to Cádiz. Confined naked below decks, two hundred Indians died. When Bishop Fonseca put the rest on the slave block beside the Torre del Oro in Sevilla, most of them were sick. Tahíaca lived.

The good bishop, seeing something special in the high-browed Taino girl, decided she would make an appropriate gift to the Queen; he hoped the gift would induce the Queen to give her consent to the Indian slave trade. So in June 1495—about the time the hurricane was destroying Fort Isabela—Tahíaca stood on the terrace overlooking the gardens of the old Moorish Alcázar in Córdoba. She did not know she was supposed to curtsy when being presented to the Queen.

"What is happening?" demanded the Queen, pursing her lips to contain her anger. "Does Bishop Fonseca think he can get around my orders by giving me this heathen girl as a present? I, the Queen, have decreed my Indians shall become Christians, not slaves!"

"But my dear wife," argued King Fernando, "the

Indians are prisoners of war. We did not scruple to sell Moorish captives after Islam fell. Are your Indians more deserving of mercy?"

Isabela paced up and down the terrace, followed at a discreet distance by her lady-in-waiting, Doña Luisa Castro de Sandoval, Condesa de Córdoba. Isabela always enjoyed walking in the old Alcázar gardens, listening to the splash of the fountains in the lily-padded pools, wondering what the Alcázar had been like when Córdoba was the capital of Andalucía's Moslem empire.

Following their victories during the Moorish wars, King Fernando and Queen Isabela had always returned to Córdoba to celebrate. Now as she looked out over the gardens, she remembered the triumphal balls—the lutes and guitars of the strolling minstrels, the knights and ladies dancing, the couples whispering together as they strolled along the marble paved paths in the formal gardens. The Queen liked Córdoba best of all her royal cities.

From Córdoba they had directed the wars against the infidels, planned the siege of Granada and the building of Santa Fé. Beside these sparkling pools she had first heard Don Cristóbal's dream of Cathay. Here they had danced the fall of Islam, city after city—Málaga, Ronda, Jaén, Antequera, and finally Granada. Here members of the Holy Brotherhood and weary clergymen refreshed themselves during the long ordeals of the acts-of-faith held on the parade grounds just beyond the gardens.

"Your Highness." Fernando called her back from her reverie. He loved her dearly, and she had kept her vows to love him, but sometimes Isabela could be a stubborn woman. "Your Highness, we are waiting."

"Yes, Fernando, I know," Isabela walked around the Indian girl, modestly clothed now in peasant dress in deference to the Queen. "Well, as the Saints preserve us, you are an Indian. What are you called?"

Tahíaca had picked up enough Spanish to know what the Queen was saying, but she chose not to reply.

"What is she called, Fray Dominic?" asked the Queen.

"Tahíaca." Fray Dominic rubbed his hands together,

eager to please the Queen, remembering that Holy Thursday in the Alhambra when she had knelt and washed his feet.

"Her Christian name?" asked the Queen.

"The girl has not yet been baptized, Your Highness."

"Why not, pray tell?"

"No sponsor, Your Highness. She was very ill when she arrived in Sevilla, and since her recovery no one has had time to instruct her in the Faith. Perhaps Your Highness would—"

"Must the Queen do everything?" Isabela demanded.

Nothing had seemed to go well lately. In spite of her victory over the Moors and the Christianizing of the Jews, there were always problems; highwaymen, sodomites, heretics, and that inept explorer Cristóbal Colón—the Admiral Don Cristóbal Colón, if you please. When he had come back to report his discovery, the King and Queen had honored him by having him sit in their presence. He had promised them such rich treasure, but so far they had seen no profit from the venture. Colón would be sure to come back next time with his hand out, too, and there were no more rich Jewish financiers to pay the bills. If it hadn't been for the confiscations of estates of convicted heretics, they would not have been able to finance Colón's second voyage or to send out supplies.

Isabela had little patience with incompetence or with selfishness. She had always put Kingdom and Church first. Plans to restore the Holy Office of the Inquisition had been completed in her quarters in the Sevilla Alcázar only a short time after the birth of her son Juan Fernando, heir to the throne. In the illusory and beautiful little Patio of the Dolls, where some nameless defiant Christian workman had concealed two darling little faces among the arabesques, Isabela had received Bishop Ojeda and Grand Inquisitor Torquemada and given her consent to the implementation of the Papal bull.

In all her married life, she had never had time to be just a wife and mother. With Juan Fernando only a few months old, she had braved the Extremadura winter to direct a war against Portugal, securing the peace by betrothing her older daughter Isabela to Don Juan, heir to the Portuguese throne. During the siege of Granada, when she was pregnant with Catalina, she had raised supplies for the troops.

Isabela could go on and on with her personal sacrifices for God and Country. The Princess Isabela had grown up in army camps, and poor little Juana wandered around looking so much like a solemn old woman that Isabela teasingly called her "Mother-in-Law." If she, the Queen, could put ruling the nation and serving the Church before the welfare of her own family, why couldn't her Admiral put governing her Indies before the pursuit of his dream? Much as she loved Colón, she would have to do something very soon, something drastic.

"Doña Luisa," said the Queen, turning to her lady-in-waiting.

"Yes, Your Highness," said Doña Luisa, giving a curtsy.

"Would you and the Conde de Córdoba like to sponsor this Indian girl?"

"Oh, Your Highness," said Doña Luisa, who knew her husband's fondness for young girls. "I do not know, the bishop has given her to you."

"And I shall give her to you and to Don Miguel."

"You have already been too generous," protested Doña Luisa. "Making my husband the Conde de Córdoba and head of the Holy Brotherhood in this province. Giving us the Castle of Almodóvar and funds to decorate Az-Zahra. Your Highness is too kind. Entirely too kind."

"Please, Doña Luisa, think no more of it," said the King. "No knight distinguished himself more than Don Miguel in the siege of Granada. No one serves the Holy Brotherhood more diligently. With men like your husband, our land may soon be purged of heretics. Besides, you deserve compensation for the loss of your son Rodrigo."

Rodrigo? Tahíaca's heart beat faster at the very sound of his name. Rodrigo might be dead, but to Tahíaca he would live forever. Surely they were not talking about the same Rodrigo.

"Speak of it no more," said the Queen. "The girl is yours. Take her to La Mezquita to be baptized, Fray Dominic. No, wait, I shall go with you. I like walking among the pillars where infidels used to pray. Praise the Blessed Virgin, La Mezquita is now a cathedral, and the synagogue on the Street of the Jews is a hospital for hydrophobics."

"Very appropriate," said Doña Luisa, curtsying again. "The Conde joins me in gratitude for your generosity. What Christian name shall we bestow on the girl?"

"You may call her Isabela, if you so desire," said the Queen in a burst of generosity.

"With your permission, Highness," agreed Doña Luisa.

Tahíaca had been impressed by the gardens of the Alcázar, as she had been impressed by everything she had seen in Andalucía. She was used to waterfalls, rivers, and tumbling streams, but she had never seen rectangular pools with water spraying up into the air. She wondered if anyone ever bathed in those pools, and she longed for the sweet smell of cabo leaves.

She had grown used to buildings made of stone, but she had never seen anything like La Mezquita. She wondered why they had enclosed trees inside the Patio of the Oranges, as she had wondered why they enclosed flowers in the Córdoban patios. Why not build houses in the forest instead of trying to bring the forest into the houses? When she saw the marble pillars inside the Great Mosque, she could not believe it. A man-made forest stretched away into the dim recesses of the vast building. Row after row of red-and-white arches like branches of trees laced together. Who had dreamed of this marvel?

Tahíaca was baptized under the rampant lions in the Royal Chapel of La Mezquita, in a ceremony she did not understand. Fray Dominic pressed the chrism into her forehead, mumbling a formula so old no one said it distinctly.

"Isabela." Fray Dominic blinked his vacuous eyes and peered closely at the Indian girl to see if she understood the importance of her new name. "Your name is Isabela."

"Tahíaca," she insisted, speaking for the first time, but in her native tongue. "Tahíaca, daughter of Anacaona, wife of Caonabó."

Almodóvar Castle guards the southeastern approach to the valley of Córdoba, standing so high on the steep promontory that the village of Almodóvar del Río cannot cluster up against its walls, but must nestle at the foot of the hill. For countless centuries, this stronghold had been fortified. The Romans called such heights *castros,* and the Arabs found the castro already marked by a crumbling round Visogothic tower. The castle the Arabs built and called Almodóvar rises stark and square from the stern rock crowning the hill—its gray walls and tower topped by crenellated battlements. Below on the hillside a few goats graze, and olive orchards skirt the hill just above the village.

In the rock beneath the castle lies the dungeon where Peter the Cruel jailed his sister-in-law long ago, before he had her beheaded at Sevilla. Here Henry III imprisoned his uncle the Duke of Benevente. At Almodóvar Henry IV fought his brother Alfonso. Here Queen Zaída took refuge when the Almohades invaded Andalucía. Seldom had Almodóvar had a lord more suited to its dark and infamous history than Don Miguel Sandoval, Conde de Córdoba, although Don Miguel was seldom in residence. His services to the Holy Brotherhood kept him away most of the time, but he sometimes kept a few prisoners in the dungeons for a while to soften their resistance before turning them over to the Inquisition.

One day shortly after her arrival at Almodóvar, Tahíaca happened upon a portrait of her lost love Rodrigo, hanging in the dim recesses of a cold cavernous hall. She caught her breath sharply, staring to see if it was an opia sent to frighten her. In her halting Spanish she asked one of the Moorish slaves who he was. The slave told her he was the dead son of the Conde and Condesa who had been killed in the massacre at Navidad by that cannibal Cacique Caonabó.

Tahíaca wanted to cry out and defend her father, tell them who had really killed Rodrigo and set the story straight, but she did not think they would believe her—and even if they did, she was afraid things would not go well for her once they knew. So she kept her memories of Rodrigo enshrined in her heart.

Tahíaca could not believe her Rodrigo could be the son of the popeyed, suspicious Don Miguel and the alternately cold and lustful Doña Luisa, whose spirit seemed as deep and dark as the dungeons beneath the castle. Tahíaca never saw them laughing and playing together as Caonabó had laughed and played with all his wives. They always treated each other as coldly and formally as if they were strangers. How had they ever mated?

Both lived off the husks of love. Doña Luisa devoted herself to the spiritual guidance of the many pages entrusted to the Conde for education and training for knighthood. Don Miguel had mistresses in every village under his jurisdiction and bastard sons and daughters in most of the provinces of Spain. Yet the Conde and Condesa of Córdoba were two of the loneliest people in all Andalucía.

When the Queen gave Tahíaca to the Sandovals, Don Miguel thought the girl might assuage some of his loneliness. He saw her as a savage virgin of a lost Eden, noble and uncorrupted. Several weeks passed without Don Miguel putting on the tall hood and cloak that masked his identity and allowed him to do the work of the Holy Brotherhood. Doña Luisa grew more and more irritable with her pages, who laughed behind her back and wagered with each other over who would be taken to her rooms for private instruction once the Conde left the castle. Finally, she took two pages with her to Az-Zahra, where she always stayed when there was a religious festival at La Mezquita. That night Don Miguel sent for Tahíaca.

Tahíaca felt a revulsion for him the moment she entered his room. He was pulling his shirt over his head, and she had one glimpse of his flabby muscles before he blew out the lamp. He groped for her in the dark, pulled up her skirt, thrust two fingers up her vagina and probed cruelly, then threw her on the bed and mounted her.

No tender murmurings...no kisses...not even a pretense of love. Just groping, pounding, gasping; then, after the sudden disgorging, he lay still, breathing heavily. Tahíaca also lay very still, trying not to remember Rodrigo. Go away, my love. Go back beyond my heart where first love lurks....

Don Miguel sat up, pulled on his stockings and his shirt, then lay back down beside her in the darkness, not touching her.

"Oh, Blessed Virgin," Don Miguel groaned.

Tahíaca knew he was not talking to her, for he did not know she could understand Spanish. She lay still, not speaking.

"I am so lonely," he whispered. "Oh, little Tahíaca, if you could only understand me."

He always called her Tahíaca, although his wife Doña Luisa insisted on calling her by her Christian name, Isabela. Poor man, she thought. He was her husband now. Anacaona always said wives must sense a husband's needs. Tahíaca would try to bring her new husband some happiness. After all, he was Rodrigo's...No! Go away! You are dead, Rodrigo!

"San Antonio, help me," Don Miguel whined. "Blessed Virgin, have mercy on me."

The whining disgusted Tahíaca. Caonabó never whined. Caonabó gave so much love to all his wives and children that he slept peacefully every night. Would she ever see Caonabó again? Ever go home to Cibao?

"Why should I feel guilty?" Don Miguel asked whatever spirit was tormenting him. "Even the bishops keep women, and their bastards go into the Church like their fathers. Some of them even take the choir boys into the sacristy and..."

Don Miguel did not finish his thought. Having dealt with his conscience, he wanted Tahíaca again. He wanted to see her as he imagined Colón had seen her.

He lighted the lamp and ordered her to disrobe. Her body shone golden in the lamplight, like a bronze Madonna.

"Santa María de Guadalupe has appeared to me in a vision!" he murmured, almost reverently.

"My husband," Tahíaca said in Spanish, timidly touching his cheek.

His bug-eyes bulged. His face turned red. He slapped her, knocking her to the floor.

"No! Do not ever say that. I am not your husband, you little heathen whore. Marriage is a sacrament. Doña Luisa is my wife before God. You are...you...you belong...the Queen gave you...Sweet Jesus, I do not know what you are to me! Get out of my bedroom. If Doña Luisa should return and find you here..."

Tahíaca was more angry than hurt. She had only tried to help him. He had no right to treat her this way. She knew how men thought. She hugged her clothing to her breast and backed out of the room, smiling her knowing smile. As she turned to leave, she twitched her hips as she used to twitch them at the traders under the ceiba. From that moment, Don Miguel was in her power.

"Por Dios, she is a little whore," he groaned.

Tahíaca spent the night in the dungeon, and Don Miguel paced the battlements until almost dawn.

CHAPTER 2

Córdoba, 1496

TAHÍACA ALWAYS adjusted herself to her current world, making it seem to all who saw her that she had always belonged there. During the year she had been at Almodóvar Castle, the men of the village below had taken to sitting on the rocks at the foot of the hill hoping to catch a glimpse of the promise of her sixteen years. Watching Tahíaca inspired some of them to go to the Indies, where such girls were rumored to run nude through the forest. Yet Tahíaca seemed to belong uniquely to Almodóvar Castle, as if she had always lived there and always been mistress of the invisible world in which she moved.

Tahíaca learned Spanish ways almost as rapidly as she learned Spanish. When Doña Luisa's wrath came down on her, she learned not to mingle too freely with the pages. Yet the pages liked Tahíaca, for she was always finding little ways to please them. The Moorish slaves, who were usually a surly, close-knit lot, helped Tahíaca learn her work. Soon the fate of her people on La Española seemed like an opia dream. Sometimes she would slip down to the cavernous hall and stand watching Rodrigo's portrait, but he, too, had taken his proper place in the secret places of her heart. Don Miguel was the man in her life now, and although she did not like him, she looked for ways to bring some happiness into the crafty old man's life.

Don Miguel had been faithful to his marriage vows ever since the first night he had sent for Tahíaca, but he took her with him almost everywhere he went now—even to meetings of the Holy Brotherhood. He liked to make other men envious of showing off his beautiful high-browed Indian girl, dressed in silks and a tall, pointed capriote without a face mask, but with long trailing silk scarfs. Tahíaca attended the needs of his guests and tasted his food and wine for poison; when she saw how the men of the Brotherhood carefully ignored her, she took a particular delight in walking her special walk and watching them avert their eyes.

Doña Luisa hated Tahíaca. She wanted to rid Almodóvar of the girl permanently, but she knew she would have to do it without arousing Don Miguel's anger. Her husband had become entirely too attached to the girl. Meanwhile, Doña Luisa wisely ignored her husband's interest in Tahíaca. To keep herself busy, she plunged into preparations for Holy Week.

Doña Luisa always felt very Catholic during Holy Week in Córdoba when Christ's Passion took on a festive air. She moved her household to Az-Zahra and held court for other noble families, attended parades, and wept during High Mass in the as-yet-unfinished cathedral hidden inside La Mezquita. Despite two and a half centuries of renewed Christian worship since Moslem rule had fallen in Córdoba, no one called the cathedral by its name, La Asunción de la Santísima Virgen. Everyone still called it La Mezquita. Beloved mosque it had been, and beloved mosque it would always remain.

Don Miguel and his Holy Brotherhood, carrying lighted red tapers and wearing tall capriotes with narrow slits for their eyes, led the parade past old Roman walls where Seneca had played as a boy, over the Roman Bridge built by Julius Caesar and around the Tower of Bad-Death—built by a penitent Spanish nobleman to honor the wife he had executed after erroneously accusing her of adultery. Aram Torres and men like him bowed their backs under the platforms carrying the anguished plaster virgins who cried glass tears. Aram's heart ached as they passed through the narrow cobbled Street of the Jews, and by the darkened and ruined synagogue, where hydrophobics were sometimes chained until they died. Jews had worshipped in that synagogue longer than in any other place on European soil.

Tahíaca watched the parade from one of the balconies the people of Córdoba had decorated for Holy Week. Córdoban patios were banked with tiers of flowering plants, and pictures of saints were enshrined on their balconies amid cascades of perfumed blossoms. Men like Don Miguel worked out their private anguish by walking barefoot and chained beneath somber black robes.

All the members of the Holy Brotherhood wore hoods and robes, for the Brotherhood was the right arm of the Inquisition, and its members were in constant danger of assassins. While Don Miguel paraded, his eyes peered through the slits in his hood, watching for suspected heretics. Holy Week offered excellent opportunities for spying out judaizers—anyone less than enthusiastic, anyone making light of images or holy relics, anyone not kneeling when the Host passed by, even anyone showing too much zeal. Heretics were becoming harder to find, but Don Miguel had been watching Aram Torres, the Jew doctor who kept a bodega and owned vineyards near Jerez de la Frontera, where they made such fine sherry that even the abstemious Moors had not destroyed the vineyards. Don Miguel had been suspicious of Torres ever since that day he had bought Az-Zahra from the rabbi going into exile. Don Miguel suspected Torres was practicing judaism in secret, but he had not yet been able to prove it.

Now that Jews like Rav Joseph had all left the country, devout Catholics had turned their attention to rooting out those Jews they called Marranos—the ones who had converted but who still practiced their abominable rites in secret. One of the principal duties of the Holy Brotherhood was the discovery of such heretics. Tonight after the parade, the Brotherhood would meet with Fray Dominic in La Mezquita. Don Miguel would take Tahíaca with him to the meeting, as usual.

La Mezquita terrified Tahíaca. The Holy Brotherhood met in a dark corner where Arab professors used to sit on cushions leaning back against marble pillars teaching the fundamentals of mathematics on which the astrolabe had been designed. Without the astrolabe, Colón would never have been able to venture out of the Mediterranean onto the Green Seas to discover the New World.

Tahíaca knew nothing of the history of La Mezquita, but she felt the strange disembodied eyes of the brothers sitting crosslegged on the floor. She recognized Don Miguel by his protruding eyes, but she felt as if the opia might have taken him too, leaving nothing except those eyes. When Fray Dominic entered, followed by altar boys carrying a small table and an enormous chair, Tahíaca was glad to see their unhooded faces; but soon they vanished behind their echoing footsteps, and Fray Dominic's vacuous eyes began to trouble her. Only she and Fray Dominic wore no hoods. Tahíaca tried to make herself small behind a pillar.

Fray Dominic took his time arranging his papers on the table and adjusting his ornate chair. Fray Dominic loved his work—all the details of ritual devotion, the comforting certainty of the Roman Catholic hierarchy, the grandeur and pageantry that had almost obliterated his memory of street life.

"First, let us consider the woodcutter's bill," he said after calling the meeting to order. He held the paper close to his eyes. "His bill for the last act-of-faith was entirely too high."

Fray Dominic looked at the undulating hoods. He liked not seeing them clearly. They were merely part of the mechanism for doing God's work. He also liked not having to see clearly during an act-of-faith. When the Church "relaxed" a heretic to the civil authorities, She expressly prohibited shedding of blood, but the secular powers were expected to pronounce and carry out the sentence of death by burning, thereby absolving Mother Church of any guilt in the death of the "relaxed" heretic. Protected by Church and State, Fray Dominic could participate in things he would never have had the courage to carry out on his own, but even so, he was glad he could not see very clearly.

"How much wood can it take for three relaxed heretics, two disinterred corpses, and five effigies?" he asked, using business details to further insulate himself from painful truths. In order to confiscate the property of suspected heretics who had fled the country or died in prison before their convictions, the Inquisition often convicted them posthumously or in absentia. In that case, either their corpses or their effigies were burned. "The Inquisitor works on a budget, you know. Not all confiscations come into our treasury. Most of them go the Crown. No, the woodcutter's bill is much too high."

"Perhaps someone should investigate the woodcutter," suggested Don Miguel.

"No one is above suspicion," Fray Dominic said.

"His Highness wants an accounting of all confiscations," said Don Miguel.

Fray Dominic sat very still, stacking and restacking his papers into neat piles, blinking his eyes while the men in red hoods stared. Long ago an Arab physician had ground pieces of glass and fixed them in frames to improve his sultan's sight. Fray Dominic wished there were still such physicians who could make marvelous glasses, so he could see the eyes of the man accusing him. Fray Dominic kept very careful records enabling the Inquisition to keep a large share of the confiscated estates, but he had never kept a dishonest maravedi, the smallest of Spanish coins, for himself.

"Read the Statement of Confiscations, Fray Dominic," commanded Don Miguel coldly, for he had never learned to read himself.

"From Carmina Perona, a pair of gold bracelets hidden by her mother who was relaxed... the sale of three fields and two vineyards belonging to Rafael Montero, the money to defray his expenses while under arrest and investigation, living in the house of the Inquisitor... payment of five thousand maravedis by the wife of Juan Cardoza, who is waiting to be relaxed—partial payment for his confiscated fields, the rest to be paid in monthly installments..." On and on he droned, holding the document close to his face, reading the list of property confiscated from the heretics.

Tahíaca tried to understand what they were talking about, but no matter how intently she listened, she kept missing the meaning of the word *relax*. All she knew was that evil was here. In Cibao, men wore masks only to frighten the enemy.

"You can see for yourself it is all accounted for, Don Miguel," said Fray Dominic, with special emphasis on his name so the Conde would know he knew who had made the accusation.

"Use no names here!" Don Miguel reproved him. "The Holy Brotherhood cannot do its best work without anonymity. Let me see the statement."

Fray Dominic reluctantly turned it over, although he did not like having his work scrutinized. He was above reproach, and the Conde de Córdoba should have known it—should never have asked for an accounting. Fray Dominic did not know the Conde could not read.

"His Highness expected much more," Don Miguel said, pretending to study the document. "These expeditions to the Indies are very costly. If we cannot raise more money somewhere, perhaps His Highness will have to stop authorizing them."

"Oh, no!" cried Fray Dominic, who had been thinking of volunteering for the next voyage. "All those poor lost Indian souls. How can His Highness turn a deaf ear to souls crying out in perdition!"

"Then the Inquisitor will have to come up with more money," said Don Miguel. "What do your investigators tell you? Who is a likely prospect? Who practices Judaism secretly? Better make it someone with more property than a woodcutter."

"We have several people under observation," said Fray Dominic defensively, his dark face growing darker still.

"Good! Have you considered Aram Torres, the physician whose bodega is in the Street of the Jews just down from the synagogue?" asked Don Miguel. "Torres is a defiant name, chosen by the family to remind good Christians of the hundreds of Moorish towers that once guarded the frontiers. The Jews have a sly sense of humor. They think they are so superior. Chosen people, indeed!"

"Aram Torres?" said Fray Dominic cautiously. "Surely you do not suspect Torres. He gives substantial sums toward building the cathedral in La Mezquita, and he attends Mass there every Sunday. He even helped carry the Virgin in today's parade."

"Just the kind of man to watch," said Don Miguel. "Some say he has been seen standing with his son Daniel looking at the ruined synagogue where they keep the hydrophobics."

"But his son has been baptized," objected Fray Dominic, as if baptism settled everything.

"Of course! Perhaps also circumcised. Before Torres converted, he kept all the Jewish laws. Don't forget, his wife's brother is a rabbi who fled to Portugal."

"You think Torres has reverted to Judaism?"

"His son is almost twelve, isn't he? Some Jews begin teaching their children about that age, when the child is old enough to be trusted to keep quiet."

"You are right, of course," said Fray Dominic. "Aram Torres certainly bears watching. He has become rich selling amulets and prescribing potions. Who knows what evil ceremonies he conducts in the rooms behind his bodega?"

"Perhaps a few hours on the rack..."

"Do not profane the sanctuary with descriptions of your tortures!" cried Fray Dominic. "The Church will have nothing to do with such methods. That is the business of the Holy Brotherhood."

Verily, Father, thought Don Miguel, but he dared

not voice his sarcasm. You cannot let your right hand know what your left hand is doing.

Sometimes Tahíaca could feel the Evil in Córdoba like a living presence pressing down on her like the air before a hurricane. The people of this land were more superstitious than her people. She found it almost impossible to keep their myths and legends straight. Everywhere she turned she found lifelike statues of their cemís, always with anguished faces as though they did not believe in the right to be happy. People seemed always to be celebrating areítos for some cemí or other—that or planning pilgrimages.

Pilgrimages offered unusual opportunities to people whose most exciting entertainment for centuries had been crowding into castles to escape the ravages of some marauding army. To travel, to meet new people, to escape their humdrum daily lives, the people made pilgrimages to Santiago de Compostela; or, if rich and under suspicion for heresy, some went to Jerusalem and never came back. Sailors like the Admiral Don Cristóbal Colón preferred pilgrimages to the shrine of the dark Virgin of Guadalupe.

Our Lady of Guadalupe performed miracles, stopped plagues, calmed seas, forgave the most heinous crimes, and was especially sought after by kings and military leaders. Her history was as dark as Her skin, for She had been buried and resurrected at least twice. Supposed to have been carved by Saint Luke, the Virgin had been buried in Extremadura to hide Her from the Moors, only to be resurrected six hundred years later in a miraculous appearance to a simple cowherd. Once before that, in Constantinople when Christianity was threatened, She had lain buried for a long time. Two resurrections from subterranean sleep had left the Virgin with skin tinged by Spain's African heritage. The Virgin of Guadalupe answers the hunger in the Spanish soul for God the Mother.

In June of that year, the Admiral Don Cristóbol Colón, having built the first sailing vessels ever constructed in the New World, arrived in Cádiz—returning to face royal displeasure before laying plans for a third expedition. He wanted the Indians he had brought to Spain to see the dark visage of Our Lady of Guadalupe, and to be baptized at Her shrine before he traveled to Burgos where Their Catholic Highnesses were currently holding court. He already doubted he would be able to persuade them to finance another voyage, for the Infanta Juana was marrying the handsome Austrian Prince Philip and must be given an appropriate entourage. Too much money had already been spent on useless expeditions and costly Moorish wars.

When Don Miguel learned Colón was going to Guadalupe, he decided to leave the fate of heretics like Aram Torres in the capable hands of Fray Dominic and make the pilgrimage to Guadalupe, taking Doña Luisa and Tahíaca with him. One morning in the summer of 1496, he laid his plans before his wife.

"No!" she said firmly. "I will not go to Guadalupe. Those mountain roads frighten me. Why do you want to go to Guadalupe?"

"To confront Colón and get satisfaction for Rodrigo's death. They say Cacique Caonabó who massacred the men of Navidad is among his captives, and I want to plant my dirk in his evil heart."

Tahíaca held her breath. She had been in Andalucía for more than a year now, and she had given up hope of ever going home, or of seeing any of her family again. Now Don Miguel said Caonabó might be here in Andalucía. Tahíaca could forget all Doña Luisa's recent abuses if she could only see her father.

"Caonabó has been brought back a captive?" Doña Luisa was startled. "The heathen who murdered our son?"

All the nobility had offered their sympathy and pledged their swords to avenge Navidad after Antonio de Torres brought back the stories of the massacre, which Colón had tortured out of Cacique Guacanagarí. To Andalucíans, Cacique Caonabó was the most notorious of all the cannibal chieftains. Neither Don Miguel nor Doña Luisa suspected Tahíaca had been the cause of their son's death, nor that she was Caonabó's daughter.

"Very well. We shall go to Guadalupe, but Isabela shall not go with us." Doña Luisa still insisted on calling Tahíaca by her baptismal name, although everyone else had given up and called her Tahíaca.

"Tahíaca not go? Why?" demanded Don Miguel, who always called her Tahíaca, partly to irritate Doña Luisa and partly because Isabela seemed so inappropriate for his free-spirited Indian girl.

"You think I don't know why you want to make this trip?" accused Doña Luisa. "To show off your little Indian whore to the Holy Brotherhood in every city we pass through. What is it you men do with her in all your late-night meetings? No, Isabela shall not go!"

Tahíaca felt a wave of panic. Not go! When Caonabó might be so very near? She had to think quickly. She decided to take a chance and tell them the truth.

"Thank you, my lady," Tahíaca said, looking down demurely as the Moorish slaves had taught her to do if she wanted Doña Luisa's favor.

"Thank me? You do not wish to go to Guadalupe? Why not?"

"Oh, my lady, do not force me to go. I am the daughter of Cacique Caonabó. My father is a proud man, my lady. Proud like Don Miguel. To see my father in chains would bring too much pain to my heart. I shall do whatever you ask without complaining—empty your slops every morning without being reminded. I shall not ask to bathe, but shall wait until you tell me to do so."

Tahíaca had found not bathing several times a day the most repulsive of Spanish customs. She longed for the ritual cleansing and the smell of fresh cabo leaves. She was homesick—oh, so homesick—and she had not realized it until now.

"No! I have changed my mind. You shall go to Guadalupe. It will put you in your place to see you father in chains. Perhaps you will not tempt the men with your smile or be ready to walk so sinfully," sniffed Doña Luisa. "Prepare to leave!"

Tahíaca's homesickness overwhelmed her that night, and she passed easily into the Taino spirit world—mysteriously transported back to the green forests and flowering valleys of Haiti, land of mountains, beautiful land where Tainos danced everlasting areítos. Tahíaca walked with Rodrigo and watched Anacaona dancing Caonabó's areíto while he sat under the sacred ceiba. The butterfly on Mayabaño's brow lighted on Tahíaca's hand, fluttering its wings in the sunlight until a sudden gust of wind blew it away. Tahíaca awoke to the dark chamber reserved for the slaves, and she bit down on her fist to keep from sobbing.

After several days of traveling, the Sandovals took quarters in a small village beside the Río Guardiana. Next morning, Doña Luisa was dawdling over her coffee, reluctant to begin the tortuous ride up the mountains. Don Miguel had gone to oversee saddling the horses, and Tahíaca was preparing to empty the slops when she heard the parrots.

Parrots? Here in the mountains of Extremadura? Caonabó! It must be Caonabó! The Admiral always brought back cages of brightly colored birds. Tahíaca dropped her bucket of slops, splattering Doña Luisa. With the Condesa shrieking at her, Tahíaca ran out of the room and down the stairs—racing like clouds before Huracán's winds.

The narrow street was jammed with people, but Tahíaca could see the tip of Caonabó's winged crown above their heads. Villagers snatched at the parrot cages, and the poor birds beat the feathers out of their wings trying to escape. The Admiral led the procession, his hair gray now, his shoulders a little stooped, his hands and his feet crippled with arthritis—clad in the plain habit of a mendicant friar.

"Caonabó!" Tahíaca shouted above the noise, shoving, keeping her eyes on the tall, winged crown. "Caonabó! Papa! Oh, Papa!"

Then she stood face to face with the man wearing Caonabó's crown and the nugget necklace Caonabó had given her mother, but the man was not her father. He was her uncle, ruler of a distant village, who had visited Cibao only once or twice. Tahíaca grabbed his arm.

"Caonabó?" she pleaded. "Where is Caonabó? I am Tahíaca, daughter of Anacaona. Where is my father?"

The man, whom Colón had christened Diego, looked at Tahíaca long enough to show he recognized her, then he turned and shuffled off, dragging his chains. He looked back over his shoulder just before the crowd closed around him again and spoke to her in Taino language.

"Huracán has taken Caonabó," he said.

CHAPTER 3

Córdoba, 1496

RAFELLA SÁNCHEZ de Torres had just returned from Friday night vespers in La Mezquita. Quickly she spread the lace Sabbath cloth on the table, then stirred the pot of garbanzo stew—enough for tonight and tomorrow. Crusty brown loaves of bread, still warm from the oven, lay on the mantel; the acrid smell of the pinch of dough she always threw into the fire still seemed to hang over the house. She picked up one of the candlesticks and rubbed at an imaginary spot, wondering why Aram had not come home yet.

In the four years her brother Rav Joseph and his family had been in exile, Aram had grown more and more withdrawn. Rafella worried about him because he never really laughed anymore. He would smile and pretend to be happy to keep up her spirits, but the life had gone out of him.

Aram didn't even enjoy his work anymore. Last year he had not made his annual trip to the mountains around Granada to gather medicinal herbs. For centuries, physicians from all over the world had made that trip, not trusting anyone else to select the herbs at the peak of their potency. Now Aram bought his medicines from itinerant traders. His supply of amulets was running low; when some of the leeches died, he had not bothered to replace them. This morning when the woman came saying her husband had been gored by a wild bull and the wound in his side was festering, Aram had barely been able to find enough leeches to bleed the man. Rafella had tried to get Aram not to go with the woman. Gorings almost always resulted in death, and Aram was sure to be blamed. No one had been able to forget they were Jews, no matter how devout they tried to appear. Now it was past sundown, and Aram was not yet home.

"Daniel," Rafella called. "Daniel, come here."

"What is it, Mama?" Daniel answered. "I'm busy."

"What are you doing?"

"Just reading, Mama. Reading the last letter from Rachel." His not-yet-man's voice broke into a higher register.

How that boy had grown in the past few months! He was almost as tall as his father now, but still thin and gangly. The broad shoulders and firm thighs would come later. He had re-read Rachel's letter a hundred times since it came. Few letters had been smuggled through, and Daniel treasured every one. Rafella, too, treasured the few letters. She missed her brother, but most of all she missed the Friday night services in the little synagogue when she would sit with Sefira gossiping with the ladies in the women's gallery and watching the children wander in and out, while in the room below ten men prayed. Poor Sefira! She should have been the one who stayed in Córdoba. How lonely it was being a Jew in Córdoba, especially an underground Jew. Yet how else could they survive? Perhaps Aram had made the wrong choice.

Rav Joseph had written that things were better in Portugal. Jews lived in the judería called the Alfama, on the hill across from Saint George's Castle; but except for a few sneers from the Christians when they went down into the city, no one bothered them as long as they stayed to themselves, worked hard, and always had money to pay. Rachel was growing into a pretty girl who turned the heads of the young men and gladdened the hearts of the old. She was a joy to her father, who had not married again. She took care of everything like the little Matronit she had become, and she would make someone a fine wife someday, but so far she had shown no interest in anyone. She, too, read the few letters from Daniel over and over again.

Rafella did not like to interfere in Aram's decision, for she was not a wife who bossed her husband. She had wanted to stay in Córdoba. She had been born here and grown up here, and she had been glad when she did not have to leave the only home she had ever known. But she knew a Jew's home was with the family, and the family—like so many Jewish families throughout history—had gone into exile. Rafella had been thinking about suggesting they sell the bodega and go to Lisbon. Surely a good physician like Aram could make a living anywhere in the world. Perhaps tonight, after Aram finished working on the room he was going to use for Daniel's yeshiva, Rafella would have a talk with him. It would be so good to hear him laugh again!

"Daniel!" Rafella called again. "Go find your father. I am afraid something might have happened to him. You have seen those men following him about."

"Yes, Mama, I've seen them. Why do they follow Papa? What has he done?"

"Nothing, Daniel. Don't worry! Your Papa has done nothing wrong. Now go and find him, hurry!" Rafella tried to keep the panic out of her voice.

"He's probably just standing in the old synagogue building looking at the walls," said Daniel. "I don't know why he always stops by there on Friday nights."

"Perhaps tonight he will tell you why, son. You're almost old enough to know. Now, hurry, go find him and bring him home before supper gets cold."

Aram Torres stood in the ruined synagogue staring at the west wall. Even in the dark he could read the Hebrew inscriptions, for they were engraved on his heart: "To Yahweh, Majestic and all Powerful..." Aram ran his fingers over the cool Hebrew letters, then touched his fingers to his lips. Tears trickled down his face. "Majestic and all Powerful..."

The abandoned synagogue was just up the street from Aram's bodega, and he had been stopping by here more and more often lately. Over the entryway the inscription began "Blessed is the man who hears me..." and ended with "...Open these doors and enter into the Nation of the Just..." Where was the Nation of the Just now?

Aram often came here after the night watchman had cried the hour and moved on. He would stand silently, weeping as Jews had wept at the Wailing Wall in Jerusalem for hundreds of years. Aram knew he had made the wrong choice. To live a double life was to live no life at all. Daniel was growing into a man, and he didn't even know he should have been circumcised. The only salvation for a Jew was to be a Jew!

The other converts knew that now, too, although the gates had been removed from the judería and all were free to come and go, it was necessary to honor the plaster saints in La Mezquita. Aram had tried to be a good Christian, but every time he looked up at the glittering Madonnas, he remembered the commandment: "Thou shalt not make unto thee any graven images." How could he worship the Virgin Mary with these words thundering in his ears: "Thou shalt have no other gods before me."

The new converts could not even support each other now, lest they be accused of judaizing. Yet they kept coming furtively to Aram's bodega for amulets to cure their sicknesses: Lilith the Night Demon to hang over a sick child's crib, and the Shekhina-Matronit to bless a bridal chamber. No minyan could meet in the synagogue for prayer, and no one sat in Elijah's chair with a son to be circumcised; but still the people clung to the old ways, and still they came to Aram Torres for remedies for the sickness of their hearts.

For a while Aram had tried to tell himself it did not matter, but he had kept hearing the Shema: *"Hear, O Israel, the Lord our God, the Lord is One..."* If he had only one life to live, he wanted to live it teaching his son Daniel to love God with all his heart, with all his soul, and with all his might. The Shema exhorted him to: "...*teach them diligently unto thy children*..."

"Papa," Daniel called into the dark building—his voice part man's part child's.

"...*when thou sittest in thy house*..."

"Papa, come home," said Daniel, wondering why his father was standing here mumbling to the wall.

"...*when thou walkest by the way, when thou liest down and when thou risest up*..."

"Papa, Mama says come home. Some men have been lurking about the street and she is afraid."

"...*for a sign upon thy head*..."

"Please come home, Papa. Mama needs you."

"...*between thy eyes*..."

"Papa, do you hear me?"

"...*upon the doorposts of thy house and upon thy gates.*"

Aram finished his prayer, turned and laid his hands in benediction on Daniel's head. Then, without even glancing up at the inscription beside the niche where the Torah had once rested, they left the synagogue. Aram did not like to think about that inscription. "A little sanctuary and house for the confirmation of the Law, dedicated in the year 75..." it began, and ended triumphantly, "Be ye lifted up, O God! And hasten the time of the rebuilding of Jerusalem." The Children of Israel were being scattered abroad in yet another diaspora, and Jerusalem was no closer to being rebuilt. Aram's shoulders sagged.

"Why do you come to this old building, Papa," asked Daniel, "at night when it is so dark? Aren't you afraid a stone will fall on your head?"

"Better a stone on my head than this stone in my heart," said Aram.

"What is the matter, Papa? Why is Mama afraid? Why are the men always following you about? What is it about this old synagogue?"

"You know it is a synagogue?"

"Of course, Papa. All the kids throw stones at it.

175

That is where the Jews used to practice their blood rituals."

"Don't ever say that, Daniel. Lies, all of it. Jews never sacrificed little children. Never! Lies! All lies!"

"Don't get so upset, Papa," said Daniel. "Why be upset over some old building and some old Jews who don't even live here anymore?"

"Come with me, my son," Aram decided. "It is time you learned who you are!"

The next few weeks were precious in the lives of the Torres family. Aram knew he might have little time left, so he made the most of it—evenings after the street noises had died down and the patio gates had been rattled at least once by the watchman, Sundays after Mass in La Mezquita while the rest of Córdoba settled down for siesta, Sabbaths while his wife watched for customers in the bodega. Aram Torres the physician became Aram Torres the rabbi, binding the words about his forehead and next to his heart.

"Hear, O Israel, the Lord our God . . . the Lord is One . . ."

By the light of candles in the windowless room, Daniel learned about his people . . . of Abraham and the covenant he made with Yahweh . . . of Sarah and Hagar . . . of Daniel and Nebuchadnezzer . . . of Joshua, and of the sons of the Maccabees. Of the Mishnah . . . and of Maimonides and Rabbi Akiba. Of the Rivers of Babylon, and of Isaiah and the promised Messiah.

Weaving the myths and legends, the wisdoms and mysticisms that bind a people together, Aram Torres tried to lead his son in the way he should go, so that when he became old he would not depart from it. He told him about the Kabbala and the Tree of Life. He tried to explain the unspeakable, incomprehensible name of the omniscient, omnipresent, omnipotent God— the Most Holy One, blessed be His Name, who has chosen Israel to be His People. Aram Torres gave his son a heritage his heart would remember when his mind chose to forget.

It was not easy, there in that little secret room.

God has chosen you, Daniel Torres y Sánchez of Córdoba.

To what purpose?

Only the Most Holy One, blessed be He, knows.

To suffer...to question...to learn...to obey...to live...to love...to keep Holy what is Holy lest man forget anything is Holy.

Aram knew he had so little time.

How can you teach a boy to become a man, to know and love his heritage, while at the same time warning him never, never to let anyone know he is who he is?

Be proud, my son. You are a Jew, chosen of God.

Hush, my son, someone may be listening.

Don't tell them we change our linen on Friday. Don't tell them we light candles in this little room and let them burn through the Sabbath night. Don't tell them we have found a butcher who observes the laws, who prays for the animals before slaughtering them, who slaughters nothing unclean.

How shall you always answer? How but with a question?

What does it do to a man to always answer question with question?

Can you learn to be evasive? To take the offensive, throwing your enemy off guard?

Trust no one! No one!

Even Jews may not be Jews anymore. Brother informs against brother, daughter against mother, son against father, even wife against husband. If the Holy Brotherhood comes, never admit you are a Jew. Never! Sing "Salve Regina." Cross yourself and swear to make a pilgrimage—to Jerusalem, if possible; but never, never admit you keep Jewish customs.

Aram Torres had so little time. Only time enough to begin making a man out of his son.

"Papa, will we ever see Rav Joseph and cousin Rachel again?" asked Daniel one Sabbath eve when they had finished the lessons.

"If God wills, my son," said Aram, though he doubted he would see his friend this side of the resurrection. "Rachel sent you another letter the other day."

"Another letter? I didn't get it. Where is it?" Daniel's eyes glowed with excitement.

"Mama has hidden it somewhere. She has been so worried lately, she must have forgotten to give it to you."

"I know, Papa. Someone follows her wherever she goes. They follow me too, now," Daniel announced proudly, as if that made him a man like his father. "Please, Papa, may I have Cousin Rachel's letter?"

"You set great store by Rachel, don't you, my son?" asked Aram.

"I am going to marry with her someday," Daniel announced.

"Marriages are arranged by matchmakers," teased Aram. "Perhaps no one will consider you suitable for a rabbi's daughter."

"Don't joke, Papa. I shall marry with Rachel and take her to Colón's New World, where we shall be proud to tell everyone we are Jews."

"What makes you think things will be different for Jews in the New World?"

"Because we will make them different," Daniel said confidently.

Rafella had hidden Rav Joseph's letter, to which Rachel had attached a short note. She was afraid the Inquisitors might somehow find out. What did it matter if Rav Joseph were her brother? One of her grandfathers had been Rabbi Solomon Levi, who had converted and become a Bishop of Burgos—but her other grandfather had been an Abravanel who had been financial advisor to the King. Not even his high court position had saved him when he refused to convert, and he and his family had had to flee. How could you balance out two such grandfathers when you stood before the Inquisitors? Finally, at Aram's insistence, Rafella produced Rachel's letter. Daniel read it over and over again.

Rachel Sánchez of Lisbon to Daniel Torres of Córdoba

Greetings, Cousin Daniel:

Portugal is not much different from Andalucía, except it rains a lot. We must still wear the red badge of shame because we are Jews, but Papa calls it a badge of courage and says we should wear it proudly.

Are you proud to be a Jew, Daniel? I am.

Papa says we may go to the Indies now that Mama has joined the curtain of souls around the Throne of Glory. Papa depends on me more and more now, but I have told him I will not go across the Green Seas without you. Do you still want to stand under the canopy and marry with me so we can be best friends forever and ever?

May the Lord bless you and keep you while we are absent one from the other, Amen.

Daniel tried to remember Rachel's face, but he could not. All he could remember was her laughter and how she crossed her arms when she was angry, and that she liked licorice roots. If he ever saw her again, he must remember to have a licorice root in his pocket. He tucked her letter under his pillow and blew out his candle.

"Do not worry, Rachel," he murmured to the darkness. "I am learning how to be a Jew."

CHAPTER 4

Córdoba, 1496

AFTER THE meeting of the Holy Brotherhood when Don Miguel had aroused Fray Dominic's suspicions about the Torres family, the friar had begun to watch them closely. He despised all Marranos, hypocrites who professed with their lips but loved not in their hearts. He remembered that none of the Torres family had attended High Mass nor taken communion. The doctor claimed they were all sick with the flux. To Fray Dominic, not partaking of the Holy Eucharist was heresy.

Before he had been baptized Dominic, five-year-old Abdu-l-Rahman was caught one day eating the round flat wafers and drinking from the bronze wine bottle used to prepare Mass—not realizing he was eating the body and drinking the blood of Our Lord—which, of course, he was not, because the bread and wine had not yet been blessed. The bread tasted flat and the wine was sour, but Abdu-l-Rahman was hungry. He drank too much wine, then began chucking candle wax at blurred Virgins. A tall, spindly-legged cleric hauled him before the Monsignor, who threatened him with hell-fire for practicing such desecrations.

"Well, what have you to say for yourself?" asked the Monsignor after the lecture, surprised the boy neither cringed nor cried. "Speak up, boy, what is your name?"

"Abdu-l-Rahman," replied the boy, "but my mother calls me Abdul."

"Abdul is a heathen name," said the Monsignor. "What is your Christian name?"

"Abdu-l-Rahman," the boy repeated. "My name is Abdu-l-Rahman. It is the only name I have."

"A Muslim child," said the Abbot. "Who is your father?"

Abdu-l-Rahman shook his head.

"Who is your father?" repeated the Monsignor.

Abdu-l-Rahman looked down, scrubbed his bare toe on the floor.

"Who takes care of you?" the Monsignor asked.

"My mother, but she is sick now and cannot work. Please, sir, is there any more bread and wine? My mother and my brothers...Please, sir, we are all hungry. Could you give me a little more bread and wine?"

"The Church has enough for everyone who hungers and thirsts after righteousness," said the Monsignor.

"What is righteousness?" asked Abdul.

"We will take you to the Dominicans at Triana," the Monsignor decided. "You shall learn about righteousness. Such big black eyes. Such a face—neither smiling nor frowning. You will make a good Dominican."

"What is a good Dominican?" asked Abdul.

Patiently the Monsignor told him of the founding of the Dominican Order and of their mission to restore purity to the Church. He made the Church sound like one of those Arabian gardens Abdul's mother sometimes told him about—a beautiful Heaven with fruits of all kinds from the Tree of Life and bubbling fountains of Living Waters. Abdul wanted very much to live in such a place. Of course, Abdul had to be baptized first.

"What shall be his Christian name?" asked the Monsignor.

"Dominic," the boy announced proudly. "I shall be called after Saint Dominic."

A few months later, after the plague took his mother, young Dominic turned to the Dominicans, who became his family. The Church was the mother he never questioned. Dominic soon learned to confess freely and frequently all sorts of imaginary sins. He wore the hair shirt, slept on cold flagstones, ate sparingly. Full grown, he stood not much taller than a boy. His vacuous black eyes stared out of a death's-head face.

Perhaps because the Eucharist had brought him to the Church, when Fray Dominic elevated the Host he felt closest to the mystical union he craved and would crave all his life. *"Take, eat, this is my body...drink, this is my blood."* His consuming passion was to complete the work of the Church on earth: to bring all men unto Christ and to search out and destroy all the enemies of Christ's Bride—especially the enemy within, the hated Marranos.

If Fray Dominic watched the Torres family closely, he was sure he could collect enough evidence to bring charges against Aram Torres for judaizing. The Inquisitors liked to build a strong case before making an arrest, even if they never told the accused what evidence they had or allowed him to face his accusers.

The vast blue early-summer sky over Córdoba was filled with billowing clouds. Flocks of sparrows soared on the updrafts above the olive orchards on the mountainsides. Fray Dominic, oaken bucket in hand, stood in the shade of an old mill watching Daniel Torres fishing upriver. The Guadalquivir, once navigable here, now flowed lazily past Córdoba, silted by the centuries of runoff from the ring of blue mountains. Beside Julius Caesar's bridge, the watermills stood like giants on mudflat islands. At the bottom of the river, cockles fed in the silt, standing upright on their heavy hinges to protect themselves from being crushed.

Rafella Torres had sent her son to fish. The Torres family had not dared eat meat on Friday since the men began watching them so closely. Daniel had caught only a few small fish, not enough for supper. He decided to try another spot. As he passed close to the mill where

Fray Dominic lurked, he stepped on a cockleshell buried in the mud and hopped about on one foot for a moment before going on to another pool. Fray Dominic smiled. Daniel's face had been a blur, but his actions had registered clearly. The boy had not stooped to pick up the cockle.

Daniel Torres had not retrieved the cockle because he knew his mother would not cook unclean things like cockles, or crabs, or crawfish, or pork. Daniel had a small string of fish, but he wanted to catch at least one big one. As Daniel threw out his line again, Fray Dominic took off his sandals and began wiggling his toes for cockles.

Fishing with his toes took Fray Dominic back to his boyhood, when sometimes all they had to eat was cockles. Fishing for cockles was much easier than other things Fray Dominic enjoyed doing—like poring over old Arabic histories, which strained his eyes. He didn't need good eyesight to fish for cockles, nor for parasitic heretics who burrowed under his skin and lay festering there. By the time his bucket was full of cockles, he had worked his way to the island where Daniel stood fishing.

"How is the fishing, my son?" Fray Dominic asked.

"How are the cockles, Father?" Daniel countered.

"Fine, just fine. I'll trade half my cockles for half your string of fish."

"How do you know I have a string of fish?"

"I have been watching you, boy." Fray Dominic's vacuous eyes seemed about to swallow Daniel.

He knows, Daniel thought. He knows I am a Jew. Mama wants this fish, and she won't cook cockles. They are unclean, but Papa says never tell a Christian any food is unclean. You may have to eat it.

"Well, boy, do we have a bargain?"

Daniel's throat closed, and he thought he was going to vomit at the thought of eating cockles dug by Fray Dominic's bare toes. He knelt and pulled up his string of fish.

"Here, Father, take my fish. They are a present for the Church . . . and for the Inquisitor."

"Don't you want my cockles?" Fray Dominic grabbed Daniel by a bony claw. He looked as big as Goliath himself, although he was not much taller than Daniel. "Doesn't the Torres family like cockles?"

"What family doesn't like cockles?" asked Daniel.

"Just like a Jew," Fray Dominic muttered. "Answer a question with a question. Do you want my cockles or not? Yes or no!"

"Yes," mumbled Daniel, not looking at the friar.

"Yes, what?"

"Yes, Father."

"Yes what, Father?"

"Yes, thank you, Father."

"That's better," Fray Dominic held out his bucket, then accepted Daniel's string of fish before he strode off toward the watermills.

Daniel watched him out of sight behind a mill, then tipped the bucket and poured the cockles back into the pool. Fray Dominic, squinting through his eyelashes from behind the mill, knew then that the Torres family were judaizers. A few days later during confession, the Arab girl who served Rafella as a housemaid confessed that Aram Torres and his son spent a lot of time in a secret room behind the bodega.

Fray Dominic's mind wrestled with God. Evil fascinated him, and the more he thirsted after righteousness, the more disappointed he felt. Accepting the Church as his defender, he hid himself behind the confessional to participate vicariously in a host of sins.

After vespers that Friday night, Fray Dominic strode down the dark Street of the Jews to the gate of Aram's bodega. Wrinkling his nose against the smell, he dipped his hand into a bucket of slops. Feeling a strange sense of elation, he drew a few quick strokes on the wall beside the gate. If the Holy Brotherhood could not see the badge of shame, they would surely smell it. He emptied the rest of the slops through the gate into Rafella's beautiful little flower-decked patio, wiped his hands on an old rag, then strode proudly back to La Mezquita.

When Aram Torres returned from tending a patient, he saw the badge of shame scrawled on the wall. He held his nose, gingerly opened the gate, and stepped around the refuse on the patio flagstones. So, it had come!

"Aram, is that you?" Rafella called from the balcony above the patio.

"Yes, my life, it is your husband Aram."

"Close the gate quickly and lock it," Rafella urged. "I heard someone outside just now."

"Don't be afraid," Aram assured her.

"The smells from the streets are very bad tonight," said Rafella as he kissed her. "Even my blooming jasmine cannot mask the foul odor."

"When the wind is from the river, you can smell the burning place," Aram said. "We haven't had much rain lately to wash the streets clean."

Not all the sweet jasmine, not meadows of heliotrope, could mask Andalucía's putrefaction, thought Aram. The whole country was gangrenous. Aram savored Rafella's garden, looking wistfully at the flowers, perhaps for the last time. Rafella had flowers everywhere—in little tubs on the flagstones, potted on walls and up pillars, on the little well curb, trailing up stairways and spilling over the balcony. Romans might have designed the atrium, but Sephardic Jews had given it heart. When a man walks into his walled garden, he can rest in the bosom of his family and stand proudly before his God.

"Papa, you are late. It is the Sabbath already," scolded Daniel, stopping just short of embracing his father.

Manhood had left Daniel not knowing how to behave. Each night he wrestled with Lilith the Night Demon. Sometimes she had a familiar face—even Rachel's, or his mother's. Daniel would waken red-faced, ashamed of his soiled bed.

"I know it is the Sabbath already, my son," Aram said, putting his arm around Daniel.

Daniel looked up at the bittersweet sadness on his father's face. Someday, he vowed, when he grew up, he would build a caravel and fill it with Jews. He would sail out onto the Western Ocean. Every time they came to an island, Daniel would ask for a cross. When he came to an island where the people asked Daniel what a cross was, he would anchor his caravel and lead his people ashore.

"Are we going to read the Torah tonight, Papa?" asked Daniel.

"Yes, my son," said Aram.

"Eat first," said Rafella.

"Not tonight, Rafella," Aram said firmly. "Come with us into the secret room. We must hurry to keep the Sabbath one more time, because if the Jews keep the Sabbath, the Sabbath will keep the Jews."

Rafella had never felt the presence of the Shekhina-Matronit so keenly as she did when she followed her husband and her son into the little schoolroom. How she loved Aram Torres, her childhood playmate, her lover, her husband. If God truly becomes united with His Shekhina when a righteous man takes his wife into his arms, then Aram Torres had contributed his share to the Restoration.

Aram smiled at his wife over the flickering candle as he unrolled the Torah. If only the Holy Brotherhood would not come until he had taken her into his arms just one more time, Aram knew he could go with them— afraid perhaps, but unbowed.

"Eleven o'clock and all is serene! Eleven o'clock and all is serene! Eleven o'clock..." The call of the watchman died away.

Aram had read about Moses and the ten plagues, and as usual, he tried to answer Daniel's questions. Not being a rabbi, he gave simple answers, but he did the best he could.

"Papa," Daniel asked. "I am puzzled about the frogs."

"Well, you see, my son," said Aram, "when Pharaoh got disgusted with frogs in his house, in his bed, in his ovens and his kneading troughs, he asked Moses to petition God to take the frogs away. Then when Moses asked when the frogs should be taken away, Pharaoh replied, 'Tomorrow.'"

"That is what puzzles me. Why did Pharaoh want to spend one more night with the frogs?" asked Daniel.

"Who knows, my son?" said Aram. "Perhaps he had grown too accustomed to sleeping with frogs. Why didn't all the Jews leave Andalucía? Perhaps we, too, have grown too accustomed to frogs."

Suddenly they heard clattering hoofbeats echoing down the cavern of the narrow street. The front gate splintered, and hooded riders filled the patio, trampling Rafella's flowers. As the Conde de Córdoba rode down the door of the secret room, Aram put his arms around his wife and son.

"May the Lord watch between me and thee . . ." Aram prayed.

"The Inquisitor is expecting you," said Fray Dominic as Don Miguel herded the frightened family into the Patio of the Oranges. "Tie your horse to a tree and come with me."

Don Miguel dismounted. Aram Torres put his arms around his wife and son, and they followed Fray Dominic into the black-marble forest. Their footsteps echoed through the building. Only a few isolated lamps cast eerie shadows over the red-and-white-striped arches. Fray Dominic's flickering candle only increased the frightening shadows.

"Papa, are you afraid?" Daniel whispered.

"Are not all men sometimes afraid?" Aram countered.

"What are they doing to us, Papa?"

"Finding out whether or not we are men," said Aram.

"Am I a man, Papa?"

"You are almost thirteen. Behave like a man and you become a man."

"Silence!" ordered Don Miguel.

Aram tightened his hold around his wife and son. Daniel looked to see if dragons might be lurking in the marble forest. In a moment they stood before the glittering gold and lapis lazuli façade. Arched over the doorway and running along the top of the walls of the octagonal mihrab ran an inscription reading "Allah is great. Allah is good. There is no god but Allah."

"Wait inside the interrogation room," ordered Fray Dominic, who had been appointed notary for the interrogation. "Disrobe. The Inquisitor will join you presently."

Don Miguel and Fray Dominic disappeared, leaving the little family in almost total darkness. Even so, Daniel demurred at disrobing before his mother, until she reminded him he had come naked from her womb. They undressed, talking in whispers, but their very whispers were amplified by the dome of the mihrab. The Inquisitor had chosen his interrogation room well. Family members were usually separated for questioning, and the echoing cries of the tortured sometimes loosened the tongues of concerned relatives.

While they waited, not daring to put on their clothes again, Daniel picked a day in his life to live over again—the day the red-haired Cristóbal Colón had come to the bodega to meet Don Luis de Santángel. What a happy day that had been! Rachel helping him tend store...Rachel teasing for a licorice root...Rachel stamping her foot and saying that of course girls could sail across the Green Seas. Who said she was afraid?

Oh, Rachel, Rachel, where are you? thought Daniel, but he was sure in his heart that they would someday stand beneath the wedding canopy. Rachel, you and I will go together to that New World.

"Listen," warned Aram. "I hear them coming back."

"I hear nothing," said Rafella. "Nothing except the echo of our own voices."

"Hush! Listen!"

"I see a light," said Daniel. "Yes, they are coming. Oh, Papa, what shall we do?"

"Stand tall, my son. Be brave. Admit nothing. You are a baptized Christian, nothing more. They will see that you have never been circumcised."

"But you are circumcised, Papa."

"Yes, son, a long time ago when I was man enough to be a Jew," said Aram. "Now make me proud of you, Daniel."

"Yes, Papa." Daniel's heart beat so loudly he heard it echoing throughout La Mezquita.

Daniel's mind drew a protective curtain around the rest of that night. He remembered a table with a board running down the middle, and a pitcher wrapped in a cloth sitting on the table. Someone held Daniel while they strapped his father on the table with his back over the board and stuffed the cloth into his mouth; but mercifully Daniel did not remember the rest.

Daniel did not remember running away. He remembered the marble forest and the feel of a cool alabaster pillar as he leaned against it to catch his breath. He remembered frightful noises echoing as red-and-white arches flashed overhead, He saw a light and raced tiptoe over creaky old wooden floors. Racing, racing toward the light. He ran out of La Mezquita just as day announced itself and Doña Luisa Castro de Sandoval arrived for morning Mass. Daniel ran straight into her arms.

"Well, well," said the Condesa, staring at the black-eyed boy with the mop of curly hair and the beautiful body of an alabaster saint. "We shall have to speak to the Inquisitor about you."

Doña Luisa liked rescuing young boys from the Inquisitor.

CHAPTER 5

Córdoba, 1497

DURING THE year Daniel Torres had been at Almodóvar
Castle, Doña Luisa had filled her life with domestic
duties, Christian causes, and reminiscences of regal
splendors. Through a special arrangement with the Inquisitor of Córdoba, several young Jewish boys like
Daniel—whose parents were under indictment for heresy—had been turned over to Doña Luisa to raise as
Christians. Except for requiring more personal service
of them, she treated them little differently from her
pages. Every Tuesday she catechized them all, and when
they had been properly schooled in Spanish gallantry,
she dressed them in gold brocade, satin and velvet, and
showed them off on special occasions.

Doña Luisa liked weddings. Seven years ago she
had accompanied the royal entourage to Lisbon for
the wedding of Princess Isabela to Don João, heir
apparent to the Portuguese throne. She had wept bitterly when the Princess had been widowed shortly
afterward, but she still lived in the afterglow of that
royal wedding—talking about it as if it had happened
only yesterday.

"Poor darling Princess Isabela," she would tell her pages after catechism. "Barely twenty years old and already a widow. What great things might have happened if her husband had lived! Just think of the Iberian peninsula ruled by one Christian family!"

Doña Luisa's pages would squirm, trying to hide their impatience as she instructed them in the ways of royalty and nobility with tidbits of gossip, some of it centuries old. She would mingle talk of the Lisbon nuptials, the balls, and the hunting trips to Sintra Castle with stories of the long-ago-widowed Arabian queen who had once taken refuge in Almodóvar Castle.

Doña Luisa would fold her arms over her ample bosom and stare at her pages with her dark Spanish eyes, then she would warn them it was not prudent to gossip about royalty until after they were dead, or when they were safely away in a foreign country. Arabs loved a good story, as we all do, she would say, but you must remember the magpies—Portugal's good-luck charm.

"Once a Portuguese king in residence at Sintra Castle was seen kissing a maid in the garden," Doña Luisa would whisper, as if telling fresh gossip. "When someone repeated it to the Queen, the King called the gossips magpies and had them banished from court. Then he built a new room in the women's quarters and covered the ceiling with painted magpies to remind court women to watch their tongues."

Doña Luisa would look sternly at her pages to make sure they understood her meaning, then reinforce it by telling about the austere bedchamber in old Sintra Castle where a Portuguese king had once been imprisoned by his own wife for fifteen years.

"Royalty, too, has its burdens," she would warn.

Women like Doña Luisa ruled their castles with little interference from their husbands, who were often off on the business of knighthood. The rocky prominences the Romans had called *castros* dotted the Spanish countryside. The castro of Almodóvar had been thrown up beside the Guadalquivir before the world solidified in the mind of God—isolated, aloof, not easily assailable. Doña Luisa was also a castro—solitary, buttressed, vigilant, defensive.

Beneath such rocky fortresses as Almodóvar lay cavernous dungeons filled with the ghosts of past vengeance, and beneath Doña Luisa Castro de Sandoval's stern exterior lay a cavern as cold and as empty, filled with ghosts of what she might have been. She showed her feelings in cruel ways, like imprisoning Tahíaça in the castle dungeon when she learned the Indian girl was the daughter of Cacique Caonabó. Moorish slaves guarded Tahíaca, but some of the Jewish pages like Daniel felt sorry for her and did special favors for the Moorish guards to get to talk with her.

Tahíaca had been at Almodóvar almost two years now, and during her year in the dungeon, she and Daniel Torres had developed a deep friendship. Sometimes, when Daniel had nightmares, he would slip down to the dungeon to talk with her. She would tell him about Anacaona and Caonabó and life on Haiti, and he would tell her about Rachel and Rav Joseph and the life he planned when he went to the New World. Seldom did he mention his parents, from whom he had had no word during these long months they had been prisoners of the Inquisition.

Both Tahíaca and Daniel were happy when Doña Luisa and Don Miguel went to Toledo for the April wedding of Prince Juan Fernando to Princess Marguerita. Don Miguel, as a member of the cortes, came back puffed up with the importance of associating with other Spanish grandees also representing their cities in the cortes—Spain's legislative body. Doña Luisa preened herself before important clergymen and visiting foreign dignitaries, and came back with new tales to tell after catechism.

"Such a brilliant wedding," said Doña Luisa. "All the royal infants will soon be married except poor widowed Princess Isabela. Such fetes, such tournaments, such splendid clothes as we saw in Toledo. Even one impressive act-of-faith. Not all was gladness and light, though. One poor man was killed tilting with a lance. Nobility does have its price to pay."

When the seven-year-widowed Princess Isabela finally consented to marry her lovesick brother-in-law Prince Manoel—now heir apparent to the Portuguese throne, Doña Luisa looked forward to more celebrations. Don Manoel had been so in love with Princess Isabela he had agreed to convert all the Jews in Portugal so the entire peninsula would finally be Catholic. Because it was a second marriage for the Spanish Princess, Queen Isabela decided on private nuptials and only a small entourage, of which Doña Luisa was not a part.

Not to be denied her celebration, Doña Luisa used her influence with the Inquisitor of Córdoba to arrange an act-of-faith on the parade grounds beyond the gardens of the Alcázar of Córdoba. Familiars and notaries of the Inquisitor traveled about the countryside advertising the act-of-faith. They passed through Almodóvar-del-Río beating their drums and blowing their trumpets; then they carried the standard of the Inquisition up the steep hill to read the proclamation at the gates of Almodóvar Castle—formally announcing the act-of-faith in honor of the future Queen of Portugal. Several heretics were to be relaxed, including Aram and Rafella Torres.

Doña Luisa gloried in the fetes preceding the act-of-faith, presiding in the Hall of the Khalifs at Az-Zahra—where the celebrated arc lamp had once dazzled people who cringed from its magic—presiding in a manner befitting the Queen herself. Special indulgences had been promised by the Bishop to all who attended the act-of-faith, and people came from as far away as Málaga. The five miles from Córdoba to Az-Zahra blossomed gaily with decorated tents as they had during the reign of the Moors. No one slept much. Doña Luisa entertained almost constantly. She had even relented and allowed Tahíaca out of the dungeon, believing it would do the girl good to witness an act-of-faith, and she enjoyed showing off both the beautiful Indian girl and her handsome new page, Daniel Torres.

"What is an act-of-faith?" Tahíaca asked Daniel one day while they waited to serve amontillado to Doña Luisa's guests. "So many strange words make it difficult for me to understand."

"I don't know," Daniel said truthfully. "I used to ask my father, but he would never tell me. He would go, of course. Everyone had to go. But he is a doctor, and he would say my mother and I were sick and could not attend."

"But what is an act-of-faith?" Tahíaca persisted.

"Some kind of important celebration, I think. Lots of people come and no one gets any sleep. You could hear the noise all night long. I think there is a big bonfire of some kind at the end."

"Perhaps it is like an areíto," said Tahíaca. "Areítos are so much fun. All the neighboring villagers come. They feast and play ball, dance, and perform areítos praising past caciques. If they wish, I can dance the areíto of Cacique Caonabó. I do not sing as well as my mother, but I remember the dance steps. I can dance the Huracán dance, too. Do you think they will let me dance Caonabó and Huracán at the act-of-faith?"

"I do not think an act-of-faith is much like an areíto," said Daniel, who had the feeling it was something horrible. "My father always came home sad-faced, and my mother would cry for days."

"I wish they would have an areíto instead," Tahíaca said. "Caonabó was a very great Cacique. People here should know who he was so they can remember him."

"You may dance Caonabó's areíto for me sometime," Daniel offered.

During the week preceding the act-of-faith, Don Miguel rode from tent to tent renewing acquaintance with his comrades-in-arms, reliving Moorish battles, and speculating on the Enterprise of the Indies. Doña Luisa reigned at Az-Zahra, serving amontillado to guests. If such festivals served no higher purpose, they did display Spanish hospitality at its best. Tahíaca served wine, while Daniel and the other pages carried messages. Both listened, trying to make sense of the gossip.

"My dear, no one wants to go to the Indies now..."

"Doña Luisa, how can you let that heathen Indian girl stay near you? Didn't you lose a son at Navidad? The girl is charming, Luisa, utterly charming, but can you trust Don Miguel..."

"A little more wine, if you please..."

"No one can ever do for Spain more than Their Catholic Highnesses have done..."

"Still, weddings are expensive, and I hear the treasury is almost empty."

"With all the confiscations the Inquisition makes, where does the money go?"

"I hear this upstart Genoese, Colón, wants nearly three million maravedis to outfit another voyage. Three million! Says he needs six ships this time, to take out settlers, if he can find them..."

"Did you see Juana's wedding armada? Such a splendid flotilla, with the colors of all the noble houses and all the religious orders hanging from the gunwales. Now that King Fernando has assumed Grand Mastership of all the Orders, we shall no doubt see more such spectacles..."

"A splendid entourage, but so expensive..."

"Colón wants settlers now, does he? Who will go? Who really believes there are fortunes to be made there now? No one respectable, I assure you."

"Criminals, that's who! They are talking about permanent pardons. You know, ship the criminals over there and be rid of them."

"I can tell you one thing. Queen Isabela will insist on sending priests this time. Fray Buil was not the right man. The Queen is very concerned about the souls of her Indians. She is a very pious woman. Why, she wouldn't let Princess Isabela marry Prince Manoel until he agreed to make Portugal as Catholic as Spain."

"Why should he hesitate to do that? Portugal should never have let Jews settle there. No Christian nation of good conscience would have received them. If they rejected our Blessed Lord, why shouldn't we reject them?"

"Money, my dear. Lots of money. You know how rich

all Jews are. A few gold castellanos placed in the right hands..."

"They had to go somewhere, poor things. After all, they're human."

"With your permission, we must run along. It's almost dawn, and we must get a little sleep before tonight's Parade of the Green Cross. I hear the Bishop of Burgos, Don Juan de Fonseca, will be leading the procession."

"Isn't he the one in charge of outfitting expeditions to the Indies? He's a good man to know. Three million maravedis to spend for sheep and horses, cattle and pigs..."

"Santángel has the exclusive trade in horses. There are no horses in the Indies, and so they fetch a good price. Santángel will undoubtedly grow richer than he already is."

"A little more wine, ladies?"

"No, thank you. It's time to go. Until then, thanks for your hospitality."

"It's nothing. Until then..."

So it went throughout the week, crowds milling around seeing and being seen, drunks stumbling through narrow streets serenading the moon, ladies devouring conversations—pouring out words and storing them up for the coming lonely months in their castros. Nothing was quite so uplifting and inspiring as a public act-of-faith. For the Procession of the Green Cross, Doña Luisa had secured seats beside the old Roman Bridge.

Aram Torres had not seen his wife Rafella for nearly a year, for the cells they rented from the Inquisitor were far apart. Much of Aram's modest estate had been depleted to pay for their food and lodging while in prison. Not that it mattered. His belongings would all be confiscated anyway. Daniel, if they spared him, would have to fend for himself, making his way in the world under the cloud of his parents' heresy conviction.

Just before the Procession of the Green Cross, Fray Dominic brought Rafella to his cell. Aram looked deeply into his wife's eyes and knew she had remained steadfast. He put his arms around her briefly. How thin she was, and she was trembling. How Aram loved her! Rafella tried to cling to him as the Inquisitor pulled them apart and put them on opposite sides of the cell.

"Do you confess your sins before God and the Church, asking to be reconciled to the Holy Faith?" asked the Inquisitor.

"What sins?" asked Aram. "What are the charges against us? Who are the witnesses? Let us face our accusers."

"To persist in this heresy, unrepentant, will cause you to be relaxed."

"What have we to confess?" cried Rafella. "Tell us!"

"Do you know that when you have been relaxed, the Church in all its mercy can do nothing to save you? Do you understand, Aram Torres?"

"Who does not understand?" Aram asked in a tired voice.

He had been through it so many times in the past year. He knew all their tricks, and he had withstood all their tortures. He knew all the fabric of lies constructed of clever words to rid their consciences of the evil they were doing.

"Do you, Rafella Torres, understand the weight of your obstinacy?" asked the Inquisitor, turning his crenulated face to her.

"What would you have me understand?" asked Rafella, yearning to lean against Aram just once more, to absorb some of his strength.

"Do you understand how it grieves Our Lord when Jews reject Him as the Messiah? Do you understand your prayers cannot be heard so long as you continue in your evil ways? Do you understand how much the Church loves you? How our hearts yearn to see you reconciled? Do you know the Church cannot harbor in its very bosom enemies of Our Blessed Lord? Do you understand, Rafella Torres, the Church cannot continue to stand between sinners and an angry God?"

Rafella looked at the bitter, lined face of the Inquisitor—as twisted and contorted as his mind. He really believed what he was saying!

"Do you understand, Rafella Torres? Do you understand?"

Rafella straightened her shoulders and lifted her chin. Aram had never seen her look more beautiful. She looked the Inquisitor straight in the eye until he shifted his gaze; but if she had opened her mouth, torrents of rage would have poured forth, and she would not give them that satisfaction. She fought them with the only weapon she had, her awesome silence.

"Very well," said the Inquisitor through pinched lips. "Fray Dominic, you have been appointed to be their familiar—to walk beside them during the procession, to stay with them during the night, and to exhort them to repent and escape the terrible penalty awaiting those the Church is forced to relax to the civil authorities. If they persist in their heresy, may God have mercy on their souls."

Fray Dominic gave Aram and Rafella the short black san benitos of the convicted heretic, painted with red devils and flames licking up from the hems. Their tall conical corozas were also black, with red flames that seemed to frame their faces. Fray Dominic modestly turned his back while they donned their san benitos for the procession.

"Next year in Jerusalem," whispered Aram, placing the coroza on Rafella's majestically held head.

"Come, come," said Fray Dominic, handing them the tall staffs topped with Green Crosses. "We must not keep Bishop Fonseca waiting."

Tahíaca had never seen anything so solemn and impressive as the nighttime Procession of the Green Cross with candles flickering like twinkling stars. Mendicant friars, two by two, walking chanting the Miserere...the Bishop in his magnificent robes...the Green Cross lifted high above the streets...women leaning out of balconies to touch the Cross as it passed...mayors, justices, commissioners, members of the cortes...knights, squires, pages...abbots, priors, nuns, friars...the Inquisitor and his clerical staff walking slowly and solemnly behind the crimson Inquisitorial banner, with its Royal Arms, its sword and olive branch, its gilt staff and long gold and silver tassels...long black coffins and poles with effigies bobbing like cemís. People carrying smaller Green Crosses, and other people carrying tall yellow tapers...cherubic boys singing areítos. Nothing like this had ever happened in Haiti!

Daniel had one glimpse of his father and mother carrying the Green Crosses, and, although he had never seen an act-of-faith, he knew by their faces and strange clothing that something bad was happening. He was thirteen years old now—a man! What had his father said last year when the Holy Brotherhood arrested them and took them to La Mezquita? "Act like a man, and you become a man." Daniel felt he had to rescue his parents, but he did not know how.

Was he Joshua blowing trumpets to level walls? Or Gideon with lamps in pitchers? Or David with his sling against Goliath? Joshua and Gideon, and even David, had had armies to back them up. Was there an army that would fight for the Jews now?

The procession moved on, snakelike, through narrow streets, past Judah-ha-Levi Plaza, circling the Mezquita, past the Alcázar and over the Roman Bridge; then back again to the Roman walls and the burning place in the Field of the Martyrs. They planted the great Green Cross next to the stakes piled with faggots. Don Miguel and the knights of the Holy Brotherhood would guard this hallowed place through the night.

Don Miguel had a bitter taste in his soul—the taste of dry bones and pitiful old Jews dropping careless words, washing their hands after meals, burying their dead before sundown, associating with relatives who were known or suspected heretics. Did Spanish honor require a man to stop doing what he had done all his life? Must everyone eat pork? The Inquisition had not yet rid Spain of Jews who thought up new taxations. Such clever men, cleverer than Aram Torres, still sat at the King's right hand—good Catholics now. Santángel had the exclusive right to trade horses in the New World, and had used his influence to escape being charged with the assassination of the Inquisitor Pedro Arbués. Money and brains made the difference, not honor. What these Jews were guilty of was not having brains enough to keep their mouths shut, or money enough to bribe the Inquisitor.

Don Miguel had lived all his life as a Catholic knight, doing his duty without question, but sometimes, when he was alone, doubts surfaced. He looked up at the sky above the ring of mountains around Córdoba, trying to pierce the veil. Are you there, God? Did Jesus ascend into Heaven on a bolt of light? Was Mary a virgin? Do saints' bones perform all those ridiculous miracles? As always when such heretical thoughts came to him, he stopped himself from thinking. The machinery of the Inquisition creaked a bit, but it would unmercifully grind anyone who voiced such doubts. Perhaps he had served the Holy Brotherhood too long, heard too much, seen too many Jews tortured, smelled too much smoke.

"Five o'clock and all is serene," announced the watchman.

Almost morning, and all serene. Serene? Not deep in the Spanish soul where a man had to answer to himself. Don Miguel reminded himself he was a good Catholic and must leave such matters to the Church. He shrugged off the early morning chill, left his subordinate in charge, and went to the kitchens where chefs had worked all night preparing refreshments for visiting dignitaries.

People who usually slept late were up early this morning to get good seats. Acts-of-faith were all-day affairs, with music and sermons and processions, before the final reading of the charges and the sentencing. Seldom did the people of Córdoba have such exciting entertainment. Doña Luisa, flanked by Tahíaca and Daniel, sat high up on the stands, waving at latecomers in their finest velvet breeches and brocade doublets, their tallest capriotes with long flowing scarfs. Knights in polished armor stood guard. Dignitaries milled about, seeing and being seen.

First came the soldiers, harquebuses at their shoulders, marching smartly with swords rattling at their sides. They formed two lines flanking the stage. Then

201

came two acolytes: one solemnly tolling a bell, the other carrying the Church's immense processional cross. Behind the cross a Dominican friar scourged a penitent in a ragged yellow san benito with double red crosses on back and front. She had been sentenced at some previous act-of-faith to be publicly scourged on Sundays and feast days and special occasions for the next seven years—excepting, of course, during her required pilgrimage to Santiago de Compostela.

Then came the penitents who, under torture, had confessed to heresy and asked to be reconciled today. They wore long yellow san benitos with red crosses, and were flanked by Dominican familiars. They would wear these san benitos until they died, and then the rags would be hung in the Cathedral to remind others of the dangers of heresy. Next came two coffins of a couple charged posthumously, followed by three straw-stuffed effigies carried by solemn young clerics—effigies of people who had fled to escape trial. Property of dead and fugitive heretics could not be legally confiscated until the ceremony of burning had been carried out.

Finally came Aram Torres and his wife Rafella, the only two people who had remained steadfast under torture, who had neither confessed nor repented. Even now Fray Dominic and one of his brothers walked by their sides urging repentance. By confessing now, they would be mercifully strangled before being burned.

Daniel Torres did not remember the rest of the ceremonies—the city officials mounted on prancing caparisoned horses, the jewel-bedecked representatives of Their Catholic Highnesses, the Bishops, the black habits and brown habits, the black-and-white habits—marching solemnly two by two and chanting the Salve Regina.

Nor did Daniel hear the long sermons, nor see the people chatting with each other around the platform, nor the dignitaries going back and forth to the refreshment stands, nor vendors selling sweetmeats behind the stage where the coffins were stacked. Daniel did not hear the charges, or see the crimson velvet box with the gold fringe or the friar who opened the sentence box with a gold key. Nor did he see his parents kneeling in front of the pulpit to hear for the first time the charges brought against them.

"Rafella Torres de Sánchez, you are charged with being a judaizer. To wit: changing your linens on Friday before sunset, preparing on Friday food enough to be eaten on Saturday, pinching off a bit of dough and tossing it into the fire before baking bread, searching out meat slaughtered according to Mosaic law, refusing to cook cockles or mussels...

"Aram Torres...for introducing your innocent son to Jewish rites, for keeping feast days, for placing your hands on his head without making the sign of the cross, for standing against the wall of the old synagogue praying as is the custom of the Jews...

"Aram Torres...Rafella Torres, for your heinous crime of heresy you are hereby relaxed to the civil authorities for sentencing. May God have mercy on your souls."

Daniel remembered none of this. His eyes glazed over and his ears refused to hear. He traveled in his mind back to that night when he had come to fetch his father and found him praying in the old synagogue—his father's face half in shadow, and the moonlight playing across chipped Hebrew inscriptions. He felt his father's hands on his head and his father's arm around him as they walked up the deserted Street of the Jews. Daniel could see warm light streaming out of the secret room.

Daniel walked woodenly beside Doña Luisa to the burning place. His eyes were open, but he did not see the flames nor hear Tahíaca scream as she saw what was happening and wrestled with the guards, who kept her from interfering. The Most High, blessed be His Holy Name, blotted out Daniel's memory, never to be revealed until the hour of his death.

CHAPTER 6

Córdoba, 1497

FOR CENTURIES Iberia had been the mystic battleground between Good and Evil as Jews, Mohammedans, and Christians all sought in their own ways to comprehend Life and the great Nothingness of Infinity. Evil is but an absence of good, and the fiercest battles are fought in the soul of a single man. Don Miguel Sandoval, Conde de Córdoba, lost his final battle at the burning of Aram and Rafella Torres.

Don Miguel began drinking when he returned to Almodóvar; yet the more he drank, the more the stench filled his nostrils. He vomited, then drank again. Across the blurred landscape of his mind rode his son Rodrigo astride a white horse. Don Miguel started, called out. Rodrigo faded away.

Don Miguel poured himself another cup of wine, and Rodrigo rode by on a red horse brandishing a dripping sword. Don Miguel sat very still this time, hoping his son would speak to him. Rodrigo faded away.

The oil burned low and the lamp wick sputtered, plunging the great hall of the castle into darkness. Into that darkness rode his son on a horse blacker than darkness itself—balancing the two halves of the world on a scale.

Don Miguel sprang to his feet, looking for his sword to avenge his son. He swore by Santiago to trade his soul for vengeance. He knew what he had to do. One act alone united man and Creator: Love! And the opposite of Love is Lust.

Tahíaca, too, awoke from a fearful trip into the spirit world—the valley beyond Death where the opia live. Suddenly he sprang upon her. He pounded her, tore her legs apart, drove deep within her. He tried to lose himself in her in order to hide the love tormenting him. She fought, knowing without feeling for his navel that he had been born without Mother and without Love. The more she fought, the more he enjoyed the fight. She was fighting for her life, knowing he meant to kill her before he knew it himself.

To Don Miguel this she-cat was all the harlots outcast from Christendom—the fallen virgins, the Jezebels, the betrayers. Laughing wildly, he vented the lust denied at all the shrines. He tried to banish evil so female purity could live again. He tried to destroy the Mother so he could destroy the son. He wanted to return to Nothingness so he could stop the torment of being alive.

He poured his burning dregs into her and left her barely conscious on the floor of the dungeon. He felt an exuberance that the sword of his body had been enough to kill her. Then Tahíaca groaned. He turned to go for his sword. Standing in the door like an avenging angel was his wife, Doña Luisa.

"Holy Mary, Mother of God!" he muttered.

Doña Luisa was beyond caring how many women Don Miguel had or how many bastards he had fathered, or even that he had taken this girl under her own roof. She was immune to whisperings now—insulated by the scars of too many hurts. She moved Tahíaca to the tower so she would have a few days to find some way to rid the castle of the girl before Don Miguel wanted her again. She did not ask herself whether she was protecting the girl or her husband or herself. She reasoned nothing out, for reasoning might have plunged her into despair. She only knew she must get rid of the Indian girl.

Tahíaca lay in a stupor on the floor of her tower prison. She neither knew nor cared how long she had lain there. Then she heard the music. Someone was strumming a mandolin and singing a lusty country tune, stopping now and then to scold a dog and call to a herd of swine. Tahíaca had never felt such a call to life. She had to see who was singing and perhaps join him in his song. Painfully she sat up, finding she could move if she did not move too quickly. She tried the door to her tower prison, but found it locked. She pushed a bench against the wall and climbed up to look.

Coming through an olive grove on the slope below the castle, she saw a young man with a pack on his back, carrying a mandolin and seeming to float on a sea of hogs. Big hogs and little pigs, fat pregnant sows and big mean-tusked boars. Little piglets ran alongside big-titted sows, and lusty shoats tried to mount everything in sight. Black hogs, red hogs, spotted hogs— grunting and snorting, snuffling and squealing, running away and being chased by the dog, getting underfoot and being kicked by the man.

Amid all the confusion walked the swineherd, jauntily strumming his mandolin, shaking his long black hair out of his eyes, smiling as though he were the King himself. Something about the swineherd reminded Tahíaca of Caonabó before the invaders came. Caonabó had always moved amid flocks of parrots and crowds of children. Caonabó would sling his hammock over his shoulder and go to the gold rivers. Love twisted Tahíaca's heart, and the pain of seeing the swineherd walk free captivated her soul. She sat down in the corner of the tower and sent her spirit out to walk among the swine. She was still sitting there when Daniel opened the door.

"Come quickly," he said. "Doña Luisa wants you."

Tahíaca followed Daniel down the spiral stairway of the old Visigothic tower and into the courtyard—overrun now with swine rooting in the flower beds and defecating on the flagstones. Doña Luisa stood by the fountain arguing with the swineherd.

"Is this the Indian girl?" asked the swineherd, looking at Tahíaca and liking what he saw. "Someone has been mistreating her. Are you sure she is a good worker?"

"Yes, I tell you. The very best. She will do whatever you wish," Doña Luisa tilted her head slyly. "Whatever you wish, understand?"

"Then why did you beat her?"

"My husband..." Doña Luisa stopped. "A condesa does not need to explain to a swineherd. I have offered you a good bargain. Leave the sow and her piglets, but get the girl out of my sight."

The swineherd started out the castle gate, not looking back at Tahíaca but expecting her to follow. Tahíaca could not believe her spirit had arranged things this quickly. Was she really free to go with him? She looked at Doña Luisa, who was gingerly working her way around the droppings.

"Well, why are you standing here?" Doña Luisa asked. "Go! And never come back!"

The swineherd was still strumming his mandolin and singing when Tahíaca caught up with him. He paused long enough to ask her name.

"Tahíaca," she said, then remembered her manners. "But my Christian name is Isabela."

"Tahíaca is a very good name," he said. "I am called Ramón. Ramón Fuentes, the swineherd, but someday I am going to be somebody."

"Where are we going, Ramón?" Tahíaca asked.

"To Sevilla, where I am going to sell my hogs to Don Cristóbal Colón. I, Ramón Fuentes, am going to see the New World!"

Like the other women who ruled Spain's high mountain castros, Doña Luisa was a stained-glass mosaic made up of bits and pieces of colorful visions, daydreams, and memories—ever-changing, living patterns. What she might have been and what she longed to be had become fragments of what she was—jagged scraps fused together in the crucible that had been her life. Passionate as only women of warm southern climes and Oriental heritage can be passionate, Doña Luisa might have made a fine whoremonger if life had not cast her as a Spanish matron.

When she thought about her son Rodrigo, she thought about the day he would come riding up the hill victorious from his conquest of Colón's New World. When she thought about her husband Don Miguel, she refused to think about all the women he bedded, but she thought about all the romantic things he had done during their courtship. So long as he made even one romantic gesture once in a while, Doña Luisa was happy. In the meantime, she had her pages.

Doña Luisa did not know how deeply she loved Daniel Torres, but she looked forward to Tuesdays when she could pick out his face in the group and concentrate on teaching this poor boy the Christian catechism. Today she was annoyed because the transaction with the swineherd had made her late. As she swept into the little chapel, the pages scurried to their prayer rails. The chapel at Almodóvar was a small anteroom off Doña Luisa's bedchamber. The pages nudged each other as she hurried through the ritual, knowing that when she hurried it was because she had decided one of them needed private instruction. Daniel had answered all the questions correctly, or so he thought as he sang the last notes of the Salve Regina and turned to leave.

"One moment, please, Daniel." Doña Luisa's voice had a strange throaty quality.

"Yes, Doña Luisa, at your service." Daniel bowed low with a flourish as she had taught him to do.

The pages snickered. Don Miguel had ridden away yesterday, and the Condesa had paced the battlements all last night. They had all witnessed the scene in the courtyard with the swineherd. Attending Doña Luisa at such times had been part of their education for knighthood, so the pages knew what Daniel could expect.

"Come with me, Daniel." The Condesa swept by the other pages as if she did not see them. "We must review your catechism."

One of the pages stuck out his foot to trip Daniel, but Daniel deftly stepped aside.

"Daniel is going to be circumcised, not catechized," simpered another page.

If the Condesa heard these taunts, she ignored them. Nothing mattered now except the hunger kindled in her that morning at La Mezquita when she saw the rising sun shining on Daniel's alabaster body. Doña Luisa did not like being obvious, nor did she wish to rush. Tuesdays were to be savored.

In her private sessions, Doña Luisa always scrupulously catechized her pages, providing herself with endless opportunities to straighten their souls while admiring their bodies. She would question them rigidly, pacing her chamber like a hungry lioness—scolding and chiding, praising and rewarding. For wrong answers she gave a smart slap on the hand with a leather strap; for correct ones a hearty hug and kiss.

Today Daniel gave many wrong answers to escape the nausea that overwhelmed him when she folded him against that smothering, overgenerous, unwashed bosom. Daniel could remember the sweet, fresh-washed smell of his fastidious mother hugging him on Sabbath eve. He remembered Rachel's fresh Sabbath laces peeping out from under her skirts.

"Daniel, you are not paying attention," Doña Luisa said crossly, taking another sip of wine from the silver cup. She always drank heavily during these private sessions. "I promised the Inquisitor to be like a mother to you. To raise you up in the Holy Catholic Faith. You really must try harder."

"Yes, Doña Luisa." Daniel looked down at his bare feet.

"Don't you think it is warm in here?" asked the Condesa. "I'll just loosen my blouse a bit."

As if Lilith the Night Demon had swept into the room, Daniel felt himself incapable of looking at Doña Luisa. He knew the nipples would be standing out against the black embroidery on her white undershirt. Oh, Rachel, sweet Rachel. Daniel raced on spirit winds searching for his lost love, his chosen girl for the canopy. Where are you, Rachel? Sweet Rachel.

Noon brought stifling heat to the sultry castle, but no relief from the endlessly repeated questions and answers. Doña Luisa drank steadily, pacing her bedchamber, discarding piece after piece of clothing, clutching wildly at Daniel, crying and calling him her love, her little lost love.

"Pour me some more wine, beloved," Doña Luisa mumbled, abandoning the pretense of catechism. "Pour your dear mother a few more drops of wine."

Daniel tipped the goatskin wine bottle, but only a few dregs dribbled onto the bottom of the cup. Doña Luisa made a face and poured them out on the floor.

"Fetch another bottle," she ordered. "But don't tarry too long, sweetmeat, I have something very interesting to teach you."

The smirk on her face followed Daniel from the room. Did he dare leave the castle? Just walk out the front door? Find Tahíaca and the swineherd and run away to Sevilla? No, Doña Luisa would send the guards after him if he did not return. Oh, Rachel, sweet Rachel. Daughter of Israel. Mother of my future sons... Rachel...little lost Rachel...

Daniel selected a large bottle of wine. He wished he had some of the herbs his father used to mix as sleeping potions. If he could get her to sleep, get her drunk enough...Reluctantly, he returned to the bedchamber. Doña Luisa had taken off all her clothes and was stretched out on the bed with her eyes closed. Daniel shuddered at the sight of the doughy gobs of fat. Hoping she was alseep, he put the wine bottle on the table beside her bed and started backing out of the room.

"Ah, beloved, what took you so long?" Doña Luisa roused from her doze.

Daniel stared at her fascinated and horrified as she lay there stroking the black forest between her legs. His stomach turned, and he could hardly keep from retching. Quickly he filled her cup and held it to her lips while she drank, insisting she drink it all. Dribbles fell on her breasts. She clutched at him, but he arched backward. She grabbed thin air, then grabbed again. Her stench filled his nostrils.

"Come closer, baby," she whispered, taking one bulbous breast in hand to offer him the nipple.

"Have a little more wine, Doña Luisa," he urged.

"Not until...not before...Oh, love, come here to me! Doña Luisa is so lonely, so lonely...so tired and lonely..." Her voice trailed off into gibberish. "Rodrigo...my son...my baby boy..."

Doña Luisa was snoring loudly as Daniel hurried out of her bedchamber, through the chapel, and down the back stairs into the courtyard. It was siesta, and not even the servants were about. Daniel knew he must waste no time in finding Tahíaca and the swineherd. No one would look for a Hebrew boy tending hogs.

CHAPTER 7

Lisbon, 1497

KING MANOEL of Portugal signed the edict on a rainy December day only a few months before Aram and Rafella Torres were relaxed in Córdoba. In keeping his marriage contract to make Iberia Christian, he gave Jews like Rav Joseph and his daughter Rachel ten months to convert or leave Portugal. He also opened the way for his heir to occupy the combined thrones of Spain and Portugal, for Prince Juan Fernando, the only male Spanish heir, had died shortly after his wedding to Princess Marguerita of Austria.

Almost immediately, King Manoel launched a campaign of forced conversion, for Portugal had prospered since the Jews migrated from Spain, and King Manoel did not want to lose such an industrious people. He ordered all who planned to leave to embark from Lisbon, then he bottled them up in the Alfama awaiting permission to go.

Every day bearded patriarchs like Rav Joseph crowded into the little split-level triangular Plaza of the Jews in the Alfama to argue now about something besides Talmudic interpretations.

Rachel Sánchez was eleven now—more matron than child, having taken care of Rav Joseph since her mother died. Rachel hated Lisbon in winter when so much rain fell that even church tiles turned moldy gray. Clothes could not be hung out to dry, and the twisted, overcrowded anthill called the Alfama always smelled sour. Jews lived in one small section, crowded two or three families to a room, with more and more arriving every day. No amount of ritual purification could mask the musty smell.

Rachel could scarcely find a corner to read to Rav Joseph, whose eyesight was failing and who wanted to memorize as much of the precious Torah as he could before the light went out entirely. When news came of King Manoel's edict, pandemonium had broken out in the Alfama, and the people had jammed the little plaza to hear Rav Joseph's advice. Rachel had led her father through the crowd and up to the platform on the top level. Rav Joseph raised his hands in benediction, and the crowd quieted. He cleared his throat and spat.

"The Most High, blessed be His Holy Name, will not leave His children comfortless," he began. "Trust in Him. Keep His commandments, and..."

"Don't mouth platitudes, old man," said a disgusted fisherman. "They ran us out of Jerusalem, and they ran us out of Spain. How many places are there for Jews to run?"

"Perhaps He will perform a miracle," said Rav Joseph.

"Like the Red Sea parting, or the Walls of Jericho tumbling down? You know, Rav Joseph, I believe God is about out of miracles. I spit on God."

"Don't allow your troubles to cause you to blaspheme, my son. Remember how the hand of the Lord smote the Egyptians, and how the Shekhina-Matronit sustained our people through forty years in the wilderness of Sinai. Are our afflictions any greater? No, I tell you. It is our faith that is weak."

Rachel looked up at her father with adoring eyes as he calmed the fears of the restless, bewildered people. Surely, if God was a Father, He was something like

Rav Joseph. Didn't He also need His Shekhina-Matronit to give him a little nudge once in a while? Rav Joseph had always seemed so strong to his people, and only Rachel knew he had doubts and fears. On the day of the edict, however, Rav Joseph had had no practical solutions for his people, and they soon fell to disputing among themselves.

Rachel had never had time to be a child, not since that day five years ago when their leaky little boat had landed safely in Lisbon, and Rav Joseph had kissed the marble paving stones in municipal square. The refugees had landed only a short distance down river from Belem, the little chapel where Prince Henry the Navigator used to pray. There he had built his school for navigators, and there, as the Portuguese like to say, the New World begins. Half the ships' captains of Europe had learned navigation in Prince Henry's school.

Rachel had followed her father that day, wide-eyed, as he led his weary little congregation up the hill to their new home in the Alfama where the rabble eked out a living: fishermen, Moroccan pirates, thieves, beggars, prostitutes, sodomites, and Jews. The dregs of mankind found a refuge on the maze of snakelike streets contorting around themselves through garbage-spattered passageways paved with slimy cobblestones. Here a windowbox full of flowers defied the squalor. There curses rained down with slops from second-story windows. Flies swarmed up as ragged urchins ran by, then settled back on yesterday's fish—oblivious of the screeches of old women the children had just robbed. Idle fishermen strummed heart-shaped lutes for dancing Gypsies. At the foot of the hill lay the Monastery of Saint Vincente de Ferrar, where a few people from the Alfama attended Mass. On top of the opposite hill, in solitary splendor, Saint George's Castle brooded over Lisbon's seven hills.

Rachel was growing to womanhood shaped by the Alfama. Already she could deftly escape clutching hands, and already she could cleverly turn aside seductive comments. She dreamed of having Daniel's children as she heard what passed for lovemaking in the crowded dark, and already she had learned to masturbate.

Rachel was practical, resourceful, self-reliant — sometimes scheming, always compassionate, ultimately fatalistic. She kept Daniel's few letters hidden behind a loose stone in the wall. Sometimes when life became too burdensome, she would take Daniel's letters down under the old Roman Bridge at the end of the street where the locked gate marked the limits of the judería. She would read his letters over and over, looking up from time to time at the wide bay formed by the mouth of the Tagus River.

Rachel was under that bridge daydreaming about Daniel and the New World across the Ocean Sea, so she missed being rounded up by the soldiers who came to the Alfama to carry all the children to Saint Vincente's to be baptized. King Manoel had mistakenly believed if he baptized the children, the parents would follow. When Rachel realized she had miraculously escaped baptism, she bought a cross and began wearing it. If she saw someone looking suspiciously at her, she would slip into the monastery chapel and kneel with her hands folded until they went away satisfied.

Of course, Jews did not convert as easily as King Manoel had hoped. They had already uprooted themselves from one country, and they began writing to relatives in Turkey and North Africa, in England and the Low Countries. While they waited in the Alfama for permission to leave, food became scarce. However, Rachel always managed to find enough to feed Rav Joseph and herself, with a little left over to make the blessing of sharing. She would be at the docks at daybreak when the fishing fleet came in, and she seemed to hear the rumble of farm wagons before they reached the foot of the hill. Sometimes she even managed to find a pinch of saffron to add to the stew, but she hadn't had a licorice root in so long she had forgotten how much she liked them.

Even packed in on top of each other as they were in the Alfama, and with a threatening exile hanging over their heads, the Jews of Lisbon found ways to celebrate.

As spring greened the hills, the little triangular plaza sprang to life. Hands clapped the rhythm of the lute and feet danced away the cobblestones. With little to fill their bellies, they found much to fill their souls; they leaned together to resist King Manoel's forced conversions.

Rachel and her father had one of their few quarrels over the subject of conversions. Rachel saw no harm in obeying the law and going through the motions to avoid deportation. In fact, she had been going around the Alfama urging others to be baptized, or at least to wear the cross and give the appearance of being Christian. Rav Joseph, of course, was bitterly opposed to such hypocrisy. When he found out what Rachel had been doing, he confronted her. When she admitted it, he spat in her face and called her a curse and an abomination who should never have been born. Rachel slowly wiped the spittle from her face, put her hands on her hips, and looked Rav Joseph straight in the eye. She had known he would find out, and she had rehearsed what she would say.

"What use is a dead Jew?" she asked. "Can he be counted to make up a minyan? Can she make a blessing? If Jews run away again and again, soon we will have no place to run. We will be Ezekiel's valley of dry bones."

"Don't quote the Prophets to me, you Jezebel. You monger for the Great Whore of Babylon. I have seen that badge of shame you wear around your neck under your dress. I followed you once to Saint Vincente's when you took a family to be baptized. You are no daughter of Israel, and you are no daughter of mine!"

"I am alive!" she said. "Alive! Do you hear me? And so are you. We eat every day, don't we? Do you think they sell food to Jews?"

"Better to starve the body than starve the soul," said Rav Joseph, turning his back on her. "Get out of my sight. You do not keep the Law—the first Commandment given to Moses: 'Thou shalt have no other gods before me.' You are no longer flesh of my flesh. Your mother would turn over in her grave."

217

Rachel paled. Her fingers seemed to feel the chill of her mother's cold cheek, and she could almost see the startled "Oh" on her mother's dead lips. She walked around Rav Joseph as he kept turning away.

"Leaving her home killed my mother," she said accusingly, and Rav Joseph stopped walking. "Don't you know that, Papa?"

"A Jew has no home except Jerusalem," he said, but his voice was full of discouragement and his shoulders were slumped. "Your mother was true to herself and true to the Most High, blessed be His Holy Name. She was born a Jew, and she died a Jew. She never desecrated her body by wearing a cross around her neck. That, and not the badge they make us wear, is the true badge of shame!"

"You call this cross a badge of shame, and you think wearing it makes me a Christian?" Rachel removed the cross and dangled it in the feeble rays of the midday sun. "Is it what you wear around your neck, or how you feel in your heart? I was born a Jew. I will die a Jew. But until that day comes, I will live. I will live, Father, do you understand me? By whatever means I can. Someday I will marry with Cousin Daniel, and I am not leaving Lisbon to go where he can't find me. I am no more of a Christian than you are, and you know it!"

A crowd had gathered around them now, and Rav Joseph wanted to stop the embarrassing argument. He could see some truth in what she said, but he knew he could never convert, no matter what they did to him. As rabbi of the community of Israel in the Alfama, how could he counsel his people to be baptized? Rav Joseph was speechless. He shrugged his shoulders and turned away once more. Rachel put the cross back around her neck and went down the hill hoping to find a farmer with a few turnips.

As the deadline for deportation neared, panic sent some Jews to the baptismal font, but a hard core held out. Rachel now wore a cross and attended Mass daily, to conceal the fact that she had not been baptized, and she stubbornly refused to leave Lisbon. Rachel ducked into the monastery when King Manoel's soldiers came into the Alfama to arrest the holdouts, including Rav Joseph, imprisoning them in the dungeons beneath Saint George's Castle until they agreed to be baptized. Meanwhile, they were held without food.

Rachel went every day to Saint George's to take food to Rav Joseph. The guards always took the food, and after a few visits, Rachel stopped urging Rav Joseph to be baptized. Finally, starvation weakened the resistance of all but a handful of old men. Rav Joseph might have held out too, and gone with them into exile in North Africa, but at the very last he could not bring himself to abandon Rachel. After all, no matter how mature she seemed, she was still only a child.

Rachel was waiting in the castle parade grounds when they brought Rav Joseph up from the dungeons. He was so emaciated he could not walk without help, and his eyesight was so near gone he did not even blink in the sunlight. He leaned on Rachel as he stumbled down the hill to the monastery, but she turned her back so she would not have to see him baptized. That night, after she had fed him and put him to sleep, she took both their crosses and tossed them into the pot of slops. All the rest of their days in Lisbon, their crosses smelled slightly putrid.

Rav Joseph tried not to think of the handful of old men who had held out for North Africa. He concentrated on finding a new place each week for the secret services. Wherever God's Torah rested, there the Shekhina shed Her presence over the Ark, comforting the people.

Early in the fall, just as it began to rain again, a letter came from Santángel. He was sorry to inform them, he wrote, that Aram Torres and his wife Rafella had been relaxed in an act-of-faith. Their son Daniel had been given to the Condesa de Córdoba to be raised a Christian. Rachel read the letter aloud to her father, without crying. Then she rolled it up neatly and put it behind the stone with the others.

CHAPTER 8

Carmona, 1497

"BLOOD OF the Moors"—so Andalucíans call the great
red splotches of wild poppies spangled over the hills
and valleys between Córdoba and Sevilla. Ramón
Fuentes was an important man with two servants; he
strutted along the winding Guadalquivir River watching farmers burn wheat stubble, strumming his mandolin, and singing romantic Spanish ballads—poignant,
sweet ballads, foot-stomping, hand-clapping ballads.
How Ramón loved to sing!

Ramón Fuentes never hurried. Life was too short to
hurry. If he and his ambling herd of swine did not reach
Sevilla in time for Colón's third voyage, Ramón would
wait for the next, or for whatever supply flotillas might
sail in between. Hogs did not like to be hurried, and
neither did Ramón. No matter how much he might
hurry, he knew he could never become an hidalgo, for
he had both Moorish and Jewish blood in his ancestry.
A man had to prove eight generations of Christian blood,
untainted by Moor or Jew, in order to become an hidalgo
(short for "hijo-de-algo," which meant *son of someone*).

Ramón knew he could never be an hidalgo, but he was determined to be the someone his sons were sons of.

"The children of my children's children will be hidalgos," he would tell Daniel and Tahíaca, "strong men to fight for the New World, beautiful women to set guitars playing outside barred windows."

Slowly they made their way down the river valley. Sows jostled along grubbing under the oaks while suckling pigs nuzzled for their dinners. The granddaddy boar ambled along unaware of his destiny, trying to ignore his great noisy brood. Sometimes he would accept the challenge of a frisky shoat, but after a few strokes of that massive head with its upcurved tusks, Ramón would be peddling fresh pork, and Tahíaca would be turning ham hock over an oak fire. Daniel knew he shouldn't eat pork, but he liked the sweet savory taste of roast pork the way Tahíaca cooked it, with a few cloves of garlic tucked under the skin.

Ramón and Daniel sometimes hired out to the reapers, or helped them burn stubble and plant watermelons, or helped strip bark from cracked old cork oaks— leaving the trunks bleeding red. Tahíaca heard the soul of the tree cry out the first time she saw Ramón strip away bark, but he told her the tree would heal and grow a new skin even finer-grained than the first. The tree would choke if the bark was not peeled away, he told her, but still Tahíaca could not bear to watch.

Sometimes they camped with Gypsies, and Tahíaca taught them the Huracán areíto. Gypsy women taught Tahíaca to sew ruffles on her skirts so when she danced the skirts would billow like the wild surf during a storm.

Ramón decided to winter in Carmona. He found an abandoned house inside the walls of the castle of Peter the Cruel, who had imprisoned three of his lovers in the castle atop the hill. Ramón and Daniel hired themselves out to help with the castle restoration—a project Their Catholic Highnesses had undertaken because they admired the view from the hill. Tahíaca soon had their patio blooming with flowers like the patios of the Córdobans.

Sometimes Tahíaca would go outside the castle walls

while it was still dark and sit beside an old olive tree with twin trunks to watch dawn push back the world. First there would be only a black velvet sky sprinkled with stars, then there would be Tahíaca and the olive tree. Then the patchwork farms where Gypsy campfires sparkled like stars, and earth and sky seemed to blend together in one sea of infinity. Tahíaca liked best the time, the briefest of moments, when she and the tree floated in a blue-lavender universe alone with the stars.

A hundred years ago this olive tree had been four sprouts planted close to each other, so if some died the others would grow and bear fruit. Two died, two lived, twining around each other. Tahíaca felt she and Ramón might be like this olive tree someday. Rodrigo had been too vibrant and exciting to live, but Ramón was a man for twining a life.

Every evening in their patio in Carmona was an areíto. Gypsies would gather in the lamplight among the flowers, laughing and singing and dancing on the marble flagstones. Ramón would play his mandolin, and Daniel would sing the old plaintive Andalucían ballads. Tahíaca would pick up a pair of cockleshells and begin dancing Huracán's dance, Anacaona's areíto Andalucían style.

Tahíaca danced Huracán, father of winds, creator of order out of chaos...dancing feet...whirling arms... billowing skirts...tapping heels...clicking cockleshells...Tahíaca would bring down the Voice of Heaven into the patio of Carmona. One hand curved over her head, one curved around her stomach in the old, old symbol of Creation—of the Chaos from which all things come, of beginning and end, of destruction and regeneration...of Force beyond control...of Huracán—omnipotent God of the Winds come to dwell among men.

Tahíaca would dance faster and faster, stamping her heels and waving her arms while her face mirrored both her awe and her sorrow, and the layers of ruffles the Gypsies had sewn to her skirt rippled like the waves of the sea as her fast fingers clicked the cockleshells into a tumult. Ramón caught her rhythm, adding plaintive melodies, and soon beautiful Gypsy girls were dancing Anacaona's song. The waves of the past, the indomitable waves of Huracán Himself, blended with the waves of the future in the patios of Andalucía in a dance the Gypsies began calling *flamenco*. Thus, Anacaona's areíto spread itself abroad on the winds, seeding Huracán on Andalucían hillsides among the poppies.

Everyone wanted to learn Tahíaca's dance. Men danced it with a particular wild flavor, and soon people were giving it variations and teaching it to each other. Tahíaca now began to feel she belonged. Rodrigo faded into a misty dream, replaced by the laughing Ramón with the shock of curly hair falling over his forehead. He was a small man, like her people, the Tainos. Tahíaca could almost believe she had been born to Andalucían life inside crumbling castle walls. When she thought of Caonabó and Anacaona it was to remember the good things—the rides on her father's shoulders when she had gone to meet him in the forest, and the dance her mother had danced with such gravity and grace.

One morning Tahíaca awoke with Hurácan tearing at her belly with his four-fingered hand. She clutched the belly as if it had a life of its own. She had managed to keep the cemí the old buhuitihu had taken from her body when he healed her after Rodrigo was killed. She knew the tumbling meant Huracán was creating another being out of nothingness, so she clutched her cemí and prayed as homesickness overwhelmed her.

For the first time in her life she felt she was not where she belonged. Oh, to be in Haiti where Caonabó would cut down a sturdy mahogany tree and fashion headboards so his grandchild's forehead would be tall and broad. Caonabó's wives would make an areíto, and all the caciques would begin choosing names for Caonabó's first grandchild. But Andalucía was not Haiti, and Caonabó was dead. The child Tahíaca carried was neither Taino nor Carib.

For a while Tahíaca carried her homesickness alone, keeping to herself among the swine she herded out the gate of the castle and down the hill every morning, moving shadowlike through the village when she returned at eventide. The women at the washing pool noticed Tahíaca's moodiness and smiled slyly at each other. Then one day, as Tahíaca bent over to wash one of Ramón's shirts, she felt the baby move—life calling to her from within herself. Quickening of generations past, awakening of generations future. Not Huracán now, but a living human being. A baby! Tahíaca dropped the wet shirt on the scrubbing stone and ran barefoot up the steep narrow cobblestone streets between lime-washed walls, past a pile of hay a farmer had left in the plaza where three streets came together, up and up the hill to the old homage where Daniel and Ramón were working. Ramón was overjoyed.

"My hidalgo!" He kissed Tahíaca and patted her stomach, waving his stocking cap at the other workmen. "Come, amigos, no more work today. I, Ramón Fuentes, am to be a father."

The workmen dropped their tools and crowded around Ramón, clapping him on the back, glad of an excuse not to work. Daniel kissed Ramón on both cheeks.

"I, Ramón Fuentes, am not the last son of a poor Catalan swineherd. I, Ramón Fuentes, am the founder of a family. Come to the bodega. Ramón Fuentes, the father of hidalgos, will buy wine for everyone to celebrate the coming of his son."

The workmen crowded around Ramón, pushing Tahíaca aside and almost smothering her, but Ramón pushed them away, put his arm around her, and walked proudly beside her to the bodega.

"Wine for my wife," he ordered. "Of the fino, not the amontillado. Only the best for the mother of my sons. A toast, amigos, to the most beautiful wife in the world."

Tahíaca felt warm and loved and protected. He had never before called her his wife. Now he told her they would be married in Giralda Cathedral as soon as they reached Sevilla, where his future son would also be baptized. He bragged to one and all about his future family, buying wine for all the villagers who had heard about his good fortune and crowded into the bodega to enjoy his hospitality.

"Hidalgos, do you hear?" he said. "I, Ramón Fuentes,

have founded a family—a family of first importance for the New World, a family of wealth, of position, a family to walk in the forefront of Holy Week parades, a family of magistrates, a family of soldiers. The sun of Andalucía has never shown on sons greater than my sons shall be."

On and on Ramón bragged about the pure-blooded dynasty of hidalgos his lusty nature had started in Tahíaca's body. Not once did he remember his son was already tainted with Taino blood, and not once did he credit his descendants' future great deeds to their Carib heritage. Anacaona's song became a whisper, and Caonabó faded into the Father of Winds—Huracán, Master of Chaos, omnipotent Creator.

In the joy of anticipating her coming child, Tahíaca forgot all past sorrows. Fixed for a moment in Huracán's eye, she had a time of peace with no cruel Don Miguel, no vindictive Doña Luisa, and no sad remembrances of Rodrigo. No hounds tearing at bare flesh, and no fires of the Inquisition. No plaintive areítos in Haitian mountain glades. Nothing now except Huracán's eye watching over her growing child.

One day Daniel found Tahíaca chipping the charred end of a piece of wood she had found on the bank of the Guadalquivir. The New Year had brought cold winds, and Tahíaca huddled near the brazier wondering why anyone would live this far from the sun's warm path.

"What are you making?" Daniel asked, studying the board Tahíaca was polishing so carefully with lard and a bit of sheepskin.

"Headboards for my baby," she replied.

"Headboards? What are headboards?"

"To strap on the baby's head so his forehead will be high and straight like yours, not round and low like the Ciboney servants."

"Why do you want to change the shape of your baby's head?" asked Daniel, whose face was assuming the rugged good looks of the Sephardic Jew—broad, high forehead; firm, determined jaw; wide-set eyes and sturdy nose.

"You can always tell the people who rule," Tahíaca replied. "They have high foreheads and tall lean heads. A mother must be careful to keep the headboards tight, even when the baby cries. To have a high forehead is very important."

"King Fernando has a round face, and his forehead is not very high," Daniel reminded her.

"I have heard it is not King Fernando who rules, but Queen Isabela," said Tahíaca. "I do not know Spanish customs, but I do not want my child to be mistaken for a servant when we reach Haiti."

"You have some very strange beliefs," Daniel said.

"Not strange to me," Tahíaca said. "My baby must have his chance to become a cacique."

"What is a cacique?" asked Daniel. "A sort of Messiah?"

"Messiah?" Tahíaca looked puzzled. "I do not know that word. What is Messiah?"

"The Messiah will..." Daniel hesitated, unable to tell Tahíaca what he had not yet sorted out in his heart. "I am not sure I know what a Messiah is. My father had only begun to instruct me in the Law when they...when he..."

Daniel choked up, turning away from Tahíaca, embarrassed by the tide of feeling sweeping over him, threatening to cut off his breath, banishing every thought, leaving only the familiar white-hot rage. He could not let himself examine the source of that rage, so he fought to suppress it, knowing if he let it surface it would consume him.

Tahíaca kept chipping away at the board, using the old Taino method of fire and knife to fashion wooden objects. Daniel watched her, thinking the Most Holy One must be fashioning Israel the way Tahíaca fashioned her baby's headboards—fire and water and sword. Burn, scald, scrape away—fashioning Himself a people. Would His fashioning never end? Would His people never be fit for whatever purpose He had for fashioning them? By putting his mind on God, Daniel brought his rage under control.

Gradually Daniel shared with Tahíaca all he knew

of the Messiah, the Anointed One of Israel who would end the Exile and restore Israel. Messiah—descendant of prophets and companion of soldiers. Wiser than Solomon, stronger than Samson, more courageous than Daniel in the den of lions. Behind such a man, the shattered remnants of Israel would rise up from their valley of dry bones and become a mighty army. Armed with the flaming sword, led by the Shekhina-Matronit in a pillar of fire, this righteous man would re-establish the Kingdom of God on Earth.

As Tahíaca listened, she thought of Tainos in the grip of their Spanish conquerors. Perhaps Huracán would also raise up a Messiah. A mighty warrior to drive the invaders back into the sea. Perhaps even the child who slept beneath her bosom. The more she thought about it, the prouder she was to be bearing the grandchild of Anacaona and Caonabó.

"My son shall be the Messiah of my people," she announced one day. "Tell Ramón we must hurry to Sevilla to find the Admiral Don Cristóbal Colón. My son must be born in Haiti."

Daniel did not want to disillusion Tahíaca by telling her the Messiah would be born Hebrew, destined to lead the Hebrews to glory. From what he had heard of the Indians, they also needed a Messiah. If believing her son would be that Messiah made Tahíaca happy, what harm did it do her to dream? Perhaps everyone needed to believe in the Messiah.

When Ramón went to Sevilla, he left Daniel in charge of Tahíaca, whose delivery time was too near to make the spring journey. Tahíaca's pregnancy affected Daniel strangely. He wrestled often with Lilith the Night Demon. Not only at night when she would leave his bedclothes stained, but also during his private hours when she helped him ease the demands of his newly discovered passion. He wished for his father, or Rav Joseph, or a man of his own people to help him understand.

As Tahíaca became bigger with child, Daniel's imagination was captivated by the child's conception. First he imagined himself an observer, then a third-party participant. He blushed with shame. He followed Tahíaca around doing little things to help her and to quiet his conscience, but he treated her like a Madonna.

He chastised himself for his thoughts, finding new fascination in the word *adultery*. "Thou shalt not commit adultery"...adultery...adultery! Oh, what a glorious word—*adultery!* Daniel lay all one afternoon under the shade of the olive tree reveling in the word *adultery*.

"Thou shalt not covet thy neighbor's wife"...wife ...wife! Wife? What Daniel Torres needed was a wife, but he was only thirteen, miserable thirteen—the unholy age of fornication.

Daniel had known all his life he would marry Rachel, but now he had these burning images to contend with, and they had nothing to do with standing under a wedding canopy and drinking wine together—an act supposed to sanctify these flaming lusts and put a holy stamp on the act of conceiving.

Oh, to conceive! To know! What glorious words: conceive and know! What did it mean for a man and woman to know each other? Daniel imagined he was Adam in Eden, seeing Eve-Rachel for the first time and knowing her. Was Rachel also becoming a woman now, developing breasts and thighs? Ah, Tahíaca's thighs! Even pregnant, Tahíaca walked as sensuously as she had walked when traders came to sit under the ceiba in the batey of her father's village.

Daniel sat under the olive tree one day while the pigs rooted for acorns under nearby oaks. He was trying to compose a letter to Rachel. Sometimes Daniel was glad Rachel was in Portugal. He was sure he could not get beyond his flaming lusts to the heart of sweet Rachel. He hated himself for clasping Lilith to his bosom. He lost himself in that stream of self-pity that keeps Israel alive. He came close to remembering the fate of his parents that spring afternoon. He went with them to La Mezquita, but something kept him away from the burning place. He vowed not to forget the Inquisition, and someday to come back to Spain and ransom them. He set his face toward the West, and he determined to take Rachel with him. He composed numerous letters in his head before he finally wrote the one he would send if he could find a messenger in Sevilla.

Daniel Torres of Córdoba to Rachel Sánchez of Lisbon,
Greetings:
I am going to the Indies with the Admiral Don Cristóbal Colón. You remember he came to our bodega one day to meet Cousin Luis de Santángel.
Someday I hope you can come to the Indies, too. Perhaps they will let Jews live there in peace, but not here. The Inquisition has arrested my father and mother, and I do not know what they have done with them.
May the Lord bless and keep thee, Amen.

Daniel was not satisfied with the letter, but it had been the best he could do. His heart had been so full of all the things he could not say to her. How could he share in the letter the fiery dreams and aching hopes that can only be shared in the marriage bed? Rachel! He clung to her very name. He understood now why no one is allowed to know the name of the Most Holy One, blessed be He. To say a name gives possession.

"Rachel," Daniel whispered. She came to him out of the olive tree, standing so near she was a sweet ache inside his very soul.

Tahíaca's delivery time came not long after Ramón left for Sevilla. She fingered the sandstone carving of Huracán as the pains came faster, wishing she could call the buhuitihu. She prayed the cemís would forgive her for not communing with them under Mother Ceiba. In Haiti, pregnant women always went daily to commune with the ancestors, for from out of the past comes the future. Ceibas had not yet been transplanted to Spain.

Tahíaca had woven a tiny hammock and suspended it near the hearth. Under the hammock stood the polished headboards, with Caonabó's royal iguana carved on each side. On the mantel sat a jar of sweet-smelling herbs Tahíaca had gathered during her walks—not cabo leaves, but fresh and clean-scented leaves for her baby's first ritual return to living waters.

Daniel had been unable to find a doctor, and he did not even have an amulet of the Shekhina-Matronit to give to Tahíaca, but the Matronit Herself wrought a miracle, spilling warm April sunlight into the room and warm maternal love over the women of Carmona crowding into the patio.

"Poor dear!" they muttered affectionately. "What pains! Poor dear. She has no mother! How sad!"

Daniel was shooed out of the patio while the women of Carmona clucked over Tahíaca as they clucked over their own daughters, as Caonabó's wives and concubines would have clucked over her if she had been in Cibao. Could these loving hands have raised sons who set dogs on her people? Could these be the country-women of Don Miguel and Fray Dominic?

Tahíaca kept expecting the women to vanish like the opia, but the women of Carmona were still there for the final searing ecstasy of the baby's birth. The loving hands of the eternal sisterhood caught his wet, sticky body. When his lusty cry rang out, all the women of Carmona smiled as if he were their own. Thus does the Matronit work Her miracles!

The women of Carmona protested when Tahíaca reached for her son and started toward the river, but they followed, curious to see the heathen rites. Daniel carried the herbs and the headboards. Tahíaca chose a warm, sunny pool for her baby's baptism.

Mother and child returned together into the waters of life. Tahíaca let him kick free, but stayed near. He held his breath and looked wide-eyed at the new distorted world. When he began to struggle, she lifted him up. His cry of rage rang over the Guadalquivir. Citizen of two worlds now, he could only go home to the water for ritual cleansings.

Tainos always built their villages near rivers. Water supported them, sustained them, transported them, revived them. Three times a day they returned to the water to give thanks to Huracán, all-powerful Creator.

He who destroys in order to build again. To ride Huracán's winds is to ride the Chariot of the Gods.

Tahíaca counted her baby's fingers and toes, pushed back his foreskin, touched the umbilical cord proving he was not an opia. She played with her son while the women of Carmona sat on the river bank frowning. When his little fingertips puckered, she knew it was time to leave his water world. Neither Tahíaca nor her son could live in the past. Already it seemed natural to Tahíaca to wear clothes. She rubbed her baby with fragrant herbs and cushioned his head snugly into the headboards while the women of Carmona shook their heads in disapproval.

She nursed him as she walked back up the mountain to the gates of Carmona. She laid him in his hammock and the netting held him like a womb. She rocked him back and forth, humming Anacaona's song as softly as Mother Ceiba sings to her children.

Bonded now to her son, Tahíaca painted her face red to show her joy, plaited chicken feathers into her long black hair—wishing she had bright parrot feathers instead—then waited for Ramón to come home so they could have a naming ceremony. Perhaps someone would give her son Caonabó's name.

CHAPTER 9

Sevilla, 1498

ALTHOUGH RAMÓN had seldom hurried, now that he was to be the father of a family of hidalgos he walked swiftly and purposefully toward Sevilla, hoping to be back before Tahíaca had the baby. On the third day he saw the landmarks—Giralda Tower and the Torre del Oro, built three centuries ago as a lookout tower for the flat Sevillian plain and the broad sweep of the Guadalquivir, navigable from here to the sea. When Ramón came to the Torre del Oro, he saw three small caravels riding at anchor just beyond it. Ramón wondered if they were large enough to cross the Ocean Sea, having at best sixty-ton capacity.

Ramón doffed his cap at the Torre del Oro, then set it at a rakish angle as he picked his way among bales and barrels, holding his nose because some of the goods had spoiled. He approached a stevedore rolling a barrel.

"With your permission," he said, politely. "Where can I find the Admiral Don Cristóbal Colón?"

The stevedore squinted his eyes and jerked his head toward the tower without stopping the roll of the barrel. Ramón started to thank him, but the barrel had already rolled past. Ramón climbed the steps to the tower door, but it was locked; so he sat down to wait, strumming his mandolin. He saw an urchin pick something out of the stores and hurriedly stuff it into his shirt.

"Boy!" Ramón called. "Come here."

The thief turned, poised to run, then sauntered up to Ramón, fascinated by the music.

"Let me play your mandolin," he said with a half-sneer on his face. "I can play much better than you."

"Where can I find the Admiral?" Ramón asked.

"What do you want with the Admiral?" the boy countered. "What will you pay me to tell you where to find the Admiral?"

"A sharp rap on the head if you don't, and saying nothing about what you have under your shirt if you do." Ramón began strumming again. "I am going to the Indies with the Admiral to found a family of hidalgos."

"Why do you want to go to the Indies?" asked the boy, who had talked with many others like Ramón. "There are cannibals there. They eat everyone except friars, who give them a bellyache. If you go to the Indies, be sure to take a friar with you."

"Thanks for the advice. Now, where can I find this great man, Don Cristóbal Colón?"

"Here he comes now, arguing with that old bastard Bishop Fonseca."

"Don't you know better than to call a man of the Church a bastard?"

"Why? Most of them are bastards. Some are bastard sons of other bishops and cardinals, and even popes. Everyone knows that."

Ramón did not argue with the boy. Everyone did know that. Even the Franciscans had been living in licentious luxury before Queen Isabela initiated her church reforms. Ramón saw the Bishop, flanked by two friars, one a Dominican not much bigger than the boy, and the other a Franciscan. But where was the great explorer Don Cristóbal Colón?

"Don't joke with me, boy," warned Ramón. "And don't let my mandolin fool you. I cut the heart out of an Arab once, so don't make little jokes with me."

"No joke, Señor, I swear by the Blessed Virgin. The Franciscan? That is Colón. He dresses like the friars at La Rabida now, but that is him, I tell you."

"Truth?"

"Truth!"

Ramón had expected a giant of a man, a dignified man before whom men would doff their hats. Here was a gray-haired man, slightly stooped, limping from arthritis. He looked more like a beggar than the discoverer of the Indies, as he gestured with a gnarled claw toward the caravels riding at anchor.

"The royal cédula calls for six caravels," Colón whined. "Where are the other three?"

Bishop Fonseca scowled. He had been appointed by the Queen to oversee shipping to the Indies, but he had no stomach for his work. The Neapolitan Wars and the royal weddings had emptied the King's treasury. The Queen's Church reforms had sent a thousand friars into exile in Barbary rather than give up their concubines and their luxurious personal estates. No substantial revenues had yet come from the Enterprise of the Indies. Nothing except a few golden artifacts and some contraband Indian slaves, most of whom could not endure the Andalucían climate. No, the Bishop of Burgos was definitely not happy with his assignment. How could he outfit six caravels with no funds?

"You have six caravels, or you will have when we secure one more," said the Bishop. "The *Niña* and the *India* cleared San Lucar weeks ago."

"You know very well the *Niña* and the *India* were provision ships," Colón said impatiently. "My cédula from the Queen calls for three caravels to transport settlers and three others for my own use in exploration."

"Have you money to pay for these other three ships?" asked the Bishop. "Perhaps you can perform a miracle like the loaves and fishes."

"Miracles are the business of the Church," retorted Colón. "Are you not concerned about the souls of the Queen's Indians?"

"It is you who show no concern," the Bishop cried. "Did you take any friars with you on your voyage of discovery? No! Did you provide for the souls of the Queen's Indians on your second voyage? No! Even the friars who went with you that time came back reporting you are unfit to govern."

"And came back without baptizing any Indians," Colón charged.

"Perhaps you, Don Cristóbal, are more interested in discovery than in salvation. Or in bringing back gold to help pay the bills. Where are these riches of the Indies you have promised the Church and the Kingdom?"

"I am on my way to make my will," said the Admiral. "My eldest son Diego will, of course, inherit my interest in the New World; and someday the tithe of the income from all the lands I have discovered will make the Church rich."

"We have yet to see such a great sum," sneered the Bishop.

"Someday there will be gold enough to gild the great altar of Giralda Cathedral from floor to ceiling," predicted Colón. "Out of my own revenues, I am ordering a church to be built on La Española where Masses will be said daily for my soul. I am providing for four Masters of Sacred Theology to instruct the Indians. Someday there will not be an Indian who does not know the sign of the cross."

As Colón spoke so fervently, the young Dominican friar beside him stared with a raptured look. A sly smile came on Bishop Fonseca's face.

"Fray Dominic will go with you on this voyage," said the Bishop. "The good friar has distinguished himself in service to the Holy Office of the Inquisition. If anyone can stamp out heathenism among the cannibals, it is Fray Dominic."

"Then get me caravels and men," said Colón. "Impress them if necessary. Empty the prisons. You cannot convert the Indians until you have pacified them, and it takes hard hearts for the work of pacification."

Colón started to walk away, but Ramón tugged at his sleeve. Colón looked at the slim young troubadour. It had been a long time since Colón had sat around a patio listening to romantic ballads.

"Admiral Colón?" Ramón asked. "You are the great explorer Admiral Don Cristóbal Colón, true?"

"Yes, strange as it may seem, the old man you see here is the Admiral of the Ocean Sea." A twinkle came into Colón's eyes.

"Are you looking for settlers for your New World?"

"For La Española? You want to go to La Española? Why?"

"To see what is there," Ramón replied.

"That is a good enough reason," said Colón, "but why should I take you? What can you do there?"

"I am a swineherd," said Ramon. "I have a herd of swine, and I can raise meat for the other settlers."

"Suckling pig would make a welcome change from jutía and Muscovy duck, but we have no money to pay for your swine. I couldn't even pay for the last shipment of wheat I ordered."

"I would not expect you to pay me for them now," Ramón added hastily. "I have been working this past winter. I can pay for their food. Just take me along and give me a little piece of land on Hispañola where they can root for their own food."

As Ramón stared earnestly into Colón's eyes, the old explorer saw some of the spirit of adventure that had sent him to sea when he was only fourteen.

"I play the mandolin and sing a little," Ramón added hopefully.

"Music is always welcome aboard ship."

"My wife dances a fine dance the Gypsies are calling flamenco," said Ramón.

"We have no money to pay passage for women," said Colón. "She would have to earn her keep."

"Oh, Tahíaca is a good worker. Cooks not only Spanish but Indian food."

"She is Indian? Where did you get an Indian woman?"

"Traded a sow and her pigs for her, but I plan to marry with her when she gets to Sevilla." Ramón showed Colón the paper Doña Luisa had given him proving he owned Tahíaca. "She is to be the mother of my sons, who will someday be the fathers of hidalgos."

"Very well," said Colón, looking at the brash young

man and wondering how long it would take the world to rob him of his confidence. "Six thousand maravedis a year to pay you as a farmer, but nothing at all for your woman. You will be paid when you return to Sevilla."

"I also have a young swineherd who works for me, a convert named Daniel Torres."

"Daniel Torres? From Córdoba?" Colón seemed surprised.

"Yes, son of a physician relaxed by the Inquisition, a man named Aram Torres." Ramón had learned from Tahíaca about their fate.

"Aram Torres? Relaxed?" Colón had difficulty keeping his voice steady.

"Did you know Aram Torres?" asked Ramón.

"Once, long ago. The Advisor to Their Catholic Highnesses came to Torres's bodega to meet me one day long ago. It was Santángel, the man who talked the Queen into approving the Enterprise to the Indies. You might say there would have been no discovery if I had not known Aram Torres. Santángel now has the exclusive to export horses to the Indies." Colón shook his head sadly. "Aram Torres dead?"

"Daniel does not remember that his father and mother are dead," warned Ramón. "If he comes with us, you will not tell him. He would find the knowledge too painful."

"Of course not," said Colón.

"May I bring my swineherd and my woman?" asked Ramón.

"Yes, yes," Colón said. "Sign your name as their sponsor on Bishop Fonseca's crew manifest."

"I cannot write my name, Admiral, sir." Ramón twisted his cap in embarrassment. "But someday my sons will be great men in the New World."

Colón left for the city to make his will, but in it he made no provision for Doña Beatriz de Harana, mother of his illegitimate son Fernando. However, one of Doña Beatriz's brothers was captain of one of the caravels on this voyage. Ramón Fuentes made his mark on the crew manifest and went back to Carmona to collect his wife, his friend Daniel, and his swine.

* * *

The women of Carmona met Ramón on the steep mountain road leading to the castle gates. They plucked at his clothes, pouring out torrents of gossip about the strange ceremonies surrounding his child's birth, especially the wooden headboards with the devils carved on the side. The faster the women talked the faster Ramón walked. They were right behind him when he burst into the room, snatched the baby from his hammock, and tore off the headboards. With an oath to the Blessed Virgin, he threw the boards into the fire.

The baby jumped and began screaming—flailing his little arms and legs and stiffening his back. Ramón stalked around the room shouting, holding the baby up like a banner while the women of Carmona crossed themselves. He snatched the little hammock off its hooks and added it to the fire, then threw the pungent herbs onto the pyre he had made of Tahíaca's past.

"Hidalgo!" Ramón shouted. His son was an hidalgo. Son of El Cid. Son of Ramón, the swineherd whose family would one day be somebody in the New World. Ramón raved about bad blood, forgetting he had Moorish ancestors and that the blood of Caribs flowed in his son's veins. The Church, he said, the Church always decided whose blood was pure enough to become hidalgos. His son would be baptized in Giralda.

Who said the son of a swineherd could not be an hidalgo? Wasn't there a family named Cabeza de Vaca who had taken their name from the placing of a cow's skull at a certain crossroads to guide a Christian army to victory? Of course, Ramón's son would become an hidalgo. Right after his baptism.

Ramón bundled his wife and son on a donkey and set out for Sevilla. Daniel Torres walked meekly behind the donkey, hoping Ramón would not remember he was a runaway Jew. They arrived in Sevilla during Holy Week when penitent heretics were being scourged through the narrow streets behind floats of Virgins, and the nobility scrambled for the best positions behind the Bishop carrying the Elevated Host.

Some came barefoot and in chains, carrying heavy wooden crosses, and wearing hair shirts. Some fulfilled vows—repaying God for presumed favors. "My ship was sinking. I cried and the Virgin calmed the waters." "My crops withered until the Virgin sent rain." "My child was sick..." "My wife was barren..." "My business was failing..."

All the grateful parades ended at Giralda, the tower of the old mosque where a few years ago, during Holy Week, Alonzo de Ojeda had pirouetted on one foot high above the cheering crowd. Everyone talked about Ojeda, who had captured that cannibal cacique Caonabó.

With Sevilla possessed by such fervor, Ramón Fuentes had difficulty finding someone to marry him with Tahíaca and to baptize his son. The Bishop was entertaining visiting nobility, friars were scourging heretics, and everyone was attending parades. The cathedral was empty most of the time. Finally Ramón found Fray Dominic, who was at loose ends until the sailing of Colón's next expedition.

Tahíaca followed Ramón and Fray Dominic into the gloomy cathedral where san benitos hung like flags from high beams. Daniel, the baby's godfather, carried him toward the altar, looking furtively behind every pillar as if haunted by memories of La Mezquita Giralda echoed with their footsteps. Fray Dominic could not see Daniel well enough to recognize him, but Daniel recognized the friar. Daniel hung back in the shadow of a pillar, trying to quiet the fretful baby while Ramón and Tahíaca said their marriage vows. Then he handed the baby to Fray Dominic and stepped quickly back. Fray Dominic mumbled the formula and pressed his thumb into the baby's forehead. The baby's outraged protest rang through the lofty gloom. Tahíaca gave the baby her breast as they turned to leave the cathedral. "Is this the naming ceremony?" she asked.

"Yes," said Daniel. "Ramón has called his son Jesús."

"Jesús? What means this name Jesús?"

"Jesús was a man of peace," said Daniel.

"Jesucristo, our Crucified Lord," said Ramón proudly. "Jesús is a good name for an hidalgo."

Tahíaca looked down at her baby. He was half asleep now, and a bubble of milk appeared in the corner of his mouth. When Tahíaca tried to take the breast away, little Jesús made sucking motions. Tahíaca smiled.

In the spring an event older than Holy Week comes to Sevilla—the annual horse fair started by the Romans, who also used horsepower to subdue the world. For perhaps two thousand years, horse breeders had been coming to Sevilla with the best two- or three-year-olds; knights came from Castilla, León, Aragón, Navarre, Granada—even from France and England—to haggle for horses. So Daniel and Ramón left Tahíaca with the baby and went to the horse fair, where Daniel met Luis de Santángel, who had come to Sevilla to buy horses to export to the Indies. Santángel had used his influence with Their Highnesses to secure this exclusive, and he expected to grow rich exporting horses. Without Santángel's horses, the Indians would never be pacified.

Daniel recognized his flamboyant distant cousin from his rich flowing velvets and rustling gold brocades, and from the many jeweled rings on his fingers. Daniel sidled up to Santángel hoping to give him the letter to Rachel. He waited until Cousin Luis had stopped arguing with a Gypsy horse broker, then he tugged at Santángel's velvet sleeve.

"Don Luis?"

"Yes, yes, what is it? Can't you see I am busy?"

"I am Daniel. Daniel Torres."

"Daniel Torres? Little Daniel Torres of Córdoba? Aram Torres's son?"

"The same," said Daniel. "Remember the day you came to my father's bodega to meet the Admiral?"

"Does a man remember what he did yesterday? I am sorry about your father and mother."

"Perhaps you can help me find out what has happened to them," said Daniel. "They were arrested by the Inquisitors, but I do not know what has become of them."

Daniel's face clouded over with pain, and Santángel looked at him quizzically. The boy really did not remember what had happened, if he had ever known. It affected some people, especially children, this way. Santángel put a comforting arm around Daniel and changed the subject.

"What are you doing in Sevilla?"

"Waiting to go to the Indies with the Admiral. Can you get a letter to Rachel Sánchez, Rav Joseph's daughter?"

"Are they still in Lisbon? You know King Manoel promised the Queen to banish all Jews who did not convert. Would Rav Joseph have converted?"

"Never!" said Daniel. "Where do you think they might have gone?"

"To Turkey. Perhaps to Morocco, or even to Jerusalem," said Santángel. "Rav Joseph was always saying, 'Next year in Jerusalem.'"

"I remember," said Daniel. "Can you get a letter to Rachel if they have gone to Jerusalem?"

"King Fernando has messengers who can take a letter anywhere in the world. I will see that Rachel gets your letter, wherever she is. You are very fond of Rachel, aren't you?"

"I am going to stand under the canopy with her after I make my fortune in the Indies."

"How will you make your fortune?" Santángel asked, knowing the Inquisition would have confiscated everything Aram Torres had. "Many go out expecting gold on the beaches, but come back sick and discouraged. Say, how would you like to handle my horses for me? Keep the trade in the family, so to speak?"

"I am not quite fourteen, Cousin Luis," Daniel admitted, then drew himself up proudly in the light of Santángel's confidence in him. "But I can handle your horses like a man, if you will trust me with them."

"Is not a man in Israel considered a man when he is thirteen?" asked Santángel. "How old was David when he slew Goliath? Now give me your letter to Rav Joseph's daughter. You are now my man in the Indies. Let us see how you do at buying horses."

Daniel Torres walked proudly beside his new partner to find the Gypsy horse broker.

CHAPTER 10

Xaragua, Hispañola, 1498

ANACAONA'S LEGEND had grown during the three years
since the blue light had carried Caonabó into Huracán's
winds. As the people lost hope, they turned to Anacaona
like children turning to their mothers. As the caciques
could no longer lead their people in the old ways, they
turned to Anacaona as they would have turned to Caonabó. Anacaona sang no more areítos, but she had become famous for the lacquered mahogany bowls she
hollowed out and painted with spirit visions. She worked
on the bowls while the caciques sat about her in the
council house waiting for her decisions. She had to work
on the bowls to keep her people from knowing she was
just as frightened as they were.

Anacaona had seen the giant condors from the mainland Andes who had come to scavenge the Haitian
mountains—ugly birds who ran along the ground too
gorged to fly. Anacaona did not need to see the muti-
lated corpses of her people to know why the condors
could not fly.

She did not need to visit villages where manioc sieves
hung empty from ridge poles to know some of the ca-

ciques had exercised their prerogative of timing their own deaths, gathering their people around them for one final areíto, then compassionately taking their people with them. Better to drink manioc sap than to be executed by the Christians for not meeting the gold quotas.

"Let them have all the gold they can find," Anacaona had said when the Christians demanded an impossible tribute of a hawk's bell full of gold dust every three months, to be paid by each person over fourteen and under seventy. To be caught without the metal token certifying payment was to be condemned to death. "Let them find their own gold. We will go to Xaragua where there is no gold."

A third of Anacaona's people, a third of all the people who had lived on Haiti when the caravels came six years ago, were gone now. Some had died fighting, some had been massacred, some had been captured and shipped away. Others had fled in long canoes hoping to reach Cuba or the mainland. Some had refused to plant crops, preferring starvation to growing food for their enemies. Some, after dancing the final areíto, had drunk manioc sap.

Perhaps it was time for the people to choose death. Manioc was kinder than the dogs, faster than working themselves to death building Christian forts on steep precipices, more merciful than a mother's awful choice between leaving her children and being run down by the horses.

"Where are the children?" the people asked themselves. "Without children, we perish."

The platforms in the corn clearings had fallen down, for no children remained to flap their arms at the parrots. Older children had been kidnapped; toddlers made good sport for the hounds; infants died when fear dried up their mothers' milk. Taino mothers customarily suckled their children past their twelfth year so if famine came the race would survive, but now there were no children. The race was dying. None of the women bore children, for the cemís forbade a man to sleep with his wife for a full moon before hunting gold. Some who violated the taboo saw their pregnant wives hang themselves rather than bear children.

The race was disintegrating because the people had no will to live. Yes, perhaps it was time. Perhaps the time to die is when, having seen too much, you begin to understand too clearly.

For Anacaona the time had not yet come. She had thought about death many times since Caonabó was taken from her, but she did not want to die a meaningless death. Until she decided how to make her death an areíto to be remembered, she would try to give her people hope. A glimmer of hope had come now. A Spanish rebel named Roldán was marching toward Xaragua with seventy men, planning a revolution against the Adelantado Don Bartolomé Colón. He wanted Anacaona to enlist the caciques in his rebellion. The caciques had come to Anacaona, and now they sat patiently waiting for her decision.

"The ceibas murmur with the spirits of our people," Anacaona said, turning her bowl upside down to spill bits of charcoal on the ground.

"Should we trust this Roldán?" asked Behechio.

Anacaona remembered how Caonabó had been betrayed when he trusted Ojeda, but she said nothing. What did they have to lose by setting the Christians against each other? If they fought among themselves over the gold, perhaps they would forget about the Tainos.

"Perhaps Anacaona will go out to meet Roldán with areítos as she met the Adelantado Don Bartolomé Colón when he came to Xaragua," Hatuey said sarcastically.

Anacaona and Behechio, over Hatuey's objections, had hosted a great areíto for the Adelantado when he came to Xaragua a few months after Huracán had destroyed Fort Isabela. Anacaona herself had gone out to greet him in her flower-covered litter. The Adelantado had given every sign of being half in love with Anacaona, but after the ball games and the mock battles, after the feastings and the gifts, after Anacaona had danced her most beautiful areíto, the Adelantado had made it clear she was his subject and must pay tribute like the rest. If they had no gold, they must pay in bolts of cotton cloth. Anacaona had given him a collection of bowls it had taken her years to make, and he had told her he would be back in three months for another shipment.

"What does it matter who rules them?" Hatuey asked. "Colón and Roldán are both the same. They have only one cemí—gold. We have only one choice—fight. To the death!"

"Let me fight," said Mayabaño. "I can draw a man's bow."

"Save your arrows, my son," said Anacaona, pushing the twelve-year-old's bangs back from the butterfly on his brow. "You will know when your battle comes."

With a stick Anacaona raked a few live coals into her unfinished bowl and tilted it so the coals fell where she wanted them, then watched the smoke begin to curl. Before the wood flamed, she poured the coals back into the fire, then sat down and began scraping at the charred wood. Her hands were black and she had a streak of soot on the tip of her nose. Despite the burden of leadership and the sorrows of her thirty-five years, her still-beautiful face looked more comical than fierce.

Oh, how she did long for Caonabó. Only Caonabó's spirit could help her now. Perhaps she should not trust this Roldán. Caonabó had trusted and been betrayed. How many times had he felt this same reluctance to make decisions when the lives of his people depended on him? Yet Caonabó had led his people, and Caonabó had given her his name; so she, too, must lead them.

When men are bewildered, when mysterious powers sap their strength, when they have no simple tasks to replace the great tasks of being men, they turn to women. Gold was no longer enough for the Christians. If Tainos had food, Christians took it. If Tainos had wives, Christians raped them. If Tainos went to the moon, Christians would follow. No wonder Taino men sat sifting sand through their fingers.

When women are bewildered, they can grate cassabe roots, or scrape charred wood to make a bowl, or go out and hang themselves. Men have no such comforts. They can only sit around staring vacantly and sifting sand. The first thing Anacaona had to do was get the men working again.

"Behechio," Anacaona ordered, "meet this rebel cacique Roldán. See what he offers, then tell me what you think."

Hatuey stopped sifting sand and stood up to go with Behechio, but Anacaona held up her hand.

"Hatuey, take the servants and find the most fertile fields. Rebuild the platforms and plant corn. The old people can frighten away the parrots. Warriors cannot fight on empty bellies."

Mayabaño started to follow Hatuey, but again Anacaona held up her hand.

"Mayabaño, go into the forest and find sturdy trees for building a new council house. Higueymato, set the women to preparing an areíto. All the caciques must sit down together and decide whether or not to listen to this rebel Roldán."

Soon Anacaona had all the people working again. The visiting caciques went home smiling. They set their people to planting crops and preparing for the rebellion. Hope soared on ghostly wings over Xaragua at the coming of Don Francisco Ximénes Roldán, the first of the petty revolutionists.

To prepare for the areíto she would dance celebrating Roldán's coming, Anacaona walked in the forest at night where opia roam and ceibas move about freely talking with anyone courageous enough to venture out at night. One night Anacaona met an old Mother Ceiba. She heard a sighing among the green leaflets and yellow blossoms. Mother Ceiba, who can withstand Huracán's strongest winds, was crying.

"Good evening, Mother Ceiba," Anacaona said politely. "Why are you crying?"

"I cry because no one dances for the Guanajata-beyes," Mother Ceiba answered.

"Cry for the Tainos, Mother," Anacaona pleaded. "Cry for the Tainos!"

"The Tainos can still cry for themselves," said Mother Ceiba. "I cry for the Guanajatabeyes."

"What of Roldán, the man who speaks with two mouths promising us we will have to pay no more tribute, but promising the Christians we will become their servants? Isn't that reason enough to cry?" asked Anacaona, who knew the ceiba cried only over real tragedies.

"I cry for the Guanajatabeyes, for the people of Avan who were born with tails," said Mother Ceiba.

"What of the Tainos? Mother? Cry for the Tainos. We have no children. Cry for us. We are caught in Huracán's eye. Cry for us. Cry for our children who have not been born."

"I cry for the Guanajatabeyes," said Mother Ceiba. "If you cannot cry for the Guanajatabeyes, you cannot cry for yourselves."

"Who are the Guanajatabeyes that we should cry for them?" asked Anacaona. "Who remembers when there were Guanajatabeyes?"

"Find the Guanajatabeyes and you will find your children," said Mother Ceiba as she disappeared into the folds of moonlight shining through a mahogany tree.

Next morning Anacaona heard a new areíto forming itself in her heart—the areíto of the Guanajatabeyes who had lived in Avan and been born with tails. The Guanajatabeyes had disappeared from the Caribbean long before the Tainos had come, but Anacaona thought some of the Ciboney servants might remember them. She inquired among the oldest ones sitting on the parrot platforms in the cornfields, but none of them could tell her much about the Guanajatabeyes. Some of them remembered the old areítos about Ciboneys coming south from the mainland to conquer the Guanajatabeyes, but no one could remember whether or not the Guanajatabeyes had had tails.

Roldán and his swaggering rebels were catspaws. Anacaona tolerated their arrogance because the caciques had not yet decided whether or not to join his rebellion. Anacaona had refused to allow Roldán to marry Higueymato. She had seen him looking at her daughter as Rodrigo Sandoval had looked at Tahíaca, but one daughter lost was one daughter too many. Of course, Higueymato wanted nothing to do with Roldán.

The people had hope again, and that was the most important thing. As Anacaona saw them rubbing each other down with cabo leaves after their noonday swim, she wanted to fix herself in Huracán's calm eye and not think of the advancing bank of His endless winds.

A mighty gale almost scrapped Colón's third expedition before it started; but finally, on May 30, 1498, they crossed the bar of Sanlucar de Barrameda and sailed for Gibraltar. The Admiral took three caravels exploring and sent the other three on with settlers for Hispañola. Among the settlers were Daniel Torres, in charge of Santángel's horses, and Ramón Fuentes and his Indian wife and mestizo son—along with their herd of swine, the first hogs to be seen in the New World. Also aboard were some of Spain's most hardened criminals. Colón had been desperate for manpower. Command of the three caravels had been kept mainly in the family. Pedro de Harana, Doña Beatriz's brother, commanded one caravel, and Giovanni Colombo, the Admiral's cousin, another. The only outsider was the Mayor of Baeza, Alonzo Sánchez de Caravjal, whose city was paying his salary.

The settlers' flotilla overshot Santo Domingo and fetched up on the south coast of Xaragua, not far from Anacaona's village, where Roldán had established his headquarters. Roldán met the flotilla in the harbor.

"Gentlemen"—Roldán doffed his hat with a flourish as he stepped aboard Harana's caravel—"welcome to Hispañola. I hope you brought your pickaxes and shovels. The Adelantado needs strong backs to help build his castle in Santo Domingo."

"We did not sign on to build castles," said a surly-voiced man still prison-sallow.

"You may begin unloading supplies," said Roldán, looking greedily at Ramón's hogs.

"Who are you, and where is your authorization for us to unload supplies here?" asked Harana.

"I am Don Francisco Ximénez Roldán, Captain-General of the Expeditionary Forces in Xaragua, at your service," said Roldán with a mock bow. "And this, gentlemen, is my authorization."

Roldán drew his sword and waved it at his men on the beach. A volley of harquebus fire whistled over Harana's head. Daniel ducked behind the mast, and Ramón put his arm around Tahíaca and the baby Jesús.

"You are welcome to join our revolution," said Roldán.

"What is in it for me?" asked the surly-voiced man.

"What is in it for you if you do not join us?" asked Roldán. "Tell them, caballeros. Tell them what life is like on Hispañola under the Adelantado Don Bartolomé Colón."

"Spoiled meat and sour wine," said one of Roldán's men.

"Bugs in the flour," said another.

"If you find three gold nuggets, the Crown takes the biggest one, the Church takes the second, and the Colón brothers take the third. You are lucky to have a little gold dust left in the palm of your hand."

"Marranos, all of them," spat a third. "Colón, Santángel, Torres, Sánchez, all of them. All sons of Abraham claiming to be good Christians to get out of Andalucía."

"Careful!" warned Harana. "We are *converts*. Our father's fathers were converted by Saint Vincente de Ferrar. By the Holy Virgin, I am as good a Christian as any of you!"

"Enough!" said Roldán. "Do not fight among yourselves. The Colón brothers can't even pacify the Indians. Are you with me or not?"

"What is in it for me?" repeated the surly-voiced man.

"Want to become an hidalgo overnight? Want to lie back with your head in some pretty Indian girl's lap and have them bring your dinner on a gold nugget big enough to be a trencher? Want to own all the land you can see from the top of a mountain? Plus all the Indians who live there to work it for you? Want to never have to work another day in your lives? Join Roldán's revolution!"

"Long live Roldán!" they shouted. "Long live the revolution!"

With a small obsidian knife Anacaona sliced plantains and dropped bite-sized pieces into the stew. For as long as Anacaona could remember, such pepper pots had been kept simmering over boucans in Taino villages. Early in the morning, Anacaona had added a freshly dressed Muscovy duck—from ducks domesticated by some long-forgotten ancestor, perhaps Taino, perhaps Ciboney, probably Guanajatabey. Fat Muscovy ducks always waddled around Taino villages picking at scraps, patiently waiting to be stewed.

Anacaona found cooking soothing. She dipped a long-handled wooden spoon into the stew, tasted it carefully. It needed more seasoning. She cut a couple of slices of ginger root, then tossed in a small, fiery green pepper that gave the stew its character and its name. When she tasted again, her eyes watered. Now the stew was ready.

As Anacaona hung up the spoon, the sounds and smells of the village crowded into her mind. Fishermen cleaning fish from the little pond behind the fish weir on the lake, women chatting as they wove stout green branches into boucans, the rank odor of an iguana simmering in a pot of sweet cassabe sauce, sweet potatoes baking in the coals, children...

Where were the children? Mayabaño and Higueymato were no longer children. Anacaona felt the sharp pain of not hearing the children. She traveled old trails of memory, walking between platforms where children teased for stories. Somewhere she heard a baby cry. Anacaona shivered. Perhaps she had passed into the valley of everlasting areítos.

The baby whimpered again, and its mother crooned a soft lullaby—an old Taino lullaby Anacaona used to sing to her children. Anacaona looked up. Tahíaca stood at the edge of the village where the vines grew so thickly you could scarcely see the trees. Tahíaca, dressed in a shapeless skirt and faded blouse, bounced a restless baby in her arms.

"Mama," Tahíaca said, "I have come home."

Anacaona could not believe it. Her Tahíaca had come home. No, it must be an opia materialized in the shape most likely to enchant her. The child was clothed. Who could tell whether or not it had a navel? A Taino mother would have let her baby's body be caressed by the winds.

"Don't you want to hold him?" asked Tahíaca.

Anacaona's arms ached to hold the baby as Tahíaca rocked from side to side, soothing his fretfulness with endearments. Anacaona held out her arms, and little Jesús leaned toward her. She took him and quickly loosened his clothes until she could put her finger into his navel. Then she smiled. Here was the ongoing, the hope. Anacaona looked at his round bronze face. He opened his eyes and the blue of the Andalucían sky reflected some long-forgotten Gothic maiden. Staring at her grandson, Anacaona saw the Guanajatabeyes.

"Where are his headboards?" asked Anacaona.

"His name is Jesús," said Tahíaca, as if that explained everything.

Holding the baby, Anacaona forgot the deserted Taino villages. She forgot women who had slept under deadly manzanillo rather than bear alien children. Slowly she began dancing with the baby in her arms—dancing the generations of all the people before even the Guanajatabeyes whose connecting spirit she held in her arms. Here was a child, and the future was secure.

CHAPTER 11

Xaragua, 1498

ROLDÁN BETRAYED Anacaona, naming her chief architect of the Xaragua rebellion and negotiating a favorable amnesty for himself and his men. Those who wanted to go home received free passage for themselves and duty-free entry for their gold. Those who wanted to stay and settle received land grants encompassing ten thousand cassabe plants plus ownership of the Indians living on the land. Anacaona would not allow Tahíaca and her baby to stay in Xaragua to dance the areíto of the vanished Guanajatabeyes.

Both Ramón and Daniel were offered land grants from the Spanish viceroy who was administering the territories newly acquired by Their Catholic Highnesses. Ramón took his land and settled his family near Santo Domingo, the new territorial capital. He began dreaming of running cattle as well as swine. Daniel, however, stayed in Xaragua, having found himself a brother—Mayabaño, son of Anacaona, wife of the great Carib Cacique Caonabó and now leader of all her people. During the next three years, before the Spanish army came to pacify Anacaona, Daniel and Mayabaño grew to manhood. Their lifelong friendship began over a horse.

Daniel had sold most of Santángel's horses to Roldán and his men, but he kept a beautiful fancy-gaited black pasofino for himself. Each day Daniel would groom the beautiful horse while Mayabaño watched at the corral fence. Gradually, day by day, Mayabaño edged closer, until one day he picked up a brush and helped groom the horse. After they had finished, Daniel tossed the reins to Mayabaño, who followed him out of the corral leading the horse without once looking back, walking tall in his pride although the hairs on the back of his neck prickled with fear. Later, Mayabaño told Daniel about the rogue stallion killing the little colt. Mayabaño would ride behind Daniel, but he never rode the pasofino alone. He was happiest when he was watching Daniel put the high-stepping horse through his paces.

Daniel admired Mayabaño's butterfly tattoo, and Mayabaño admired Daniel's black fuzz of a beard. Both wore as little clothing as possible. Daniel never felt comfortable completely nude. He tried to explain sin, telling Mayabaño about the Garden of Eden and the fig leaves that Adam and Eve used to cover themselves after they had eaten the forbidden fruit.

Mayabaño laughed and told Daniel about the island of Bimini where springs of pure water would keep people forever young. Daniel said they could make a great deal of money selling such water, if the legend were true. Then he tried to explain to Mayabaño that the stories from the Torah were true, while Taino stories were only legends. Mayabaño laughed and challenged his friend to a race.

Mayabaño always won the races. Even though Daniel had developed the muscles of a man while serving on the caravel, he could not match Mayabaño's strength and endurance. Tainos were trained to run all day at a steady pace and to skim canoes over vast waters between islands. Mayabaño could even outrun the pasofino, in a short dash.

Mayabaño taught Daniel how to build a fish weir

and trap iguanas, but nothing could induce Daniel to taste the pungent meat. Daniel remembered Fray Dominic's cockles and his mother's fastidious ways of cooking. Córdoba was a dimming memory, but Aram Torres's instructions for his son's bar mitzvah were indelibly stamped on Daniel's heart. He could eat roast pork with only a twinge of guilt, but he refused the foul-smelling iguana, even though he was told it was a delicacy.

From an old buhuitihu Daniel began learning Taino healing arts—which medicine came from which plants. Watching the old man with his rattles and cemí stones, Daniel remembered something his father had said about the healing power of amulets: He who makes himself sick can also make himself well.

So passed some of the happiest days of Daniel's life—long lazy days, peaceful days preceding the final storm. Anacaona ruled Xaragua, keeping an uneasy peace only because the long peninsula lay far away from where other caciques were rebelling.

Roldán's rebellion had sealed the Admiral's fate, and Don Cristóbal Colón was brought home to Andalucía in chains. Their Catholic Highnesses appointed Don Nicolás de Ovando, Commander Major of the Knights of Alcántara, to govern Hispañola. Ovando sailed in February 1502 with the largest fleet commissioned to date—thirty magnificent caravels. Ovando's mission: Get the gold flowing and pacify the Indians.

Colón could not give up yet. He was convinced his fabled Cathay was the mainland the Indians talked about. They drew maps with seashells on the sand, so he had a good idea of where the land lay. Still wearing his chains, he knelt before Queen Isabela, imploring one final voyage of exploration. Embarrassed, Their Catholic Highnesses relented, giving him four small caravels, mandating he be treated with honor, *but forbidding him to set foot in Santo Domingo*.

Colón outfitted his four caravels beside the Torre del Oro in the shadow of Giralda. He tried to put to sea from Cádiz on May 9, 1502, but a gale kept him in port two more days. When he anchored off Santo Domingo in June, his arthritic bones told him Huracán was near.

He sent Governor General Ovando a warning not to launch the homeward-bound gold fleet. Captive aboard one of Ovando's caravels was Cacique Guarionex of Magua, perhaps communing with Huracán through Caonabó's spirit. Also aboard was the largest gold nugget ever found in the Indies. Ovando scorned Colón's superstitious warning, and denied the explorer permission to land.

Ovando's fleet sailed into the winds of a hurricane, and nineteen ships went down in the storm—taking the first large gold shipment to the bottom and yielding five hundred new souls for the invisible chorus that moans in every manifestation of Huracán's power. One ship alone reached Spain to tell the tale.

Huracán had gathered up all the souls of the great caciques: Caonabó, Guarionex, Cotubanama, even Behechio. Only Anacaona remained when Governor Ovando and seventy Knights of the Order of Alcántara set out to pacify Xaragua.

Anacaona decided against a war she could not hope to win. Instead, she prepared a great areíto, hoping to achieve peace...dancing...feasting...rival villages playing exhibition ball. Ovando invited Anacaona to a Sunday afternoon "game of canes"—a tournament invented by the Arab khalifs...hidalgos in shiny breastplates and plumed helmets riding prancing pasofinos. Anacaona proudly accepted his invitation, assembling eighty of her caciques in plumed crowns to wait her signal to enter.

At a word from the Governor, the Knights of Alcántara charged the royal bahío where the caciques waited, setting it afire. Anacaona tried to join her caciques in the burning building, but Governor Ovando had another honor reserved for her. He hanged Anacaona.

So Xaragua, last rebellious province on Hispañola, became pacified. Anacaona spread her spirit on the winds after refusing last rites offered by Fray Dominic and a pudgy young cleric named Fray Bartolomé de Las Casas, who had come to instruct the Indians in Christian ways. Las Casas accepted as his first prospect a young orphan taken slave at Xaragua, using the boy as his personal servant.

What Fray Bartolomé de Las Casas had seen at Xaragua was burned deep into his soul. Back in Santo Domingo, he dipped his quill in the tears of the Indians and began to write, and write and write. Anacaona's areíto has a new voice. Las Casas will not stop writing while he lives, nor will he ever be condemned by the Inquisition for his criticism of Spanish cruelty.

Daniel and Mayabaño managed to escape in the confusion that followed. Keeping away from the main roads, they managed to reach the seashore, where Hatuey and a few others were about to launch long canoes.

"Where are you going?" asked Daniel.

"Back home to Cuba," said Hatuey, with a grim look on his face.

Daniel longed to go with them—with his friend Mayabaño, the only brother he had ever known. He wanted to prolong his brief Eden—but he hesitated a moment too long, and the canoes began shoving off.

"May the Lord watch between me and thee..." Daniel began, wading into the surf after the canoes.

Mayabaño cut him off with a piercing Carib war cry.

"I am not to blame!" Daniel called after them, the anguish of the massacre lay heavily on him.

"You are one of the Christians," accused Mayabaño. "You are a Spaniard."

"I am a man," said Daniel. "I am your friend."

"Well, friend," said Mayabaño, the butterfly on his brow belying the pain on his face, "beware! When next you hear Anacaona's song, prepare to die."

CHAPTER 12

Andalucía, 1503

IN THE SPRING of the year in which Anacaona died, Andalucía was visited by an earthquake, accompanied by a hurricane of such frightful proportions not even the oldest person could remember its like. Queen Isabela mourned the destruction of her sumptuous new palace at Carmona.

Nothing had gone right since 1492. Nothing! The Queen's mother died in 1496. Juan Fernando, her only son and presumed heir, died in 1497. Her beloved daughter Isabela, Queen of Portugal, died in childbirth in 1498. Two years later her little Portuguese grandson Prince Miguel, heir to both thrones, also died. Her daughter Catherine, widowed after only five months of marriage to Arthur, Prince of Wales, son of King Henry VII of England, had become virtually a prisoner in England waiting to marry Prince Henry—who would presumably become King Henry VIII. Juana—poor, sad little Juana—was desperately unhappy with her handsome Austrian husband, Prince Philip.

Life was so unfair! Just when it seemed something might come of Colón's promise of riches, a hurricane destroyed Ovando's gold shipment, and no one seemed to care about the souls of her noble savages. The Queen walked the lonely halls of her many palaces with a heavy heart, accompanied only by her confessor.

In the spring of 1504, confirmation came of Juana's growing madness. She had the hair shorn from the head of a lady-in-waiting who had turned Prince Philip's head. The Queen was appalled. Juana would soon become Queen of Castilla!

In June of 1504, King Fernando fell ill but recovered. Soon the Queen was also ill. Tormented by incessant thirst, swollen with dropsy, she continued to receive ambassadors at her bedside. Even now, when she lay dying, she could not give up the reins of state.

On October 12, the anniversary of the Great Discovery, Isabela began writing her will. She named King Fernando regent for Juana—who was already being called Juana la Loca. She bequeathed marriage portions for poor maidens and ransom money for Christians captive in Barbary. She urged hastening the work of converting her Indians, and commanded redress for any wrongs they might have suffered. She cautioned her heirs never to surrender the Rock of Gibraltar.

As the court gathered anxiously at her bedside, she said: "Weep not for me, nor waste time praying for my recovery. Pray rather for the salvation of my soul."

On Wednesday, November 26, 1504, having received extreme unction from the last of a succession of confessors who had been beside her during her thirty years reign, Her Catholic Highness Queen Isabela of Castilla passed from this life. Her remains were interred in the Alhambra. Juana la Loca was now Queen of the expanding Spanish Empire.

In 1506, in Valladolid, Spain, the Admiral Don Cristóbal Colón died—a pauper in disgrace.

CHAPTER 13

Lisbon, 1506

RACHEL SÁNCHEZ had been six years old when they buried her mother on the way to Palos and eleven when King Manoel ordered the Hebrew children baptized. She was twelve when Rav Joseph came back from prison and thirteen when she received the letter Daniel had entrusted to Santángel. Immediately she had begun scheming to leave Lisbon and go to the New World. At fourteen King Manoel's soldiers had discovered her stowed away on a ship in violation of the King's edict against New Christians leaving Portugal.

For the last six years she had taken care of her father, carefully reading the Torah to him so he could keep his blindness secret from his crypto-congregation. As Rachel read, Rav Joseph recited, until the whole of the Law and the Prophets had been inscribed on his heart. He talked nostalgically of Córdoba, where long ago in La Mezquita Arab physicians had removed cataracts from a khalif's eyes. Rachel knew they would never go home to Córdoba, but such small deceits helped Rav Joseph keep hope alive.

Now Rachel was twenty, and they were fleeing an

angry mob. Yesterday a riot had broken out in the Alfama, and five hundred New Christians—as they called
the Jews—had been massacred, but the blood lust had
not been satisfied. This morning had been quiet as the
Alfama went about making its bleak living, but tonight
the zealots had come again—yelling "Tax-farmers and
money-changers, Christ-killers and blasphemers."

"Hurry, Father, hurry," Rachel urged. "It is not much
farther now."

Behind them they heard the mob, mostly women,
rampaging in the little plaza of the judería. A black
ribbon of starless sky lay over the twisted narrow street,
lighted only by fires flickering threateningly on the
moldy old walls. Ahead the street dropped off sharply,
curved, and dipped down under the old Roman bridge
to the locked gate beside the river. The crowd sounded
ominously closer.

"Give us a miracle, please," Rachel prayed, looking
heavenward.

Rav Joseph stumbled along the rough cobblestones,
clutching the Torah so tightly the silver crowns rattled.
Rachel felt to make sure the little packet of Daniel's
letters was safely tucked inside her bosom.

"A miracle," she pleaded, hurrying ahead toward the
bridge. "Only one miracle. Don't let the gate be locked!"

Rest and Rachel's good care after Rav Joseph returned from prison had restored enough of his sight
that he could see light and dark; but without Rachel's
arm to guide him in the narrow street, he stubbed his
toe on a cobblestone. He cried out, clutching the Torah
closer. Rachel turned, saw him trying to recover his
balance on the steep downgrade, but she could not reach
him before he fell and struck his cheek against a stone.
He was still clutching the Torah, but its silver crowns
had rolled down into the gutter.

"Poor dear! Poor dear!" she murmured, kneeling beside him.

"The crowns," he mumbled. "Find the crowns."

Blood was streaming down the side of his face into
his beard. He sat there looking at her like a hurt child,
disbelieving. Rachel tore off a piece of her apron and

held it against the wound. She tried to help him to his feet, but he kept mumbling about the crowns. She crawled to the gutter to retrieve them, then helped him to his feet. He leaned against her, stunned and staggering. She stopped in a little alcove to let him rest, hoping the mob would stay in the plaza until they could go on again.

Yesterday when the riot had broken out, Rachel had found them a safe hiding place. Some had not been so lucky. Even women taking refuge in the church had been dragged away, still fingering their rosaries. Hatred had been building up against the Jews for three years, when, after a scanty harvest, the people had looked for scapegoats. Now plague threatened the city, and the priests again looked to the Jews to find a reason for God's sending the plague. A couple of weeks ago, some families celebrating Passover had been discovered and arrested. Now the riot had been set off by a chance remark about a beam of sunlight. Rachel had been at the Mass and seen the last ray of the setting sun light up the bronze crucifix. She had also arrived early enough to see the friars position it on that very spot.

A miracle, proclaimed the friars.

Refracted light, laughed a tactless Jewish scientist.

Blasphemer! yelled the mob, and they tore the Jew apart and dragged his body to Rocio Square to be burned.

Heresy, cried the Dominicans, lifting up the disputed crucifix and carrying it through the streets in front of the mob, leading them deeper and deeper into the contorted Alfama. Rachel and her father had barely escaped into the little secret room they were using now for a synagogue. Luckily none of the rioters had discovered the concealed door.

"Come, Father," Rachel said now, picking up the Torah. "Take my arm. We must hurry."

Just as they reached the bridge, Rachel heard a fisherwoman's hoarse yell as the riot spilled out of the little triangular plaza where patriarchs took the midday sun and argued fine points of the Law. Rachel put down the Torah and pushed on the gate. A miracle! Like the pushing back of the Red Sea! The gate swung open.

Rachel's heart skipped a beat. A burly fisherman with a weather-bronzed face stood just beyond the gate. She hesitated, stepped back under the bridge in front of her father to protect him.

"This way," said the fisherman, bending to look under the ancient stone arch. "Hurry! My boat is not far away."

"You are not Hebrew," said Rav Joseph.

"Do I have to be Hebrew?" asked the fisherman.

Rachel held back, not sure whether to trust him or not. The Alfama teaches a woman to be cautious. Rachel had been the despair of the matchmakers, keeping men at bay with a ready laugh and the cynical remarks her people had used to shield themselves through the ages. She was readying a flip comment when the fisherman threw his net.

"Ever handle one of these?" he asked.

"No," Rachel replied. "Are you a Christian?"

"Does it matter?"

"No," said Rachel, noticing he was young and rather handsome.

"I am a Christian," said the fisherman. "Bring the net. It will be a long night."

Rachel and her father rode out the night watching the fires of the Alfama reflected on the dark waters of the Tagus. By morning they had a big catch. When they returned to shore, they learned King Manoel had sent his troops to quell the riot and arrest the ringleaders. The troops stayed to give protection to the surviving New Christians. Rachel never learned the name of the handsome Christian fisherman, who had wanted nothing more from them than the privilege of saving their lives.

Rachel made a temporary home for Rav Joseph in the burned-out judería, where fifteen years of suspicion and rumor-mongering by the Dominicans had erupted into the riot. Rachel and her father attended Mass now more faithfully than most of the Alfaman Old Christians, who usually contented themselves with dancing at the festivals, such as the festival of Saint Anthony, who had been born in Lisbon. Alfamans might carry the Cross during Holy Week, but they usually left weightier matters of Faith to the priests. They were a superstitious people desperately needing to believe in miracles, simple and easily provoked, ever quick to defend symbols of their religion.

After the riot, some of them were so ashamed they helped some of the Jews rebuild, but some still harbored suspicion and hatred in their hearts and looked for any excuse to insult Jews. Some of the more militant Dominicans were even calling for the Inquisition to be established in Portugal. Rachel knew it would not be long before hatred spewed forth in fresh violence. She went with a deputation to King Manoel to plead with him to allow New Christians to migrate to the New World. The King promised to consider letting them go.

On Rachel's twenty-first birthday, March 1, 1507, Daniel's proposal of marriage arrived. Rachel stopped her work when the letter came and sat in the midday sun reading it over and over again, tracing the very words with her fingers as if touching them brought Daniel nearer. Daniel had finally found his tongue, writing all the things he could never say before, words her heart had longed for ever since she could remember.

Daniel Torres of Santo Domingo, Hispañola, to Rachel Sánchez of Lisbon, Portugal,
Greetings:
Rachel, my beloved, will you marry me?
I know such proposals should be made through the matchmaker, but we have the same Matchmaker as Adam and Eve. As surely as God loves his Shekhina, so I, Daniel Torres, love you, Rachel Sánchez. For as long as God's love shall last, so long shall I love thee, my beloved, "for thy love is better than wine."
As you can tell, someone has smuggled in a copy of The Song of Solomon, and it has given tongue to my heart. Read the songs, my beloved, and you will hear my heart talking to your heart. My love flames up as I read, and I grow weak with love for you, "O thou fairest among women."

"Arise, my love, my fair one, and come away." Come away from all the sin and sorrow of nations that can never be cleansed. Come away to a new Eden—to the Sea of Caribbee where it is spring all year round.

But even in this Eden there are serpents, and they have hanged an Eve named Anacaona who danced before God and became a legend—a Judith who led her people. Her son Mayabaño is like a brother to me, although I may never see him again. Even in death, Anacaona is part of the ages, and I wish you could have heard her areítos. She was a sweet singer such as David used to be to Israel.

My business has prospered. I cannot import enough horses to supply the demand, so Ramón Fuentes now breeds them for me on his encomienda—where he also runs a fine herd of cattle. "Encomienda" is a polite word for slave camp, for the Indians living on the encomiendas belong to the owner of the land grant and must work for him in addition to making their own living. We Spanish have so many polite words to cover up our sins—words like *relax* and *pacify* and *encomienda*. Although everyone knows encomiendas are cruel and inhuman, I don't think even Fray Las Casas's preachments can stop the exploitation. We are like pharaohs drunk with wealth gotten from slaves who must gather their own straw to make bricks. I, myself, have not taken an encomienda.

Fortunes are to be made here if a man doesn't allow himself to be lured away by Indian tales of golden cities beyond the horizon. The land is so fertile almost anything will grow. Settlers receive free passage, pay no taxes for the first few years, receive grain and stock for their encomiendas—all paid for by the Crown—and can import and export free of duty for a limited time. The Torres enterprises are handling sale of grain and stock, and also much of the exporting. We make a nice profit. More and more merchants are chartering flotillas, and our firm handles much of the business. Soon there will be expeditions to Cuba and the coast of Darien, and perhaps eventually we will explore the mainland the Indians say lies north of here. The Admiral's fabled Cathay, no doubt. There will be Torres mercantile houses in all the new cities, and we can find work for any of the family who choose to come here.

The long arm of the Inquisition has not yet reached us, and I hope someday to find my parents and have them join us. I still do not know what happened to them after they were arrested that horrible night in La Mezquita. Hardly a ship comes to port but there is a New Christian abroad, and I always ask about them, but no one seems to be able to answer me. Whether sailor or supercargo, New Christians usually make their way to the Torres bodega for a good cup of Jerez wine and some lively conversation. Your father would be at home here.

We are Christians, of course, all of us. No one is allowed to emigrate unless he is a Christian, but we are not blessed with too many friars yet. The worst of the lot seem to come here, and many soon abandon the cloth to take up with Indian women or encomiendas. Some rabid ones like Fray Dominic bear watching, but one Fray Las Casas makes up for a passel of Fray Dominics.

You can see, my beloved, there will be plenty to keep us busy if you will only come here and marry with me. I can promise you a good life and prosperity, and, best of all—freedom. Freedom for ourselves and for our children, and for our children's children's children.

"Arise, my love, my fair one, and come away." Come stand with me under the canopy before The Song of Solomon sets such a fire in my blood the whole universe will be consumed in the flames.

May the Lord watch between me and thee, Amen.

Rachel would sleep with Daniel's letter under her pillow, dream of its poetry in her sleep, and embroider its flowery promises into her marriage contract. Long winter rains had obscured the harbor of Lisbon and nutured gray fungi on the peeling walls of the burned-out judería, only partially rebuilt. On the day Rachel received Daniel's letter, word spread through the judería that King Manoel had finally lifted the ban against New Christians leaving the country. Rachel pulled her shawl tightly around her shoulders and walked through the fog to the old Roman bridge. As she walked out the gate onto the river bank, the fog cleared. Rachel saw a Spanish brigantine riding at anchor in the harbor. The warm sun felt good, and she found herself almost running toward municipal square to arrange passage to Hispañola.

A few days later, Rav Joseph sat in the corner of the lean-to Rachel had built, cradling the Torah. Tears trickled down the side of his big nose into his beard. Rachel set her mouth in a firm line as she tied their few belongings into a tight bundle.

"Please, Rachel, please!" Rav Joseph begged, like a child with its mother.

"No!" she said grimly.

"But, Rachel, God's Torah..."

"No! The Torah stays!"

"Why, Rachel?"

"It is too dangerous. Haven't you heard about the Inquisition? Don't you remember what they did to Luis de Santángel and Gabriel Sánchez for assassinating the Canon Arbués? Don't you remember what happened to Uncle Aram and Aunt Rafella?"

"There is no Inquisition in Portugal."

"Not yet, anyway. You forget, Father," Rachel knelt down beside him, trying to soothe him. "We are Christians now, Father. Do you understand? We have to act like Christians. We are going into Spanish waters on a Spanish ship to a Spanish colony. We have to be sensible, Papa."

Rachel always called him Father when she was being stern, and Papa when she wanted to soothe and comfort him. Long ago Rav Joseph had stopped wearing his cross unless he was going outside the judería. Now Rachel hung his cross around his neck. He grimaced and tried to tear it off. Rachel slapped his hand gently, then covered it with her own to keep him from discarding the cross.

"Wear it, Papa," she said firmly but compassionately. "Though your skin turn green, you must wear it. We are Christians now, Papa. Please remember that. Now give me the Torah. I have found someone who will keep it until we can smuggle it out of the country."

Rav Joseph embraced the Torah one last time, kissing its tasseled fringes as Rachel gently pried it out of his arms. He had copied this Torah with his own hand after he learned to be a scribe, and he had used it all of his rabbinical life. It had been torn when the cart carrying the Ark overturned on the way to Palos, but he had mended it lovingly. The words of God's Law were inscribed on his heart and were dearer to him than the dim memory of the wife he had buried in the yellow Andalucían clay. As Rachel took the Torah away, a tear rolled out of Rav Joseph's gray beard and fell on the cross.

CHAPTER 14

Santo Domingo, Hispañola, 1506

WHEN THE Admiral Don Cristóbal Colón died in disfavor, the Colóns lost control of the expanding Spanish New World, although his sons continued to petition Queen Juana la Loca. Hispañola, the fulcrum, has been pacified. The New World of the Caribbean and its surroundings now belongs to men like Alonzo de Ojeda, Hernán Cortés, Francisco Pizarro, and Pedrarias Dávila. Before long it will belong to men like Fray Dominic, Daniel Torres, and Ramón Fuentes—and women like Tahíaca and Rachel Sánchez.

Colón was a tool, and the rest are tools, also. Behind the explorers come the conquerors; behind the conquerors the men wearing chasubles and carrying crosses. Behind them the men with spades and plowshares, the women with cooking pots and brooms; behind them the men with counting tables and gavels, the women with long rustling gowns peering out from behind iron-barred windows and lacy fans. Huracán moves relentlessly onward.

Daniel Torres had been in Hispañola eight years now, and the little colony of Santo Domingo could not have survived without the Torres mercantile business. When the three brigantines hove into sight in early summer, the people of the little town dropped whatever they were doing and went down to meet the fleet. Fray Dominic came to see if the Dominicans had finally sent out friars to establish an Order and build the first church. Daniel Torres came to check cargo manifests and to watch for Rachel Sánchez and her father.

Ramón Fuentes brought his mandolin, and his wife Tahíaca her castanets. Their growing brood of children would help Tahíaca dance a welcome to the new settlers—most of whom would eye the mestizo children with curiosity mingled with suspicion. A family usually had to be in the Indies for a while before the wife went home to Spain and left the husband to take an Indian woman, but, although the few Indians left now were docile, their mestizo children could be as proud as their Spanish fathers. Already the word *criollo* had crept into the language to describe anyone born in the Indies— even those of pure Spanish blood—and sometimes the sharp division between peninsulares and criollos brought wounded pride to a fighting pitch. Only Tahíaca and Ramón never allowed themselves to be affected—Tahíaca because she had never known she did not belong wherever she wanted to be, and Ramón because he was so proud of his children—the first generation of his family of hidalgos. With Ramón's music and Tahíaca's dancing, the anchoring of a Spanish fleet was a festive occasion.

Since his letter proposing marriage with Rachel Sánchez, Daniel had scanned every debarking longboat hoping to see Rachel. He kept a dried-up, scarcely recognizable licorice root in his pocket, and he wondered if he would recognize Rachel when he saw her. What kind of woman would she have become? She would surely not be the little girl who had welcomed Santángel to the Córdoba bodega to meet Cristóbal Colón. Daniel could see her crossing her arms over her chest and sticking out her tongue in defiance, saying that of course girls could go across the Ocean Sea if boys could.

Rachel would be strong-willed still, Daniel expected that. The Jews had survived because of such strong-willed women. Daniel knew he could safely put his trust in her, but he wondered how he would deal with her. The problem lay in himself and not in Rachel. He had lived too long in the woman-scarce world where most Spanish men took Indian wives. He had wrestled so successfully with Lilith the Night Demon that he was afraid of what might happen when he no longer had to restrain himself.

He had dreamed of standing under the canopy with Rachel, but he wanted her so desperately he was afraid he might be completely in her control if he let himself go. When he thought of having her for his wife, his mind seemed to stop working and the demands of his body took over. Even when no fleet was in sight, he would find himself staring out to sea—not thinking consciously of Rachel, but floating on the euphoric cloud of his own love for her.

Now, as the crowd gathered on the beach to watch the fleet furl sail, ship oars, and drop anchor before lowering the longboats, Daniel Torres was oblivious of the music and the chattering of the excited Santo Domingoans. He strained his eyes for a glimpse of the passengers lining the rail, but he could not distinguish faces, for the ship had anchored too far out.

"How beautiful!" said Ramón.

"Eh? What? What did you say?" asked Daniel.

"See how the sun sparkles off the water dripping from the shipped oars," said Ramón.

"Not only a swineherd and the father of hidalgos, but also a poet," said Daniel, clapping his friend on the back, glad of something to take his mind off looking for Rachel.

"Is that a caravel out there?" asked Fray Dominic, squinting at the blurred shapes in the blue void.

"No, only a small pinnace," said Daniel.

"A brigantine," Ramón disagreed.

"Brigantine? Pinnace? Not much difference in size," said Daniel.

"I was just telling my swineherd friend—"

"Not a swineherd, amigo." Ramón feigned pain. "My son Jesús will inherit the most prosperous encomienda on Hispañola. He will be a man of stupendous wealth. Land...cattle...tobacco...indigo...sugar-cane...cocoa ...hemp. I will soon have to scour the out islands for Indians to keep up with the work. Tahíaca will have to make many sons to help spend all the wealth I will make."

"How many sons have you now?" asked Daniel.

"One for each year we have been in Santo Domingo. Ah, what a wife! When my Tahíaca wiggles her hips—yii...yii! What man could resist a woman like my Tahíaca?"

The men laughed, and Tahíaca cocked her head and danced a few provocative steps. The ladies fanned furiously, giggling behind their fans, and young Jesús Fuentes looked embarrassed.

"You are a lover, eh, Ramón, not a swineherd," Daniel teased.

"Ramón does not tend swine. My Indians tend swine—when they are not off bathing in the river."

"You tolerate such heathen practices!" Fray Dominic eyed Ramón with confessional suspicion. "Bathing every day has been forbidden by the Governor General. It is unhealthy to bathe so often. Robs the skin of natural oils. Makes you susceptible to the miasmas from the marshes."

"You think bathing causes the black vómit?" asked Daniel, using the Spanish term for yellow fever.

"Black vomit is God's judgment on a sinful people," Fray Dominic snorted.

Daniel sometimes argued with Fray Dominic, although he always felt uneasy talking with the irascible friar—as though he were in one of those dreams where no matter how he tried to run, his legs would not move fast enough to outdistance whatever it was bearing down on him. He knew he had seen Fray Dominic the night his parents had been arrested, but the memory was fearful. No matter now Daniel steeled himself against his fears, they always returned like a latent fever.

Being with Fray Dominic made Daniel feel guilty without knowing why. Perhaps it was taking over the encomienda when he had sworn not to become part of that system—but the owner had been heavily into debt to Daniel for supplies when he had given up and gone back to Andalucía. Daniel had taken over the place to recoup his losses, and he had consoled himself by saying someone had to look after the Indians before they were carted off to an encomienda less humanely managed. Already a brisk slave trade had sprung up as enterprising Spaniards raided the other islands to replenish the diminishing work force on Hispañola.

"Indians are a wicked and sinful people, and must be converted from their evil ways. Lazy and indolent people, stupefying themselves with smoke and worshipping idols in roach-infested caves, destroying unborn children by committing suicide. Taking two lives and condemning themselves to perdition. Promiscuous, naked savages! Cannibals!" Fray Dominic's voice had been rising in pitch.

"Did you ever see an Indian eating human flesh?" Daniel asked.

"No, but the tales are many."

"Tales—ah, yes, tales!" Daniel murmured, remembering the tales they used to tell against the Jews. "Who cannot set the blood afire with tales? Fray Bartolomé de Las Casas seems to disagree with you, Fray Dominic. He has gone to Rome to plead for the Indians. He thinks they should be allowed to live free in their own villages."

"Preposterous!" said Fray Dominic. "How can these ignorant children govern themselves when they can neither read nor write? Fray Las Casas oversteps himself. His Holiness Pope Julius will soon set him straight."

"Or give him his own encomienda with lots of Indians to convert," Daniel retorted.

"Look!" interrupted Ramón. "They are lowering the longboats."

As the longboat neared shore, Daniel saw the girl

sitting beside the old bearded man dressed in black. Rachel! His heart sang as he imagined her in a walled garden filled with rue and sweet basil. She would make sweets for Purim festivals, set aside a coin for the poor, and make the earth shake as they stamped out Haman—all the Hamans and the Isabelas and Torquemadas who had ever tried to destroy the children of Abraham. Daniel would embrace Rachel and their children would be like the sands of the seashore for number.

When Rachel saw the man pacing the shore, she knew he was Daniel. No mistaking that Sephardic look—the narrow skull with the high sloping forehead, the oval face made longer by the thick, curly darkbrown beard. The dark, almost almond-shaped eyes. His ancestors might have come from the East when Iberia was called Tarshish, but twenty-one centuries in the peninsula had stamped Spain indelibly on Daniel's countenance. He would be as wise as Solomon, as learned as Maimonides, as mysterious as the kabbalists, as passionate and poetic as David, as sensuous as the khalifs who had carved elaborate ceilings of alabaster and gold and lapis lazuli so they could lie beside their loves in their great alcázars and listen to the music of tinkling fountains.

Rachel looked for some sign of the little boy who had chased her around the bodega in Córdoba, but she saw only the man with the sparkling eyes promising her children. She liked the confident set of his shoulders under his rich brocade doublet. Obviously he had become a man of substance.

As the boat neared shore, Rachel saw Daniel glance beyond her to the horizon. Yes, he was a Hebrew, all right—forever looking beyond. She would have to look well to her household while he went wandering, and keep Sabbath candles burning to lure him back. A freshening breeze brought the scent of flowers, and Rachel smiled. Her heart had found a resting place, as near a home as is ever given the people of the Exile.

As the boat scraped bottom, Rachel stood up and crossed her arms over her breasts. In that moment the little girl Rachel came out of the bodega in Córdoba and settled herself into Daniel's heart. He reached in his pocket to make sure he had the licorice root. Then he waded out to the boat, ruining a perfectly good pair of Córdoban leather boots.

"Rav Joseph Sánchez?" he asked, doffing his floppy velvet hat with a wide flourish. "Daniel Torres, at your service."

"Were you speaking to us?" asked the girl, and Daniel caught the warning in her voice. "Perhaps you have mistaken us for someone else. My father is Señor José Sánchez, a *Christian* physician from Lisbon. I am called Rachel."

She held out her hand, and Daniel bowed—bringing her fingertips within a breath of his lips. He will do, she thought. Then she caught a whiff of garlic pork. He has been a convert too long, she decided. He will have a lot to learn before I can marry him.

"May I carry you ashore?" Daniel offered, holding out his arms.

"My father cannot see well," she replied. "Carry him, please."

Daniel picked up the frail rabbi, wondering how a man could weigh so little and still be alive. He had heard about the privations after the riot in Lisbon, but he hadn't dreamed they had been this bad. He carried the frail man ashore, then turned back to fetch Rachel. She had taken off her sandals, pulled up her skirts, and was wading ashore. Daniel wanted to leap into the air and kick his heels for joy, but he merely smiled, took Rav Joseph's arm, and walked away. He knew Rachel would follow.

True to herself, Rachel refused to marry Daniel Torres until he had returned to his heritage. Masses and crucifixes might preserve their lives on earth, but keeping Jewish traditions would preserve their souls. Daniel unfolded like a beached sponge as he soaked up Sephardic Judaism. He studied with Rav Joseph those things the Holy Brotherhood had kept him from studying when they broke down the door of his father's secret room. Soon he could dispute the relative merits of Babylonian and Jerusalem talmudic scholars.

Daniel's head sometimes ached from trying to puzzle out cosmic kabbalism—reflecting on whether evil will finally destroy or be destroyed, on whether man can find his way back to God. He embraced the Law and the Prophets as a man embraces his bride. Rav Joseph warned Daniel against delving too deeply into the kabbala lest he come up against the flaming sword God had placed outside Eden.

Daniel was full of questions, not only about the Hebrews and their Exile, but also about Anacaona and the dying Tainos. For every question Daniel raised, Rav Joseph had either a scriptural quotation or another question.

Rachel slipped easily into housewifely traditions. By day she tended the bodega, and by night she embroidered her marriage contract. She looked to her household, supervised the Indians on the encomienda—making sure none of them broke the laws of the Sabbath. Rachel had studied mathematics in Lisbon, and she burned her candle low over ships' manifests, listening contentedly to her men dispute weightier matters like individual accountability to God, and whether or not we are our brother's keeper. Who is my brother? Is the Messiah a promise or a symbol? Rachel felt comforted with everything in place—the storage jars on the mantel full of wine and sweet olive oil, freshly baked bread on the Sabbath table, and two well-fed men with time to expand their minds.

Gradually word spread among the Jews that the blind man in Daniel Torres's house was a rabbi, and soon a small congregation of crypto-Jews gathered each Sabbath to pray. You could always find a minyan if you included the women. They smuggled in books in bales of cloth: Maimonides, Isaac Luria, Judah-ha-Levi, the *Zohar*—even a translation of Aristotle. And finally Rav Joseph's own copy of the Torah, wrapped in a fine Persian carpet Daniel had ordered especially for the Governor's new palace. They built an Ark and hammered out a menorah—hiding these sacred objects behind false fronts in heavy Spanish furniture, moving their synagogue from place to place, often meeting under the protection of gigantic ceibas. They had to worship in secret, for they were subjects of Juana la Loca.

Daniel wallowed in family, in his sense of Hebrew destiny—all the sufferings wrapped so tenaciously around their shoulders and not shared with others who could not possibly know the meaning of suffering because they had not been Chosen, all the poignancy of the Exile that had turned them in upon themselves and made them examine themselves and refine their thinking and find ways to control their destiny even when disaster hung most heavily over their heads, all the personal anguish that translated itself into art and music and poetry and laughter—bittersweet laughter and deep family jokes understood only by fellow sufferers of their persuasion, all the heroic legends preserved so carefully and purified of all dross in the rarefied righteousness of a people who have captured the suffering heart of all mankind and made it uniquely their own. All these and more warmed Daniel, soothed Daniel, fortified Daniel against the moment when God would choose to reveal to him that awful day in Córdoba.

Daniel had begun building a stone house for his bride before he wrote his letter of proposal—one of the first stone houses in Santo Domingo, with the warehouse and the bodega on the lower floor and living quarters above, all built around a patio so the house could breathe. The house was almost finished now, with its intricately scrolled delicate black ironwork brought all the way from Toledo, and its patio shaded by a ceiba and hung with pots of blooming bromiliads. Upstairs were two bedrooms with straw mattresses laid on benches built against the wall Indian style. Hidden under the clothes in the cypress clothespress were the lace Sabbath cloth and the preciously smuggled Torah.

Downstairs was Rachel's big kitchen with its heavy table and its plain sturdy chairs, and on the table a finely wrought pair of silver candlesticks. Some of the settlers' Indian women would peep in the door just to see Rachel cooking on the open hearth under the broad chimney, turning her meats on the upright wrought-iron grill, and rocking back and forth on the little three-

279

legged hearth chair. Bracketing the hearth on three sides were stone benches topped by a ceramic-tiled shelf holding jars of all sizes filled with wheat and barley, olive oil and vinegar, honey and brown sugar, dried lentils, herbs, spices, coffee, and cocoa beans. Hanging in the corners were dried peppers, garlic, and onions. A fine open-door oven had been built into one side of the hearth, and on the other a wrought-iron warming oven. Rachel kept all her iron polished against the salty air of the capital city. Along the walls, Daniel had built shelves, plenty of shelves, for the dual cooking utensils and serving dishes required to keep kosher.

While Daniel recaptured his lost heritage with Rav Joseph, they shared the new house as cousins, but not as lovers. Rachel finished her wedding contract and began sewing yards and yards of fine lace into a wedding dress and a ruffled canopy. When both were finished, Daniel showed no eagerness to set a wedding date. He had settled too quickly into the family. Rachel tried to talk with him, but he often seemed to be talking on another plane, so most of the time she carried on her conversation and he carried on his. She often found him just sitting and looking out over the bay.

"What is out there, Daniel?" she would ask.

Most times he did not answer at all. His spirit had gone walking on Anacaona's winds, or following the Admiral, who—some declared—had left his bones in Vallodolid so he would not be hampered in his explorations. Daniel also seemed to need far horizons. Part of him always seemed farther away than when she had lived in the Alfama, and she would read his letters over and over to find the Daniel she loved. Rachel realized she might never stand under the canopy if this kept up.

One night Rachel walked up behind Daniel and laid her hand on his shoulder. Rav Joseph was expounding on predestination. Does mankind have a choice, or does he follow the destiny laid out for him from before time began? Rav Joseph liked the neat patterns of the kabbalistic Tree of Life, while Daniel was still young enough to believe he had a choice.

"Daniel," Rachel said hesitantly.

"Surely you cannot believe the Lord God has ordained such sufferings!" Daniel insisted, ignoring
Rachel.

"Who can understand the ways of the Most Holy One,
blessed be His Name?" asked Rav Joseph.

"Daniel," Rachel tried again.

"One moment, Rachel," Daniel said, patting her hand
without looking up. "We are discussing things beyond
a woman's understanding."

Rachel pulled her hand away as though it had been
burned. She folded her arms, but her hand still burned.
Tears welled up in her eyes. Why had she ever come to
Hispañola? She could have stayed in Lisbon if she
wanted to listen to old men disputing unanswerable
questions. If Daniel did not want to marry with her,
why had he sent for her? She had spurned a Portuguese
nobleman or two who favored ghetto girls. Rachel turned
away quickly and tried to finish her accounts, but the
figures ran together on the page. Above the din of their
arguments, she heard the insistent night sounds of the
Lisbon judería.

"That's good! Oh, so good...so-o-o-o good! Don't stop!
Please don't stop."

Stacked together two or three families to a room in
thin-walled houses piled on top of each other, the people
in the judería knew life. A girl growing up there learned
early the poignant savagery of human love...the grunts,
the hoarse breathing, the pounding, the cry and whimper, the pleadings...the long silences of kisses...the
awful agony of orgasm...the mysterious enticement of
hearing others making love...the future calling to the
past through the urgency of the present. Rachel had
learned early to explore her own sweet pleasure to those
primitive rhythms; but she wanted more, much more.

Rachel had kept the men of the judería at bay, waiting for her Daniel, and now she was tired of waiting.
Her womb cried out for his children, and the night demons troubled her—bulls, snakes, slowly opening doors
against which she pushed with all her strength. She
would awaken in a sweat, her crotch sticky, her nipples

rigid. The rabbis did not have a personification for Rachel's night demons. Perhaps no one had ever told the rabbis women had such visitations.

"Good night, Papa," Rachel said, picking up the candle. "Good night, Daniel."

Neither of them wished her a good night. They argued on, not seeming to hear her, lost in eternal verities.

Rachel lay in her bed, slapping at mosquitoes, fingering herself to ease some of the tensions, listening to her men argue. Finally Daniel spread a blanket on the floor beside Rav Joseph's couch. Rachel waited until she heard both men snoring, then she slipped out into the starry night and hurried across the patio to the warehouse. Rachel pried open a case and lifted out an exquisite little alabaster vial of Arabian perfume.

Lilith the Night Demon had never come to Daniel so enticingly sweet or so exquisitely sensual. She floated into his dreams on an arabesque mist. She touched him, and he swelled with love. He reached for her, but this time she did not mock him. This time she was a flesh-and-blood woman with a navel, and her name was Rachel!

"Rachel! Oh, Rachel!" he breathed, knowing he should stop himself, but having no power to do so.

He poured his longing into her in short quick spasms, ashamed he could not hold himself back. He fell across her exhausted from his virgin effort. He did not know what he had expected of love, but surely more than this. Rachel covered his sweaty body against the rising sea breezes. He lay with his head on her beautiful breasts, longing to begin again but too languid to follow his desire. She slipped out from under him and rose to go back to her bed. Her father was still snoring softly.

"Don't tell anyone," Daniel warned.

Rachel smiled.

Tahíaca and Ramón helped Daniel and Rachel prepare for their wedding—their real wedding under the canopy, not the vows they would say in church when the Dominicans finally came to Hispañola. Ramón,

like many Catholics, was satisfied with a few ceremonies; for the rest he believed each person was entitled to his own customs. He knew Daniel and Rachel
were secret Jews, just as he knew Tahíaca sometimes
went to the caves of the ancestors to commune with
the cemís. What the friars didn't know couldn't hurt
anyone.

Rachel planned her wedding as carefully and as methodically as she planned everything else in her life—
making lists, setting schedules, working tirelessly to
create the chaos out of which she would create order.
Ramón erected the four posts for his friends' wedding
canopy, choosing a place deep in the forest beside a
stream of water. Rachel herself attached the ruffled lace
canopy, and Tahíaca draped the posts with white orchids. Jesús, a self-important eight-year-old, guarded
the narrow pass into the canyon.

While Rachel took her ritual bath, Ramón sat behind
the rocks playing old Sephardic love songs. Tahíaca
talked about times past when her people came reli-
giously to these waters. Rachel stained her nails red,
decked herself with flowers and jewels, and garlanded
her head with honeysuckle imported from Spain. Jesús
carried Rachel's white veil with its long golden tassels
hanging almost to the ground. As the dying sun dropped
below the mountains, Rav Joseph unrolled the heavy
linen marriage contract Rachel had embroidered so lovingly. Only a few trusted guests heard him read the
contract and pronounce the prescribed blessings. Afterward they feasted on bollos and rumcakes, drank
Madeira and sugarcane rum, and danced the night away
in a bit of old Sephardic Spain. Ramón accompanied
the newlyweds to their bower, singing an old Spanish
canticle.

Inside the bower, Rachel had laid a satin coverlet
over a fine Persian carpet. On each side of the door,
where vines were crossed, stood tables with alabaster
jars wafting heady Arabian perfume. Overhead hung
a blue silken canopy with silver threads twinkling like
stars. Not the ceilings of the Alhambra, true, but an
inducement to her lord to lie back and look up. Daniel

looked up in awe at the tents of Abraham in the wilds of Hispañola. Whither thou goest....

They tasted love's fruits as dawn filtered into the glade, and the birds took up where Ramón's mandolin left off. Daniel cupped her breasts in his hand and rolled her nipples in his fingers while he kissed her. His tongue explored the sweet recesses of her mouth. She touched that throbbing rod that would soon unite them. Their bodies glowed like alabaster as Daniel parted her thighs and entered the secret place her love had made ready for him.

Tradition teaches that God and His Shekhina are reunited every time a man makes love with his wife. Daniel and Rachel felt very close to God on their wedding night. Daniel did not need Rav Joseph to tell him about God, for God is Love.

CHAPTER 15

Santo Domingo, Hispañola, 1511

FOUR YEARS passed before Rachel and Daniel could wed officially in the chapel of the New Dominican Monastery. On the same day, their three-year-old son Samuel Alfonso received the sacrament of baptism. Most of the important people of Hispañola came to help celebrate the Torres wedding and Alfonso's christening.

The little boy had been called Samuel in the bosom of his family, but even Rav Joseph agreed it was too dangerous to circumcise little Samuel. Neither could he be taught his heritage until he became old enough to be devious. So the Torres-Sánchez family would practice their rites secretly, and the boy would be christened Alfonso to protect him from the growing spectre of the Inquisition. Samuel Alfonso would grow up thinking he was a Christian.

Alfonso was an old, respected Christian name. Most of the kings who had stopped the worshippers of Allah in the mountains of Asturias and left the rest of Europe to the Christians had been named Alfonso, in honor of the first King Alfonso—successor to Pelayo, the Christian warrior who, with only a few men, had successfully defended a rocky crag from the Mohammedan hordes. Some credited the downfall of the Moslem empire seven hundred years later to the living spirit of this handful of Christians unwilling to surrender. Yes, Alfonso was an honorable name, for the Alfonsos were defenders of the Faith.

"Well, well, child," said Governor Diego Colón as he swung Alfonso high into the air. "How does it feel to become holy and legitimate in one day?"

Alfonso giggled, knowing nothing of holiness or legitimacy. He felt the weightless thrill of flying through the air, and his dark eyes sparkled. Rachel looked on fearfully. Why did men have to toss babies into the air? Alfonso's mop of curly hair ballooned as he fell, and the Governor caught him just in time.

"Did your father ever tell you we go back a long way?" asked the Governor.

Three years ago the Colóns had returned in triumph to Hispañola—all of them except the Old Explorer, whose restless bones lay for the time being in the Franciscan convent at Valladolid. Don Diego Colón, the Admiral's eldest son and therefore his heir, had married the daughter of the Duke of Alba, who had interceded with King Fernando on his son-in-law's behalf. King Fernando ruled as regent for the demented Queen Juana.

Samuel Alfonso Torres y Sánchez had been born the same year Don Diego returned as governor—shortly after a hurricane had leveled the capital, including the governor's palace. The Torres bodega had been one of the few buildings left standing after the storm, and the Governor sometimes conducted state business from a table in the bodega while they were rebuilding the capital.

Superstitious people had crossed themselves and declared the storm was Caonabó's revenge, urging the capital to be moved again. Disaster had caused the Spanish to abandon Navidad and Fort Isabela, but nothing could keep them away from the gold now being scientifically mined in Cibao. An estimated three hundred thousand pounds of gold per year now poured out of Cibao. Giralda's cathedral had a main altar glittering from floor to ceiling with Caonabó's gold, and Sevilla had become a city of women left behind by men flocking to Hispañola to take up encomiendas and send Indians down into the mines. Queen Isabela's death removed the last obstacle to Indian exploitation.

Fray Bartolomé de Las Casas had pleaded eloquently, but futilely, for the Indians. The Church, now under the firm control of the Spanish throne, which collected tithes and made ecclesiastical appointments, had sent an investigating committee to Hispañola. Former Governor Ovando had convinced the committee that the Indians would isolate themselves from Christians if they were given their freedom, thereby removing the opportunity to preach the Gospel to them. The Indians were enslaved to save their souls.

Only a few thousand Indians were left, and only a few of them had been baptized before the Order of Saint Dominic came to Hispañola. The Dominicans had arrived a few months ago, after stopping briefly in the Canary Islands to exorcise a demon who warned them: "Beware, He who made me holds the secret of the future!" The Dominicans had built their monastery and established churches on the now-pacified island of Hispañola, converting the now docile Indians so successfully that the King of Portugal invited the Order to his colonies to preach the Gospel to his hostiles. Fray Las Casas had been given an encomienda where he could experiment with more peaceful methods of persuasion, and Fray Dominic had welcomed his Order to the Caribbean. Fray Dominic never left the Church like so many opportunistic friars. He found ample satisfaction for the moment in helping the Order manage its own encomienda.

Both Fray Dominic and Fray Las Casas were at the Torres bodega sipping amontillado and congratulating the newlyweds with the handsome little son. Alfonso looked up at the Governor, teasing to be tossed again. The Governor shook his head and sat the child down on the flagstones. Then he turned to Daniel in a nostalgic mood.

"Remember that day my brother Fernando and I came with the Admiral to your father's bodega in Córdoba?" he asked.

"Why should I not remember?" Daniel asked guardedly.

"A day to live in history," the Governor continued. "If Santángel had not believed in my father's dream, none of us would be here today."

"Thanks to the Blessed Virgin," Daniel said piously.

"How is your father, Daniel?" the Governor asked, and Fray Dominic moved in closer to listen. "You never speak of him. Is he still living?"

"So far as I know," Daniel said, a spark of near-memory clouding his eyes. One had to be careful not to inherit the stigma of heresy. "I have not been back to Córdoba in many years, and you know how the mails are. Who knows when it may please our Lord to call him home? My father was a true servant of God."

"Like his son Daniel," said Fray Las Casas, whose family had been converted during Saint Vincente de Ferrar's campaign more than a century earlier, and who would never in his life be accused of heresy, even if he was highly critical of both Church and throne in the matter of the Indians. "No one has worked more diligently than Daniel to build the monastery, and no one has a purse more open when we come to collect alms for the poor."

"But I have noticed you seldom do much work on Saturdays," said the vacuous-eyed Fray Dominic.

"Attention, amigos!" said Ramón Fuentes, picking up the guitar he had substituted for his mandolin. "My wife Tahíaca will now dance the famous Huracán dance, called by the Gypsies of Andalucía *la flamenca*."

Everyone applauded and moved back to watch Tahíaca dance. Ramón had carved a pair of mahogany castanets to take the place of the cockleshells. Several of the ladies of Santo Domingo had studied with Tahíaca, and soon the patio was a sea of whirling ruffled skirts and tapping heels. Everyone clapped and sang the Indian words they only half understood. When the dancers had been appropriately applauded, Ramón sang a sad ballad about Granada. Then Rachel signaled the servants to pass bollos and empañadas and to refill the wine cups.

"Have you seen Alonzo de Ojeda since he returned from Darien?" asked the Governor as he sipped amontillado.

"He comes in from time to time for cassabe beer," said Daniel.

"And to hide from creditors, I wager," said Ramón.

"Yes, Ojeda is a broken man. Always without money, always half drunk, always bragging or challenging someone to a duel. They will find him cut to ribbons by a Toledo blade one of these dark nights. He is like the ghosts that haunt the site of Fort Isabela."

"Did you know Ojeda captured the famous Cacique Caonabó?" asked the Governor. "My father told me about it. Ojeda tricked the cacique with a pair of Biscay handcuffs—told the cacique they were wives."

"Wives do tie a man down," said Ramón. "Take my Tahíaca. Now, there is a woman who handcuffs me to the bed. Did you know she is the daughter of the famous Anacaona?"

"Probably Caonabó's daughter, too," said the Governor, "although how can a man ever be sure who fathers his children?"

"Careful, Governor!" said Ramón, smiling the cold Spanish smile that always precedes a challenge to a duel.

"Ojeda is a braggart." Daniel turned the conversation away from Ramón's injured pride. "Brags about pirouetting atop Giralda. Brag and complain, that's Ojeda. He can't go home to Spain because the Bishop would demand his head for his debts, but he can brag about how he played the game of aperrear with the Indians, and complain about how Balboa and the others cheated him out of Darien."

"I heard Ojeda abandoned his starving companions to the cannibals," said Fray Dominic.

"Ojeda went to Jamaica for a load of slaves," sniffed

Fray Las Casas. "How long will we continue to sell our Indian brothers into bondage? The answer lies in Africa. We must bring in Africans to do the work. They survive the hard work much better."

"Please, Fray Bartolomé," chided Fray Dominic. "No preaching at a party."

"Lieutenant Governor Velázquez will soon be taking an expedition to pacify Cuba," said the Governor.

"Cuba!" The men crowded around to hear more. "Is there gold in Cuba?"

"Who knows?" said Colón. "My father thought so. Cuba is a big island, and it will take a large force to pacify it. Pánfilo de Narváez will be commanding the cavalry. They will need plenty of horses, and a good hostler to handle them. Are you interested, Torres?"

"Perhaps," said Daniel, the old wanderlust seizing him. He wanted to see Mayabaño and Hatuey. Then he saw little Samuel Alfonso threading his way in and out among the stockinged legs, looking up at the parade of velvet bloomers. Rachel stood with a pitcher of wine, one hand on her hip, listening apprehensively.

"Velázquez needs a man with some knowledge of healing," said the Governor. "Didn't you learn Indian cures from the buhuitihu during your years in Xaragua?"

Apparently the Governor knew everything. Daniel practiced a little medicine on the side. There were no trained physicians in Hispañola, and the people turned to Daniel for help. He even kept a supply of amulets.

"Well, didn't you learn a little medicine from the Indians?" Colón repeated.

"Yes, and from my father-in-law, who was a physician in Lisbon before he came here," Daniel said.

"Then it is settled. You will go to Cuba," said the Governor.

"Perhaps, if I didn't have responsibilities...a wife and child...my blind father-in-law...the bodega... two cousins recently come from Sevilla who have to be settled in Jamaica..."

"You have a business already in Jamaica?" the Governor was astonished.

"Shouldn't a man look after his own interests?" asked Daniel.

"Then you must go to Cuba," said Colón.

Rachel confronted Daniel that night as they were undressing for bed. "You are not going to Cuba, are you?"

"Did I go to Darien? Did I go to San Juan de Puerto Rico with Ponce de León to look for his magic springs? Did I go to Jamaica?"

"You did!"

"Only after the islands had been pacified. Only long enough to establish a trade in cassabe and cotton. The women of Jamaica make very fine hammocks, and hammocks are fashionable in Spain now. The Casa de Contratación will revoke Santángel's exclusive if we do not keep up the exports. Sugarcane is hardly enough to keep a business thriving."

Control of trade to the Indies was now firmly in royal hands, under the direction of the three-man board called the Casa de Contratación, headquartered in the new wing built onto the Alcázar in Sevilla. No business could be transacted with the Indies without their approval—no exporting or importing, no exploration or pacification. No flotillas could sail except from Sevilla and Cádiz, and no contracts could be let without the board's approval. The Casa de Contratación would control the Caribbean for centuries to come.

"Ramón seems to do very well raising sugarcane and horses and cattle, and he never leaves home."

"Ramón can depend on me to buy all he can raise. I owe a great debt to Ramón Fuentes and his wife Tahíaca. I hope my family never forgets that debt."

"What do you owe your own wife and son?" Rachel cried.

"Can a man prosper who does not look for new opportunities?" Daniel asked, taking Rachel into his arms as men always do when they want their women to agree against their will. "I will only be gone a few months.

We have to have new businesses for all the cousins who keep coming out."

"Oh, Daniel," Rachel sighed, leaning weakly against him, knowing she had lost. "Will you never change?"

"I certainly hope not, my life," Daniel called her the Spanish man's most precious endearment—my life.

Rachel knew Daniel would go. Only the Most High, blessed be His Holy Name, had kept Daniel from joining the disastrous expedition to Darien with Ojeda and Amerigo Vespucci. Everyone had wanted to go to Amerigo's lands, but not many men had come back. Daniel had filed a complaint with the Casa de Contratación to collect the debt owed by Vasco Núñez de Balboa, who had had himself shipped over in a barrel to escape his creditors. The Torres-Santángel firm would be years collecting the bad debt. In the meantime, they would have to work Balboa's abandoned encomienda to try to recoup their losses.

Everyone wanted to get rich quick now. Mention the mythical seven cities of Cibola and everyone saw himself parading past Giralda dripping jewels. Rachel knew how to prosper. Sell supplies to the gold-smitten hidalgos. Raise a large family to take care of you in your old age. So far there was only Samuel Alfonso.

Yes, Daniel would go to Cuba. A true son of Abraham, he spent too much time looking beyond horizons for the Promised Land. It was the ominous shadow of the Inquisition that caused Rachel to agree Daniel should go to Cuba. A man couldn't have too many businesses scattered in different parts of the world, nor too many places of refuge in case of trouble.

Haiti had become Hispañola now—a dearly beloved miniature Spain of saints and siestas, of forts bristling from hilltops and pueblos laid out around plazas where families strolled in the evening, of whitewashed churches and houses built around patios where guitars played and women danced. Spain was not the cavalcades of armored knights, nor the fiery fervor of friars, nor armadas and eldorados and cities of gold. Spain was walled gardens, hidden grottoes with mudejar ceilings, and love beside murmuring fountains. Spain was families.

Families thrive in walled gardens buffered from the world. The Fray Dominics, shut up in their cloisters away from such families, never know the blessings of family. Small wonder their eyes grow dim and their hearts warped.

Daniel Torres was so busy with preparations for the Cuban invasion he scarcely had time for siesta now. One afternoon when the city was shuttered, Rachel waited for little Samuel to fall asleep then slipped past her snoring father and down the stairway. The iron rail was too hot to touch. Two recently-arrived cousins sat gossiping quietly under the ceiba. Rachel watched Daniel stroke his neatly trimmed Spanish beard as he checked cargo manifests.

"Aren't you coming up for siesta?" she asked.

"We need a hundred more sides of pork," Daniel said.

Rachel knew it was going to be one of those conversations where they each talked to themselves, yet each knew what the other was avoiding saying.

"We will miss you, Daniel," she said, trying to circumvent his retreat by being direct.

"Fuentes will just have to bring along more live pigs," Daniel said, choosing not to listen. "They thrive where other animals can't find food."

"I want another baby, Daniel. A little girl."

"The flotilla is ready to sail, and you know I don't really want to leave you." Sometimes they switched sides like that in the middle of a conversation.

"Pigs!" Rachel almost spat the word. "God forbid! 'And the swine, though he divide the hoof, and be cloven-footed—'"

"Don't quote Torah to me now, Rachel," Daniel said, looking over his shoulder as if expecting to see Fray Dominic.

Daniel had been jumpy ever since the Dominican Order came to Hispañola. He had managed to push Córdoba into the dark maze of his mind for years, but now he had begun having nightmares—masked raiders, dark-robed familiars, smoke and fire, the dark marble forest... Anacaona hanging from a tree while the caciques cried out from the burning bahío. Daniel would awaken drenched with sweat, clutching Rachel to him as if loving her would destroy the demons he knew he had not dared face up to even in his dreams. Daniel and Rachel never talked about the Inquisition, yet it shadowed everything they did. Daniel's restlessness lay in his need to find a land where men could worship God in peace.

Two years ago, to encourage trade and immigration, King Fernando had lifted the ban against New Christians coming to the New World. Daniel and Rachel had been swamped with relatives. The catch was that New Christians could only stay two years, so Daniel had kept ships shuttling back and forth. He had kept making trade agreements and establishing new trading posts in conquered lands. Both he and Rachel had returned to Spain last year, but they had not visited Córdoba. Instead they had visited Guadalupe, Virgin of the Restless. Now, with the Dominicans in Hispañola, could the Inquisition be far behind?

"Are you going to Cuba with Velázquez?" Rachel asked, pulling the question from some deep vein of courage.

"Perhaps I can do some good. Persuade Mayabaño and Hatuey it is useless to resist. See if Higueymato is still alive," Daniel had told Rachel about Anacaona's daughters and son—the brother and sisters he had never had.

"Give them over to Pharaoh?" Rachel asked.

"They are not Hebrew, and this is not Egypt!"

"Isn't it? Does God only favor Hebrew children with His chastening rod?" Rachel's cold voice was bitter with sarcasm.

"'Whom He loveth, He chasteneth,'" Daniel quoted.

"You know what is happening to Indians. Why will you be part of it?" Rachel asked. "When will men beat their swords into plowshares?"

"So you quote Rav Jesus now?"

"Rav Jesus often spoke the truth. It is not what the

prophets say, it is how people twist what they say that causes trouble. Fray Las Casas also speaks the truth."

"Las Casas is going with the expedition to Cuba," said Daniel.

"So it is an expedition now, is it?" Rachel mocked. "How cleverly we mask our sins with words! Expedition sounds so much more humane than invasion. And *pacification!* Ah, that is a lovely word—*pacification.* Almost as lovely as *aperrear!*"

"Relax, Rachel, relax! You are getting upset over something you do not understand."

"Don't tell me to relax. Don't you ever use that word in my presence again! And I do understand! Would to God I did not understand!" Rachel was shouting now.

Daniel had never loved her more. He knew they were not quarreling over the Inquisition, or over the coming invasion, or over the injustice to the Indians. They were quarreling over the coming exile from each other. From Rachel's love came her wrath. Daniel reached out, not quite touching her, leaving a pregnant gap between them.

"Oh, Daniel," she cried, leaning against him. "Don't leave me! I look strong, but I am not. Not without you. I need you, Daniel."

Rachel stood there trembling, knowing she would be only half alive while he was away. Daniel pulled her to him, nuzzled his face between her ample breasts. How sweet she smelled! Like ambergris in a dark chapel. How she trembled! Daniel spread his doublet on the hard-packed floor. He tasted the honey of her breasts and savored the salt of her loins. He plowed her like a wild bull plows a heifer. He rode her like Neptune riding the wild sea.

The sun hung low in the west when the cousins closed the door to the patio so little Samuel would not stray into his parents' haven. Afterward Daniel held Rachel close while she cried. Daniel would go to Cuba, and Rachel would let him go—neither of them knowing why. While Daniel was gone, Rachel would bear their daughter, who would be stolen out of her crib by Lilith the Night Demon. After the death of their daughter, Rachel would bear no more children.

CHAPTER 16

Cuba, 1511

HIGUEYMATO HAD always been the shy one of Ana-caona's children. If traders eyed her as they eyed Ta-híaca, she would hide behind a tree. If the young men of the village flirted, she blushed and ran away. After the Spanish came to Haiti, she spent much of her time hidden deep in the forests.

Higueymato suffered greatly from her shyness, for she wanted to be as loved as her mother and as popular as her sister, but her shyness saved her from a spurious marriage to the rebel Roldán, who would surely have abandoned her. Shyness also saved her life, for when the Christians were playing aperrear, not even their trained hounds could find Higueymato.

For all her shyness, Higueymato loved her people fiercely. Mayabaño had to force her to leave Xaragua after the massacre, for she wanted to prepare her mother's body for entombment in a wicker cemí basket. She also wanted to help nurse the wounded back to health as she had often done after other battles and other massacres.

When Cacique Hatuey and the Haitian refugees arrived in Cubanacán in their long canoes, they soon established themselves in Anacaona's old village. Before long Mayabaño married a beautiful girl from the village of Caonao and settled down to raise a family; but Higueymato began preparing places to hide, knowing the Spaniards would come.

She was a gentle girl of quiet strength, as enduring as the rocks. She had not married, although Mother Ceiba had told her she would someday rule a mighty nation of peaceful people and have a daughter as beautiful as her mother. Higueymato thought it strange she should be chosen to rule, but she never questioned the cemís. She was so in tune with herself and with her world she never let anything trouble her for long.

She was twenty years old when the invasionary forces of Velázquez came to pacify the island, and she retreated high into the mountains of Southern Cubanacán. She was certain her Mother the Earth was protecting her, for the Christians landed on the tip of the island at a village called Baracoa, so ringed with mountains it was completely cut off from the rest of the island.

For as long as areítos had been sung, this island had been called Cubanacán. The Admiral had renamed it Juana in honor of Prince Don Juan Fernando, then heir apparent to the Spanish throne. Now, for obvious reasons, it could no longer be called Juana, so its official name became Fernandina in honor of the regent King Fernando. Cubanacán stubbornly resisted the changing of its ancient name, finally accepting a compromise. Everyone called it Cuba.

Adelantado Diego Velázquez, veteran of the Xaragua campaign, used all he had learned under Ovando in the pacification of Cuba. His expeditionary army consisted of three hundred troops, plus support personnel: cooks, hostlers, blacksmiths, carpenters, baggage handlers, friars—each of them eager to corral an encomienda. Fray Dominic and Fray Las Casas accompanied the army; so did Ramón Fuentes and his hogs and Daniel Torres and his pasofino horses. Daniel had his hands full, for the cavalry under the command of

Pánfilo de Narváez had tough going in the thick forests of the mountains the Spaniards called the Sierra Maestra.

Two Sandoval brothers, bastard sons of the Conde de Córdoba by a La Mancha chambermaid of questionable blood, served with Velázquez as Sandoval bastards had served and would serve with most of the Spanish invasionary forces in the New World. Orlando was a lancer of unusual daring and ability, and Francisco, called Paco, was an alabardero. Like many Spanish sons disenfranchised by monogamy and the inheritance right of the firstborn, the Sandoval brothers had to fight for their futures.

Handsome young men the Sandovals, all of them, even the bastards. Thirsty for harem thighs, hungry to be sons-of-somebody. Wearing shiny armor and riding blooded pasofinos given them by their titled father, they arrived in the Indies just in time to distinguish themselves in the invasion of Cuba.

The lancer Orlando always rode with his visor up, and sixteen-year-old Paco always carried his alabarda at a jaunty angle over his shoulder, but gripped just right to swing in a deadly arc. An alabarda carried three cutting instruments attached to a longstaff: a four-sided point, a half-moon axe blade, and a pick. A good Toledo artisan could work an alabarda into an artful design of curlicues and half-circles twisted around themselves in a tangle of points, each edge so sharp the instrument offered a dozen or more cutting edges. Paco Sandoval, for all his youth, was the best alabardero in Velázquez's Cuban army.

When the army fortuitously landed at Baracoa, Hatuey made the most of the additional time. He gave the last great areíto in the Caribbean, and the spirit of Anacaona animated the dancers. Mayabaño and Higueymato sang Anacaona's songs in her own words; for no one had been able to tell their history so majestically as Anacaona—now elevated by her martyrdom to an unassailable position of legendary power.

After communing with his cemís, Hatuey made a speech recalling Spanish atrocities and reminding his people the Christians worshipped only one cemí: Gold! He urged his people to hide behind every tree, lie in wait behind every rock, and rain arrows down on the enemy from every hilltop. If the Cubanacáns must be sacrificed on a golden cross, let the ceibas be watered with Christian blood. Then Hatuey threw all his golden ornaments into the Río Cauto and led his people in the war areíto, calling on Huracán—Who broods over the waters, Who destroys and raises up as He pleases. Many Taino spirits would soon whisper among the ceibas, cry on the winds, and spread themselves through eternity to await their time of vengeance.

Hatuey delayed the "pacification" of Cuba, for the invaders made little progress as long as he led the resistance. Even the parrots mocked the Christians, but most of the Indian arrows fell harmlessly on Spanish armor. Hatuey finally saw the futility of fighting and fled to one of Higueymato's hiding places in the mountains, taking with him a small band prepared to die of starvation rather than surrender.

Velázquez needed to make an example of Hatuey— so when Paco Sandoval captured one of Hatuey's people, Paco drew on centuries of traditional Oriental torture and soon Hatuey was in the hands of the tormentors.

Higueymato escaped to watch from a mountain hideout as the Spaniards prepared to execute Cacique Hatuey. Fray Dominic kindly offered him last rites and salvation, but Hatuey declined. If the Spaniards peopled the Christian Heaven, Hatuey wanted no part of it. Anacaona and Caonabó would be waiting for him in the land of everlasting areítos. Hatuey was burned at the stake, and Higueymato fled deeper into the forest.

After Hatuey's death, Velázquez's army swept through Cuba, founding seven cities, from Santiago de Cuba to Havana, and parceling out encomiendas to the victorious conquistadores. One village they named Matanzas, which means massacre, because shortly after eating a meal kindly provided by the Indians, Paco Sandoval had shouldered his alabarda and begun slaughtering his hosts. Others joined the fun. During the massacre, Fray Las Casas ran about begging the soldiers to stop, but before the swords were sheathed, a thousand Cubanacáns lay dead—among them Mayabaño's young wife, his two concubines, and his four young children. The village had once been called Caonao, in a province called Camagüey.

For Velázquez, the pacification of Caonao somewhat compensated him for the feverish death of the young Spanish wife he had married shortly after establishing his headquarters in Baracoa. Or perhaps it made up for the loss of Moctezuma's Aztec riches, for he had quarreled with Hernán Cortés and felt he had been cheated. Being sent to conquer Cuba was not an honor to Velázquez, but an insult. Everyone knew riches lay on the continent. But the Matanzas incident may have cost the Spanish Empire the whole of the North American continent, for when he returned from patrol to find his family dead, Mayabaño knew he had found his war. He plucked the hairs from around his butterfly and for the rest of his life wore a white buzzard tuft—Carib style.

Mayabaño fought a suicidal war after the massacre at Caonao. He painted his face and his body half-red, half-yellow—with broad black bands framing the megaluccus on his chest. He stuck duck bones into his nose and ears. He froze his grief into the reservoir of dead memories he had been building since his sister Tahíaca was brought home half dead. He coolly and methodically set about entrapping and massacring Spaniards, making it his life work—knowing he had little chance of final victory, but fighting anyway. Wherever Mayabaño went, Higueymato shadowed him—never visible, but always ready for the day he would be killed or injured.

Mayabaño ambushed Narváez and a small cavalry troop in the woods south of Havana, setting a trap with the branch of a giant mahogany. He climbed the tree and waited. Thanks to his friend Daniel Torres, Mayabaño was no longer afraid of horses. As Narváez passed under the tree, Mayabaño released the branch, sweeping Narváez off his horse. With a Carib war cry, Mayabaño dropped on the stunned Narváez, putting a sharpened digging stick to the captain's jugular vein. He could have killed Narváez, but he wanted to savor the terror he saw in the Spaniard's eyes.

His hesitation almost cost him his life as Paco's alabarda whistled in a wicked arc—striking Mayabaño a glancing blow, but laying open the megaluccus tattoo from neck to waist. Paco rushed in to finish the job, but Narváez waved him away. He wanted to watch the young Indian bleed to death. Paco turned away, disgruntled, just as Daniel Torres and Fray Las Casas hurried into the clearing.

Seeing the butterfly on the high broad forehead, Daniel knew he had found the only brother he had ever known. Grabbing his medicine bag, he knelt beside Mayabaño while Fray Las Casas shoved a rosary into the warrior's blood-covered hands.

"Out of the way, Padre," ordered Narváez. "Finish him, Paco!"

Paco Sandoval came slowly across the clearing, swinging the alabarda in menacing arcs around his head. Daniel and the padre stood their ground.

"Move, Padre," ordered Narváez again, "unless you want to tangle with that alabarda."

"For the love of God," cried Las Casas. "The man is dying! Do you want another Indian soul on your conscience?"

Narváez hesitated. Mayabaño's strength was ebbing, but he looked at the Spanish commander with venomous hatred. Better kill me now, he thought, or someday I will kill you. Something of Mayabaño's determination must have communicated itself to Narváez, energizing the Spanish love of mortal combat between two evenly matched enemies. Suddenly Narváez wanted Mayabaño to live to fight again. Over the captain's face came that sweet saintly look Spanish men sometimes have in their portraits. He waved Paco Sandoval away again.

"He is your Indian now, Padre. Save him if you can."

With Fray Las Casas's help, Daniel refused to let Mayabaño die. He packed the gaping wound with a compound made from the stone the Arabs called shrankh, mined in the mountains of Córdoba. During the wars with the Christians, the Moors had carted it out in mule trains. The gob of red compound kept slipping off a spurting artery.

What was it the prophet Ezekiel had written? The scripture Rav Joseph had said you should repeat to stop bleeding? Daniel remembered hearing his father use it once, but he could not remember the exact words. He turned to Fray Las Casas.

"Padre, there is a verse in Ezekiel about blood, said to stop bleeding. Do you know what it is?"

"Does a son of the Covenant forget his heritage when he becomes a Christian?" asked Las Casas, leafing through his Bible.

"Hurry!" said Daniel. "Can you find it? Hurry!"

"Here it is," said Las Casas. "*'And when I passed by thee, and saw thee polluted in thine own blood, I said unto thee when thou wast in thy blood, Live; yea, I said unto thee when thou wast in thy blood, Live.'*"

"Live!" commanded Daniel. "Live, Mayabaño! I say unto thee, Live!"

Fray Las Casas began telling his rosary, and Daniel mulled the Shema over in his mind as they waited for the bleeding to stop. Daniel wished he had become a real doctor like his father Aram, wished he had studied with the great Arab physicians who used to teach at La Mezquita, wished he had some of the scientific books Their Catholic Highnesses had burned at Granada, wished he could have sat at the feet of the great Jewish physician Maimonides—himself born in Córdoba.

Daniel had saved as many people as he could during this disastrous pacification campaign; and he had turned his face away from those he could not save, to keep his anguish from stifling him. If he had been a real doctor, he might have bled Mayabaño, but he was not a real doctor.

"Live! I say unto thee, Live!" He refused to turn his face away from Mayabaño.

Gradually the remedies began working. The blood dried around the edges of the rusty compound. Mayabaño would live.

When Higueymato saw Narváez leave, she timidly came out of the woods to watch the men working over her brother. With her help they found a cave where they could hide Mayabaño until he was well enough to travel. Higueymato knew the time had come when the cemís wanted her to take command, so she found ten oarsmen and a long canoe. She also recruited a buhui-tihu to accompany them across the ninety miles to the Cayes. Mayabaño leaned on his friend Daniel as they walked down to the choppy waters of Havana Bay.

"Where will you go?" asked Daniel.

"To the Cayes, then on to the mainland," answered Higueymato, who had taken full charge.

"What about hurricanes?"

"Should a Taino fear to call on the great god Huracán?" answered Higueymato.

"What will you do when you get there?"

"Warn my people." Mayabaño spoke up in a voice surprisingly strong. "Warn you, too, my brother. Beware if you come with them to the mainland. To take an island like Cuba is a small matter, but to take that vast continent will cost blood enough to make the seas run red. We will be ready!"

Mayabaño stepped into the canoe, and Higueymato spoke to the oarsmen. Daniels heard them singing Anacaona's song as the canoe skimmed swiftly over the water, taking the Cuban refugees to Florida.

BOOK III

Some New Thing of Great Value

It must be followed up, because it is certain that if not now, then later, some new thing of great value will be found.

ADMIRAL DON CRISTÓBAL COLÓN;
from
The Life of the Admiral Christopher Columbus
by his son Fernando Colón.
translated by Benjamin Keen

CHAPTER 1

Santiago de Cuba, 1539

IN SANTIAGO DE CUBA, the island's capital, Rachel and
Daniel settled into a tug-of-war marriage held together
by genuine love and concern and torn apart by un-
realized dreams. Rachel no longer cried for her lost
daughter or for the children she might have had. Instead she schemed for the day she would have grandchildren.

During the quarter century following the pacification of Cuba, the Torres enterprises spread throughout
the Caribbean isles and the conquered lands named
after a writer called Amerigo Vespucci—Central and
South America. Now the new governor of Cuba, the
Adelantado Hernando de Soto, had arrived to make
final preparations for another invasion of the land called
Florida—the eastern half of the North American continent. Three previous invasions had failed.

Rachel cared more about finding a wife for her thirty-
one-year-old son Samuel Alfonso than she cared about
conquering armies or expanding Torres enterprises.
Most of the suitable Jewish girls who came to the Caribbean were already betrothed, and Samuel seemed

content running the family business. The men of Santiago puffed their cigars and said the Torres boy would never marry since he couldn't marry his own mother, who obviously ran her son's life as she ran Daniel's life. If Alfonso sometimes strayed to a nearby Indian village as most of the young Cubans did, he and his mother never mentioned it, but the family had almost stopped associating with Ramón Fuentes and his wife Tahíaca because Samuel had once looked favorably on one of the Fuentes daughters. Rachel would never tolerate Samuel's marrying outside Judaism, even though no one attended Mass in the cathedral more faithfully than Rachel Torres y Sánchez.

A rather plain Jewish girl named Sarah Cabrera y Cohen came to Cuba with her father, who set up his weaver's looms and soon had a thriving trade in fine brocades. Immediately Rachel started matchmaking, but she had had little success before Soto's army arrived. Now, even at the "game of canes" given by the people of Santiago in honor of their new governor, Rachel could not pass up an opportunity.

"Have you asked Sarah to the masquerade ball tonight?" Rachel asked her son as they waited for the opening parade.

"Please, Mama," begged Alfonso. "Stop trying to marry me with every Jewish girl who comes to Cuba."

"You are thirty-one years old," cried Rachel. "Who will carry on this family if there are no grandchildren?"

"I know, I know!" said Alfonso. "Father Abraham's covenant: '...as the sands of the seashore in multitude.' Wouldn't it have been better if you had had another son?"

"Why must you plague your mother, Samuel?" asked Daniel, using the family name even though to use it in public was dangerous. "God did not see fit to open Rachel's womb after Lilith took away your little sister."

"Sarah is a fine girl who keeps feasts and fasts," said Rachel.

"Sarah is plain, Mama," objected Alfonso. "Couldn't God have sent me a pretty one? Her nose..."

"So what! Look in the mirror. You have the beginning of such a fine nose. Look at your father's nose. Getting bigger year by year. What is an Israelite without his nose?"

"A man who minds his own business," said Alfonso.

"Samuel, careful!" warned Daniel.

"Sarah has pretty eyes," said Rachel.

Alfonso looked toward the end of the field where the parade was assembling. He wished his mother would stop. Sarah did have beautiful eyes, fringed with long thick lashes and rimmed with kohl like the eyes in a sultan's harem—those eyes disturbed Alfonso more than he admitted to his mother. Sarah had two assets: her beautiful eyes and her eagerness to please. Many a time Alfonso had discovered his wine cup miraculously full, while Sarah stood nearby holding a wet cloth around the pitcher to keep the wine cool. When she saw him looking, she would duck her head to hide her nose, but love would shine out of those marvelous Andalucían eyes. Such overwhelming love and devotion only made Alfonso uncomfortable.

"I wonder if Mayabaño made it to Florida," said Daniel, changing the subject to diffuse the tension between Alfonso and Rachel.

"Look, Papa, the Adelantado," said Alfonso.

Adelantado Don Hernando de Soto entered the tournament field at the head of his army of six hundred men, half of them cavalry on Cuban horses. The Adelantado rode a pasofino mare with a gait as delicate as a ballerina. She had red plumes on her bridle and gold tassels on her caparisoned silks—a fitting mount for the man who had brought the Emperor of the Incas to his knees. The people of Santiago had hardly stopped celebrating since Soto's flotilla arrived from Spain. Now the world would finally notice Cuba! Soto had a commission from the Casa de Contratación and the Emperor Carlos to govern Cuba and explore and pacify Florida. Cuba would be the capital of the vast untamed North American wasteland and Cuba would at last be known to the world.

Nothing stirred the blood of Santiago's citizens like a military parade. They cheered as the flags trooped by: the military orders of Santiago, Calatrava, and Alcántara; the Emperor Carlos's coat of arms; the flags of the provinces with sons in the expedition; the family crests of the noble hidalgos; and finally the adelantado's banner—the golden eagle with bloody talons. Imperial birds were the eagles, rapacious by nature, fit symbols for the conquistadores from the mountains of Extremadura—Balboa, Cortés, Pizarro, and Soto.

Following the color guard came the Portuguese knights astride prancing horses—lancers and swordsmen whose polished armor fractured the June sunlight. On their burnished shields and polished sword hilts were hammered obscure Arabic decorations no one knew how to read: *"With the help of Allah, thine enemies shall surely die"* and *"Allah is great. There is no god but Allah."* Soto had not allowed the Spanish knights to ride in the parade, for they had shown up in Sevilla on blooded horses wearing silks and brocades instead of armor. After Soto castigated them for not dressing like soldiers, they traded their fine horses for spavined nags to raise money to buy second-hand chain-mail rusty from the Moorish wars. Soto had invested his Peruvian fortune in outfitting this venture, but each man had to furnish his own arms and horses.

So the chastened Spanish knights marched with the infantry: the harquebusiers, the crossbowmen, the alabarderos, and one lone Englishman carrying a longbow. Bringing up the rear of the parade came the artillery: a single lombard on a mule cart. Paco Sandoval sidled up to Daniel Torres as the parade retired for the jousting to begin.

"What's happening, Jew peddler?" he sneered. "Are you rich enough to wager two castellanos against the lancer wearing the orange plumes?"

Daniel stiffened. He had hated Paco Sandoval on the day he worked so hard to save Mayabaño's life after Paco cut him down with an alabarda, and twenty-five years of watching Sandoval's behavior in the Indies had not changed his mind. Daniel looked straight ahead at the playing field, hoping Sandoval would go away.

The horses thundered down the field toward each

other, and when they met, one freshly cut bamboo lance splintered harmlessly against the shield. The rider in the orange plumes emerged victorious. The "game of canes" had been invented by the Moors. It was a spectacular show of horse and horsemanship—an armored art bequeathed by the Persians to the rest of the world when they first encased horse and rider in bronze, an Oriental war game in which men only occasionally died. The "game of canes" was war purified by the pretense of play, retaining its thrill and glory without its bloody reality.

"Well, Torres," said Sandoval again. "A little wager."

"Should Daniel Torres toss away his hard-earned money?" asked Rachel. "My Daniel is no gambler."

"No gambler?" Sandoval bowed to Rachel. "Madame, everyone is a gambler. Fray Las Casas tells us Africans can stand hard work better than Indians. So what happens? I bring in half a dozen slaves from Portuguese Africa, and they make themselves a drum, go into the mountains, and eat manzanillo. Take five of my very best Indians with them. Committed suicide, all of them—even a pregnant woman. Robbed themselves of any hope of Heaven just to get out of a little work. Now, can you say life is no gamble?"

"Try treating your slaves like human beings," suggested Daniel.

"Human? They're animals. Can't read. Can't write. Can't even say their Hail Mary or cross themselves properly. You cannot tell me they're human. Indians didn't even have the wheel until we came."

"Can you read and write, Paco?" asked Daniel.

"Don Francisco to you, Torres," said Sandoval. "Hidalgos don't have to know how to read and write. A sword buys someone who can. By God, all life is a gamble."

"Don't blaspheme the Most High, blessed be His Name," said Daniel.

"Looking for the Inquisitor, are you, Jew peddler?" mocked Sandoval. "Remember what happened to one of Cortés's men who turned out to be a judaizer. Not even Moctezuma's gold would have saved him from the fire."

Daniel paled. The Inquisition had come to Mexico, where the first act-of-faith had been held eleven years ago. Much as he hated the Sandovals, Daniel could not afford to arouse Paco's suspicions.

"Two castellanos on the black knight," said Daniel warily.

"You're carried," said Paco, and stood watching the horses ready for the charge. "My brother Orlando was a man who knew how to gamble. Got tired of his Indians dying in the worked-out copper mines, so he sold me his share and went to Florida with Narváez. Never came back, but he's a Sandoval like our father the old Conde de Córdoba, so I wager Orlando is in Florida somewhere fornicating with some Indian princess."

Daniel let the crudity pass, but Rachel pulled her lace mantilla up around her face. The Indians were almost gone in Cuba now, except for a few fierce tribes in the interior. They had been killed off by hard labor, or were victims of their own despair. More and more raids were being made on the mainland to bring back Indian slaves. Vasco Porcallo, who had the horse-factoring contract for Soto's expedition, was going only to capture and bring back slaves. Daniel Torres had never dealt in slaves, although some of the cousins thought him a fool not to do so. Mayabaño must have made it to Florida, for none of the three previous official expeditions had been successful.

The black knight triumphed, and Sandoval grudgingly paid his debt. The crowd cheered as Soto awarded the man a gold trinket, and the band played the unhorsed loser off the field. Daniel wiped his face. The June heat was scorching.

"You're getting rich off sugar and tobacco, aren't you, Jew peddler?" asked Sandoval. "I hear your Indians made you a wooden machine to grind the cane."

"Yes, a trapiche," said Daniel, wishing Sandoval would move so he could enjoy the tournament with his family.

"Can Indians stand up to pulling a trapiche?"

"I use oxen," said Daniel. "I plan to clear a few more acres for cane next year. My Indians have already slashed the trees, and they'll soon be dry enough to burn."

"Using Indians would be cheaper than using oxen," said Sandoval. "You don't have to feed them so much. Is there any real money to be made in sugarcane, Torres? Or in tobacco?"

"Not much in sugar. I raise it mostly for Rachel's pastries and for making a few kegs of rum. Tobacco's getting more profitable. Sailors smuggle it out in their hammocks. Pay a good price for it. Tobacco's getting very popular in Europe. Rum, too."

"No real money to be made in Cuba," said Sandoval. "Not without more slaves. But you keep on growing cane and making rum. I'll sharpen my alabarda and help pacify Florida. Man might get himself a title out of this expedition. You going, Torres?"

"You could be right about the title," said Daniel, not answering whether or not he would go with Soto's expedition.

Mayabaño's butterfly face under the white buzzard tuft seemed to float into Daniel's mind, and he could almost hear Anacaona's song. The Indians had to make a stand somewhere, and they had made it in Florida. Hernán Cortés had conquered Mexico after a big battle with Moctezuma, and Francisco Pizarro had conquered Peru with Soto's help, but Florida had conquered Juan Ponce de León, Lucas Vásquez de Ayllon, and Pánfilo de Narváez. Daniel wondered if Mayabaño had been the one to kill Narváez. If he had, Paco Sandoval might have a hard time earning that title.

Soto had taken over Cuba's capital city of Santiago, quartering his army in the homes of the citizens. Six hundred men with their morisco body servants, their wives, and their dark-skinned mistresses. Not all were soldiers. Some were coopers, blacksmiths, carpenters, cooks, sailmakers, shipbuilders. A few were clergymen, among them Fray Dominic—gray-haired now, with the same malevolent eyes and a face as dour as Torquemada's, a drawn face, pinched by life's cheating and determined to make someone pay for the cheating.

Santiago women woke early to start the cooking fires. Men stayed up late drinking rum and debating politics. Officials planned festivities. Encomienderos rode over the mountains leading strings of horses, some not saddle-broken. Almost every household expected to profit from this expedition; families slept in hammocks to give their beds to Soto's hidalgos.

Santiago had few excuses to celebrate. French corsairs frequently besieged the port, hurricanes battered their flimsy straw village, and earthquakes leveled their hastily built stone churches. Loneliness held them together, and backbiting tore them apart. Disappointed that copper and not gold abounded in the Sierra Maestra, they worked their Indians to death in the mines, and raised cattle, hogs, and casabe to trade for a piece of the action in an expedition like this. To make their fortune. To go back to Spain in style. Who wanted to live in Cuba when the Seven Cities of Cibola lay waiting to be conquered? The Cubans were in high spirits as they feted Soto while he made his plans to move Cuba's capital to Havana. The expedition had brought a little bit of home, a little bit of the pageantry and glory of chivalrous Spain. Soto landed in Santiago in June, but he did not leave for Havana until the end of August, and August in the Caribbean belongs to Huracán.

Soto's army traveled overland, pacifying Indians and hacking its way through dense forests. His wife, Doña Isabela de Bobadilla, daughter of the infamous Governor Pedrárias Dávila of Panama, sailed around the island to Havana. Some of the citizens of Santiago sailed with her, including the Torres family, who were moving their business headquarters to the new capital. Sarah Cabrera y Cohen went also, having had little trouble persuading Rachel she could be useful in the business. A hurricane blew the fleet off course, but they survived to reach Havana.

Soto's army did not reach Havana until the end of the next March. Shortly before they arrived, French corsairs attacked the city, burned the church, and carried off its gold plate. The new Bishop of the Caribbean, who had almost drowned when he stepped into the sea while disembarking in Santiago, had refused to move the bishopric to Havana, but he commanded Soto to rebuild Havana's church with his own funds. Soto grumbled to his wife that the bishop lived in luxury with six African slaves and twenty Indians on an encomienda given to the Church, while he had to spend part of his rapidly dwindling Peruvian gold to rebuild the Havana church. Daniel Torres contributed heavily when Soto took up a collection.

Soto sent Juan de Añasco to scout a suitable landing place in Florida, but Añasco also suffered a hurricane. His crew returned to Havana so shaken by their experience they crawled on their knees from shore to church to hear Fray Dominic say a thanksgiving Mass. Añasco lost one ship, but found a suitable harbor—perhaps the one used by Narváez. He also brought back four captured Indians to train as interpreters.

Rachel knew before Daniel did that he was going to Florida with Soto. She had seen him look up from his reading and stare out over choppy Havana harbor with the familiar wanderlust in his eyes. Daniel had not admitted to himself that he wanted to go, because he doubted Soto would come back. Daniel had read Cabeza de Vaca's account of the disastrous Narváez expedition—of the poverty and hunger of the wandering Indian plains tribes. Cabeza de Vaca had not been able to wear clothes when he first returned to Spanish civilization after twelve years as a slave to the Indians, nor could he sleep except on the ground. Soto knew nothing of this, for Emperor Carlos had refused to let Soto read Cabeza de Vaca's report, but Daniel had read it when the explorer was in Cuba before he went back home to Spain. Daniel knew Mayabaño was waiting in Florida somewhere, waiting with all the other Caribbean refugees who had made it to Florida. Yet, apprehensive as he was, Daniel would go, and Rachel knew he would.

"Florida," Daniel mused one day in late May, putting

aside the *Zohar* he had been reading and leaning back against the shady wall of the patio. "Soto is going to Florida."

"Careful of my plants," Rachel warned.

"Surely Mayabaño made it to the Cayes," Daniel said, more to himself than to Rachel.

Rachel sat quietly embroidering while Sarah clacked the treadle of her loom, and Samuel Alfonso sat at a table in the corner going over the books. For years now, Rachel and Daniel had talked without bothering to answer each other, knowing what was going to be said before it was said. They carried on these multifaceted conversations oblivious of anyone else present.

"Nice masquerade ball we had in Santiago," said Rachel.

"Why do you think a certain Samuel Alfonso took a certain young lady to the ball, but hasn't paid her any attention since then?" asked Daniel, looking meaningfully at his son.

Alfonso ducked his head deeper into the ledger, and Sarah blushed and flung her shuttle with such force it became entangled in the threads. Sarah's family had once been weavers for the sultans. No one knew Sarah was planning to use the fancy brocade she was weaving for a coat for Alfonso. She had begun working on it while they were still in Santiago, and she was hurrying to finish it before Soto's expedition left. Sarah and Alfonso had talked more often than Rachel and Daniel suspected, and Sarah knew Alfonso would go with his father if Daniel decided to go to Florida.

"Samuel should ask a certain fine Jewish girl to marry with him," said Daniel. "Does he think Abraham's seed spring from the sands without help?"

"Daniel!" Rachel chided, missing a stitch.

She stuck her finger with the needle and soiled the white linen Sabbath cloth she was embroidering to give Sarah and Alfonso as a wedding present. Rachel sucked her finger until the bleeding stopped, then covered the spot on the cloth with a flower.

Samuel Alfonso stared at his accounts, but the figures ran together. He had never disobeyed his father and mother, although he had sometimes wanted to. He had taken over the family business right after Rav Joseph died. Daniel had been so devastated by the rabbi's death that he had turned to mysticism. While Daniel pored over the mysteries of creation and redemption as taught by the kabbalists, Rachel and Alfonso operated the Torres enterprises—with the burden of management falling to Alfonso. Perhaps Daniel had left too much of himself in Córdoba, or perhaps Anacaona's people weighed too heavily on his mind. Daniel loved her, of that Rachel was sure. Their Sabbaths were sometimes glorious times, but even at the peak of their joy, the Daniel she wanted would be just out of reach—caught up in a web he was powerless to untangle.

"You are going to Florida with Soto," Rachel said, and it was a statement, not a question.

Sarah looked up, startled, darting a glance at Alfonso, who was staring intently at her face. Yes, she had beautiful eyes. Eyes that burned deep into Alfonso's soul, stirring Abraham's seed. Eyes he could look at for only a moment, but eyes he could never forget. When Alfonso broke their gaze, Sarah looked down at her loom.

Now it had been said. Daniel was going to Florida, and Alfonso would go with him. North where cold winds blew. Out of sight of Sarah's eyes, but not out of reach of her warmth. She was weaving him a coat of fine wool, imported from Spain, and she would embroider it with griffins and unicorns and garlands of flowers twined around scrolls and ancient Arabic love letters. Her love was the warp, her compassion the woof, and every stitch a love poem her heart could not utter. Weaving the Shekhina's own mantle of love, Sarah prayed for Alfonso's safe return with her busy feet on the treadle of her loom.

"Since Soto has moved the capital to Havana, Sarah's father has been successfully running the business in Santiago," Daniel said. "Alfonso can help you with this one."

"No," Rachel said, crossing her arms over her chest. For a fleeting moment Daniel saw the little girl in the

317

bodega in Córdoba. "If you go to Florida, Alfonso goes with you."

"Nonsense! You need Alfonso here. Jesús Fuentes is taking his father's herd of swine, but Ramón will stay here. Tahíaca is not well, and women should not be left alone."

Tahíaca and Ramón kept more and more to themselves as a society divided itself into the criollos, who had been born in Cuba and were often of mixed blood, and the peninsulares, who were born in Spain of certifiably pure blood. Two societies had emerged, and both were proud. Ramón still bragged occasionally that he had founded a family of hidalgos who would make their mark on the Caribbean, but his words rang hollow, for the peninsulares were already in firm control. Tahíaca had gradually dropped out of Havana society, slipping into melancholy because she could no longer go wherever she wanted to go. She no longer danced the Huracán dance, but Spanish dancers had already made the flamenco their own, insisting it had originated in the Basque country.

"Alfonso goes with you," Rachel insisted.

"Jesús can help me with the horses. Swine can fend for themselves. Alfonso stays. Suppose he should decide to marry with Sarah? Would you disappoint the Shekhina?"

"The Shekhina can wait. She has had plenty of practice," Rachel declared. "Sarah can help me with the business. She has to learn sometime."

They glared at each other, having come to a standoff in their continuing tug-of-war. Neither of them could gracefully give in, yet both knew Rachel would have her way. She always did in the little things, but she had always been wise enough not to oppose Daniel in anything of importance. Her heart ached because he was going, and she was sure he would never return, but she would not have tried to get him not to go. That tug-of-war would have put their love to a test she could not bear. Rachel sighed, and watched the wanderlust creep into Daniel's eyes.

"Perhaps Alfonso should go," said Daniel. "A young

man should see God's handiwork before man spoils it all. Walk through the wilderness before it is all gone."

Havana had some eighty households, and everyone joined in the bustle of outfitting the flotilla, speculating on the fortunes to be made. Most of the hardware had been secured in Spain: arms, munitions, spades, pickaxes, and crude iron needed for blacksmith forges. Baskets and ropes and foodstuffs had been partially secured in Cuba—including twenty-five hundred shoulders of bacon furnished by Ramón Fuentes and crates of casabe bread which would keep for months, plus three hundred hogs on the hoof, three hundred or so horses, and the descendants of the pack of hounds that had worked out so well in pacifying Hispañola.

The dry stores had been stowed away, and on Saturday, May 17, 1539, Fray Dominic stood by the seashore wrinkling his nose as he swung the censer, sprinkling Holy Water as he blessed three hundred hogs. Jesús Fuentes, assisted by a detachment of men under Paco Sandoval, tried to herd the swine up the gangplank into longboats, but the hogs protested—squealing, grunting, running everywhere except up the plank.

Sandoval did not relish this duty, but he accepted it to secure his position with the expedition. He expected to come back rich enough to buy a title. Soon Sandoval began enjoying himself, making a game of it, running through the surf after the slippery swine—catching one by the ear, another by the tail, matching his hog-catching skill against that of the raw recruits until all their fancy breeches were soaked in brine and their particolored hose hung in soggy shreds. After the last hog had been loaded, they slung their ruined leather boots over their shoulders and strutted into Havana to the Torres bodega, clapping each other on the back and making ribald jokes.

"Wine!" they demanded as Sarah came to wait on them.

As Sarah served the wine, Paco slapped her on the hips and made a remark about her nose, after which

Sarah refused to serve them again. Alfonso came into the bodega, glowered at the rowdies, and told them they should be ashamed to call themselves Spanish gentlemen. At that moment Alfonso almost decided to disobey his mother and remain in Cuba to see that Sarah need never be insulted again, but he was too well schooled in the Commandments, and he knew his mother would never let his father go without him.

"Tell me, Torres," Sandoval said. "Are you the judaizer who is going to be our hostler?"

"Does my Hebrew ancestry make me a judaizer?" asked Alfonso, in a guarded tone. "King Fernando himself was descended from Jews. My family are old Christians. My father furnishes all the oil for the churches in Cuba—imported olive oil, nothing but the best. He helped rebuild the cathedral in Santiago after the earthquake, and the church in Havana after the corsairs burned it. No woman attends Mass more faithfully than my mother."

Sandoval grinned a knowing grin, winked at his companions, and drained his cup. Alfonso hated it when his worlds collided. He had no knowledge of his grandparents' martyrdom, because his mother never mentioned it and his father did not remember. Sometimes Alfonso wondered who he was—the Jew Samuel at secret services in the bosom of the family, or the Christian Alfonso running a thriving mercantile business. Alfonso knew he had to be careful of men like Paco Sandoval, but he wanted to say: "I am a Jew! Make what you will of it!"

The very success of the Torres family made them suspect, as success had always made Jews suspect. Alfonso dared not be so bold, yet he hated feeling guilty for being born a Jew. He hated most of all the feeling that he should somehow blame his parents. Perhaps this was why he had never married. How could he place this burden on an unborn child? He would be happy when the fleet sailed. With a continent to pacify, who would bother about whether or not Samuel Alfonso Torres was a Jew?

* * *

Adelantado Don Hernando de Soto lost count of the people waiting to board—a couple hundred caballeros, four hundred or so infantry, another couple hundred support personnel; plus African and morisco body servants, Indian slaves trying to get back home, mestizo mistresses, and the camp followers who always manage to swarm around an army. Soto made a wild guess of fifteen hundred and a conservative estimate of a thousand, not forgetting the clerics and friars and their slaves, and the four Indians Juan de Añasco had captured on his scouting voyage. What did it matter how many there were, or that Soto had not fulfilled his charter commanding him to take food enough for eighteen months? Hadn't armies always lived off the land? Soto had invested all his fortune in outfitting this venture, and if he couldn't commandeer supplies, he wouldn't make a profit.

Just before he allowed the final boarding, Soto addressed the assembly from a longboat. Following a short Mass, he read aloud his charter from the Casa de Contratación and His Catholic Majesty Emperor Carlos. The Sunday sky was Caribbean blue and the friars' vestments green overlaid with white and gold satin chasubles. Flags flew from the ships and nobility banners hung from every rail, as Soto began reading the three-thousand-word document in a dry voice—a document providing for the conquest and governing of the eastern half of North America known as Florida, and establishing Cuba as its capital:

"'Inasmuch as you, Captain Hernando de Soto, set forth that you have served us in the conquest, pacification, and settlement of the provinces of Nicaragua and Peru, and other parts of our Indies...'"

He was to take, at his own expense, officers of the King's exchequer and such ecclesiastical personnel as were necessary for the instruction of the natives in the Holy Catholic Faith, paying their passage and providing for their subsistence. Ransom of any caciques captured was to be divided one fifth for the King, one seventh for Soto, and the rest among the conquerors. The crowd, which had been noisy during most of the reading, hushed as Soto read the King's instructions about the spoil:

"'Likewise, that all the gold and silver, stones, pearls, and other things that may be found and taken, as well in the graves, sepulchres, and temples of the Indians, as in other places where they are accustomed to offer sacrifices to their idols, or in other concealed religious precincts, or buried in houses, or patrimonial soil, or in the ground, or in some other public place, whether belonging to the community or to an individual, be his state of dignity what it may, of the whole, and of all other, of the character that may be and is found, whether finding it by accident or discovering it by search, shall pay us the half, without diminution of any sort, the other half remaining to the person who has found or made the discovery...'"

Soto's voice droned on, reading the license—nay, the command—to steal, rob graves, and desecrate places of worship in the name of God and King. He paused to let his audience absorb the provisions before reading the rest. He skipped the regulations forbidding maltreatment of the Indians. Most of Soto's people had served with similar missions and knew what to expect. The regulations would not be obeyed; reading them was unnecessary.

Soto rolled up the sheepskin. He had not read the last few sentences—the penalties if he, Soto, failed to carry out the charter issued in the name of the King by the powerful Casa de Contratación. If he failed to pacify and populate Florida as agreed, the King would: *"...order that you be punished and proceed against you as against one who keeps not nor complies with, but acts counter to, the commands of his natural king and lord."*

Soto, like all the other conquistadores, had sunk all he had into this venture, all the gold he had captured in Peru. Conquest was a business from which a man expected to profit. If Soto failed to pacify the Indians, he would be a ruined man afraid to go home to face his creditors, a disgrace like Alonzo de Ojeda, who had ridden so high when he captured the cannibal Cacique Caonabó.

As Soto finished, the crowd surged forward to board. Rachel clung to Daniel, tears streaming unashamedly down her face.

"Don't go, Daniel, please," she pleaded, losing all the composure she had cultivated these past months. "Please don't go. I know I will never see you again. Never!"

"Nonsense! What can happen? I will be far from the fighting. Besides, think of the profit we will make from the Florida trade—duty-free, the King promises, for eight years."

"Will profit warm my bed on Sabbath nights?" asked Rachel. "You will not come back. I feel it."

"I will be back before winter for a load of trade goods. You will see. I will write often. Florida is not so far away from Havana. Now dry your eyes and blow your nose like you used to do in Córdoba when I gave you licorice roots. Then say good-bye to our son Sam— to our son Alfonso," he corrected himself. He must be careful now.

"Take care of your father, Alfonso," Rachel ordered. "Make him wear a stocking cap when he sleeps. And watch what he eats. He sometimes eats things he shouldn't. Do you think God does not know what goes on in Florida?"

Alfonso hugged his mother and kissed her on both cheeks, then turned to find Sarah looking at him with those Oriental eyes and pressing a wrapped package into his hands. He stammered a refusal, ashamed to have Sarah give him a gift, but when he saw that shimmer in those marvelous eyes, he hastily took the package and kissed her on both cheeks.

"Go with God!" Sarah said.

"May the Lord watch between me and thee," Alfonso muttered, turning away red with embarrassment.

In the midst of the confusion of boarding, Daniel suddenly became bold. What did it matter now whether someone suspected him of judaizing? As he stepped into the longboat and pushed off, he said proudly, loudly enough for anyone to hear who might have been listening:

"Next year in Jerusalem!"

Sarah and Rachel clung together as the fleet sailed out of the harbor. Rachel strained her eyes as long as she imagined she could see a sail. Her heart told her she would not see Daniel again until the Shekhina-Matronit gathered up all the people of the Exile and brought them into the shimmering curtain of souls around the Throne of Glory.

"Next year in Jerusalem," Rachel murmured to a soaring seagull.

CHAPTER 2

Florida, 1539

Huracán fills the gulf guarding the long peninsula. Jove's universal all-seeing eye prepares to layer life and death...Mother and Father—impregnating, conceiving, nourishing, devouring in the endless cycle of Creation. One God, indivisible—the Beginning of that which has no beginning, and the End of that which has no end...

The Infinite withdrawing into Himself, away from Herself for the time and space needed for creation...God manifest suitable to purpose—now animal, now human...now cataclysm, now nothingness—the Nothingness in which everything abides...the Great I Am— Eternal, Infinite, Inscrutable...the Nameless whose unspeakable name contains all...

Huracán broods over Florida...

Florida is millions of lives briefly lived in sweet verdant summers...plant eaters and meat eaters...one-celled animals oozing up, swimming, crawling, standing, falling—shaking underground labyrinths with thundering crash of great bodies. Snarling, biting clawing, devouring each other as extinct species emerge into new life forms.

Isolated into islands by inundation of melting polar ice and elevated into mountains as earth retreats from searing solar power—submerged or not, Florida is irrevocably part of the Caribbean.

Think not to contain God, nor to limit Creation. Another breath and you, too, become part of the Great I Am.

Huracán broods...

CHAPTER 3

Bay of the Holy Spirit, 1539

HALFWAY UP the gulf side of the finger-shaped peninsula lay the port Añasco had selected as point of de-
barkation for Soto's expedition. When the hurricane
finally abated, the air had a fresh-washed look and the
sea a variegated sparkle. The fecund smell of the bruised
land guided Soto's fleet to the mouth of the bay they
named Holy Spirit. They anchored just outside the bar
on Whitsunday, May 25, 1539. As they dropped anchor,
all hands crowded the rails and hung from the rigging,
shouting unanimous praise to God for such a Paradise.

The flotilla—five ships, two caravels, and three small
brigantines—anchored outside the deep-throated harbor—a landlocked maze of shallows and shoals, of false
inlets and wide rivers and enough islands to hide a
painted heathen army.

Daniel Torres watched uneasily as Indian smoke signaled their arrival. He stood on the deck of the brigantine selected to explore the bay, half expecting to hear
Mayabaño's Carib war cry. Alfonso stood in the bow
helping a sailor with the sounding. The ships and car-

avels could not cross the shallow bar until the horses were debarked.

Soto sent Captain-General Vasco Porcallo ashore with a scouting party; they had orders to round up some Indians for the formal ceremony of taking possession. Then he sailed back across the bar to pick up the soldiers and priests necessary to possess Florida in the name of Carlos V, Emperor of the Holy Roman Empire.

Receding tides from the hurricane had left the rock weir teeming with fish. The Timucua family had built additional boucans to smoke their catch, chatting happily as they worked. Smoked pompano, mackerel, and bluefish would tide them over until the green corn was ready. The young husband and the old father waded out to spear more fish. The old mother carried a wooden platter of freshly smoked fish toward a piney hummock where the young mother sat nursing her baby. A small boy squatted beside a tree with a drawn bow, waiting for a squirrel to come within shooting distance. At the edge of the clearing a deer grazed patiently as her flag-tailed fawn nuzzled her from time to time.

The young woman smiled as the baby stopped nursing. The woman playfully tickled the baby's nose with the tip of her shiny black braid. The old woman scolded, so the mother laid her baby in his hammock in the corner of the sturdy bahío with the raised log floor but no walls. Before she joined the old woman, she diapered the baby with fresh moss gathered from the trees around the clearing.

A chameleon scampered up the post as the mother set the hammock swinging. She hummed a Taino lullaby until the baby sighed. Then she went to help the old woman store the fish in a deerskin pouch.

The boy sat so still the squirrel became too brave. Twang! The boy ran gleefully toward the twitching squirrel. A roseate spoonbill soared up from a pond left by the storm, frantically beating its wings to clear the treetops.

Paco Sandoval rode with Porcallo's seven horsemen

in the scouting party, chain mail rattling as he swam his horse ashore, splashed through a reed bog, and galloped through a patch of sea oats onto a hummock covered with sea grapes. Paco plucked a bunch of green berries, which grew on the trees with rusty red trunks and big coin-round leaves; their branches arched every which way to make pine-needled grottoes. Snowy egrets flew up as the troop hacked its way through the hummock with swords. A roseate spoonbill frantically treaded water, flapping its wings to get airborne.

The two Timucua men heard the commotion and fled to the trees, where they turned and drew arrows from their coiled hair to rain on the Spanish. The caballeros retreated, and the Timucua jubilantly followed, hurling spears after the arrows were exhausted. Knots of feathers designed to protect their elbows fluttered in the breeze as they defiantly waved their empty bows. Their faces and shoulders were painted black to keep off mosquitoes; they wore loincloths woven from moss.

"Attack! Attack!" ordered Porcallo when the Timucua retreated toward the hummock for a fresh supply of arrows.

Lances and alabardas became hopelessly entangled in vines and tree limbs, delaying the charge, but the knights caught the two Timucua at the edge of the clearing. Porcallo drew first blood, impaling the young man on his lance. With one pendulum swing of his alabarda, Paco Sandoval dispatched the old woman and the boy and nicked the old man on the shoulder, knocking him down.

The young woman ran screaming into the woods. Very beautiful, Paco thought as he watched her disappear. He saw the cradle rocking in the breeze and knew she would return. As the old man tried to stand up, Paco roped him and dragged him half-running, half-stumbling through a clump of sea oats while the others cheered. The young mother peered from behind a palmetto clump, then darted across the clearing toward the baby's hammock.

Sandoval caught her just before she reached the bahío, gagged her to stop her screaming, and tied her behind his saddle. As the troop left the clearing with the old man and his daughter-in-law, a cardinal flew down to sit on the strings of the baby's hammock, and the doe who had been frightened away came back to graze. The fawn ambled over to peer curiously at the sleeping baby.

When Porcallo's troop returned with the Indians, the Adelantado Don Hernando de Soto was waiting on shore with his infantry and his clergymen. As the troop dismounted, Porcallo's horse fell dead—an arrow embedded deep in its belly, unseen beneath caparison and saddle. They had lost twenty horses to the hurricane, but this was their first battle casualty.

Soto's troops stood at attention in six companies of fifty as friars in gold-trimmed vestments chanted the Te Deum, solemnly planting the ornate iron cross against rusty trunks of sea grapes. Flanking the cross stood the color guard carrying the banners of Santiago de Compostela, His Catholic Majesty Emperor Carlos V, and Soto's own bloody eagle. Somewhere back among the islands an alligator trumpeted and a cottonmouth moccasin slithered up a cypress branch.

The men could not keep from ogling the young woman's bare breasts as Fray Dominic chanted. The bewildered Indians tried not to look frightened as Soto unrolled the sheepskin to read the *Requirements*—a royal document the Spanish conquerors were mandated to read to Indians whenever they took possession of new territories. He read, of course, in Spanish, hurriedly slurring the words the Indians would not have understood anyway.

"'On behalf of King Carlos V, grandson of Their Catholic Highnesses Don Fernando and Doña Isabela of Castilla and León, etc.,...we, their servants, notify you and make known as well as we are able, that God, our Lord...'"

Soto's voice droned on, to the increasing bewilderment of the Indians, spelling out the conditions and listing the justification for seizure of their lands, their property, and their lives. The *Requirements* proclaimed belief in God, Creator of the universe, and in the established spiritual descendant of Saint Peter called the Pope—ordained by God to rule over all mankind no matter where scattered over the earth. This benevolent Pope had appointed Their Catholic Highnesses, through Soto and his men, to receive the services of the Indians on behalf of God, to instruct them in the Faith, and to bring them into the Church.

If they submitted, they would be received with love and charity and allowed to continue working their lands under ownership and for the benefit of the caballeros, and to pay tribute to the Crown and tithe to the Church. If they resisted, Soto's army would—with God's help—make war upon them, take their persons and their wives, their sons and their daughters, and make slaves of them. The choice belonged to the Indians. It had all been carefully stated in this document. Neither Pope nor Crown, Soto nor the caballeros would be to blame for what happened if the Indians chose to resist. The young woman and the old man, who had been chosen to represent all the Indians of eastern North America, understood not a single word.

After the ceremony, the new Governor General of Florida gave the young Indian woman to Paco Sandoval as a reward for his daring. Sandoval chained her to a tree to keep her from running away while they debarked the horses. He tossed her the squirrel her son had killed and ordered her to dress it and cook it for supper. The stiff squirrel, still impaled on the boy's arrow, fell unnoticed at her feet. Her eyes had glazed over to mask the turmoil boiling inside her.

The first day of occupation was almost over. The setting sun was haloed by cumulus clouds, and the water outside the bay glowed orange, as Alfonso debarked the last horse from the flagship *San Cristóbal*, alternately coaxing and cursing Soto's prize pasofino to cross the unsteady gangplank to the brigantine. The mare neighed, walled her eyes toward the high poop deck, then backed into the Canary Islands Negro shoving on her rump. He cursed in guttural gibberish and buried his fist in her flank. The mare kicked out, sending the Negro sprawling against the mainmast. Daniel shouted at him for not being more helpful to Alfonso, and the burly man gave both men the evil eye before he picked himself up and began shoving and cursing again. He wished he had the legendary Canary Islanders' ability to fly.

They had lost twenty horses to the hurricane, plus Porcallo's mount killed by the Indians. Soto would play aperrear with any men who lost his prize pasofino. Swimming horses ashore from so far out was impossible, so they could only be transferred to the brigantines by the gangplank.

The mare gingerly put one foot on the gangplank and pranced across as if on parade. Alfonso hurried across the plank, and Daniel followed, relieved that this was the last load of the day. The tide would soon be going out, and Soto would be stuck inside the harbor away from the main fleet until the next high tide. Tall masts with sun-gilded sails cast a network of shadows across the iridescent water as the brigantine pulled toward shore. Indian smokes ringed the darkening mouth of the bay.

Alfonso wondered how many horses he had coaxed across that gangplank today. His aching muscles said several hundred, but his head-count tabulated only eighty-one—plus those carried on the brigantines. They had started out from Cuba with three hundred, so tomorrow would be another trying day.

Daniel clapped his son on the shoulder, proud of his adaptation to outdoor life; he was glad he had brought Alfonso to Florida, glad they did not have to unload arms and supplies—especially the hogs. How would Jesús Fuentes get three hundred hogs down that gangplank?

As they sailed across the bar between two islands, a manatee surfaced a few yards away, flipped over on her side, and began suckling her quarter-ton baby. Gulls circled overhead, wheeling and scolding. On one of the small islands a tiny deer with miniature antlers zigzagged through a series of puddles, spraying up liquid gold.

Everyone hugged the cookfires to keep away swarms of mosquitoes. Tree frogs played concerts, accompanied by an owl in the sea grapes. Silvery-gray wraiths of moss swayed from cypress branches. Daniel's heart contracted with the beauty of his first Florida sunset.

He dropped to the ground, too weary to stand. He must be getting old, he thought, if helping debark a few horses could tire him so. He recalled that day at the Sevilla horse fair when he had met Santángel and made his contract. He had been so unsure of himself because he was too young, now he was equally unsure of himself because he was too old. He plucked a streamer of Spanish moss and rolled it into a pillow. He looked at the puffs of Indian smoke, wondering how long it would take Mayabaño to know they were here.

Where would Mayabaño pitch his battle? If he attacked tonight, he could wipe out the command post and perhaps abort the expedition. Daniel had no doubt that Mayabaño had been responsible for the failure of the three previous expeditions—Juan Ponce de León, Ayllon, and Narváez had all been killed. Mayabaño might have evened up his score with Narváez for killing his family and almost having him killed.

Possessing Florida might not be as easy as reading the *Requirements* before a couple of Indians. Daniel lay on a soft cushion of long needles, picked up a handful of soil, and sifted it through his fingers. Partly sand, mostly broken bits of seashells, a small animal bone, and a pebble or two of coral—Florida lives lived long ago.

Daniel thought of Rachel as men growing old always think of their wives of many years—young! Sweet Rachel. Seductive Rachel. Little Rachel of Córdoba sucking on a licorice root.

"Rachel, beloved," he murmured to tree frogs and mosquitoes. "Next year in Jerusalem."

When Alfonso walked up behind his father with a plate of food, the old man was snoring softly.

* * *

The Indian woman lay slumped against a cypress tree a few feet from the spot where Alfonso stood watch. Her wrists were caked with blood from jerking at her iron fetters. Alfonso pulled his embroidered coat, Sarah's coat, out of his bedroll as the cool sea breeze came up. Round fan-shaped palm leaves rustled overhead, and Alfonso inhaled the perfumes of the white blossoms. He whistled an old Arabic love ballad to keep himself awake as he watched the dozing horses tethered to the remuda line.

A panther screamed, somewhere in the direction of the clearing where Sandoval had captured the woman— then another panther, and another. Soon the pack was snarling over its find. The woman cried out, pleading in high-pitched gibberish. Sandoval sauntered over and cuffed her. Alfonso jumped to his feet, then hung back, knowing it was foolish to rouse Sandoval's ire. The woman jabbered again, her pleading eyes fixed on Alfonso. The panthers were quieter now, snarling only once in a while. Sandoval hit the woman again. She stopped jabbering and began whimpering.

"Leave her alone, Sandoval," Alfonso ordered.

"Mind your own affairs, Jew peddler," Sandoval said.

"Is this how a caballero treats a woman?"

"She is Indian. A wild savage. Given one chance, she'll knife you."

"Leave her alone, I say," Alfonso insisted.

"Soto gave her to me. I will do with her as I please," Sandoval snarled. "If you have any complaints, take them up with the Adelantado."

Alfonso heard rather than saw the woman struggling, but he saw Sandoval lower his body upon her. Alfonso turned away, not able to help and unwilling to watch. He could not afford to strike a caballero. Not one of the other caballeros would consider Sandoval in the wrong. Alfonso's face burned with shame, but this was the first night of a long expedition. He could not take on all the troubles of the Indians. Yet he was ashamed of being Spanish, and ashamed of being a man, but most of all ashamed of being a helpless Jew.

"Listen, Jew peddler," Sandoval jeered as he pulled

up his clothes. "What will you give for a little piece of her?"

"Bastard! Rum bastard!" Alfonso muttered, using the old derisive Arab name for Christians, but not loudly enough for Sandoval to hear.

One of the panthers screamed again, but the woman was past crying. Perhaps it was just as well she was chained and could not go back to the clearing.

At midnight Alfonso shook Jesús awake to relieve him on watch. Before he lay down to sleep, Alfonso spread his new brocade coat over the shivering Indian woman. His father still snored softly, and Alfonso was asleep almost as soon as he lay down.

The panthers had finished their meal now. A raccoon scampered through camp carrying a rodent to the water. Overhead a spider spun a hurricane-shaped web—a slender, silvery trap. Soon a couple of fireflies winked in the web.

Lilith slipped easily into Alfonso's dream, sliding down a wispy Spanish moss, holding a wrapped bundle in her hands. Her body was the Indian woman's body, but her eyes were Sarah's eyes. Lilith smiled as she handed Alfonso the present, but he laid it aside unopened as he reached for her. Lilith evaporated in his arms, melting like fog until only her smooth navelless belly shone in the darkness.

Lilith's eerie laugh lingered as Alfonso reached for the package. The brocade wrapping fell away as he clutched his own penis—circumcised miraculously, but still recognizable by touch as his own—hot and hard and throbbingly familiar. Oh! So familiar.

Oh, God! How many times had he spilled his seed upon the ground? Forgive me, he breathed through raspy nostrils as he began to masturbate. He evoked the image of the Indian girl to ease the pain of his loneliness. Try as he would, he could not blank out Sarah's eyes. As warm semen spurted over his hands, he felt a palmetto bug crawl up the back of his neck.

Toward morning Daniel woke suddenly, hearing a panther scream. It sounded like the plaintive echo of Anacaona's song. Daniel sat up and looked at the sleepers until he could distinguish his son Alfonso. Before journey's end, many of them would be dancing to Anacaona's music. Daniel lay down and tried to go back to sleep, but he couldn't. He kept listening to the Indian woman crying softly.

CHAPTER 4

Bay of the Holy Spirit, 1539

MAYABAÑO HAD been running all night—ever since he had seen the smoke message—pacing himself carefully, as his legs carried him toward the village at the head of the bay where Hirrihigua and the other Timucua caciques would be waiting. Ever since Juan de Añasco had captured the four Indians to take back to Havana, Mayabaño had known the cross-worshippers were coming. Now they were here, and he was ready.

Half of the fifty-five years registered in the knotted cords tied around Mayabaño's waist had been spent preparing the people of Florida to repel the Christians. Someday, after Mayabaño's spirit had spread itself upon the winds, the invaders might succeed, but not while he lived. Not while people remembered Anacaona's song.

Mayabaño still wore his hair plucked so the butterfly showed beneath the white buzzard tuft. The jagged scar across his chest gave the megaluccus tattoo a sinister look. A war club, circled by three crescent moons, in turn circled by stars, was tattooed on his right forearm. The war club signified his pledge to fight the invaders. Warriors from villages all over the land had such tattoos and were awaiting Mayabaño's orders. They would fight the common enemy, regardless of old tribal animosities. Crescent moons indicated caciques who had participated in defensive campaigns, and stars were earned by showing the scalplock of an invader. Mayabaño wore in his nose the finger bones from his most notable victory—the killing of Narváez.

Higueymato had guided the long canoe across the ninety miles of water from Havana to the Caye of Bones, and she had patiently nursed Mayabaño back to health before they began their mission of warning people of the continent to resist the Christians. While Mayabaño was recovering, Higueymato gathered conch shells. When he was well enough, they worked their way from key to key trading. In every village Higueymato sang and danced Anacaona's song.

Since then they had traveled all over the southeastern half of the continent from the big river Chucagua to Cofachiqui—trading baskets, sharks' teeth, smoked fish, turquoise, copper beads, deer-horn spoons, salt, flint, persimmon cakes, pet squirrels, mockingbirds, anything and everything anyone wanted to trade. Mayabaño played football and stickball, chunkey and hide-the-arrow and toss-the-beans. Higueymato cheered the ball teams, danced their dances, and sang with them their burial songs. Mayabaño sat respectfully in temples and ossuaries looking at the images of caciques dead hundreds of years; he thoughtfully examined tribal arsenals and war arks.

In Cofachiqui Higueymato met the handsome young nephew of a cacique, a man in line for tribal leadership if his people approved. When Higueymato saw him, her shyness vanished. Mayabaño could not believe how boldly she flirted, or how she schemed to get the warrior to notice her. Higueymato knew what she was doing, for the man was the only man in the world for her. At first she embarrassed him by the intensity of her devotion, but soon he realized she was the well of his pleasure. He came to that well many times to refresh himself before he finally married her.

Mayabaño took War as his wife and warriors as his

children. Many caciques loaned him their favorite wives so his brave blood would flow in the veins of their children. The Indians called him War Man Who Talks With Wind. Perhaps he did. Perhaps Huracán himself gave Mayabaño advance notice of the invaders, sent breezes to whisper when the cross-worshippers were seaborne.

Mayabaño had repelled three invasions. Ponce de León had staggered home to die. Ayllón's colony met similar fates. Mayabaño himself had presided over Narváez's lingering death—using all the tortures learned from the Christians, tying Narváez to a tree and dismembering him slowly, roasting the conquistador's flesh and eating it before his eyes. After Narváez died, Mayabaño cleaned his bones and put them in his trading pack; not even when the bones were scattered in temples all over the land did Mayabaño's hate diminish.

Hirrihigua and Mocuzo were waiting for Mayabaño in the longhouse atop the cacique's mound at the head of the bay. After running most of the night, Mayabaño sat down in silence while the caciques passed the pipe from one to the other. Important decisions could not be made hurriedly. They sat without speaking until the sun was well up in the sky. Finally, with very little talk, they settled on a plan of action. Mayabaño knew from previous experience that the invaders could best be defeated by wearing them down, before moving in for the kill.

Hirrihigua would abandon his village and retire with his people to the glades, sending messengers up the peninsula with Mayabaño's knotted-thong war messages. Mocuzo would make friends with the Adelantado, delaying him as long as possible in Hirrihigua's village and giving him the captured Spaniard Juan Ortiz as interpreter. Ortiz had been saved from death by the cacique's daughter, and during his years living with the Indians had made for himself a place of friendship and trust. The invaders were not evil if they were not more numerous than the Indians, and if they were not armed and mounted. Ortiz would unwittingly lead the army to Cacique Anhiaca's Apalachee village, where they would have to winter. The warriors in Timucua villages in between here and Apalachee would fight delaying battles. Cacique Anhiaca's warriors would further reduce their numbers during the winter.

Mayabaño sent knotted deerskin thongs to all the caciques informing them how many warriors would be needed for the final battle. When his army was ready, he would send other knotted thongs to guides who would lead the cross-worshippers into his trap. In the meantime, the invaders would be easy to mislead with rumors of gold. When Mayabaño was ready, Soto's army would be led westward to Mauvilla where the war-club society would be waiting.

CHAPTER 5

Bay of the Holy Spirit, 1539

NEXT MORNING the young Indian woman was awakened by the ache of milk-filled breasts; she pulled the fancy coat up around her shoulders for a few moments, staring dry-eyed as dawn blotted out the stars. She sighed deeply as she unbraided her hair, then she pushed back the coat and sat up. Slowly and with great effort, she disarranged her hair to indicate mourning. Her husband had called her Topokeegee Yungee, which means Happy Place, but she knew she would never be called that name again. Before she gathered branches to build the boucan for cooking Sandoval's breakfast, she carefully covered Alfonso with Sarah's coat.

Dull eyes looked out of her tear-swollen face, and milk oozed from her breasts and ran down into her moss skirt. As she leaned over Sandoval to serve the grilled mackerel, he playfully pinched one breast. A feeble stream of milk shot into his mouth. The men laughed, and he milked first one breast, then the other, while the woman stood immobile. When Paco Sandoval tired of the game, the woman shuffled away on shackled feet.

Alfonso had been watching, clinching his fists so tightly his nails dug into his palms.

"Rum bastard!" Alfonso muttered. "Lazy Rum bastard! Who does he think he is—the high mukaddam?"

Islamics had always called Christians Rum, and a *mukaddam* was the van leader of Mohammedan armies. Alfonso relieved himself against a bush, imagining it was Sandoval's face. *Piss on you, Rum bastard! High mukaddamuk, piss on you!*

The June morning soon became steamy, and although Sandoval donned his chain mail, he refused to wear armor plate. He dumped the armor on the Indian woman before he went off scouting with Porcallo. The four interpreters Añasco had brought to Havana had run off during the night, and Soto needed replacements. They also needed bearers for the baggage, and Porcallo was beginning to assemble a slave shipment to send back to Havana.

"Here, let me help you with that," said Alfonso as the woman struggled with the armor.

She clutched the armor to her, surprised. Men hunted; women carried. She looked over her shoulder, afraid Sandoval would beat her. She was Sandoval's woman now.

"It is all right," Alfonso assured her in a soothing voice she could understand, even if she could not understand Spanish. "It is all right. Sandoval is a warrior; Alfonso is a carrier and hostler. Alfonso can help you."

Each time he said his name, he pointed to his chest. Finally she let go the armor and let him tie it across the back of a horse.

"Alfonso," he said again, pointing to himself. "I am called Alfonso. Al...fon...so. Alfonso."

"Al...fon...so...?" she repeated, quizzically. "Alfonso?"

"Alfonso! Very good. What are you called?"

She turned away. One must not say one's name. Others decided by what name you should be called. No one knew she had been called Happy Place, and the name no longer suited her.

"Ruth," Alfonso decided. "I shall call you Ruth, the

Moabitess. 'Whither thou goest, I will go;...thy people shall be my people, and thy God my God.'"

Of course, she did not understand he wanted her to follow him faithfully, as the biblical Ruth had followed Naomi. Ruth could become his concubine...after Sandoval tired of her. But what of Sarah? Alfonso tried to put Sarah's dark eyes out of his mind. Sarah did not belong in the Florida wilderness. The sun was up and the day was warm. Alfonso shrugged off Sarah's embroidered coat and tied it across the pack horse.

"Ruth," he said, pointing to her.

She nodded her head. Ruth, she said to herself, but it would not be good to say her new name aloud. She looked around to be sure Sandoval was not watching her talk with another man.

"Ruth," Alfonso said as the vanguard mounted up, "You have a baby. Where is your baby? I will get it for you."

Her milk-filled breasts told him she suckled a child, perhaps two. Indian women often suckled their children until they were twelve or thirteen years old, so if famine struck, the young would survive and the tribe would not die out.

"Baby?" he repeated, cradling his arms and rocking back and forth. "Baby? Where is your baby?"

Tears came into her eyes, and she shook her head.

"Don't you have a baby?" he asked again.

She shook her head vigorously, wiping away a tear that trickled down her nose. Then Alfonso understood. If the woman had had a baby, Sandoval had left it behind. Last night the panthers...

"My God!" he cursed. "That bastard! That Rum bastard!"

As Ruth shuffled away, Alfonso slammed his fist into a sabal palmetto.

As the trumpets blew and the vanguard moved out, Alfonso noticed a bright green chameleon sunning itself—trying to look like a leaf, but spoiling the ruse by flashing its bright orange sun. As the clanking, creaking, centaurianlike army moved through the mud flat into the tangled forest, a flock of snowy egrets alighted on a dead tree—silvery, surrealistic leaves fluttering in the golden sun of the Florida morning. Alfonso knew then that he would never get Florida out of his blood. He had been bewitched, and he would pass the enchantment down to his children and his children's children; so that no matter where they were born or raised, if they ever came to Florida they would know they had come home.

Florida lay too near primeval mists for most of the Spaniards, who were looking for another Iberian peninsula of castle-rock mountains overlooking rolling savannahs—places like Hispañola and Mexico and the great American Southwest. They would not grieve to leave Florida. They wanted gold more solid than sunshine, lapis lazuli more malleable than cerulean lakes, and precious gems more lasting than tree orchids and air plants.

Soto occupied Hirrihigua's deserted village at the head of the bay—eight or ten common houses, each large enough to house a hundred people; a temple–charnel house topped by a wooden bird with gilt eyes; and the cacique's house built atop a terraced mound near the beach. They leveled the forest a crossbow's distance from the village and commandeered Indian corn stores. Then they brought the fleet into the harbor and unloaded cargo.

Soto ordered the cacique's mound excavated for possible treasure, but they found only shells and bones and pottery shards. The Indians had built their main defense on a pile of garbage! The temple–charnel house contained only a few charred pearls, plus Indian bodies neatly laid out on shelves. Soto ordered the heathen temple destroyed.

Luckily they found Cuban refugee Juan Ortiz—a survivor of the Narváez expedition who had lived in Florida so long he was mistaken for an Indian and was about to be killed before he cried out in Spanish. Ortiz became their interpreter and brought his benefactor Mocuzo to Soto's camp. Soto questioned the friendly cacique about gold and whether Indians living inland cultivated corn. The army could not move inland without adequate food supplies along the way. Mocuzo, following Mayabaño's instructions, spun a tale of gold just beyond the horizon—a story Soto was to hear from every cacique who wanted the marauding army out of his territory.

In early June, Soto sent most of the ships back to Havana to be sold, left a detachment to guard the supplies in Hirrihigua's village, and marched inland with the main body of the army. Before he left, two treacherous guides had to be thrown to the dogs.

With great apprehension and mounting enthusiasm, the Adelantado Don Hernando de Soto ordered the trumpets sounded on the morning of June 15, 1540, and the armored companies moved out: vanguard, color guard, battle guard, rear guard...horses...hogs... mules...the battle wagon carrying the lone lombard...Indian women with baskets strapped to their heads, baskets filled with doublets, breeches, pikes, shields, helmets—all the accoutrements of an army of caballeros...ropes, hammers, chisels, saws...for building bridges over rivers, and for the fort in their mythical Cibola where they would settle down and build homes, plant gardens, and raise more swine.

Soto's army had camped six weeks in Hirrihigua's village, and they took from the fifteenth of July until the sixth of October to travel the hundred leagues to the Apalachee nation—traversing piney groves and dense forests so wildly beautiful they made the heart ache, and swamps so forbidding and desolate they argued over turning back. Most considered Florida worthless—without defensible mountains or promise of gold. Only neat Indian farms covered the fertile hummocks—with rows of beans, pumpkins, corn, and squash growing among fallen trees. Mayabaño's warriors fought them tree to tree, hiding in cane brakes, rising out of lakes, harassing the Castilians in a ceaseless battle. The Indians' honor demanded they retire when they outnumbered the Christians, leaving the fight evenly matched, but the Castilians were not so chivalrous. Except under trees, horses gave the Christians the advantage, but Indians soon learned to shoot through chinks in the armor.

Soto's centipedelike army crept along eating everything in sight, leaving the Indians without food for the winter. League by league through villages bearing names of caciques—strange names like Urriparicoxi...Tocoste...Ocale...Irarahatata. Joke-provoking names. Who could respect a people who did not give their villages pronounceable Castilian names?

They named some places themselves: River of Discord, where a serious dispute arose; River of the Deer, where friendly Indians presented them with dressed deer; Town of Bad Peace, where a cacique who had exchanged himself for thirty prisoners later tried to escape, causing Soto to play aperrear with him. Once they kept a handful of defeated Indians in a lake until their bodies were white and bloated.

Soto was setting the pattern for the rest of the expedition. He expected to live off the Indians. He demanded bearers and women to service his men—usually the same women did both. He took caciques captive, but released them at the edge of the next village. Some villagers he threatened to burn alive, and some he threw to the hounds. Many villages he found deserted. Mayabaño's guides led the army over treacherous country where small bands of warriors waited to pick them off. Soto, of course, did not know about Mayabaño—but Daniel Torres was sure he was waiting for them somewhere.

Soto was more humane than previous conquistadores; he never understood the hostility of the Indians or their reluctance to give up their villages and provide food for the army. Didn't they understand an army had to eat? Nor did he stop to baptize Indians, though later they set up a few crosses.

By the time they reached Anhaica Apalachee in the rolling hill country at the north end of the long peninsula, word came to Soto that Indians were gathering together an army, but Mayabaño was not yet ready, so

Soto saw nothing to confirm the rumors. Cold winds caused Soto to decide to winter in Apalachee—the most prosperous and best cultivated of the Indian provinces—thus guaranteeing sufficient winter corn for the army, if not enough for the Indians. Soto sent Añasco back to the Bay of the Holy Spirit to break up the settlement and bring the remaining ships to nearby Apalachee Bay.

It had been Soto's custom to release the woman bearers as soon as a new work force had been commandeered, but some, like Ruth, stayed with the army rather than face going back home. She served Sandoval faithfully and uncomplainingly, so he kept her until they settled in for the winter, but with the new women of Apalachee to amuse him, Sandoval turned Ruth out to go home. Having no home and no family, she hung around camp hoping Alfonso would notice her.

Ruth could never go back to the Timucua. She had been only a child when her Taino parents came from Cuba to the Cayes in a double-hulled canoe. She had grown up among the Calusa and had been lucky enough to have a young Timucua man want her for a wife, but she had never been really accepted by his clan, the Alligator Clan. Now she had violated their taboo against adultery. Not that she could have done otherwise—but the Alligators would never forget that her husband's killer had also been her lover, and they would avenge her husband as if he were alive.

She would be imprisoned until the next Green Corn Dance; then, after the cacique had cut off her hair, she would be sent naked between two lines of people trying to explain to each in turn why she had committed adultery. They would insult her and throw garbage at her, then she would be exiled from the province. A ban would be put on anyone who helped her. Some clans stood an adulterous woman against a tree and used her for target practice, but the Alligator Clan was more merciful. Of course, men who violated marriage vows were never punished. A husband might bring a new woman into the house, and the wife had to live with her.

Ruth chose to remain with the Christians rather than face those penalties. She bided her time, doing little things for Alfonso and Daniel when they were not watching, much as Sarah used to do. They would awaken in the morning to find a basket of freshly ground corn-meal on their doorstep.

Ruth traded some of her beautifully woven baskets for bird feathers and copper rings to wear in her ears and her hair. She traded one especially big basket for a clay jar filled with clarified bear grease. She dyed her hair red black, then made it shiny with bear grease, piled it high on her head and adorned it with pink flamingo feathers. She painted her cheekbones with high red spots and her neck and shoulders a delicate shade of pink, then she waited one day beside the spring where Alfonso liked to bathe—a silvery spring bubbling up from underground limestone caves.

It was a bright crisp Florida morning when fog babies lie cradled in hollows and flocks of migrating birds call flight directions. Alfonso undressed and stood for a moment bathed in sunshine, then plunged into the icy water. He swam quickly to the bank and hauled himself out, gasping and shivering, shaking his mane of curly hair before plunging back into the water, to warm himself.

Soon Alfonso was swimming vigorously, as he used to swim in the Río Cauto near Santiago de Cuba when he was a boy—swimming and splashing, diving down into the silvery depths where the sun changes color and everything has an unreal look. He was at home in Earth's womb—at home with the fish and the living limestone formations. His skin tingled, and the blood surged through his body. He had never felt so alive. Again and again he plunged into the soothing waters, unaware of the eyes of the beautiful Indian woman.

Ruth hesitated only because she had seen the beautifully embroidered coat Alfonso wore on chilly nights—the coat he had spread over her the night Sandoval captured her. Alfonso was a good man, Ruth knew that—

kind and gentle, a hard worker strong enough to protect her if she were his woman. She had seen him trying to conceal his wrath when Sandoval mistreated her.

Yet Ruth wondered who had made the coat for him. Sometimes Ruth had seen Alfonso staring into the distance, absentmindedly rubbing his fingertips over the intricately beautiful designs. A look would come over his face—the love look. Ruth promised herself not to think beyond the end of this journey, when Alfonso would surely go back to his woman.

Finally Alfonso pulled himself out of the water and lay down on a sun-warmed rock. Soon he drowsed off and drifted into that other world—the dream world the mind creates for itself between waking and not waking, the fantasy world where all things are conceived before they exist.

Ruth came to Alfonso on the waves of his fantasy, and he did not know whether or not he dreamed her. Not even when he held her in his arms, not even when he tasted her sweet mouth, not even when he took her nipples and rolled them one by one over his tongue, suckling as he had suckled his mother. Oh, Woman!

Alfonso gently opened Ruth's legs and joined himself with her in the only marriage ceremony God Himself ever ordained. They frolicked all afternoon, playing hide-and-seek in the woods. Alfonso could never catch her, for Ruth was fleet as an antelope. Nor could he hide from her, for she always discovered him by crushed fern or upturned pebble. Once a party of Anhaica's warriors came near them, but they were too happy to know danger. The leader of the war party ordered his men to leave them alone. Here was a Spaniard who knew how to make a woman happy.

Ruth awoke next morning in time to salute the rising sun. She paid her respects to the four winds, thanking them for blowing this man her way. Quickly she filled a hollowed-out pumpkin with fresh water, then dropped in hot stones. The pumpkin was cooked to a steamy softness by the time Alfonso and his father awoke. When Ruth heard them stirring, she scooped two servings into wooden bowls, poured over them some sweet bear-grease,

349

then knocked politely on the doorpost of the bahío. She served Daniel first, so the father of her new man would be pleased his son had found such a good woman. For the first time in many months, she had not awakened thinking of the little hammock in the clearing.

"Why is Sandoval's woman serving us breakfast?" Daniel asked.

"She is no longer Sandoval's woman." Alfonso blushed and turned away.

"Oh? Whose woman is she now?"

"She is my woman," murmured Alfonso, who still lived under the shadow of the Fifth Commandment.

"What did you say? I do not think I heard you correctly."

"She is my woman," Alfonso said, a little more firmly.

"What do you mean, she is your woman?"

"She is my woman, and her name is Ruth," Alfonso repeated.

"Is that all you can say? 'She is my woman, she is my woman,' over and over again? 'She is my woman.' Do you think your old father is stupid?"

"I was lonely, Papa," Alfonso said.

"What will your mother say? She is not of our people."

"Now I am not so lonely," Alfonso said, though it seemed a lame thing to say.

"She is not of our people," Daniel repeated. "Why did you not take a woman in Cuba? Why must you take a woman who is not of our people? We do not need anyone to carry our baggage. Why do you need this woman?"

"What is wrong with needing her?" Alfonso's voice was almost defiant. Perhaps he had lived too long under the shadow of his father, by the skirts of his mother.

"She will conceive, and you know the Law. Any child of hers cannot be considered a child of Abraham. It is through the mother the seed passes on. Why could you not wait for some nice Sephardic girl like Sarah? Señor Penis is king now, eh? You think your Señor Penis is the only one to get hard? How many times I have wrestled with Lilith you cannot know! You want an Indian woman should take the place of your mother?"

"Papa, you wouldn't!" Alfonso was outraged as children are when confronted by their parents' sexuality.

"No, I wouldn't, but I have been tempted many times. You think you have found the only beautiful Indian girl? You should have seen Tahíaca when she was in Almodóvar. I crept into her bed the night...the night...She came to me once when my spirit dwelt in sadness." Daniel felt perspiration on his upper lip, although the day was chilly.

What had he almost remembered? Something awful. Something too terrible to be remembered...something that would deal him a blow too great to survive.

"Papa, many men have taken concubines. Many were the wives of King David, yet the sages say he was a man after God's own heart. Even Father Abraham knew his wife's handmaiden."

"Yes, and see what trouble our cousins have caused with their Prophet Mohammed and their 'Allah is great, there is no God but Allah.' All Andalucía felt the heel of Hagar's sandal. Woe is the day Father Abraham let her into his tent. Do not bring such woe upon our household."

"She is just an Indian girl, Papa. Not a girl for the canopy. When we go back home to Cuba, she will go back to her people. Meanwhile, what harm can it do if she makes me happy?"

Daniel had turned away and covered his head with his prayer shawl. He began fingering the fringes as he recited the Shema, *"Hear, O Israel, the Lord our God, the Lord is One..."*

Cold winds had begun blowing during the night, and even the sun had not taken the chill away. Alfonso shivered, and Ruth was beside him holding out Sarah's coat. Alfonso leaned forward so she could put it around his shoulders. It felt good.

CHAPTER 6

Anhaica Apalachee, 1540

BECAUSE ALFONSO and Daniel sheltered Ruth in their bahío and shared what food they had with her, she was one of the few captive Indians to survive the winter. Most of the Indian slaves died of exposure and starvation.

Florida peninsular Indians built towns around artificial mounds fifty feet high—flat topped, with the cacique's house atop mounds accessible only by wooden stairways fifteen or twenty feet wide. Important people lived around a plaza below the mound, and commoners around the fringes on neatly laid-out streets. During attacks they retired to the mound to defend the stairways with volleys of arrows. When the Christians came, the Indians abandoned their towns, trusting the protection of swamps and woodlands.

Native Floridians fought the invaders courageously. Hunted down by horses, they could loose a quiver-full of arrows while a crossbowman reloaded. Their bows were so powerful that arrows penetrated two coats of chain mail; they used reeds that split, and aimed for eye holes in helmets. Consigned to the hounds, they could tear a dog's mouth in a grip not even death could loosen.

When the detachment arrived in Anhaica after breaking camp at the Bay of the Holy Spirit, they carried five men who had been wounded in the genitals. Several others had been left behind in the swamps; their scalps provided entry into Mayabaño's war-club society. Daniel did what he could to help the wounded, and Fray Dominic did what he could to help the dying— Christian wounded and Christian dying; the Indians they left to the buzzards.

Twice during the winter Indians set fire to Anhaica. High winds quickly spread the fire, burning two-thirds of the village to the ground—including medical supplies and clothing. Some Christians began dressing in animal skins. Alfonso managed to save the coat Sarah had woven for him, but not before fire burned a large hole in the sleeve.

Ruth patched the coat with marten skins and added a fine fur collar. She also made Alfonso a pair of deerskin strips to be wound around his legs in place of the particolored hose. He looked very funny with his puffed velvet breeches atop the buckskin leggings. Ruth traded for a pair of buffalo-hair garters to tie the leggings in place.

Patrols went out only to confiscate more corn. Tempers flared as boredom galled the idle caballeros. Indian women walked a thin line, and sullen-eyed Indian men had to be kept chained. Even the friars grew restless. No one baptized Indians because no one would be around to instruct them. Frairs scrupulously said Mass, hoarding the last of the wheat flour for making the Host— which, of course, could not be made from Indian cornmeal.

Fray Dominic spent some time in the hospital wards. He and Daniel developed an uneasy, wary companionship. Fray Dominic had forgotten Daniel was the little boy on the mud flats in Córdoba, and Daniel had blanked Córdoba out of his memory. Still, Daniel always felt uneasy when Fray Dominic came around, but Fray Dominic seemed to need someone to talk with besides the clergy, some of whom thought he was a bit strange—too much of a zealot, too eager for mystic manifestations.

Fray Dominic had studied the history of the Mohammedan dynasties in Andalucía, and if Moslems had not been weakened by luxury and begun fighting among themselves, Fray Dominic might have been Khalif of Córdoba, living in luxury and having special prayers said for him on Friday nights in La Mezquita. Fray Dominic was descended from the Omayyads and carried a most illustrious name: Abdu-l-Rahman, scion of the builders of the Great Mosque in Córdoba. Sometimes Fray Dominic liked to talk of another age, another time of Arab glory—repeating the saying that Africa begins at the Pyrenees.

As a Christian, Fray Dominic was dour and taciturn, but as the Arab Abdu-l-Rahman, he fulfilled the prophecy of Allah's gifts to different races: to the Greeks, brains; to the Chinese, hands; to the Arabs, tongues. Men weary of the long winter, tired of gambling and bored with fantasizing about gold would gather quickly around Fray Dominic when his black Arabian eyes began to sparkle.

"You know," Fray Dominic said one day, "Arabs used to say that because God forbade Christians to enter celestial paradise, he gave them Andalucía."

"True! True!" said men homesick for rolling Spanish hillsides covered with olive and almond groves. Perhaps Soto had chosen to winter in Anhaica because of the rolling hills.

"No people on earth are as proud as Andalucíans," he continued. "To call a warrior an Andalucían is to call him a man of honor."

"True! True!"

"None is so unwilling to bear tyranny, none so quick to disobey their rulers when treated with contempt. Who can make an Andalucían bow his neck or submit to oppression?"

"No one! No one!"

Every man in Soto's army saw himself a king after this conquest; if not a king, then leader of a new conquest. A little money, a few followers also eager to become kings—presto, a new kingdom. Hadn't the Arabs taught them that?

"And no man falls prey more easily to the charms of a beautiful woman!" said Fray Dominic.

The men groaned, thinking of girls left behind, or imagining girls they could have if they found the Cities of Cibola.

"Lust caused the Christians' downfall in Andalucía," Fray Dominic continued. "Lust gave Arabs the victory—unbridled Christian lust for the beautiful daughter of Ilyan, Sultan of Tangiers."

Soto's men drew nearer. Even mixed with a sermon, they liked a spicy romance. The Spanish would cling to romance and chivalry longer than any other people, cleaving a sharp line between home and harem.

"The Sultan Ilyan was a merchant of hawks and horses who, according to the custom of those days, sent his beautiful daughter across the Strait of Gibraltar to be educated in the court of the Christian King Roderic—one of the sultan's best customers. The Gothic king betrayed the sultan's trust. He fell hopelessly in love with the Arab maiden; when she resisted him, he had his way with her by force."

Fray Dominic waited for appropriate expressions of outrage over this breach of chivalry.

"So Ilyan swore to send Roderic such hawks and such horses as he had never before seen. True to his word, the Islamic hawks swept through Iberia on Arabian horses—all the way to the gates of Toledo. Nothing more was ever seen of Roderic except his jeweled sandal on the bank of the Tagus River. They captured Toledo only after Roderic had broken the magic spell protecting the city, and they carried away all its treasures, including Solomon's emerald table—which was never seen again. Some said the table was solid emerald, and some said it had feet of silver, but all agreed it was inlaid with rubies, diamonds, and pearls."

The men's eyes glittered as if this fabled treasure awaited them in the Florida wilderness. Encouraged, Fray Dominic continued. "Every time a new sultan came to power, he enriched himself plundering Christians and burning their villages. If an Arab soldier died fighting for Allah, he was promised a place in Paradise that very day!"

Fray Dominic continued to whip up their fighting spirit as his brethren had done so successfully for centuries—telling of the valorous El Cid and all the Alfonsos who had turned back the Moors and after seven centuries had driven them out of Iberia. He did not neglect to arouse anti-Semitic feelings by pointing out that Jews had sometimes opened the gates of the cities for the Moslems, who then left them in charge and made them trusted court advisors, but he neglected to tell them Jews had fought equally bravely for Christian kings and had been also their trusted court advisors. He told of Pelayo, the hero of the rocky cliffs of Galicia.

"Never question what can be done with a handful of dedicated men," said Soto, who had moved up through the crowd. "Christ himself had only twelve disciples, and Mohammed started with only his wife and a couple of servants. When Francisco Pizarro was going to Peru, he drew a line on the ground with his sword. Behind lay the safety of Panama and the certainty of poverty; ahead lay hardship and danger, and the riches of the Inca. Only thirteen of us stepped across Pizarro's line, but we conquered Peru!"

The men cheered, and Daniel wondered if a few dedicated men could really conquer a country or stop an army. If so, perhaps Mayabaño could keep Florida out of the hands of the Andalucíans. Daniel went back to his bahío to write another letter to Rachel. Soto was sending the brigantines home to Havana with orders to rendezvous at Apalachee Bay with supplies, come next October. Alfonso tried to write a letter to Sarah, but he could find nothing to say. Daniel poured out his heart.

Daniel Torres, hostler with Soto's Expedition to Florida, to Rachel Sánchez y Torres of Havana, Cuba, Greetings:
  Beloved wife, keeper of the walled garden of my

heart where Sabbath light filters through the lace mantilla of your deeds, how I long to see your beautiful face once more, to kiss you and hold you and tell you all the things I seem able to say only in letters. I love you, Rachel, and I have loved you ever since you were a little girl in Córdoba sucking licorice roots.

January in 1540 was bitterly cold, and February offers little warmth; but we are not too uncomfortable. An Indian woman Alfonso calls Ruth does for us. Soto thinks nothing of pressing Indian women into labor after capturing their caciques, but because of tribal taboos, the women can never go home again. This woman Ruth makes us comfortable, and Alfonso seems to have found a manhood I fear he will sorely need before this journey is over.

How arrogantly we Spanish claim the world, assuming the Pope had the right to parcel it out between his two favorites, Spain and Portugal. Soto behaves as if he owned this land and all its inhabitants. We confiscate all their food supplies, leaving them to face months of starvation. Small wonder we face constant hostility.

Mayabaño is out there somewhere, and when it storms, I can hear Anacaona's song in the wind and see Caonabó's iguana face on the clouds. If there had been enough men like Caonabó and enough women like Anacaona, we would never have gotten a foothold in the Caribbean.

We are a passionate people, we Andalucíans—so fervent in our devotion, and so arrogant in our convictions. Perhaps for this reason the Spanish soul has been chosen for the everlasting battle between Good and Evil. When we choose good, we want to be saints; but when we slip into evil, hell has no better champions! How long will we deceive ourselves?

Fray Las Casas is right—all people are one. We are all children of the Most High, blessed be His Holy Name—fragments of one Eternal Soul, destined to live over and over again until we get it right. The Indians have such a legend. They believe after death evil ones are turned back to be born again, and good ones go to Heaven to live in bliss for ages until they grow old and tired and ask to be reborn. Suppose they are right. Will we who are now killing our brothers come back as the condemned race—to be oppressed and killed?

In the mosques the Imams used to preach: "There is no power or strength but in God! God is master of all lands and dominions, and gives them to whomever he pleases." If we pacify this land and take it for ourselves, how long will it be before God gives it to another people? Life is but a breath of Huracán, say the Indians.

Yet they do not fully cultivate this fertile land, and I am sure it could feed many people. Soto seeks only gold, but I see crops and thriving cities and merchant ships. Florida sunshine has more gold than all the Inca treasure houses. Would we could reap that treasure without incurring a bigger debt than our children may be able to pay!

Beloved wife, you shall not hear from me again this next year while we explore this vast land. I am sustained by your love, and I will write you when I can. Remembrance of our Sabbaths brings me nearer to the Most High, blessed be His Shekhina.

Next year in Jerusalem, Amen!

CHAPTER 7

Havana, 1540

RACHEL PICKED her way among the rocks, watching the spray break, clutching her black shawl around her shoulders. Women in Havana dressed in black as if they were already in mourning. Daniel and Alfonso had been gone almost a year, but no matter how busy Rachel kept, she would sometimes find herself staring at nothing, thinking of nothing, feeling nothing but the awesomeness of her own particular Exile—not the Hebrew exile from God, but the physical exile from Daniel's love, the exile that destroys slowly but surely.

Rachel determined not to let her loneliness destroy her. So, when its oppressive weight bore down too heavily, she would leave Sarah in charge of the bodega and walk down to look at the sea. The infinite blueness, the blurring of the horizon at the point of hope, the endless breaking of the seas, soothed her.

Havana Harbor was choppy that day, the kind of seas Cubans called "chorrera." Already the port itself was being called "Old Chorrera" because north winter winds whipped seas to a froth. Rachel shivered and turned back toward the village. Up the street she saw a young seaman serenading a barred window, and behind the bars she glimpsed flushed ivory cheeks and flashing black eyes. She was almost overwhelmed with envy of the young lovers; she had never felt so lonely. Daniel had never serenaded her, and now he never would.

Women alone keep busy. Most stayed safely behind barred gates except when they wore black lace mantillas to church to kneel on Persian prayer rugs and pray for the safe return of the Soto expedition. Women alone have little to do except pray and gossip. They met in patios after siesta to embroider and lament the rise in the number of loose women since the treasure ships had brought idle seamen into port.

Sooner or later they always talked about Doña Isabela de Bobadilla's young niece, who had been seduced by Don Nuño de Tovar on the voyage out from Spain— telling the story over and over again until the poor girl's ears must have burned with shame. Of course, Nuño de Tovar had done the honorable thing and married with the pregnant girl, and Soto had demoted the young hidalgo as a fitting tribute to Spanish honor, but now the girl and her baby had to live with the disgrace while the men were away.

Some women had little time for gossip, among them Sarah and Rachel and Doña Isabela de Bobadilla, acting Governor of Cuba in her husband's absence. Doña Isabela carried on running battles with Creole city officials, with workmen building Morro Castle, and with Havana port authorities who, for a healthy bribe, allowed foreign ships to unload in direct defiance of the Spanish Crown's exclusive-trade edict. Everyone knew how they did it, and everyone knew Rachel Torres was behind it. Ships sailed into port and were quarantined, their suspected cargo stored overnight in conveniently unlocked inspection sheds. Next morning cargo barrels—empty barrels—would be reloaded. As long as enough money changed hands, no one objected, and Cubans lived the better for goods Rachel sold at reduced prices.

Rachel was proud of her accomplishments since the

Soto Expedition went to Florida. Daniel had established Torres enterprises, but Rachel was now the prime mover. Not only was she doing a thriving business in Havana, where Spanish ships carrying Mexican and Peruvian treasure laid over to sail in convoy to protect themselves from French corsairs, but Rachel had also made a deal with one of the corsairs to buy his prizes at a port near Bayamo, where the cousins would store the cargo for redistribution in the Spanish New World. Rachel had bid successfully on the ships Soto sent back to be sold; now her crews were carrying contraband into most of the ports of the Caribbean, using the bribe system she had worked out so successfully in Havana. No ships based in the New World could legally carry cargo from one port to another, and struggling colonists would have starved without Rachel and other enterprising people, but the Crown called all of them corsairs.

By now Rachel had little reason to respect Crown edicts, and she circumvented them whenever she could. Some said Doña Isabela de Bobadilla received the Governor's cut of the bribes, just as some said Morro Castle would never be completed because Doña Isabela had pocketed most of the money appropriated by the Crown for building up Havana's defenses. However, no one blamed Doña Isabela. Cuba was not rich in gold and silver like other Spanish colonies. The only way governmental officials could make their fortunes and return to Spain in style was to look out for their own interests whenever opportunity presented itself. Doña Isabela de Bobadilla had been well taught by her father, the infamous Pedrárias Dávila of Panama.

But in spite of all her success, seeing the young lovers had made Rachel heartsick. She had had so little romance in her life; now Daniel had gone to Florida, and Rachel knew he would not come back. She pulled her shawl tighter around her shoulders as she trudged toward the bodega. No matter how hard she worked she felt empty and useless; glimpsing someone else's happiness made her so lonely for Daniel she wanted to cry. If men only knew what it did to women to be left alone...

Rachel was not a crying woman. She was a woman

who took charge of things. Now she took charge of herself. She straightened her shoulders and lifted her chin and went back to the bodega to keep an eye on Sarah. Too many young seamen had crowded into Havana, and one of them might find Sarah attractive and start serenading outside her window. Sarah, too, was human; Alfonso was far away. When the fleet was in port, Rachel would watch Sarah carefully, for in her mind Alfonso and Sarah were already married.

Sarah was at her loom weaving a hammock when Rachel returned. A few seamen sat idly drinking wine, but one of them stood watching Sarah. He was a potbellied man with heavy jowls, not a man Rachel would have found attractive, but Sarah was blushing at his attentions. Rachel knew plain girls were far more vulnerable than pretty ones. Rachel watched for a moment, trying to find a way to interfere that would not embarrass Sarah. Rachel loved Sarah dearly, and would defend her as quickly as she would have defended Alfonso.

"Ah, Sarah, how beautiful!" Rachel said, leaning over to inspect the weaving. "I have seen some beautiful Indian hammocks in my time, but never one so beautifully fringed. Don't you think so, Señor?"

Rachel smiled at the potbellied man, and Sarah blushed again—blushed now for Madame Torres, who was making a fool of herself over this seaman. It was unbecoming to an old woman to flirt. The man, of course, preened himself; like the gallant Spaniard he was, he wondered how he could seduce both women. He had learned long ago that ugly girls and old women were far easier to seduce, and provided just as much pleasure as young pretty ones. He did not know he had little chance of seducing either one of them, for Rachel had learned about such men in the Alfama.

"Sarah, would you go up to the castle and see if Doña Isabela's lookouts have sighted a sail? Take one of the servants with you," Rachel requested.

"Oui, Madame," said Sarah, who liked to show off what little French she had learned.

"Would you do me the honor of allowing me to accompany you, Señorita?" asked the potbellied man.

"Sarah cannot be seen on the streets of Havana with a strange man, Señor," Rachel chided. "Surely you understand how that would set the tongues clacking. You would not wish to compromise a lady, would you, Señor?"

"By no means," he said, caught in the trap of his own chivalry. "Forgive me, Señorita. Of course I meant no such thing. I only thought you might need my protection."

"In Havana, a lady's honor is her protection," said Rachel. "Perhaps, while we wait for Sarah to return, you would play a game of dominoes with an old woman."

"With much pleasure, Señora," he said, bowing deeply and clicking his heels. She was a sly old woman, he thought. Sly and rigidly virtuous. After one game to satisfy his honor, he would go find an easier woman.

Sarah left the bodega with a vague sense of disappointment. She was grateful to Rachel for not letting things get out of hand with the man, but she had enjoyed the small flirtation. She sometimes wished she had the courage and the opportunities prettier girls always seemed to have. Alfonso might never come back, and she might become an old woman without knowing love. Sometimes she envied the mestizo women who earned their living in the arms of sailors. Women alone are so very lonely, and to be an ugly old woman alone would be the loneliest of all, Sarah thought, as she hurried toward the castle as if trying to escape her loneliness.

If only another ship would come with letters. Alfonso seemed so far away, and it was possible he would never return. If Sarah had had any other proposals of marriage, she might not be waiting for Alfonso. It irritated her that Rachel always managed to block any opportunities, even harmless flirtations. Sarah did not even like the potbellied man, but he had made her feel alive. Why did men have to leave their women alone?

Tahíaca was rolling cigars on her thighs when her nose began to itch. Usually when her nose itched she killed a fat Muscovy duck and make a big pot of pepper stew, because she knew company was coming; but today she sent one of the children to find Ramón. When he came, she told him they must go to Havana to meet the ships from Florida and get word of their son Jesús. Although Ramón and his family lived in the country outside Havana and could not possibly see the ocean, Ramón began loading the donkeys with trade goods for the journey. Tahíaca's nose was never wrong.

Tahíaca and Ramón seldom went to Havana now, for she had finally created a little world where she was content to belong. All of their sons except Jesús worked on Fuentes land and lived with their wives and children in bahíos much as Anacaona's people had lived before the Spanish came. None of their daughters had gone to live on the streets of Havana as so many of the mestizo girls did. Tahíaca knew things were changing, and she raised her daughters as strictly as any Spanish matron.

While they sat beside her rolling cigars, Tahíaca would tell them about Anacaona and Caonabó, and about Mayabaño and Higueymato. Because one or two of her daughters had her own roving eye, Tahíaca never let them out unchaperoned. All of her daughters could expect to marry well—not hidalgos, but substantial Cuban-born businessmen with their roots in the soil.

Ramón still liked to brag that he was the father of hidalgos, and certainly he was the father of a large and prosperous family, but his wealth was in land, and they still lived like a simple swineherd and his wife. Tahíaca was happy. Although she knew she was not welcome in the halls of the Governor General of Cuba, she had her own world. Never would she walk by the beach or pace a tower looking for her lover to come back. Every night when she went to bed, she had Ramón. What woman could ask for more?

Everyone in Havana followed Ramón and Tahíaca down to the shore, and shortly before sunset a sail came over the horizon. The stars were again coming out when the ships anchored in the harbor and the longboats came ashore. People crowded around begging for news.

366

Doña Isabela had to order them to stand back while the man in the longboat distributed letters. Everyone talked at once, and everyone wanted to read every letter for whatever scraps of news they contained. No one was selfish enough not to share a letter, although many, like Rachel, held back certain personal passages. When the last letter had been distributed and read, Sarah still stood looking expectantly up at the caballero in the longboat.

"Is that all?" she asked, and she could not keep the disappointment out of her voice.

"Yes, Señorita, that is all."

Sarah turned away holding her head high, trying to hold back tears. She could not bear to be pitied—for her plainness or her loneliness. Why hadn't Alfonso written? Perhaps the Indian woman who cared for Alfonso and his father...Sarah did not want to finish the thought. Rachel came up and put her arm around the girl she had chosen to bear her grandchildren. Men could be so thoughtless. Rachel, too, suspected Alfonso was...she, too, did not want to complete her thought.

As they walked slowly back toward the bodega, they saw the potbellied man walking with a mestizo girl. He lifted the girl up and sat her conveniently on an unfinished part of the castle wall; then he positioned himself between her legs, put his arms around her, and began kissing her and murmuring meaningless endearments.

Rachel sniffed her disapproval, and Sarah looked the other way, but both of them secretly envied the girl—at least for the moment. They walked a little way in silence before Sarah spoke.

"Why didn't Alfonso write to me?" she asked, and her voice was full of anguish. "Why?"

"I don't know," said Rachel, who had received more comfort from Daniel's many letters than she had from all her long marriage. "Men express their feelings in different ways. Wait until Alfonso comes back. Just wait!"

Sarah wasn't satisfied. She wanted more assurance than anyone except Alfonso himself could give her. Although she had no prospects for the moment, she felt she was being cheated by waiting for Alfonso. She wanted to throw away all her Sephardic upbringing for a few moments on the castle wall with some man, any man. Sarah wanted to be touched.

No one ever touched her except Rachel, and Rachel's touch was not the loving touch Sarah craved, but only a restraining touch on the hand, or sometimes a companionable touch on the shoulder. Sarah could always feel Alfonso just beyond Rachel's touch, and that made her even more lonely. Sometimes, when the loneliness grew too sharp, Sarah would accidentally brush up against one of the men as she was serving wine in the bodega. Then she would burn with shame and apologize profusely. For a while afterward, she would make sure to keep just the right distance between herself and the customers, but the coldness of that distance was like the winter winds over chorrera. Sarah didn't think Rachel could understand what it was like to feel lonely, never to be touched.

"I had to wait a great many years for my Daniel," said Rachel. "The fishermen in the Alfama were always trying to get me under the old Roman bridge, but I never went with them. I waited for my Daniel."

Sarah said nothing.

"Some men are worth waiting for," said Rachel.

Sarah wasn't so sure.

CHAPTER 8

Anhaica Apalachee, 1540

PREGNANT SPRING wove an intricately beautiful arabesque over the rolling hills around Anhaica. Arab ar-
chitects must have dreamed of a country like this and
translated it into alabaster and gold and lapis lazuli as
they carved the pleasure domes of Andalucía—the Alhambra and its summer palace. Live oaks and hickory
interlocked with wild cherry and magnolia. Fingers of
sunshine combed waving tresses of Spanish moss. Pur-
ple clematis and honeysuckle entwined with dogwood
and wild plum. White water lilies on emerald pads
floated in sapphire lakes. Bees and butterflies, bluejays
and cardinals swirled around the opulent bosom of
Mother Earth. A mockingbird trilled as the vanguard
rode forward into position, and the lumbering beast of
an army prepared to move out.

"Forward! Forward!" Soto commanded, and the
trumpets blared.

Soto traveled east from Anhaica. Shortly before they
were scheduled to leave their winter quarters a fortunate thing happened. Two caballeros captured an Indian
boy they called Perico, who told them of a land called

Cofachiqui ruled by a cacica of great wealth and beauty, a land of gold and silver, and of pearls so numerous the army would not be able to carry them away. This land, said the new guide, who had been sent by Mayabaño, lay toward the rising sun—which the Indians of that region worshipped as a goddess. Blinded by the glitter of the rumored treasure, Soto and his men willingly followed Perico into a swamp. Meanwhile, Mayabaño was completing his fortification of Mauvilla west of Anhaica. As soon as he was ready, Mayabaño would send Perico the knotted thongs.

As the army began to unwind, caballeros stuffed suckling piglets into their saddlebags and foals gamboled around mares. Grumbling infantry shouldered the last of the Indians' corn, a half-bushel to a man— an irksome burden in addition to the armor they would have to carry until more Indian women could be captured. Few women survived the winter.

Ruth squatted by her basket and adjusted the carrying strap to her forehead, hoping the strain of lifting Alfonso's and Daniel's share of the corn would not cause her to abort. She had not yet told Alfonso she might be carrying his child, for she did not know how he would take her news. When they had first met, Alfonso had taken such joy in her company—querying her about Indian customs and beliefs, eager to learn the secrets of field and forest, and never having enough of talking with her.

Lately, however, he had become silent and withdrawn, coming to her bed in the middle of the night and leaving it before he slept. He had stopped bathing with her in the spring, and he ate his food silently and without thanks. Alfonso would go back to his people someday—to the woman who had made the pretty coat. Ruth wondered what would become of her and her child after he left.

Daniel was in charge of the cart carrying the lombard. Not once had the unwieldy cannon been used. How could a lombard be useful against targets as swift as deer? Yet Soto clung to the expensive ordnance like a talisman as his Peruvian fortune slowly dwindled away. Soto hoarded everything except time and men and Indians. Half the eighteen months given him by his charter had passed, and Soto drove his army relentlessly to make up for lost time—following Perico toward the rising sun and the rumored wealth of the Lady of Cofachiqui.

Soto showed the strain in his long, pinched face and grim mouth, looking older than his forty-odd years. Each placid pastoral village with no evidence of gold etched disappointment deeper. Soto saw nothing of value in the Florida farmland. Gold alone had value.

Almost constant rain soaked the army. Forest turned to swamps, and rivers overflowed. At one ford horses had to be drawn across with a windlass while men clung to their tails. Three days out of Anhaica the lombard bogged down. Daniel cursed, sloshed through the mud, put his shoulder to the wheel, and shouted at the mule. As the mule pulled, Daniel's face turned red above his graying beard, but the lombard lay useless. The mule slipped. Alfonso, hurrying up to help, saw his father fall on his face in the mud.

Alfonso shouted for Ruth as he picked his father up, and together they got the cart moving again. Ruth knew the old man could not stand much more. She had seen men like him slip away into the wilderness and never come back.

Daniel slogged along behind the mule, thinking of Córdoba and fishing in the Guadalquivir. He thought of Rachel, sweet Rachel, who liked licorice roots. Thank God she was safe in Havana.

I am getting old, Daniel thought. I will never see my Rachel again on this earth. He forgot how eager he had been to join Soto's army, and beat his breast asking why God had led him out of Cuba and into this forsaken wilderness.

Indians besieged the army every step of the way. One day a large band cornered seven alabarderos, then honorably withdrew all but seven of their own warriors to even the fight. Still, five alabarderos had died before the army could rescue them, and a sixth expired as Daniel extracted the arrow from his chest. The seventh, with his raw scalp his only wound, clung stubbornly to the handle of his broken shield until he died.

The route of the army was littered with discarded armor, as though some prehistoric beast had shed bits of its skin. In villages where houses had mud-plastered walls and great balconies, women cooked beans in fancy Toledo steel helmets decorated with arabic script.

Soto found villages deserted, caciques hard to capture, women and children withdrawn into the forest. The army still carried its own baggage. Horses were so scarce that caballeros were demoted to foot soldiers. In some of the villages, Soto found corncribs with remnants of last year's grain. He always apologized for taking the last of the Indian stores, saying they surely understood his army could not avoid eating.

In one province, the people were all old and near blind. Where were the youths? Soto asked. A plague, the people said, keeping from the Adelantado the news that their young men and women were training with Mayabaño at Mauvilla.

Perico accomplished the job Mayabaño had assigned him. Gold was the god of the Christians, and they followed Perico toward the riches of the Lady of Cofachiqui, who rules many provinces from her populous city on the river at the foot of the mountains. Her tributary caciques, it was said, filled her treasure houses to overflowing.

As Easter quickened the Spanish hearts, Soto's weary army stopped to erect crosses. Soto reminded the men that Juan Ponce de León had discovered Florida on Easter Sunday and named it Pascua Florida in honor of the season. Fray Dominic baked the Host from their dwindling supply of wheat flour. Daniel and Alfonso, mindful of the many pogroms that had started over a fancied slight to the Host, lifted their voices with the rest to sing the Te Deum on April 1, 1540.

Fray Dominic remembered that glorious day in the Alhambra almost fifty years ago when Her Catholic Highness—rest her soul—had washed his feet. Fray Dominic thought of following her pious example and washing the feet of some Indians, but no Indian had yet been converted—not even Perico.

Soto invited the Indians to attend Mass, telling their cacique that he, Soto, was a child of the Sun and had come from Her dwelling place to seek legendary cities as golden as the Sun Herself. The Indians, who loved a good show, gathered to watch Fray Dominic lift the Host and drink from the golden goblet. Afterward Fray Dominic made a long speech, most of which was lost in Perico's translation. The Indians, however, bowed to the cross. All agreed they had seen a good show.

After dark Daniel and Alfonso slipped away into the woods to talk of Passover, sitting on a fallen log weaving about their lonesome souls the strong fabric of their faith—talking of home in Cuba, of Rachel's paschal lamb, of family and friends, and of God's Torah. How they needed to renew the Passover triumph, to talk of Death's Angel passing over blood-spangled doorposts, and of the stench on the land of Egypt! Both Daniel and his son avoided talking of the Covenant of Abraham, and of the fact neither of them had ever been circumcised—the most important mark of Hebrew manhood, God's own brand.

"Papa," said Alfonso after they sat in silence for a few moments. "What is this strange fascination with the Crucifixion?"

"My son," said Daniel. "If there had been no Crucifixion, holy men would have invented one."

"But why? What does the Crucifixion have to do with keeping God's commandments?"

"Not everyone is mature enough to face the responsibility of keeping God's Law, my son," said Daniel. "Nothing touches this immature soul so deeply as the mystic power of the Crucifixion. Imagine! By believing in the Cross, I can kill the evil I find in myself and the evil I recognize in other people. I die symbolically, and I rise triumphantly after only three short days, victorious over death and the grave!"

"How the writers of the Gospels must have labored under that inspiration!" Alfonso said. "I can almost hear them. Don't forget He forgave His executioners. Don't forget the soldiers who gambled over His clothes. Don't forget the harlot who stood beside His Virgin Mother, nor the rich man who carried His cross. Don't forget the thief who repented, or the governor who washed his hands of the matter. Don't forget the hurricane that brought darkness for three hours, and don't forget the angel atop the empty tomb Easter morning."

"And don't you forget the story of the keys of the kingdom," Daniel said, "or that even one heretic casts doubt over the Apostolic succession and the miracle of salvation."

"Is that why they burn heretics?" Alfonso asked. "To keep from diminishing their miracle? Must everyone believe before they can believe?"

"Even one unbeliever casts the shadow of the doubt lurking in their own minds, my son," said Daniel, "and they must kill their doubts. Seven Heavens stacked on seven Heavens could not hold all the people killed in Holy Wars. When all the other gods are but half-remembered dreams, this Jesus will be hanging from a little gold cross around someone's neck."

They sat in silence for a while, listening to the tree frogs. Daniel felt a little closer to the mystery than he had before, but he knew something more waited to be revealed before he would understand. Tonight, for the first time, he had been able to talk about the Inquisition without hurrying away from some awful secret hidden in his own soul.

"Will we ever get out of this wilderness alive?" asked Alfonso, to break the silence of the things they had not discussed.

"Only He knows," Daniel shrugged, "blessed be His Holy Name, who has numbered our days according to His will."

Again they lapsed into silence.

"Soto will never find the gold," said Daniel after a while.

"He is overlooking a fortune, Papa," said Alfonso. "We both know that. Look at this fertile land. The Indians farm only enough to feed themselves, but we could teach them to feed the world. We could bring in a few bales of cloth, a few knives and trinkets, some iron pots, a few pair of good Córdoban leather boots, trade with them and make a fortune."

Alfonso's eyes were shining, and Daniel felt the stir of healthy trader greed. Give a little. Take a little. Leave some for the next trade. If you took everything, as Soto did, there would be nothing left to trade but hatred.

Before they left the village where they had set up the Paschal crosses, Ruth warned Alfonso that Daniel could not continue managing the ordnance cart. They formed a plan and went together to the cacique's house where Soto held court on the balcony. Paco Sandoval stood guard below.

"With your permission, Don Francisco," Alfonso twisted his tattered velvet cap, addressing Sandoval politely, although he had not yet earned the right to be called Don. "May I speak to His Excellency?"

"His Excellency is busy," Sandoval said. "Be on your way, Jew peddler, and take your Indian woman with you."

Alfonso started to turn away, but Ruth stood in his way.

"You must speak with the Adelantado," Ruth insisted. "Your father cannot stand much more."

"I demand to see His Excellency," said Alfonso.

"State your business."

"I will state my business to the Adelantado."

"You will never see His Excellency unless you tell me the nature of your business."

Their argument had gotten Soto's attention. He stood up, stretched, and walked to the edge of the balcony to listen.

"Very well," Alfonso said. "The mule that pulled the ordnance cart died this morning. We will need to use one of the caballero's horses to pull it."

Alfonso saw concern flicker over Soto's face. The lombard was more to him than a few pieces of iron bolted together.

"Impossible," said Sandoval. "Too many caballeros

are already walking. No one will give up his horse to pull the ordnance cart."

"Then we must leave the lombard behind," said Alfonso.

"Let me speak with the hostler, Paco," ordered Soto, anger pinching his nostrils, the corners of his mouth turning down to match his thin moustache.

Everything had gone wrong on this expedition. Too many horses had been lost to the hurricane, and too many had been killed by the Indians. When Añasco was returning to the Bay of the Holy Spirit last fall, one horse had simply refused to go on. The Indian who caught him after Añasco let him go hadn't even known what to do with the saddle. Now the ordnance mule had died.

How many men and animals had Soto lost? Too many. Only the swine seemed to thrive, and they kept straying into the woods. Too many men killed, wounded, captured, strayed. Yet, all their hardships would be forgotten once they reached Cofachiqui and the Cacica's gold.

"Harness some Indian women to the cart," Soto ordered.

"But Excellency, the men have been promised baggage carriers. Even the seven hundred women the cacique gave us are barely enough to carry everything."

"Seven hundred? He promised me two thousand Indians."

"Most of them are warriors. You know warriors will not carry. They are worse than caballeros when it comes to doing women's work. We will have to leave the lombard behind. Even Indian women can carry only so much."

"Tell him the plan," Ruth urged, tugging at Alfonso's sleeve.

"Why not leave the lombard in care of the cacique of this village? If we have to besiege Cofachiqui, we can send a detachment back for it. Cofachiqui is not too far away, only a few days' ride, even the long way round."

"We are not going the long way round," Soto said. "We are going due east."

"Oh, no, Excellency!" Ruth interrupted, addressing the Adelantado directly although she knew it was forbidden. "Do not go east! Tell him, Alfonso. He must not take us into the Land Where Death Stalks."

"Can't you keep your Indian woman quiet, Torres? It is Torres, isn't it? Torres the Marrano?"

"Torres the Christian," Alfonso assured him. "The woman will not speak up again, Excellency."

Ruth looked down at the ground. Why were men always so stubborn about taking advice from a woman? She had heard the Indians talking about the Land Where Death Stalks, a region so desolate even the animals avoided it. Even Perico had tried to warn Soto, but Soto had threatened to have Perico barbecued if he didn't lead them to Cofachiqui by the shortest route.

"The Indians are trying to trick us," Soto said. "Cofachiqui is only a few leagues away. Swamps have not stopped us before. We will take enough food for four days and double-time the marches."

"The lombard, Excellency?" Alfonso asked again.

"We will make a present of the lombard to the cacique of this village," Soto declared. "With appropriate ceremonies, of course. Remember how the Admiral Don Cristóbal Colón blasted the half-sunken *Santa María* out of the water to impress the Indians at Navidad?"

Remember Navidad, thought Alfonso, remember the men left at Navidad.

"Indians are easily impressed," continued Soto. "That is why they will always be our slaves."

Pharaoh must have said something like that when he ordered the Hebrews to make bricks without straw, Alfonso thought.

"Get ready to move out, Torres," Soto ordered. "Dismissed!"

Ignoring all advice, Soto marched due east—hurrying to find his golden city, hoarding the swine even when food became scarce. He had not allowed the men to butcher his brood stock, although he had made presents of some of the hogs to caciques to placate them for their forced assistance. Sometimes piglets strayed

377

into the forest, but for the most part the herd was intact. Now food grew scarce. The men had not been allowed time to hunt before they entered the wasteland, and now there were no animals to hunt. As they ran short of meat and salt, the men began dying.

Four days into the desolation, grains of corn became more precious than gold nuggets. Nine days out, the horses' rib cages showed. Hunger blurred the vision, amplified sound, distorted light. As bodies fed upon themselves, minds crossed the border into the fringe world. Living became one vast morass, and death seemed like a liberator.

When food ran too low, Soto turned the Indian women loose to go home, but he had to threaten to shoot them to make them leave. The men shouldered what baggage they could carry, leaving the rest for the snakes—the coral, the diamondbacks, the copperheads, and the water moccasins. Fray Dominic had a horrific vision, which he shared with no one.

Dense forests shut out the sun, and the army traveled in perpetual twilight, peopled only with bodiless echoes and savage yowls. Caballeros began charging ethereal knights riding soundlessly through the mossy cobwebs—never coming closer. Men ate vines. Only the swine seemed to thrive, rooting in the mud for food. One day Alfonso saw Daniel give Ruth a few grains of corn, which she popped into her mouth gratefully.

"What are you doing, Ruth?" Alfonso scolded. "Papa needs his food. Look how sunken his eyes are."

Ruth stopped chewing.

"Let her alone, Alfonso," Daniel said. "She needs the food more than I do."

"She is young, Papa. So am I. We can stand a little hunger, but you..."

"Don't be a fool, Alfonso. Are you blind? Ruth is with child."

Oh, God! Alfonso thought. Why now? Sarah's eyes seemed to accuse him. Too late! Too late! Who will bring up this child in the proper way?

"Are you with child?" Alfonso asked.

Ruth nodded, wishing Alfonso could be joyful as her

husband had been joyful each time she presented him with a child. She had not thought of her Indian family in a long time, but now she thought about that little cradle swinging in the breeze, and her face clouded over with sadness. Alfonso looked at her, standing so forlorn in the midday twilight of the dense forest. He put his arms around her, promising never to leave her, talking as though he were safely home in Havana and not in the forsaken wilderness even the Indians had abandoned.

"I will find you something to eat," Alfonso promised, "but don't take any more food from Papa."

"Better a child should be born than an old man go on living," said Daniel.

"Don't talk that way, Papa. I will get us out of here. You shall see."

Daniel did not answer. Mayabaño was out there waiting. God had sent Daniel on this expedition; when he met Mayabaño, Daniel would know why.

Ruth showed Alfonso where to dig for edible roots. They killed a rattlesnake, which Daniel refused to eat until Alfonso reminded him how King David had eaten the showbread when he was starving. Next day Soto ordered half a pound of pork given to each man. Daniel had never smelled anything so savory as that roasting pork.

The scanty pork rations revived the army a little, and on Sunday, April 25, Juan de Añasco returned from a scouting mission bringing good news. Ahead lay a village with provisions. Soto took the strongest horses and fittest men for a forced march to the village. The hunger-weakened army straggled behind—all walking, for their horses were too weak to carry them. In groups of ten or twelve, bunches of three or four, singly or in pairs, they stumbled along—falling sometimes and lying where they fell until life renewed itself and they could go on.

Alfonso not only looked after the spent horses, he kept Ruth and his father moving on. Coaxing the old man…"Only a little farther, a few more steps…You can make it, Papa. With God's help, you can make it."

Alfonso had become the father now and Daniel the child. Alfonso was loving, tender, cajoling, scolding, cursing Daniel for wanting to die. Hunger gnawed at Alfonso's guts, but a more painful hunger gnawed at his heart. He must get his father back to Havana. If Daniel should die here, who would give him a proper Hebrew burial? Alfonso wished he had spent more time with his grandfather, Rav Joseph, or with the rabbis who traveled around the Indies holding secret services. Great ceremonies should mark a man's death. Great tombs should be erected. Rav Joseph had said the Hebrews of Andalucía covered their graves with flat heavy gravestones to keep out the Inquisitors.

"Get up, damn you," Alfonso scolded his father. "Get up! I will not let you die! Not here! Not now! Now get up and walk!"

They had reached the edge of the Indian village before Daniel fell near a smoldering grill where Soto had cremated an Indian who could not tell him how to find Cofachiqui. Daniel sat beside the gruesome sight, muttering to himself. Alfonso picked his father up and put him over his shoulder while Ruth hurried to queue up for their rations.

"You can't have my father." Alfonso shook his fist at the sky. "I won't let You take him, You bumbling Farce! Some God you are to do this to Your Chosen People. What plans do You have for us now?"

Alfonso managed to stagger to where Soto was giving out the last of the corn from the Indian corncrib. He dumped his father on the ground and sank down beside him, too weak to move. Ruth fed the old man Indian fashion, as a mother feeds her baby its first bites of chewed food. Slowly Daniel Torres revived.

CHAPTER 9

Cofachiqui, 1540

AFTER APPROPRIATE torture, the Indians had guided Soto to Cofachiqui. Jesús and Alfonso had stayed behind with some of the Caribbean Indians and the African slaves to round up the swine and the spent horses and nurse them along to Cofachiqui. Alfonso had put his father on first one horse then another for the three days it took to get to the river bordering Cofachiqui. When they arrived, the men could talk of nothing but La Cacica, niece of the woman ruler of the nation who had fled into the mountains to escape the Spaniards. Juan de Añasco had gone to fetch the revered widowed aunt of La Cacica, but his Indian guide had committed suicide rather than betray his beloved mistress to the Christians. While she was gone, her niece ruled in her place.

"You should have seen La Cacica," said Paco Sandoval to Jesús and Alfonso as they crossed the river in one of her canoes. "She rode down to this river in a carved throne-chair on the shoulders of her noblemen."

"What name is she called?" asked Daniel with a feeling he had been transported back to Xaragua, where Anacaona had met the Governor in a flower-decked litter.

"La Cacica, what else? Do not their Catholic Majesties sign cédulas 'I, the Queen' and 'I, the King'? So regal is she that I have heard her called nothing else but La Cacica. She was dressed in white linen so thin you could see through it, with a feather mantle and feather headdress haloed around her head—three feet high it was, shimmering like an exotic bird's crest. She sat on fur cushions and wore a pearl necklace draped three times around her and hanging to her waist."

"No, to her knees," corrected a man who had walked down to the river and was helping them out of the canoe. "You should have seen La Cacica's retinue of long canoes."

"Who is telling this story, amigo?" asked Paco.

"You are, amigo, so long as you tell it correctly."

"Her barge had a woven cane canopy," said Paco. "The barge was not paddled, nor sailed, nor poled. The barge was drawn behind canoes paddled so skillfully scarcely a ripple showed on the water. Por Dios, when His Excellency saw La Cacica, he almost stood in her presence, she was so regal. Soto gave her his own ring after she had draped the long string of pearls around his neck."

"Ruby, the ring was," said his assistant. "Imagine that."

"I'm hungry," said Jesús. "Is there any food in Cofachiqui?"

"Food? You never saw so much food!" said Paco. "Corncrib after corncrib full of grain, and ten times as much more in the nearby villages, so they say. They store it up for lean years, like they store deerskins and furs. All the caciques of her tributaries pay a certain amount into La Cacica's storehouses."

"They dye the skins whatever color they wish," said the worrisome interrupter.

"Be quiet and let me finish my story. Then if you have anything to add, you may do so." Sandoval glared at the man. "They prepared a feast for us—pumpkin bread and sofkee, roast turkey and mulberries."

"There are enough mulberry trees—"

Sandoval put his hand on his sword hilt, and the would-be storyteller kept quiet.

"Enough mulberry trees to start a silk industry and put the Málaga weavers out of business," said Sandoval. "Yes, sir, we can start building pigpens and planting lettuce. Soto will surely establish a settlement here. La Cacica controls all this rolling country and yonder blue mountains too. The throne goes through the female line, and La Cacica is beautiful and not yet married. Perhaps Soto will take himself an Indian wife and leave Doña Isabela to rule Cuba."

"Any gold?" asked Alfonso.

"No, but plenty of copper. What the Indians thought silver is only iron pyrite. Crumbles in your hand."

"You can't eat gold," said Alfonso.

"But look at this land," said Sandoval. "And Indians aplenty to work it. Man could build himself an Alhambra on yonder mountains, retain a few caballeros to keep the peace, and live like one of those old Arab khalifs."

"Anything else of value besides the land?" asked Jesús.

"They say there is a temple not far from here," said Paco. "One of those charnel houses they have all over Florida, only this one is reserved for high mukaddams like La Cacica. Well, in this heathen temple La Cacica says there are so many pearls we couldn't carry them all away if we tried. Unbelievable, isn't it? Soto posted a guard until he and the King's Exchequer can see for themselves."

"Do you believe so many pearls could be piled up in some old Indian's graveyard?" asked the would-be storyteller, unable to keep silent any longer. "We have died and gone to Heaven."

A few days later, Soto and his greedy army, acting under the auspices of their Charter from the Casa de Contratación, came to the temple where for centuries the people of the blue mountains of Cofachiqui had laid to rest the bones of their supreme rulers—not village caciques, but only the reigning caciques and their families. The temple stood on a bluff surrounded by a deserted village. A recent plague had temporarily driven away the buzzard men who, with their long fingernails, picked the bones clean. A neat park separated the village of Cofachiqui from the sacred village on the bluff. Pet squirrels ran up mulberry trees, joining with bluejays to scold the Spaniards.

The hackles on Daniel's neck tingled as they walked through the deserted village. Steep roofs covered with woven reed mats kept out rain. The temple sat on a serpentine mound, sprawled out in clusters of rooms around the main sanctuary.

"Jesucristo!" gasped the men when they saw the temple.

The steep roof and thick mat-covered walls were draped with pearls—ropes and ropes of pearls like fishnet drying in the sun, with ruby-throated shells lining the edge of the roof. The temple had no windows, but when Soto opened the door, expecting dust and cobwebs, he found everything immaculate.

Twelve wooden giants, each twice the size of a man, guarded the door—standing in pairs with weapons poised, guarding the bones of their caciques with raised clubs, outsized swords, herculean battleaxes, copper-bladed pikes, and bows as tall as themselves, with arrows drawn to shoot. Each weapon was lacquered, strung with pearls, and brightly fringed. So meticulously carved were the guardians that they seemed about to attack.

Beyond them, on shelves lining the walls, lay the intricately carved wooden coffins of the caciques and their families, each guarded by life-size statues of the deceased. Down the center of the temple, stacked up like pyramids, lay box after box of pearls.

Pearls and more pearls...enough to make rosaries for all Christendom...draped around the walls, hanging in the air, supporting feathered fans...piled everywhere. How many centuries had the people of Cofachiqui been enshrining their rulers in this sacred temple? How many oysters had been cast into the fire to open and reveal this many pearls?

"Do they pray and make sacrifices in this temple?" asked Fray Dominic.

"No," said Soto. "La Cacica knows nothing about prayer and sacrifice."

"Who needs to pray?" asked the irreverent Sandoval. "Just give Saint Peter a few of these pearls, and the gates of Heaven will swing open."

Even Fray Dominic was too awed by the charnel house to react to this blasphemy. What ceremonies had attended these elaborate funerals? How many warriors had laid down their arms in solemn processions? They discovered eight rooms of weaponry—one room for each kind. Ceremonial weapons—all individually crafted, decorated and lacquered, polished to mirror brilliance, fringed and feathered and roped with pearls. A heavenly arsenal waiting for a ghostly army to come back and make war.

Daniel felt he had stepped into the *Zohar*—the kabbalistic book of splendor. Perhaps the Indians did not pray in words, but they knew how to create awe—to generate the presence of the Almighty, blessed be His Holy Name—the Unspeakable, the Unknowable. In the Indian charnel house, Daniel Torres felt he was in the Presence of the One. *Hear, O Israel, the Lord our God, the Lord is one...*

Soto did not try to restrain his soldiers. They had risked their lives on this Florida venture and deserved their reward. The hidalgos pulled the ropes of pearls down from the walls, upset the coffins, and tumbled out the bones looking for more treasure. Among the skeletons they found artifacts from the Ayllon colony Mayabaño had exterminated. They overturned the wooden guardians and emptied many boxes containing nothing but pearls. It was true there were so many pearls they could not have carried them away.

Afterward Soto shut the door on the shambles, taking only five hundred pounds of pearls so the people of Havana would believe them, and letting each man take enough pearls to make a rosary. When the men grumbled, Soto reminded them the King's taxes had not yet been paid. When they returned one day to divide the land into encomiendas, whoever received grant to the land where the temple stood would owe the King a great deal of money. All of them knew who that would be: His Excellency Don Hernando de Soto, Governor of Cuba, Adelantado of Florida, and now Marqués of Cofachiqui.

* * *

Soto made no settlement at Cofachiqui. He did not have time to turn the fertile Appalachian piedmont into gold, so despite protests from his weary men, he moved on in search of something of great value—the gold he felt sure must lie somewhere in this vast continent. Soto's army marched again the thirteenth of May, taking La Cacica prisoner to assure safe passage through all the provinces of her suzerainty.

From village to village, women, seeing their heroine in bondage, came out to place the carrying straps on their foreheads and bend their backs to the load. Most of the Castilians had stashed away some pearls, and La Cacica carried a small wooden chest full of prize pearls that had never been bored and were not fire-blackened like most of the rest. News of the ravaged temple spread on winged feet of Indian runners, festering in the hearts of the people, who watched for a chance to revenge their sovereign. Many young men and women went west toward Mauvilla.

As Soto's army left the piedmont and climbed into the blue mountains, food became scarce again. The infantry threatened mutiny because the cavalry in the vanguard always ate what little food there was before the rest of the army could catch up. They had passed out of La Cacica's territory now, but even here the village caciques knew about her and came out to do her honor.

Daniel stayed close to the troop guarding La Cacica, pondering her strange resemblance to Anacaona—the same dignity, the same bearing, the same spirit drawing other spirits unto herself—but Anacaona's spirit had long ago spread itself on the winds.

Long ago in Xaragua, Mayabaño had explained the Carib belief in immortality. After the soul broke free of the body, it could wander over the face of the earth taking whatever form it pleased, sometimes communicating with the living and sometimes entering newborn children to finish whatever had been left unfinished at death. Some of the Spanish kabbalists had similar beliefs. According to Mayabaño, evil spirits sometimes stayed near a village where someone had died, trying

386

to lure the newly released spirit to join them. A spirit hovered near its abandoned body for a full moon after death. If the festivals held in the month after death did not drive away the spirit, the village would be abandoned—as the Spanish had abandoned Navidad and Fort Isabela when they first occupied Haiti. No one stayed too near a village death had visited. In the provinces bordering Cofachiqui, Soto's army found several abandoned villages that had been visited by the plague.

Daniel sometimes reminisced around the campfire, telling Alfonso about the courageous martyr Anacaona, the brave Caonabó, and his friend Mayabaño—the butterfly boy. The more Daniel talked, the more he felt Anacaona's nearness. Sometimes he could almost hear her song on the night winds. As Daniel talked of Anacaona, the Indians of the Caribbean who had been brought along as slaves gathered around. So did some of the Africans. La Cacica sometimes sat not far away, surrounded by her maidens. Ruth translated for La Cacica, but the regal face never betrayed her eager heart.

Higher and higher the army climbed into the mountains, and hungrier and hungrier the men became. Once in a while the Indians brought them turkeys, and sometimes opossums or dogs. Daniel ate the forbidden food only because Alfonso forced him to. Soto still would not allow the men to slaughter his brood swine. He dreamed of settling near a city of gold, not knowing he had bypassed the only gold-bearing region in the mountains.

Cold winds blew down the gap the day they came to the big river the Indians called Chucagua, making it seem more like winter than the twenty-sixth of May. The infantry guarding La Cacica huddled by the fire; when she asked permission to go into the woods with her maidens, they assigned Daniel and Alfonso to watch her. La Cacica had been waiting for such a chance.

Alfonso and Daniel stopped a discreet distance away from a suitable clump of bushes; but La Cacica, instead of going in, motioned to two of her maidens, who carried the small carved cedar chest. She opened the chest and drew out a handful of unbored pearls. Smiling graciously, she held out this fortune to Daniel.

"For you," La Cacica said in Spanish.

"Don't take them, Papa," warned Alfonso. "She is trying to bribe you to let her escape."

"I know," said Daniel as he held out his hands for the pearls.

"Many thanks," said La Cacica, saluting him Indian fashion.

"Wait!" cried Daniel as she turned to leave. "Your name? What are you called?"

"La Cacica," she said.

Daniel knew he was treading on a taboo. North American Indians did not tell their names lest they give the listener power over them.

"Your true name," Daniel insisted, and Ruth translated. "The name they gave you when your soul came into your body. What is it? I must know."

La Cacica smiled. By now some of the Caribbean Indians gathered around La Cacica, evidently planning to escape with her. Among them was a big black Congo slave who had been continually maltreated by his Cuban master. La Cacica looked up, smiled sweetly at the black man, and reached to take his hand. Daniel marveled that love had flowered on such a journey. Perhaps love, like the opia, always hovers near waiting for an opportunity to manifest itself even in the darkest hours.

"Your true name, tell me," Daniel commanded. "I must know before you go."

"I am Anacaona, daughter of Higueymato," said La Cacica. "My grandmother was the famous singer of areítos—Anacaona, wife of Cacique Caonabó—and my mother is the sister of the man you call the butterfly boy."

Daniel and Alfonso turned their backs as the Cuban refugees followed Anacaona into the forest. Except for the handful of pearls, Daniel would have thought it was a dream—a vision of Anacaona—but the pearls were real. Soto sent out search parties, but they never recaptured La Cacica.

CHAPTER 10

Tascaluza, 1540

PERHAPS DANIEL had his vision of the Shekhina because he had been wandering too long in the wilderness. They had left Cofachiqui in May and had wandered through the wild beautiful land all summer and into the fall. Now in early October, they came to the province of Tascaluza—whose cacique was said to be a gigantic man. Soto was losing hope, and his discouragement infected the army.

Soto had more trouble now with his straggling army than with the Indians. How could he keep the cavalry fit to fight without starving the infantry? How could he keep Indian bearers from walking off in their chains carrying precious supplies? Armor rusted. Alabardas grew dull. Lances split. Crossbows came unstrung. Hungry men wandered off in search of food and never came back. How could he call this an army when most of the men wanted to settle down? They sickened from hunger and exposure. They died of exhaustion and arrow wounds. They gave up in the God-forsaken Florida wilderness.

In training camps armies march in formation. On

parade grounds and in "games of cane" cavalry demonstrate precise battle tactics. On the march, armies straggle. Men get blisters or leg cramps or bladder trouble or have to go off into the woods to evacuate the cook's mistakes. Some don't sleep well at night. Others think only of home while stumbling along in the mud.

Strange ammunition laid Soto's army low. Mud! Women...lack of women. Food...lack of food. Mud! Insects...weather...boredom. Mud! Forced marches ...flooded rivers...rocks. Mud! Mud! Mud!

It had rained all the fall of '39 and all spring and summer of '40. Rivers overflowed, carpeting forests in mud. It rained in September and October until the whole damn world was one big mudball studded with soggy Indian villages. Then His Excellency Don Hernando de Soto began making the troops sleep in the open—in the mud!

On October 9, 1540, the army camped in the open a league away from Tascaluza. The constant October drizzle soaked everything, chilling the men into numbness. Daniel slept fitfully, awakening often haunted by half-remembered dreams. Then he had his vision of the Shekhina-Matronit—blessed be Her Holy Name.

Perhaps she began forming Herself in Daniel's unconscious when he sold freedom to La Cacica for a handful of pearls; perhaps Anacaona Herself had made that final metamorphosis for which each soul longs, the immortal leap into myth and legend where form and substance change at the behest of each dreamer. Perhaps She came to warn Daniel, or to reveal part of the mythical secret he yearned for. Whatever the reason, She came to him as he had always known She would—the other half of himself rising out of billowing mists on a cloud crowned with fire.

She was the starry body stretching Itself across the universe, gathering Itself together out of a fire-ringed halo. When She began to dance, Daniel recognized Her. She was Anacaona, dancing astride a Red River on whose banks burned everlasting fires.

From time to time, she dipped a golden cup into the

river and drank the blood, whereupon She danced faster and faster, beating Her heels so hard the earth quaked, gathering up mists and wrapping them around Her like billowing skirts. From time to time, She snatched brands from the everlasting fires and waved them across the sky like banners, scattering flaming sparks across the universe.

From out of the fires rose ten thousand spirits, then ten thousand more, then more and more, swirling and writhing and forming themselves into one mighty Warrior—an awesome Champion dressed in shining armor. Anacaona took up a flaming sword to do battle with the Champion. The fervor of Her dance increased, and the melody of Her song was the clash of battle. Around Her neck She wore a necklace of skulls, and a panther skin formed Her robe. Her high forehead was crowned with birds whose golden wingtips brushed the sun and rested upon the stars. A cloud of butterflies swarmed around Her head, and She wore a coral snake for Her girdle.

Each time Anacaona's sword pierced the Champion's armor, a river of blood flowed forth, and the river carried flotillas of canoes filled with other Warriors, each more terrible than the first. And all the Warriors were clad in armor with their visors down so no one could recognize their faces. Anacaona danced, and the enchanted Warriors danced with Her.

Anacaona sang, and the battle was Her song. Her dance shook the earth so mountains trembled and fell, and seas gushed up to devour the land. The dance of the Warriors shook the universe so the stars tumbled from their places and great holes appeared in the sky, through which the Sun shot an all-consuming shaft targeted at Love, and the body of Love which is Pleasure.

A mockingbird sang, and a baby was born to Anacaona and the Warrior Champion. Anacaona suckled the child until he was grown. Then He dipped His own cup into the Red River.

Daniel knew he was dreaming; he wanted to wake up. He fought to wake up, to escape the horrible truth of his vision. Yet he could not wake, so he lay in the shadow of his dream—half afraid to dream again lest the dream claim him forever, reluctant to leave the certainties of such a vision for the uncertainties of reality, dreading the separation from the Shekhina-Matronit—blessed be Her Holy Name.

Daniel awoke in a cold sweat. He heard a panther scream, a plaintive echo of Anacaona's song. What was it Mayabaño had said when he left Haiti for Cuba? When next you hear Anacaona's song, prepare to die.

Daniel kept his vision to himself. To tell such dreams invites laughter. No one can stand the pain of too much remembering. No one can see the Light and not be blinded. No one can look upon the face of God and live. The Messiah will come one day after he is no longer needed.

Earlier that day Mayabaño had stood on the tower surveying the fort—his fort, his life work copied from Spanish forts on Hispañola. A cool breeze ruffled the buzzard tuft above his butterfly. He seldom smiled, because he had fifty-four years of battling the Christians, but he smiled now—a grim, mirthless smile of satisfaction.

Strength, safety, advantage, and power lay behind these tall, thick log walls covered with sun-baked plaster. Square towers every fifty feet looked out over the plain, and warriors of all nations manned the catwalks beneath shooting ports halfway up the walls. The banners of the four large nations and many smaller ones hung in front of long barracks built on wide streets surrounding the parade plaza. At fort headquarters, Mayabaño's own butterfly on a black background hung just below Tascaluza's yellow chamois banner with the blue crossbands. Inside every barracks sat the war arks tribal shamans would use to dance their prayers at tonight's ceremonies.

The great nations—the Cofachiqui, the Hirrihigua, the Apalachee, and the Tascaluza—had all sent warriors down old war trails to answer Mayabaño's knotted war summons. Many smaller nations had also sent warriors, some without being officially summoned Choicest and bravest of all the men and women in each tribe had assembled at Fort Mauvilla, carrying tempered weapons of their own making. The fort and its barracks bustled with the celibate practices of war—arms making, target practice, rigorous physical training.

Men outnumbered women, but women often shot straighter, ran short distances more easily, and could see better the slightest movement in the forest around the clearing. New recruits kept the plain surrounding the fort picked clean for a distance of two bowshots—not a pebble or a blade of grass could hide an approaching enemy.

Mayabaño had asked for two thousand warriors, but more and more had kept pouring into the fort as Spanish atrocities mounted. Some had not yet had time to tattoo the war club on their forearm. Volunteers pledged a death oath. Weaklings and cowards were sent home. Mayabaño accepted no old people—not even men as old as himself—no children, no pregnant women. He allowed no sexual intercourse and no marriages. War was the bride and Death the bridegroom.

Now Mayabaño paced the tower, looking out over his army and his fort and remembering. He had so much to remember: Navidad and the man who had raped his sister Tahíaca—raped her body and kidnapped her soul, carrying her forever into the Christian world; the Admiral Don Cristóbal Colón leading his army up the broad cultivated north plain of Haití; Ojeda tricking his father Caonabó into riding his first horse; Ovando tricking his mother Anacaona to her horrible death; Hatuey choosing death over the Christian Heaven; Mayabaño's wife and his children—and his concubines—massacred in Cuba and himself almost cut in two by the alabarda—saved from death by his friend Daniel Torres. If there had only been more Spaniards like Daniel Torres...

Only the memory of Daniel troubled Mayabaño. Other memories became hate objects giving his life meaning and purpose. The Spanish had taught Mayabaño and the other Cuban refugees to hate, and they had learned their lessons well—learning to out-torture torture, to out-trick trickery. Mayabaño had copied their tactics until he was the prototype of Iberian knighthood—of chivalry gone wrong. Except for Daniel Torres, the brother Mayabaño had never had, all of the despicable cross-worshippers deserved to die!

Unlike Daniel, who tunnelled his horrible memories back into his mind to fester in darkness, Mayabaño gnawed on the dry bones of his dread remembrances— feeding on them until he had almost convinced himself nothing good had ever happened to him. Yet once in a while he would find himself running through the forests of Xaragua with his boyhood friend. He would be swirling in the mists of near death and hear his friend's command: *Live! I say unto thee, Live!* He would be running to escape a galloping herd of horses, and Daniel would ride by and hold out his hand. Mayabaño's worst fear, a fear he confided to no one, was that one day he might have to choose whether or not to kill his friend Daniel Torres.

Mayabaño pushed his fear into the back of his mind and began thinking of the great black giant, Cacique Tascaluza. The name Tascaluza meant black warrior. Tascaluza was a giant created by the secret process of manipulating the bones of infants and feeding special herbs to the women who breast-fed them. Tascaluza's son had also been made into a giant by this process reserved only for royalty.

Tascaluza had been the first cacique to take Mayabaño's warnings seriously, to begin fortifying his villages. Tascaluza had helped Mayabaño set up his information network and his plan of battle by selected warriors—the best of all the tribes who usually fought among themselves but could now be counted upon against the common enemy. When Ponce de León landed, runners had brought the news to Mayabaño at Tascaluza's village. When Ayllon settled near Cofachiqui, Tascaluza sent warriors under Mayabaño's command to help Higueymato repel them. Spanish relics had been installed in the temple at Cofachiqui in a victory celebration. By the time Narváez landed, Fort Mauvilla was near completion, and Mayabaño was no longer an itinerant trader, but a respected war leader. Mayabaño and his warriors had killed the men of Narváez's expedition not many leagues from here, letting only a few escape to tell the tale.

Wherever the Spanish landed, Mayabaño and his warriors were ready for them. Now Tascaluza and his commanding general, Mayabaño, son of the great Carib Cacique Caonabó and his famous wife Anacaona, had laid a trap for the Adelantado Don Hernando de Soto. Mayabaño's hand-picked guides had received the war thongs telling them Mauvilla was prepared, and they were leading the unwary army into the trap. Knowing Soto had helped conquer the mighty Inca Empire, Mayabaño had administered the death oath to all his warriors—male and female. If the battle of Mauvilla was lost, it would be because there were no more warriors left alive to fight.

Tonight they would hold the purification ceremonies. Mayabaño would make himself invisible to the enemy in a special ceremony, donning a mantle of black crow feathers and painting his face black except for the butterfly. Then he would celebrate the Black Drink ceremony. All the warriors would drink the bitter black purgative until they vomited, cleansing their bodies and their souls before the battle. Tribal leaders would bring out sacred war arks, purifying and consecrating each battalion according to ancient sacred rituals. Mayabaño himself would dance Anacaona's areíto.

Tomorrow Mayabaño would go to Tascaluza's village to meet Soto, and the next day Soto's army would be led into the trap. Mayabaño did not think beyond this battle. Long ago he had overcome his fear of horses by refusing to let fear dwell in his mind, now he overcame fear of defeat by refusing to believe defeat was possible. Death might defeat him, but not the Christians!

Daniel was with the vanguard as they rode into Tascaluza's village, toward the high mound where the cacique waited, but the rest of Soto's army was scattered through the woods. All Soto's troops marched on foot now, even the caballeros. There were not enough horses to make up a company, but Soto kept three horses for his own use, and these horses were cared for and fed whether Soto and his men ate or not. Soto's pasofino could still do the Moorish battle stances: the charge, the jump, the sidestep, the rearing, the sitting-on-haunches necessary for hand-to-hand combat. Soto had to make a brave showing of horsemanship. Without horses, the Spaniards were no better fighters than the Indians, and Soto knew it.

Mayabaño had warned Tascaluza about the horses: how the Spaniards put people to flight, then rode them down; how quickly a man could be impaled on a lance held by a caballero on a charging horse. The trick was to show no fear, not to break and run, not to blink an eyelash or allow the heart to flutter. Caciques had always disciplined their emotions, stoically received deputations while hiding their fears. So Tascaluza sat impassive under his deerskin sunshade, flanked by all the caciques in his suzerainty—all wearing elaborate decorated jackets and leggings. On their heads sat tall feathered crowns. Mayabaño sat on Tascaluza's right, his butterfly almost glowing under the white buzzard tufts.

Daniel could hardly restrain himself when he recognized the lined face with the butterfly tattoo. Mayabaño, my brother! My brother! Alas, what chasms separate us. Only in memory can we be children playing together. Daniel had loved only two people since he lost his parents: Rachel and Mayabaño—his mysterious half-savage other self.

Mayabaño had not yet seen Daniel. He was watching Soto in his rust-freckled armor riding his horse up the stairway to the top of the mound. The old fear knotted Mayabaño's belly as Soto prepared for the charge.

"For Santiago and the Blessed Virgin!" shouted Soto...spurs to flanks...drumming hooves...billowing dust clouds, as the white knight brought his horse up short in front of Tascaluza's court.

Feathers stirred in the breeze, but not a fringe trembled on any of their jackets. A servant calmly fanned the gigantic Cacique Tascaluza with a sunshade banner. Soto drew his sword and made a long speech. He had lost two of his best soldiers, vanished on a scouting mission. He would burn Tascaluza and his village if the cacique did not produce the two men.

"You speak too much," Tascaluza scoffed. "Actions, not words, witness the truth. Mauvilla shall make a reckoning of this matter. Come, we will go to Mauvilla."

Tascaluza rose, and his court rose with him. Tascaluza towered over them all. He demanded a horse. Soto sent for one of the dray animals, but even on this big horse, Tascaluza's feet almost touched the ground.

As Mayabaño turned to slip out of the village, planning to move quickly to take command of Mauvilla, he came face to face with Daniel. He was shocked by the almost-white beard, but he recognized Daniel's piercing eyes.

"Mayabaño, my brother," Daniel said, putting his hands on Mayabaño's shoulders.

Mayabaño was annoyed at this opia who had come to weaken his resolve to kill all the Christians! Mayabaño's eyes narrowed. He did not smile, but after a moment, he placed his hands on Daniel's shoulders.

"Daniel...my brother," Mayabaño said sadly. "Beware of Mauvilla. If we meet there, I am pledged upon my life to kill you."

Daniel choked up and could not speak. In the look that passed between them, they poured all the yearning of their lost boyhood. Daniel gripped Mayabaño's shoulders, nodding to show he understood. Mayabaño stared a moment more, then shrugged off Daniel's hands and strode away.

CHAPTER 11

Mauvilla, 1540

DANIEL HEARD Anacaona's areíto once again on the road to Mauvilla—a road bordered by cornfields waiting to be reaped. Soto thought the singers and dancers were a welcoming committee, and he rode up beside Tascaluza to compliment him on his hospitality. Tascaluza's face was a piece of black marble.

When Soto saw Fort Mauvilla, he could not believe the Indians had been resourceful enough to build it, or foolhardy enough to risk siege and pitched battle. Running battles through swamps and glades had served the Indians too well. How could they expect to win against phalanxes of pikemen, companies of alabarderos, and troops of trained lancers—to say nothing about the men with the deadly harquebuses? Christians had been fighting such pitched battles for seven hundred years. They had defeated the Moors by besieging such forts. Soto could almost hear the exhilarating cadence of battle—the heart-stirring call to War's altar.

War is the supreme religious ritual to mankind's oldest and most powerful god. Battle is the expiating blood sacrifice—the fighting that denies dying. To kill without being killed is to defeat the greatest of Impostors, Death. Great are Thy dominions, O War. Terrible is Thy countenance to behold. All nations shall bow down and worship Thee. War is the final consuming Passion from whose service no one can escape.

When Daniel heard Anacaona's areíto, he could not yet see the singers and dancers, but he saw Anacaona in all her mystic beauty. Her spirit possessed him, and he could hardly keep from dancing. But hearing it also chilled his heart, and he turned fearfully toward his son.

"Alfonso, my son," Daniel called. "A word with you."

Alfonso was helping Ruth. Her time was near, but Soto had insisted she carry her share or be turned out of the army. So Alfonso and Daniel had constructed a false bottom for her basket and loaded it as lightly as they could. Still, the child's ungainly presence weighted her down. Alfonso thought Ruth was beautiful. He even considered giving her his share of La Cacica's pearls, the ones he was saving for Sarah.

"Alfonso," Daniel called again. "Come here. I want a word with you."

"Yes, Papa." Alfonso caught up with his father in three strides.

How he had changed, Daniel thought. In Havana he was a timid, squinch-eyed storekeeper; now he is a man—his own man, a man to be trusted with a family. A man like my father Aram. Daniel was pleased he could remember his father without pain.

"You wanted to tell me something, Papa?" Alfonso asked, respectfully breaking the silence after they had walked a short distance together.

The singers and dancers were leading Soto's vanguard toward the east gate of the fort. Alfonso whistled.

"How did they build it? It looks like they used masons' trowels to plaster the walls. Is Soto really going inside?"

"He appears to be," Daniel said. "Soto is a stubborn man."

"Is that what you wanted to tell me? That Soto is walking into a trap?"

"Yes...uh—no!" Daniel spoke with irritation. "Don't

be an ass, Alfonso. Soto will do what he is destined to do. That has nothing to do with why God has brought you and me here."

"Why did God bring us here?"

"To fulfill the Covenant," Daniel said. "Now we can keep the Covenant of our Father Abraham."

"Circumcision?" Alfonso was astounded. "Here? Now?"

"Here! In this place, as soon as possible. It is important."

"But Papa, you said New Christians dare not be circumcised. The Inquisitors look for that as the first sign of judaizing."

"Are we not Jews?" Daniel cried, loudly enough for everyone to hear.

"Yes, Papa, but be quiet about it."

"We have been quiet long enough. It will not matter now. Not after today. Now only the Grand Inquisitor, blessed be His Holy Name, will know if we have kept our Covenant with Him."

"But, Papa..."

They were standing in the middle of the road, and the baggage handlers walked around them. Some looked curiously at the old man arguing with his son.

"Don't argue with me, Samuel." Daniel used his son's Hebrew name, having spoken his Spanish name for the last time.

"As you wish, Papa," Alfonso agreed, thinking how hard it was sometimes to keep the commandment to honor thy father.

"Kneel down, Samuel," Daniel ordered. "Kneel here in front of me."

"Right here, in the middle of the road?"

"No one is paying any attention. Soto has gone into the fort, and the Indian women are busy laying down their burdens against the fort walls. Now kneel!"

"Oh, Papa, not that antiquated oath!"

"Kneel!"

The form of the oath was as old as Genesis. Father Abraham had used it when he made his servant swear not to take a wife for Isaac from among the Canaanites.

401

As Alfonso knelt and put his hand under his father's thigh, an awe came over him. He felt the strong sense of the Hebrew presence. "Thy rod and Thy staff comfort me . . . in the presence of mine enemies." Alfonso knelt in the dust of the Florida wilderness; but after touching the penis connecting him to all the generations of his people, it was Samuel who looked up expectantly at his father.

"Swear by our Father Abraham that you will not let me go to my grave uncircumcised," Daniel demanded. "Swear it, Samuel, my son. Swear it!"

"I swear it, my father," said Samuel, and his voice choked with unshed tears.

Soto rode into the fort with his vanguard at Tascaluza's heels, then ordered the munitions, clothing, and supplies stored safely inside before Indians darted out of the woods to carry them off. Supplies were short, but Soto would be meeting the ships from Havana later this month — if they came, if a hurricane did not destroy the flotilla, if Indian scouts could find the right port . . . if . . . if . . . if . . .

When the battle began, Daniel and Alfonso were storing baggage on shelves in a conveniently empty storehouse near the fort's plaza. Fray Dominic and one of the other clerics were storing communion vessels, sacred vestments, pitifully small kegs of wine, and the nearly empty flour barrel. Suddenly they heard the chilling yell of Indian warriors trying to frighten their enemy into surrendering. Then a Spaniard screamed, and they heard Soto's war cry: "By Santiago and the Blessed Virgin!"

"Quick!" said Alfonso. "Bar the door. The Indians are attacking."

Fray Dominic dropped a communion vessel and made for the door, trying to get out.

"For God's sake, Fray Dominic, don't go out there," said Alfonso. "Help me restrain him, Papa! Help me hold the door. Find something we can use for a club."

The battle re-created the army into a single-minded animal with Soto for a brain and centuries of Christian tradition for a heart. As quickly as one man fell, another took his place — moving automatically, as muscles move without being aware of how nerves transmit the message. No thought was required to load and shoot the harquebuses, to string crossbows, to swing alabardas, to keep pike ranks and charge with lances. The Battle of Mauvilla lasted nine hours: from nine o'clock in the morning, when Tascaluza disappeared into his headquarters to give the signal to attack, until almost sundown, when Soto leaned on his saddle pommel to look at the last dying Indian.

At first, Daniel and Alfonso were relatively safe inside the storehouse while the battle raged outside. Fray Dominic knelt quietly in one corner, mumbling his rosary. Daniel and Alfonso kept the door, clubbing any Indians who tried to enter and stacking their bodies along the wall.

Neither of them thought about how they might get out of here. They were not soldiers. The battle outside had nothing to do with them. They retreated, not out of cowardice, but because nothing existed outside those four log walls. Nothing except gaudily painted clowns and grotesque monsters. Nothing at all. Not Ruth, not Sarah, not Rachel. Not past, present, future. Only here and now. Only this safe ship riding out the hurricane.

After a while Soto escaped into the open and drew the Indians outside the fort, where lancers and alabardas could work more efficiently. The people in the storage room heard the women who had been Soto's bearers begging for weapons to fight the Spaniards. The last vestige of Fray Dominic's reason slipped. He wanted to go outside, lift up the cross, and preach to the Indians. Daniel and Alfonso had difficulty restraining him.

Fray Dominic had begun to believe in miracles—not past miracles requiring only slight suspension of the barrier between reality and fantasy, not future miracles requiring only fervent hope bred of desperate need, but present miracles, which require proof. He really believed the Savior would appear, the Blessed Virgin would wash all this away with Her tears, and the Indians would believe and sin no more. Perhaps he was right. Perhaps a miracle would have occurred. Fray Dominic had spent all his life hoping for just one miracle, but he never had a chance to find out if this was his miracle. Daniel and Alfonso tied him up in the corner, where he sat mumbling to himself—his rosary useless in his lap.

After noon the Indians retreated back into the fort. Soto tried unsuccessfully to storm the gates, then had his axemen chop away the mud plaster covering the trees that formed the wall. After they breached the walls, Soto set fire to the thatched barracks.

During the fierce street fighting, Soto took an arrow in the buttocks, but kept fighting, standing in his stirrups. Three crossbowmen, five alabarderos, several pages, and a couple of Indians fighting on the Spaniards' side took refuge in the storage shed. The Indians began tearing up the roof to get at them. Fray Dominic thought he was reliving the miracle of the sick man lowered to be healed by the Christ. He held up the cross, but the crossbowmen shot the Indians.

Trumpets blared, drums chattered, fifes called to arms, and Soto's rallying cry kept the troops fighting: "By Santiago and the Blessed Virgin! Attack! Attack!"

Smoke burned the eyes and choked off the breath as rising winds spread the fire from house to house. Soon the whole village inside the fort was afire. Women who had been shooting arrows from the safety of the barracks were driven into the open by the blaze. Caballeros later denied they had killed any women, but if not, Fray Dominic had his miracle. At least a third of the Indian casualties were young woman warriors who died with their weapons in their hands.

Soto finally rescued the people trapped in the burning storage shed, but as Paco Sandoval escorted them down the flaming street, Fray Dominic took an arrow in his right eye. Miraculously it did not kill him, but it left him at the mercy of the demons who visited on him the tortures of all those horrors mankind has pushed into the dark recesses of the mind.

Daniel and Alfonso carried away the raving priest so the Indians could not mutilate his body. As they approached the back gate of the fort, Mayabaño stepped out from behind a burning building. His arrow was aimed at Daniel's heart.

"Shoot, my brother," said Daniel as he saw the butterfly pale above the blackened face. "Shoot if you can, and get it over with."

Mayabaño looked at Daniel, and his bowstring seemed to be stuck to his fingers. Slowly he loosed the string. He motioned to Daniel and Alfonso to proceed out the gate with their burden. As they turned to go, Sandoval charged, impaling Mayabaño on his lance.

"Mayabaño!" cried Daniel. "God forgive us."

More than two thousand Indians died at Mauvilla. Some said five times that number. Soto's official count of Spanish casualties was eighteen dead, a hundred and fifty wounded; twelve horses dead, seventy wounded. The friars said Christian wounds healed miraculously. Daniel was too busy helping the surgeon to count dead or wounded, or to bother denying miraculous healings. Few were without wounds. That anyone survived was a miracle.

A golden October moon swathed in ice blazoned a cross in the sky at the passing of Fray Dominic, but no one noticed his miracle. The clerics stopped only long enough to give him a form of extreme unction, then went back to wringing their hands over lost sacramental vessels and lack of wheat flour to make the Host—all of which had been destroyed by the fire. Fray Dominic was blind and delirious and did not witness his miracle.

Ruth had birthed her baby in the woods, but after placing him in a moss-lined cradle strapped to her back, she came back to help with the wounded. Only curable wounds were treated. Some men were left to die, and others to heal themselves. All medical supplies, along with all spare clothing, had been burned.

Ruth foraged for cobwebs to stop bleeding, and aloe and other herbs to treat burns. They needed oil for ointment. Soto remembered how Cortés had solved his boat-caulking problem when he besieged Mexico City, so the Adelantado of Florida also ordered dead Indians rendered for their fat. Ruth calmly built a fire, found a charred iron pot, and set to work with a knife.

When her baby cried, Ruth nursed him, not worrying

405

too much about all the opia lurking around Mauvilla. Alfonso did not see his son's face until late the next day, when most of the dead had been buried and the wounds tended. They called the baby Jeremiah.

Ruth brought Daniel a cup of soup, and he ate it without asking where she had found food in the burned-out fort. Some men flayed and roasted dead horses.

Evil hovered over the fort. Panthers, bobcats, and wolves did not even wait for darkness to begin scavenging. Soto tried to keep them away until the Spanish dead were decently buried. Daniel and Alfonso looked for Mayabaño's body, but did not find it. Perhaps he had crawled off into the woods to die, or perhaps shy Higueymato had been waiting out there to carry her brother's body back to the temple in Cofachiqui. Perhaps Mayabaño was still alive!

On the third day, Alfonso built a rude lean-to against the fort walls and led a weary Daniel to rest, wrapped in the fire-charred remnants of Sarah's coat. Ruth suckled little Jeremiah before she lay down on the moss bed beside Alfonso and his father. None of them had slept since the battle.

The next morning Daniel did not get up. When Alfonso brought him breakfast, the old man stared off into space. Ruth told Alfonso to leave him alone, but Alfonso insisted on checking him for wounds. Daniel made no protest, but he had no visible wounds.

Daniel had talked very little during the days they were tending the wounded, but he had become a taciturn man. Lacking Hebrew scholars against whom to hurl his ideas, Daniel had fallen into the habit of disputing with himself. Now he disputed a matter even the sages had never agreed upon. Not one of those petty problems like how far a man is allowed to walk on the Sabbath, but the problem of the Divine Nothingness, of all the good and evil coming out of that Nothingness, and of how to reconcile them so a man could live with himself. Beware, the sages taught, of pondering too much on the kabbala, lest you see the Light and cease to exist—not die, but cease to exist—return not to the curtain of souls around the Throne of Glory, but to the single black dot of Nothingness where time and space do not exist.

The previous night Daniel had wandered again in the narrow, flower-hung streets of the judería in Córdoba. He had tried to pray in the little synagogue, but he was alone; without a minyan, his prayers echoed in the bare chamber. At La Mezquita, he washed his hands in the fountain, but refused to enter the forbidding marble forest. Then he had been transported to the glittering mihrab where hooded figures...he smelled burning straw...charred flesh... *"Honor thy father and mother, that thy days may be long in the land the Lord thy God giveth thee."*

Daniel did not cry when he realized what had happened to his father and mother, but he had not wanted to know, and knowing, he wanted to die. The shame of hiding behind the religion that had martyred his parents was unbearable. He turned his face to the wall of the fort, but God was not ready for him yet. Daniel railed silently at a God who would allow such suffering.

Daniel was too engrossed in his fight with the Almighty to answer when Alfonso tried to rouse him. The battle lasted all day behind his sullen eyes. He hated himself for being a convert—no, not convert, Marrano. Not Marrano because the Christians derisively called him Marrano, but because his heart condemned him for the deceptive swine he was.

Daniel tried to find the truth of the Exile from the Presence of God, the Inscrutable One with no name. No name? There had been many names. Yahweh, Baal, Allah, Jesus, Mary, Huracán. Yes, Huracán, the unpredictable capricious creator-destroyer, the uncontrollable all-seeing Eye. Dance dances and pray prayers, but not one gust of wind can be changed.

By bits and pieces, Daniel formed himself a creed by which to die...God, the lawgiver...God, the life-giver...God, the compassionate Savior with the money whip...God, the conqueror, the avenger. Daniel's mind sputtered trying to capture elusive Divine Light and put it all back together again—the faith of Abraham, the zeal of Torquemada, the soul of Anacaona. Somehow they all fitted together.

Lucifer, angel of light. No, not Lucifer, that fallen rebel angel. How can Lucifer be part of it all?

If there be any virtue, think on these things ...blue gentians beside Córdoban roadways, golden wheat stubble on the Sevilla plains, majestic live-oaks filled with blushing air plants, the laughter of little children playing, the ecstasy of Sabbath lovemaking, the singing and dancing in Andalucían courtyards, the splendor of armored knights riding into battle, the sweetness of a ripe persimmon, the vastness of a Caribbean sky...

Whatsoever things are just and of good report... providing a dowry for a poor girl, purchasing the freedom of a slave, giving food to a crippled old man, unchaining the slaves in Toledo dungeons and hanging their chains on the church walls, assassinating the Inquisitor Arbués as he prays in the cathedral, financing Colón's incredible voyage, fighting five hours with an arrow in the buttocks, pacifying the Indians so the land can be inhabited...

What of the Indians? What of their land, their homes, their gods? One people, one world, one God.

Hear, O Israel, the Lord our God, the Lord is One...

That awesome, terrible Oneness...one indivisible, omnipotent, omniscient, omnipresent God. Suddenly Daniel understood. One! Creation and destruction, Good and Evil, were one—all One. The Lord our God, the Lord is One!

Daniel turned his face to the wall.

Samuel Torres kept his oath and circumcised his father's body before he buried him. Ruth helped wash the body, and two or three other New Christians came to sit looking at the candle at the head of the bier. Where Ruth found a candle Samuel never knew. The Jews had little clothing left to tear, but they tore their charred rags and solemnly buried Daniel Torres before sundown on the day he died.

Samuel Alfonso tore the coat Sarah had made, poured ashes from the fort over his head, and sat shivah seven days on a low rock. Afterward, he circumcised himself and his little son Jeremiah while Ruth patched the burned, torn coat.

CHAPTER 12

Chucagua River, 1543

TWO AND A HALF years had passed since the Battle of
Mauvilla, and the remnants of Soto's army occupied an
Indian village beside the great river the Indians called
Chucagua. They had crossed and recrossed this river,
and Soto's bones had been sunk in its murky depths to
keep the Indians from exhuming and mutilating his
body. Now they had come back to this great father-of-
waters to build pinnaces to take them home to Spanish
civilization.

"Sarah!" Alfonso called as he paddled the canoe up
to the door of the house. The Chucagua had flooded in
March, inundating the land for twenty leagues on both
sides of the river. Forty days later the flood waters
began to recede, but even now, in the last of May, they
still had to use canoes or walk about barefoot.

Sarah? Had he said Sarah? Sarah was in Havana.
How could he have made such a mistake?

"Ruth!" He corrected himself. "Come help me. The
Captain-General wants the oakum and the hog-lard-
resin you mixed up. We're caulking the last boats."

Sarah, Ruth thought, laying aside the old Indian

blanket she had been shredding to make ship's caulking. So Sarah was the woman who had woven the beautiful coat. Not much was left of Sarah's work now. The coat had been torn and burned and worn threadbare. Ruth had patched it with whatever skin was available. Jeremiah lay on the bunk bed against the wall, the old coat tucked up under his chin to keep him warm.

Beyond Alfonso, Ruth could see the brown floodwaters of the Chucagua spread out among the trees. She caught the rope and tied up the canoe. Alfonso jumped from the canoe to the house. Indians on the Chucagua had learned to build their houses on stilts so their bench beds lining the walls would be safe and dry above the solid pine floors. Old people said the Chucagua flooded every fourteen years.

Twenty-eight days after the Battle of Mauvilla, Soto had led his army northward into the wilderness, afraid to risk a mutiny by rendezvousing with the caravels from Havana. They had wintered among the Chicaza, but suffered a massive Indian attack when Soto demanded baggage carriers. Mayabaño had done his work well. In April of 1541, they had fought a battle in another Indian fort called Alibamo—almost as devastating as the Battle of Mauvilla.

They had wandered through fertile land all that year, seeking the elusive gold. In October the Tula Indians attacked. They were snowbound all winter. In March of last year, Soto moved on again, and in May or June— they disagreed now about the months—they had come back to the Chucagua, where Soto died of a fever.

Moscoso, Soto's successor, had led the disgruntled army west again to a poor land where nomadic tribes followed the buffalo herds. After casting an incompetent guide to the dogs, the army turned back, wintered near the Chucagua, and began building boats to go home to Cuba. Florida had won! Spring winds sang Anacaona's song.

The floodwaters had saved them from another Indian attack. Cacique Quigualtanqui had taken up Mayabaño's cause and was massing troops from twenty tribes upriver. The Spaniards worked furiously to launch their

boats before the river receded enough for Quigualtanqui to launch his naval offensive.

Ruth had told Alfonso about Quigualtanqui's plans,
having learned them from a handsome warrior who
shaved his head on both sides and wore feathers in his
roach. The warrior often hung around Ruth when he
was in the camp during the days before the flood, spying
for Quigualtanqui.

"Ruth," Alfonso said as he loaded the last of the
caulking, "where is that bark line you were plaiting?
We're rigging the last of the boats. They must be
launched before the waters recede. Their hulls may not
stand being dragged over the ground."

"How many boats are you building?" asked Ruth,
although she knew already. She and the other Indian
women had anxiously counted the boats, while the
Spaniards were busy turning harquebuses into nails
and stirrups into anchors.

"Enough boats, don't worry," Alfonso lied. "I won't
leave Florida without you and the boy."

Ruth turned away to hide her anxiety. Alfonso never
called their two-year-old son Jeremiah; he always called
him simply "the boy." Alfonso was a good man, better
than most of the Christians, who turned their pregannt
women out, but Ruth knew Alfonso thought often of
the woman who wove the coat—Sarah.

Ruth knew, in spite of Alfonso's promises, he would
leave them behind when he went back to his people.
She tried to be grateful that he had been kind during
their wanderings, carrying Jeremiah on his shoulders
when he was almost too weary to walk himself. When
their baby daughter had been stillborn last winter, Alfonso had given Ruth the pearls La Cacica had given
his father—pearls Ruth knew he had been saving for
the coat woman. Ruth had put the pearls inside a little
doeskin pouch she wore around her neck, a pouch containing also the sky-blue stone Alfonso had gotten from
a nomadic Indian.

Ruth wore these good memories like amber beads
strung round her heart. One of the amber beads reflected the image of a clearing where a tiny hammock

swung in the breeze and a small boy squatted at the foot of a tree waiting to shoot a squirrel. The woman once called Happy Place liked to crystallize her memories in amber, creating a lovely world without battles or long marches, a world of laughter and ecstatic whisperings. Soon Alfonso would also enter her amber world.

Alfonso was a good man. Last winter, when the starving Indians had come to the stilt village begging for food, Alfonso had been one of the men who risked his commander's wrath by giving the Indians some of their own corn. Ruth loved him. So handsome he was now in the quilled shirt and fringed leggings she had made. Except for his curly hair and the beginning of a bald spot on the crown of his head, Alfonso looked like a broad-shouldered, muscular Indian.

When time came, Ruth would take her son upriver. Perhaps she and the other women left behind would build themselves a village and plant crops—corn and squash and beans. By and by hungry warriors would drop by with freshly killed deer or turkeys. Someday a man might be dancing the Green Corn Dance...perhaps a man like the Quigualtanqui warrior with the feathers in his roach...he might look at Ruth in that special way, and...

Meanwhile, Ruth had many amber beads strung on her memory necklace. She had seen mountains and this great river. She had loved a white man, and she had a curly-haired son. She had ridden the feathers of Huracán's wings and come out alive. What more could she ask?

Guilt rode with Alfonso as he paddled toward the dockhouses. He wished he had Don Diego de Gusmán's courage. The nobleman had fallen in love with his Indian woman; when he lost her in a card game one day, he had stolen her and run away. Not even Soto's cavalry had been able to find the lovers. Alfonso wished he could solve his problem as easily.

Alfonso loved Ruth and the boy—who looked like an Indian except for his curly hair, but his father had been right. Ruth was not of his people, and the boy, circumcised or not, could not be considered a true son of Abraham. Why must the bloodline be carried through the mother? Ruth had never allowed another man near her, not even that handsome Quigualtanqui warrior. Would she have betrayed their attack plot if she had been lying with the warrior?

After Alfonso left, Ruth counted her rosary. All the Indian women knew there were only seven boats, barely enough for the surviving Christians and certainly not enough for six hundred Indian women and children. Ruth had seen the priests pray successfully for rain in drought-stricken Casquin, and she hoped the Blessed Mother might listen to the prayers of her new Indian children and not leave them far from home at the mercy of strange Indians who hated them for serving the Christians. Not even Ruth's amber world softened that reality.

Between Saint John's and Saint Peter's feast days, the Christians launched their frail craft. Tomorrow, June 2—Saint Paul's Day—they would test the craft on the mighty Chucagua. The river flowed along calmly now, confining itself to its banks between dried, crackling mud. Everything was ready for an early start in the morning.

Provisions had been stored. Baskets of corn, loaves of dried persimmons, pouches of jerked horsemeat, salted hams and shoulders, skins of fresh water. Caulking, blankets for patching sail, extra reed line, moccasins, shirts, leggings, martenskin cloaks—all made by the Indian women. And thirty horses—the best of the remaining herd. The Christians had no gold, no silver, no precious metals—all they had were a few fire-blackened pearls—and no guns, no lombard, no gunpowder. Just a few hand-wrought birch lances and a few rusty crossbows. The guards paced restlessly, looking for sign of Quigualtanqui's warriors—spending one last night in Florida, but dreaming of home.

Did ladies really wear long satin dresses and smell of perfume, or was that just an Arabian tale? Did gentlemen really ride prancing pasofinos and politely joust at a "game of canes"? Were glittering Madonnas still crying glassy tears in cool dark churches? Did people read books and play guitars and march in Holy Week parades? Was there another world out there—a civilized Spanish world where the power of the monarchy and the sanctity of the Church had meaning?

Alfonso sat in the doorway watching the long shadow of the stilt house. In his lap he cradled a small beaverskin pouch containing his father's letters—letters he had found after Mauvilla, but never read. What would his mother do when she learned his father was never coming back? What had his father written on those carefully filled pages? Love letters? Alfonso had difficulty thinking about his father and mother lying down together and...

Probably a diary of the expedition. Perhaps a criticism of Soto's high-handed cruelty to the Indians. Soto had so enjoyed the game called aperrear. How many lying Indians had the Irish greyhounds devoured? If Daniel had written of this, he would surely have tried to soften the evil, to come to terms with the cruelty in the noble Spanish soul—in the human soul. Were not men like Las Casas also Spaniards, men who had written scathing denunciatios of such deeds? Was not Alfonso Spanish? And his father Daniel? And his grandfather Rav? Jews first, but also Spaniards—the Sephardim.

Ruth and the boy came toward Alfonso across the crackling mud flats. Somewhere not far away Jesús Fuentes began playing his handmade flute. Men like Jesús and his father Ramón would always find instruments to make music. That, too, was part of the Spanish soul—the music, the songs, the dancing, and the laughter. When Jesús lost his guitar to the Mauvilla fire, he had made himself a willow flute. When Jeremiah was two years old, Jesús had given him a turkey-bone whistle—and in the past six months the boy had learned to blow only one note.

As the boy drew near, Alfonso picked him up, held him at eye level, and stared into the solemn little face; then he hugged his son before putting him down. Ruth put the boy to bed while Alfonso filled his pipe with cedar bark. Ruth handed him a live coal, and he filled the air with fragrant cedar smoke, but he remembered the taste of dark Taino tobacco grown on good Cuban soil. Alfonso wanted to hold back tomorrow. No need to talk now. All the talking had been done.

Alfonso missed the talking most—the family talking, the gossip of who married whom. Filigree lineages traced out in soft feminine voices. Buying and selling and making a profit tied up in waggling beards. Age-old mysteries endlessly argued in sonorous tones. Shared sufferings and shared promises...shawl-draped minyans praying familiar prayers...feasts and fasts...his mother's honey cakes and Sarah's dark eyes...the vast five-millennial Hebrew coat of many colors Ruth would never be able to wear.

Why had Lilith tempted him into taking a gentile woman? How could he face tomorrow and leave behind a woman who had never done anything except love and serve him? How could he forsake a woman who had no other life than the one they shared?

Alfonso's mind ached with the puzzle, and his heart overflowed with love. His problem was that he loved them both, as Jacob must have loved Leah after he was tricked into marrying her before he could have Rachel, as Abraham must have loved Hagar after she bore him Ishmael. Yet Abraham had sent Hagar into the wilderness.

Alfonso sighed, and Ruth came to sit beside him, laying her hand on his inner thigh. As her fingers moved, his love sprang to life, demanding satisfaction. Alfonso groaned and buried his face in her bosom. She rocked him as she would rock a child; singing an old Taino lullaby. He surrendered himself to her, and their love washed away all his fears.

Shekhina...Lilith...Ruth...Sarah...Woman! Woman! Woman! And God created woman. Flesh of my flesh...body grafted onto my body by the rod of my continuing...wellspring of living waters...the marriage feast..."It is not good that man should be alone."

Ruth and Alfonso slept in each other's arms, and not

even the boy crying in his sleep disturbed them. In the morning Ruth gave Alfonso the doeskin pouch of pearls before they walked down to the landing, where Alfonso had to coax twenty horses into canoes—forefeet in one canoe, hind feet in another. Moscoso had ordered all the Indians left behind except those he and his staff officers were taking back as slaves. The command boat was far downriver by the time Alfonso loaded the last horse.

Ruth stood with the women, who were singing a high, keening song. Just before they shoved off, Alfonso grabbed his son and swung him aboard. Jesús held the wiggling boy. Ruth cried out in protest—a cry barely audible above the wailing women. Then Alfonso picked Ruth up in his arms and stepped over the rail into the boat.

"Entreat me not to leave thee, nor to return from following after thee..."

Quigualtanqui caught up with them two days downriver. One of nature's paradoxes is that deadly things can sometimes be so beautiful—the coral snake with its brilliant red-yellow-black bands, the glittering scales on the diamondback rattler, the tiny red dot on the shiny black rosary pea—as if God has made a pact to beautify death. Quigualtanqui's avenging flotilla was one of Death's beautiful enticements.

The Cacique rode in the command canoe, sitting under a scarlet canopy while fifty oarsmen dressed in scarlet plumes skimmed the long canoe over the surface with powerful, rhythmic strokes matched to areítos of glorious wars. The long, broad-bladed oars were lacquered scarlet, as was the canoe itself, so the whole thing looked like a great scarlet ibis about to take wing.

Horses could not have run faster than Quigualtanqui's battle barge, carrying thirty scarlet-plumed warriors with drawn bows—their long hair tied back with scarlet headbands, their bodies stained red and glistening with bear grease. Even their faces were painted scarlet. Following Quigualtanqui came other canoes almost as large, all scarlet and all with oarsmen and warriors dressed in scarlet.

Behind Quigualtanqui came twenty other caciques, each with a retinue in his chosen color—a deadly rainbow skimming over the khaki water. Moving, writhing, weaving itself into endless patterns as the oarsmen showed off their prowess. All morning they darted within a crossbow distance of the Cuban flotilla, only to dart away again, peeling off in kaleidoscopic designs.

Ruth huddled in the bottom of the boat, hugging Jeremiah. Alfonso pulled fiercely, trying to keep the lumbering craft out of danger. Fourteen oarsmen rowed each Cuban boat, every one of them chopping at the water as if he rowed alone. The accursed independence of the Spanish soul would destroy them yet—*I, myself, for myself alone.*

At noon Quigualtanqui attacked, making a pass on both sides, aiming primarily for the horses. Alfonso leaped into the canoe with a grass mat for a shield, hoping to protect the horse from the volley of arrows. He failed. The thrashing of a dying horse upset the canoe, and Alfonso jumped back into the boat just in time to take an arrow in his shoulder.

He was bleeding profusely. Ruth cut the shaft, tried to pull the arrow through so she could stop the bleeding. Just then the canoe commanded by the warrior with the feathers in his roach shot up close to the boat. Alfonso's eyes blurred as he felt himself about to pass out.

"Papa! Papa!" yelled Jeremiah.

Alfonso shook his head to clear it, and saw the warrior struggling with Ruth. Alfonso stood up, swayed, almost reached her. He staggered as the warrior put Ruth into the red canoe and the oarsmen began their taunting chant. The brown waters of the Chucagua swirled round the canoe. Alfonso saw the crested warrior club Ruth just before a blue-feathered squadron took the red one's place.

"Mama..." Jeremiah's anguished cry trailed over the water.

Alfonso shoved the boy into the bottom of the boat and covered him with his own body.

"Stay down, son," he ordered. Then he passed out, pinning the boy beneath him.

The battle lasted until sundown. All but eight of the horses were killed, and not a man escaped being wounded. Alfonso's little mestizo son Jeremiah cried himself to sleep in his father's arms, but the child had not a scratch on him.

Indians fought them all the way to the Chucagua delta. Then for fifty-three days the survivors hugged the western rim of the Gulf, sailing toward Mexico, where twenty-two years ago Cortés had conquered Moctezuma. Huracán made one last attempt to destroy them before they reached the mountain-rimmed village of Panúco. The men kissed the ground and walked on their knees to the little mud church to thank the Blessed Virgin.

Panúco took the Soto survivors to its heart, and His Excellence, the Viceroy of Mexico, ordered them to the capital, where the citizens dressed them in Spanish finery and the Viceroy gave a reception where they were allowed to kiss his hand. The citizens of Moctezuma's city were so enthralled with the furs the survivors wore that they paid a high price to see who could have fur collars on their coats. Alfonso built up a lively trade in cleaned discarded furs, but he would not sell the coat Ruth and Sarah had made. He left the new business in charge of a New Christian family when he and Jesús Fuentes left for Havana.

During the year they had been in Mexico, Alfonso often took Jeremiah to visit the great stone pyramid temple of Quetzalcoatl—messenger of the gods. Finally, Alfonso and his little son Jeremiah, almost four years old now, came home to Havana. They arrived just in time for Yom Kippur—the Hebrew Day of Atonement, a day of confession and judgment, a day for remembering martyrs, a time of beginning again.

The little Hebrew congregation of Havana, mostly women, barefoot and dressed in white, had gathered for the High Holy Days in a little grove outside the city, safely away from the Church's prying eyes. Rachel acted as rabbi, keeping the tradition alive. Cut off from the services of a trained rabbi, they did not always recite the prayers properly. Having no cantor, they sometimes garbled the melodies. To make up a minyan, they let women pray. When there were not enough women, they prayed anyway—hoping God would forgive this breach of talmudic tradition.

Rachel, her hair almost white, was leading the mourner's kaddish when Alfonso walked into the clearing leading the bronze-skinned, curly-haired little boy. Alfonso stooped to put off his shoes and the shoes of his son, and Rachel's heart skipped a beat as her voice missed a note, a word in the prayer. She continued. Not even her son's homecoming could be allowed to interrupt the prayer for the dead of one's family, and for all martyrs past and future.

Samuel Alfonso Torres joined the prayer he had recited for his father during the year after his burial at Mauvilla, and he prayed not only for his father and for all the martyrs of the Inquisition, but also for Caonabó and Anacaona and their heroic son Mayabaño. Remember, O Lord, he wanted to say, Mayabaño is the one with the butterfly tattoo who died fighting for his people.

Rachel's voice trembled. Samuel put his arms around his mother, and little Jeremiah looked up bewildered. Sarah led the response to the kaddish. Alfonso's voice broke as he looked into Sarah's eyes. How beautiful she would look under a canopy!

"Your father, Samuel?" Rachel asked when the prayer was finished.

"I kept his letters for you," Samuel said.

He handed Rachel the salt-stained beaverskin packet. Rachel clutched them to her heart, tears swimming in her eyes. She looked down at the boy.

"Your son?" she asked.

"My son, Mama," said Samuel. "He is called Jeremiah, and he has been circumcised."

Rachel put her hand on the boy's head in the traditional blessing. Sarah touched the sleeve of the coat she had embroidered, feeling the soft fur of Ruth's handiwork. Tomorrow would be time enough to ask questions. Jeremiah sat down on the grass and began blowing his turkey-bone whistle. To the little congregation it sounded as shrill and compelling as the shofar.

"Samuel," said Rachel, "will you lead the Prayer of Atonement?"

Samuel looked toward Heaven as he began the only part of the Yom Kippur prayer he remembered, the part engraved on his heart by his years in the Florida wilderness.

"God of our fathers, forgive us, pardon us, grant us atonement...we have sinned...we have trespassed, we have dealt treacherously, we have robbed...we have wrought wickedness, we have done violence, we have framed lies, we have counseled evil...we have committed iniquity...we have oppressed...we have been stiffnecked, we have done wickedly...have pity and compassion; grant us atonement...'"